SHARKS
OF THE
WASTE
LAND

Gwendolyn N. Nix

Published by Outland Entertainment LLC
3119 Gillham Road
Kansas City, MO 64109

Founder/Creative Director: Jeremy D. Mohler
Editor-in-Chief: Alana Joli Abbott
Senior Editor: Gwendolyn N. Nix

ISBN: 978-1-947659-84-1
Worldwide Rights
Created in the United States of America

Editor: Elise McMullen-Ciotti
Cover Illustration & Design: Jeremy D. Mohler
Interior Layout: Mikael Brodu

Printed and bound in the United States of America.

Visit **outlandentertainment.com** to see more, or follow us on our Facebook Page **facebook.com/outlandentertainment/.**

Dedication

To the steadfast.
To me in my twenties, when you didn't think these dreams would become
real, but thunder only happens when it's raining, so...

Now I see what there is in a name, a word,
liquid, sane, unruly, musical, self-sufficient,
I see that the word of my city is that word from of old...

—Walt Whitman "Manahatta"

I

Subject T's stomach growled in belly-aching mutiny. Cramps twisted his intestines, pretending there was something to digest. It was different from his usual kind of hunger where he knew he'd get bread in the morning, a protein shake in the afternoon, and a vitamin capsule with his greens at night. It never filled him up, but it kept him running. Now, he barely had enough energy to lift his legs out of the thick mud flats. The cold muck squished between his toes. Bubbly, dark water seeped into his leftover footprints. Vaguely—the fear a shadow of his previous terror—he wondered what kind of outsider diseases he was being exposed to.

He knew he should find clothes, something like what the wardens wore to distinguish themselves from the experiments, but he hadn't seen anyone for miles and miles since his...*escape*. Even thinking that forbidden word made him shiver, and he knew, down to his core, that while he hadn't had a say in leaving the only place he'd ever known, he *had* been a willing participant.

He scanned the coastline and heard nothing but the same familiar and satisfying silence, like that of his cell, broken by the uneasy lapdog roars of the ocean during low tide.

Here, on the outside—and he still couldn't believe he was on the *outside*—it smelled sick with the scent of decaying seaweed and overturned oxygen-deprived sediment. Everything he'd heard from the doctors and psychologists rang true: outside the Facility walls remained nothing but devastation.

White shells peeked out of the mire. He sidestepped glass shards of broken bottle heads the ocean hadn't smoothed yet. Staggering into the breach, he shivered with a sudden cold that was nothing like the stone cell he knew so well. His mouth felt padded with cotton, an indicator that his body had flushed the drugs from his system. A wave knocked him to his knees. He sank down deep, mucking through the filth to pull out his first clamshell. The clam spat murky water in his face, but he smiled—knowing it to be big-toothed and crazy—in spite of it. Somewhere in the back of his mind, he decided he would not die from starvation.

He shuffled to a half-buried corner of a cement block. Chilled mud slicking his shins, he hit the shell against the block until it cracked open like a perfect nut to reveal the meat inside. Gold. The shell's jagged edges sliced his fingertips and bent his nails backward as he pried it open, but he didn't care, not when the chewy mess landed on his tongue.

He suckled at it, choked the mucus down, and sipped at the remaining juice. Shell pieces ground to dust between his teeth. While it tasted like earth, at least it ended the hollowness inside. The clam settled thickly in his stomach, which gurgled for more.

Panting, he desperately foraged farther out in the surf. He ignored the barebones trees growing back on shore, barely noticing the one that stubbornly kept its display of changing orange and red blooms. The cuts on his hands burned as he bashed a second clam open.

"What do you think you're doing?" a voice shouted above him, and his treasure was slapped out of his hand. Landing in the mud with a splat, it was swallowed by a small wave and dragged a handbreadth away.

He bit back a mewl at the loss and licked his lips to savor every smidgen of salty energy. Looking up into the setting sun, he saw a man step in front of him: tall with dark spiky hair, clothed in layers of dirty cotton with a leather satchel and backpack snugly fit to him, his bronzed skin better suited to the hot sun than his own pale—now sunburned—flesh. Subject T wanted to speak, but it had been such a long time and talking was a privilege.

He reached out and recovered his clam—*who knew how many remained?*—but the man immediately snatched it away. Subject T whined. *Please give it back, I'm so hungry.* But the man shook the clam in front of his face like a guard would a fist before punching him. He balked, sitting hard into the mud.

"You can't eat these," the newcomer—*the outsider*—said. "Don't you know that? Look at it." He traced a greenish tinge along the clam's outer lip and pulled the layers back to show a dark brown strip.

Subject T licked his lips. *So succulent, so good.*

"Don't you see? It's bad for you. Makes you sick. It's a piss-clam. The Wallabout really must'a kept you isolated if you don't even know *that.*"

Subject T shook his head. No, he didn't know. He did know that after he swallowed, it left a metallic breath on his palate, like blood when he bit his tongue.

"You can't eat any of the mollusks here." The man wiped his hand on his thigh and side-stepped as if to circle Subject T. The stranger never seemed to stop moving, even when the movements weren't necessary. "They're all contaminated."

Subject T shivered as the clothed man reached out to him and lifted the hair off the nape of his neck to touch the tattooed letter there. The man's finger stilled against it, quieting his high-energy intensity for a brief moment.

He couldn't answer this tall male dressed like a real person with boots and a belt buckle shaped into a knot. Subject T knew about books and counting the stones in his cell and about injections. He knew about treatments and punishments and about the letter tattooed on his wrist, anklebones, and even on the inside of his thigh. But he didn't know about piss-clams.

"How did you get out of there?" this newcomer asked.

Subject T trembled more after the foreign touch left his skin. He counted the multitude of bacteria and viruses that could've been passed to him and wanted to laugh because he wasn't technically new to this land. He had been born in a cement tower and raised maybe a hundred miles away from here, yet this was his first time outside.

The clothed man took his elbow and helped him stand. "Too stupid. It'd be a crime not to help you," he muttered as he dug into one of the pockets of his leather jacket and pulled out an old plastic bag. "Us Manahattas are too sweet-hearted for our own good, but it's what made us the strongest tribe out here. Taking in pitiful strays like you." Opening the bag, he shook a cracker into his palm and offered the wafer by holding it to Subject T's closed lips, as though persuading a picky child. The outsider expected him to eat from his hands. Subject T did, no questions asked. Salty. Grainy. He chewed it to paste, let his saliva mold it into a ball, and pushed it to the roof of his mouth.

"Can you talk?" the man asked, shoving a cracker into his own mouth. "Or did the Wallabout take your tongue, too?"

Yes, he thought, watching the man tuck the food away. "Yes," he croaked.

"Mako Saddlerock," the man said, extending his hand. Subject T wasn't sure what to do with it. His education on the dangers of the outside still echoed in his mind.

"Doesn't matter," Mako said. His outstretched hand snuck back into his pocket. Subject T's eyes followed his hand. Mako snorted out a disbelieving laugh. "You don't get to touch the food until you're clean. You're filthy."

"Yes," Subject T echoed. "Filthy."

"I can show you where to clean that sludge-acid off, but that's it. I can't help no Bruykleen man beyond humanity's courtesies."

"Thank you."

Mako grunted, turned away, and tossed his head in a way that said he clearly meant to be followed. "You probably don't even know you're at Dead Horse Bay."

Subject T shook his head. He knew of old crinkled maps full of renamed lands, but he couldn't pinpoint where he was to save his soul.

"Don't even know that you're an abomination." Mako said it like a curse. "That you've probably got people hunting for you right now."

He didn't. But he didn't care. Because the sun was setting, deep with pink and orange swatches, and it was the first one he had ever seen in his life.

2

When Mako's triumphant cry pierced the silence, Subject T forced himself not to bolt for cover. Mako rushed towards a floating body that rocked with the waves. Yanking on a stiff arm, he pulled the corpse as far on shore as possible. The body lolled back and forth, bloated and blue. A mark on the body's wrist—some kind of badly inked number—made Subject T touch his own clean-edged letter.

Subject T tried to fight the cold, black dread from taking over any rational thought. Shaped by the racing dusk, the dead man reminded him of his hallucination: the skeleton lady who had stood in the distance as he crawled across concrete to the shore. His legs useless and limp, his mind cracked and addled. She waited for him. He shifted awkwardly, refusing to dwell on the parting remembrance of the bone girl urging him to reach her faster.

He watched Mako, instead. Mako, who patted the body down, dipped deft fingers into the pockets, and fingered the soaked wool of the corpse's jacket. Mako, who eyed the boots with a squint, wrestled them off, and tossed them to him, saying, "Your size, perhaps?"

Slightly too big, they scraped against the back of Subject T's heels. He shifted around in them, hating how his feet felt moist and dirty inside these dead man boots. He thought about mold growing under his toenails, but a small ball of relief settled in his stomach. He wasn't going to die. Mako knew how to survive in this wasteland, and if he could stick with this outsider, he might learn how to survive, too.

Mako tutted when he saw the state of the corpse's pants—unsalvageable, Subject T assumed—but the red jacket, heavy with sludge-acid and smelling like rot, peeled off the corpse easily. Mud pellets flew as Mako fanned it out in the deepening twilight. "Have to keep an eye out for these," he said, handing it off. A tight fit, but starvation had made Subject T's shoulders thin enough.

He raised an eyebrow at Mako, trying to copy this outsider's expressions, and shifted in his new boots again. He'd seen bodies before but never in such a state as this. Usually, expired experiments were carried out in white sack bags heavy with the outline of slack limbs.

The head a rounded ball compared to the long narrowness of legs. His coat felt unnaturally heavy. Brown water dripped from the hem.

"Poor bastard," Mako muttered with a grimace. "Did you know him?" He dipped his forefinger into the mud and swirled it around, then drew three lines from the outside of the corpse's eyes to the hairline and nudged the body with his foot until the head pointed east.

"What are you doing?" Subject T asked, a little awed by the ritual.

"You might not believe it, but I was raised to give the dead *some* semblance of respect," Mako said, a grin slowly spreading across his face. "Don't want his ghost to follow us, do we? Why, did you know him?"

Subject T shook his head. He knew people by their posture and the way they smiled, but he had never seen this particular man before.

"Looks like a guard from the prison. You know, where you came from," Mako said, tapping his wrist and inclining his head toward Subject T.

Subject T squinted at Mako, feeling his forehead scrunch up in a question. The identification letter tattooed on his wrist blazed with heat.

"The Wallabout," Mako said, waving his hand out toward the horizon. "The prison ship. Wasn't that where you were? Wasn't that where you escaped from?"

Subject T shook his head again. He had never been on a ship before.

Mako let out an exasperated sigh. "You would have had to swim. Not too forgettable."

Subject T backed away. He couldn't swim anywhere. No one taught him these things. The water seemed too unforgiving to let him survive for even one minute.

Mako shrugged, pawing the dead man's pockets again. "Story goes, that old steel hull was overcrowded with society's most vicious criminals and set out to sea when the world went bad. Prisoners or guards—although honestly the two are probably the same about now—are thrown overboard when they die and wash up here. This isn't so much of a beach as it is an unofficial cemetery. Sometimes you even luck out."

He held out a handful of coin-sized purple and white shells to Subject T. When he grinned, the freckles scattered over his nose and cheeks stood out, rendering Subject T amazed at the sudden youthful glimmer cutting through the travel-weary face. He smiled back in response, feeling a thrill at how this outsider changed from man to boy in whirlwind seconds. "And luck," Mako said gleefully, "is on our side."

Subject T knew next to nothing about outsider tradition, but he liked how this one made Mako glow. Oddly pleased, he watched Mako pack away the shells and tighten the strap of his satchel until it fit snug to his waist. His backpack, some kind of canvas and leather with tarnished buckles, barely budged.

Subject T's gaze drifted back to the sky to see the final colors fade. A dark blanket invaded the gray twilight. Faint twinkles shone through the cloud cover. He wondered if those were stars.

Another jerk of Mako's head indicated he should follow. He did so mindlessly, trying to ignore the cold shakes working their way up his legs. His stomach clenched with a churning gut sickness, and he had to lean over before he was sick. The piss-clam rolled up his throat and splattered on the mud as a pinkish glob.

He felt a pat on the back. "I told you they were bad for you," Mako said. Subject T mourned the loss. He knew he would be hungry again soon, but this was one survival lesson he wouldn't forget.

"C'mon," Mako said. "Got some good water stashed. You can clean out your mouth. Wash your hands."

"Clean," he said.

"Best feeling in the world," Mako said, his hand still on Subject T's shoulder.

Mako's clean water was a metal pail lodged deep into the sand, brimming with water-skimming bugs. "Rainwater's not the best," Mako amended. "Got all the sulfur and junk from the sky, but it's better than nothing. Here, let me."

A small ladle hung off the edge of the pail by a curved handle. Mako picked it up and filled it with water. "Hold out your hands."

Subject T cupped them while Mako poured water sparingly over his scraped knuckles. He rubbed his fingernails. He had read somewhere that bacteria liked to settle there.

Mako scooped more and held it out to him. He pressed the offering to Subject T's chapped lips. The water coated Subject T's tongue in old metal tang and refreshing wetness. It soothed the back of his throat and poured into his stomach, cold and slick. His satisfaction lasted only a moment. "More," he said, handing the ladle back.

Mako filled another cup and sipped it. Subject T wanted the ladle back so bad his fingers itched to snatch it away. He wouldn't, though. He remembered in his early word-hungry days taking another experiment's book with a dirty punch, and the isolation chamber and drooling pills that came after it. Patience was a good lesson to learn—the Facility's lesson.

Mako let him drink two more ladlefulls. They shared, passing back and forth, each sipping his share before dipping it into the bucket and spitting out the bugs that got caught in the storm. After, Mako pushed the pail further down into the dirt as if to ground it and said, "C'mon, daylight's nearly gone."

As they walked, Subject T couldn't understand Mako's purpose for gathering tall yellow grass and dried cardboard slabs. The bundle of sticks under his arm grew in size until they settled under a concrete overpass. Mako cleared a space free of debris and arranged his gathered detritus into a small triangular frame, stuffing spare leaves and grasses between the stick cage.

Subject T wanted to clap when Mako brought out a small lighter. A fire. Mako was building a *fire*. "By the trinity, this better catch," Mako said, striking his thumb on the trigger. "Only have one flare left."

The small flame stuttered, caught, and held. Subject T marveled at its fragility as it wavered precariously on an invisible wick. Quickly though, as if starved, the small flame fed on the grass and roared to life. Subject T jumped back. The light overwhelmed him. The heat painted his face, so different from the dust-smelling warmth that coughed out of the Facility's floorboards. Mako watched him with an intensity that unnerved him, then held out his hands palm-up to the flame. Subject T mimicked, fear knotting his belly as the fire cracked and shot out ember points. He flinched, but somehow Mako's calmness relaxed him enough to sit. In the heart of the fire, the embers breathed, a respiration of alternating black and orange.

He bent his knees up to his chest, delighting in the heat curling up his shins. The smoke made him dizzy. He wanted to ask questions, confirm truths his psychologist had told him, infinitely curious why Mako didn't have horrible deformities from environmental toxicity. The words bounced around in his head. He knew how to form inquires, how to mimic and respond, but putting those words into the air was the hardest thing he'd ever done. His jacket hung on a concrete jut, crackling with steam as the wet evaporated and the dirt dried out into flakes.

"Mako is a shark?" he finally asked, breathing a sigh of relief that he was loud enough for Mako to hear.

Mako's ears perked, and a wide grin spread across his face. He settled near the fire with a sigh, making a diamond with his bent bowlegs. His ankles touched. He unscrewed a tarnished flask and took a quick draw.

"Yeah," he said at last. "A nasty kind of shark. All teeth. My daddy used to hunt them. Won respect for landing the biggest monster in the whole ocean. My mama wasn't happy when he wanted to name me after his first catch. She figured Bignose Bitch would give me a lot of hell from the other kids."

Subject T nodded, wondering what it would be like to fidget like Mako, full of rough and tumble energy that kept him leaning to check the fire, whistling with his teeth, and picking his nails. Subject T only knew silence and quiet, how to blend into the shadow and remain unseen.

"What's your name?" Mako asked. "Haven't been calling you much of anything, and I figure you'll be hating that right about now."

Subject T shrugged. He really didn't have a name, except for "Subject T" by the people with clothes who spoke through intercoms and observed him through glass and metal grates. He rubbed the lettered cross on his ankle.

"Begin with a T?" Mako guessed.

"T," he said. "T like a thresher." He remembered reading about those short-nosed creatures, wide black eyes and downturned pouty mouths, tails like whips. Endangered one book had said. Extinct, said another.

Mako laughed. "You want to be a shark too?"

He nodded enthusiastically, wondering what the tightening sensation around his mouth meant. "Thresher," he said.

Mako poked the fire. "Two lone sharks in this big world and we find each other on this trash-heap beach? Guess it fits though. It wouldn't be my luck to meet someone from the same tribe, *nope*, of course you've gotta be from one we've been fighting with for years."

A bubble of laughter at Mako's expense built in Thresher's stomach—of course they weren't the *same*: such an observation was obvious baseline data; he was Facility-stock, Mako a dangerous outsider—but he held it inside. He mouthed his new name, building courage to say it out loud again. It almost hurt to hold in the battering words yearning for release. He rubbed a jagged fingernail against his thigh, seeking any kind of relief.

"Where are you headed from here?" Mako asked, hazel eyes narrowed to slits.

"Headed?" Thresher said.

"Where are you going tomorrow?" Mako clarified. "I told you, I can't help you further. My people stopped doing that a long time ago, even before the tribal wars began. I've got things to do, people to see. I won't have you holding me back. You're on your own from here."

"You're leaving me?" Even Thresher noticed the childish terror leaking through at suddenly having to face the next day alone. He didn't know you were supposed to raid dead men's bodies or find pails of rainwater for cleaning or even how to build a fire. Suddenly, the darkness around him became an overwhelming obstacle that would never end. He couldn't stop the sun from setting. He would lose all the colors.

Mako looked surprised. "Not a Wallabout, huh, and don't look like you know if you're a land Bruykleener either. Where exactly *did* you come from?"

Thresher didn't want to talk anymore. He didn't want to remember, not when freedom was more terrifying than the known. All these heavy doubts and regrets made him want to cry. He cradled his head on his knees and closed his eyes, making himself small. He wondered if this was what death felt like, a great unknown full of uncertainty with no schedule at all. He didn't know if freedom was worth it, to still feel this alone.

3

N ika's hot inhale sucked the burlap bag tied over her head into her nose and mouth. She exhaled like a punch, desperate for anything that didn't feel like suffocation. She felt the collar every time she swallowed, tight like she was a fucking bulldog, and tried to squash the low-lying tingle of panic spreading from her stomach to her brain. She wriggled her arms, but she had seen the padded bindings securing her down with big buckles. She wasn't going anywhere. *Immobile.* The uncomfortable spread of her legs, bent to fit the stirrups, upgraded to an ache. The doctors had removed her worn jeans and stained underwear, but she still wore her sweater. The unraveling cuff tickled her clenched fingers.

Clothes were the biggest difference between those born in the Facility and those brought here. She shivered just thinking about those trinity-damned experiments who had to wear the over-washed medical gowns or gray scrubs. She still had the clothes she arrived in, although now the jeans had holes in the knees and between the thighs. Her chunky sweater had faded from rich chocolate to murky pollution. Her underwear hung on in mere scraps, molded to her skin, and the underwire of her bra poked her ribs.

She wouldn't give them up for the world.

Her legs began to feel numb, and when her whole pelvis lost all feeling, she reared up in her binds and thrashed in pure terror. For a moment, she thought *I can do this, I'm strong enough to break this*, before a calming hand rested over her forehead and her head began to swim. A soft lullaby hummed close to her ear, paired with a muffled exhale breathed through a mask or respirator. She wanted to scream, but thought she might throw up all over her face instead and wouldn't that be a fine way to begin the day, eating your own bile.

The air was stale with poor circulation. She teethed an edge of the sack, lathed it with saliva, and then sucked the moisture right back out of it.

Who knew how long the procedure would last?

Before, it took a mere hour, but she miscarried three weeks later.

The cafeteria server plopped the bowl of oatmeal on Nika's tray with a half-smile, as if congratulating herself for finally providing something tasty for these prisoners, these experiments. The white puffs, even slathered in rare brown sugar with a dash of milk, stuck in Nika's throat.

She fiddled with the pilling thigh hole in her jeans. Her left leg jiggled and she catalogued the circus of the day. The young boy rocking himself in the corner. The small gang grouped around a particular table with the same scientific notation tattooed on their wrists. Once upon a time, she would've made the effort to guess the experiment behind the symptoms, but she didn't feel like there was a point anymore. Not when they were still trying to make her like one of them.

She noted the high ceiling with its barred windows. Today the sky was gray—but then again, when wasn't it? She began to think they painted it that color on purpose, paid some very stupid artist strung out on hunger to make something of himself by water-coloring an unchangeable and depressing sky.

She fingered the white paper cup beside her meal. Her experiment letter was scribbled on the side in black marker like it was her name. She rattled the pills inside, counting up the blues, reds, and purples. Her own personal mural that would paint her insides a hundred new colors and make her feel as gray as the sky. She paused. Counted again.

Hunched over in her metal chair, she examined the room a second time. Nothing out of the ordinary. Nothing different, except one pink pill missing from her daily intake.

Nika dumped the pills into her mouth. They clacked like broken piano keys against her teeth. Her tongue traced the different shapes. The candy coating dissolved into tangy bitterness. She swallowed them whole and chased them down with a quick gulp of tepid water.

Wincing, she remembered when she first refused her treatments and how it heralded blood tests with constant IVs in her wrist and back of her hand. The itchy, crusted blood. The cooing questions— why didn't she want to get better, didn't she want to be a good girl and take things that would make her well again?

She wasn't a child. The last time someone talked to her like that, she clocked him in the jaw. She wasn't a good girl—or a good fucking experiment for that matter—and she didn't want to be one. But she knew the value of submission. It meant meals, blankets, and keeping her old clothes that smelled like her memories, like the stain on the sleeve where she'd spilled tea. She sucked on the brown splotch sometimes in her cell, thinking she could taste the bergamot.

Maybe they had miscounted her pills. Unlikely. When each patient's health remained the main concern of the Facility, it seemed strange that such a misstep would occur. She rubbed a finger over the tattooed letter on her wrist, crisscrossed with small raised scars, and resisted the urge to pick at it.

She stood up, leaving the dull utensils and the sectioned off plastic tray that never failed to keep her food separated. She felt the same as before: hollow, unsure, and overfull with memories. If she truly admitted it, she would add defeated to that list.

Lost in thought, she walked past the gang at the table and clipped her shoulder against another patient. She didn't even utter an apology. He glared at her, but she couldn't be motivated to care.

During her physical therapy hour the next day, she ran fast on a treadmill, fueled by the dream of escape, and breathed hard against the reality that she never would. She had her peer-mentoring hour where she was put in a room with other Facility experiments in their buttoned-down gowns. Some of them stared at picture books while others bounced up and down and pulled thousand-page volumes from the metal shelves.

She laughed at them from her corner, nursing a print novel someone had taken a crayon to and had scribbled the words out with big loops and chaotic circles. She was in an honest-to-god zoo. She fell asleep hiding behind the book perched on her knees.

In her mental therapy hour, she sat still while doctors talked at her about the environment, toxicity, and mutations. Each week, someone told her she was making a difference, that her contributions helped to remake society. She snorted, saying our own hands had destroyed society; didn't he know about the bay full of horse skeletons and the water grayed by broken sewage lines and crumbling buildings cracking from the acid rain? She had lived in that environment, toxicity made her strong, and, if they really wanted someone to save, they should stop shoving some kind of mutated thing into her vagina. She wasn't *made* here in the Promised Land like the rest of them. She was born out *there*, on the outside, and what they were doing to her was morally wrong.

Her psychiatrist smiled, patted her knee, and motioned her to the door. Hour up.

She sat in the same spot in the cafeteria as yesterday, playing with her oatmeal and letting her spit turn it to mush on her tongue. She sipped the chlorinated water and jiggled the pills in her cup. Two were missing now.

She tipped the cup back, relaxed her gag reflex, and put the empty cup back down. Glancing around, a curl of anxiety warmed her stomach. She wouldn't dare mention the missing pills to the kitchen girls, but the mere thought of them changing her dosage—giving her more or less when she was coping just fine before—made her knees so weak she almost wanted to demand her pills, the right ones, the ones that didn't change anything.

She swallowed them anyways.

She got up and walked out of the cafeteria with her head down and arms crossed tight, when someone grabbed her elbow hard enough to bruise. Yanked to the side and into a corner, she glared at the man in front of her. At least she thought it was a man—you could never tell with these Promised Land types. He stuck a finger in her face, bright eyes liquid in the gloom, every bit of him focused on her.

"You make me sick," he said. "Do you outsiders really give up so easily?"

"Give up?" she asked. "Who the hell are you?"

"I'm one of theirs," he snapped, shaking her slightly. His hands were broad around her arms, and she caught a brief glance of the tattoos on his wrists. "I may have been made in here, but I've never seen something as pathetic as you, wandering around like you have no choice, no purpose."

Pissed off, she opened her mouth to contradict.

"Isn't that what they tell us? That you outsiders are dangerous, full of chemicals, *exposed*? All I see is a surly, baby girl who can't hold it together for shit when there's the slightest bit of pressure on her. Well listen up, you better get a hold of yourself quick because I'm getting out of here and you're going to help me."

He let her arm go and shoved her against the wall. Her shoulder blades bounced, leaving her raw.

"Enjoy your vitamin deficiency," he said, turning and walking away.

"There's a good girl," the doctor whispered above her. His elastic gloves left dry powder on her skin as he dabbed the sweat beading on her forehead.

She thought about her grandmother.

She jerked against the clamps around her ankles as something cold and metallic nudged her inner thigh.

She thought about her mother.

She felt a breach inside her, sliding in and filling up the emptiness. She wished she could be empty forever.

She thought about her brother.

"There's a good girl." Again, whispered above her.

Her brother would be heartbroken. Lost. Searching for her and never giving up, but he should, he really should, it's just ridiculous to keep looking when she'd been missing for so long—

The rod slid out slowly, carefully, and the doctor kneeling between her knees lifted the thermometer so he could read it. "Good temperature," he said. "Mucus discharge is perfect."

Something bigger nudged at her, slippery and smelling like oil, and she squirmed as the overfull feeling expanded. Who knew what kind of experiment's genetic gunk was being put in her: was it the one who had been exposed to high doses of PCB's? The drooling boy who shook all over from his diet contaminated with methyl mercury?

Maybe it was that ugly one who took her pills. Took them away because she couldn't get pregnant and he wanted to scare her a bit, show her that he knew he was wasting his semen. Maybe that's why he grabbed her and told her she was worthless. He didn't want to get out, *there was no way out*, he only wanted to frighten her. Boy, she'd gotten scared, but not now. Not anymore.

"I just don't understand the problem. The environmental conditions are absolutely ideal."

She suppressed a full-bodied laugh. She didn't want some dirty mutation's baby growing inside her. She would rather kill herself instead. It wasn't that she couldn't make a baby, she just *wouldn't*.

Mind power. That's what the ratty poster tacked up in the reading room said. Mind over fucking matter.

The thought made her laugh even more. Her chest shook in small convulsions. Both doctors watched her closely. She tried to calm down. The big overhead lights blinded her. When she blinked, she saw an expanding ring of red fire encompass the whole surgical room.

The next time she saw that piece-of-shit mutation, she was going to punch that smug grin right off his face.

Why did you want to see this?" the doctor asked, slinging his arm over the experiment's shoulder.

The experiment licked his lips, eyes focused on the outsider strapped to the table, watching the way the implantation crew hovered over her with carefully sterilized equipment and tools. Hidden away in the observation room, the darkness made both of them looser as they watched the procedure. The experiment leaned into his doctor's warmth, fighting the smile trying to curl his lips, and covered the tattooed X on his wrist. "I still don't understand why we bring outsiders into the Facility," he lied. "Doesn't it put all of us in danger?"

His doctor shrugged, trailing his fingers up and down Subject X's arm. "Yes, but that risk defines the Facility's purpose. It's our main tenet, the foundation of our—" The doctor rubbed his chin as a mocking smile curled his lips. "—*tribe*, to quote the outsiders."

"But why create all of us experiments on the inside, then? If the purpose is to save them," Subject X gestured to the trussed-up woman, "then why create us?"

The doctor gave Subject X one of those looks—oh, sweet, innocent, *stupid* boy. "It's not about saving them, per se, it's about resurrecting and maintaining overall human survival. Being separated from the outside means that we, here on the inside, are more than likely evolving differently compared to the likes of her. There aren't enough humans on the outside to facilitate healthy genetic growth. They've become weaker, sicklier, without any strong evolved traits to survive their environment. It's likely that we, without enough genetic diversity, will one day crash in the same way."

The doctor put his back to the outsider, leaning against the glass separating the observation room from the procedure room. He cradled Subject X's jaw in his hands, leaning in to gently kiss Subject X's cheek. "But we've created a human lineage through the many experiments here that, once perfected and introduced to the outside population, can thrive," he whispered against Subject X's ear. "That means that you, simply by being created, have insurmountable purpose. We have to ensure that those changes can still be compatible with those on the outside—those who have the culture and societal ties to carry these offspring and bring them into the main population. What's the use of creating children strong enough to withstand the diseases, radiation extremes, and pollution effects if we don't have the vessels to carry and care for them?"

Subject X hummed in agreement. The outsider—Subject O—thrashed and strained. He and the doctor stilled, observing her struggle, as if it were an anomaly that would soon pass. Subject X knew the Facility had pushed her too far. A limit existed to these outsiders, a point where they recognized they had become too much like experiments, and it was like a heat point where they destroyed themselves.

He had seen it happen before. The outsider had begun to descend toward it. Her skin had taken on a pallor of exhaustion. He couldn't let her be ruined. That was why he tried to incite her, push her around, create oddities in her daily procedure that might wake her up from her depression. He thought about the medicine he'd stolen from her, the pills hidden in his cell. Knowledge of the outside existed within her—the culture, geography, survival tactics—and he felt like an explorer from one of the books in the library, plotting a secret plan under the noses of everyone here. "But how has she survived this long?" he prodded. "Why does she struggle so much?"

"She doesn't understand the greater picture. To her, everything is against her will." The doctor made a pleased sound, like Subject X had done something surprising to him, and he turned back around to view the rest of the procedure. "I was surprised that you asked to view this procedure, but truly, why the sudden interest?"

"I was curious about her." Subject X paused. "And somewhat scared of her."

"You should be. Who knows what kinds of contaminants live in her blood, on her very skin? That's why we discourage interaction with her. But you've always been such a daredevil. Facing your fears."

"Only when you're with me," Subject X whispered, flashing the doctor a winning smile, and the doctor—stars in his eyes—took his hand, sneaking them both through the doors back toward the psychologist's wing of the Facility.

On the arm of the doctor, Subject X held his head up high as they passed the guards. They were used to him being in odd places. No one really thought it out of the ordinary when Subject X appeared where no experiments were meant to be. He was a favorite. He knew the place intimately, could sneak from one end of the Facility to the other, using all sorts of closed off hallways to wards, using keys temporarily stolen from the cooks and janitors and guards like a spy. He could mask illness one minute and then be the winking clown the next. He made people laugh. People liked him. People *loved* him.

It wasn't enough. The Facility was too small for him, especially now with the increased security after one of the experiments went missing. His experimental purpose was over and done with—he had been a prenatal test. Now that he'd been born and grown, the rest of his days would consist of simple data collection, keeping track of his existence. He needed more. Idleness helped craft this obsession with the unknown—with what lay outside.

Within him lay a restless anthropologist cowboy—there was a bigger world out there, and he meant to have a piece of it. But he couldn't ride his horse into the sunset blindfolded. He needed to speak the language, understand the customs. He didn't want to survive—he wanted to *live*. He needed the woman strapped to the bench to teach him, guide him, help him. He needed a name—an outsider name. A name would make her trust him.

Jailbreak would be hard, but it was the only thing he could do. That is, if the doctors didn't destroy his one ticket out first.

Somehow, somewhere, between the dying fire and his chattering teeth, Thresher fell asleep. It felt more like unconsciousness, gray and full of nothingness.

He tried to fight it, terrified that beyond the gentle chirps of insects and the wind, something waited to get him. He watched Mako plump his backpack into a pillow and zip his jacket up to his chin. His own coat cast shadows over them as it swayed on its makeshift hook. Thresher wanted to wrap up in it, but shuddered, thinking how wet it would be.

By the time his eyelids sealed shut, he felt calmer, especially after hearing Mako's sleep sounds; complete with huffs similar to those of his cellmates, familiar with the little snorts, grunts, and inhaled drool of life. Maybe Mako watched him through his slumber. If he was being watched, at least he hadn't been left behind.

A soft touch rocked his shoulder. He woke up quickly, always had, and blinked against the soft dawn. Mako stood over him, head haloed by the sun. His hair stood up on end in burnished brown. Thresher put his hand over Mako's and squeezed tight, frantically counting the freckles on Mako's nose and cheeks as if it mattered somehow. He thought freckles were supposed to make you look younger, but Mako looked sunburnt, rough, and just a little too ragged to be adorable. "C'mon," Mako said. "Get up."

Sitting up, Thresher felt his lower back tighten in pain. He gasped, riding out the stiffness.

"Do you know how to do this?" Mako asked, thrusting a length of dirtied white bindings into Thresher's lap.

Thresher couldn't speak. He bit his lip and felt like he was made of stone.

Mako sighed, knelt between Thresher's legs parted at the knees, and took a foot on his lap. "You're completely useless, you know?"

Thresher wanted to nod but he was too focused on relaxing. His muscles throbbed, hurt and angry all at the same time. He flexed his stomach muscles. *Hold me up,* he told them. *That's what you're good for.*

He watched Mako wrap the used cotton binding around his foot, Mako's warm fingers brushing against his cold toes and hesitating over the black tattooed cross on his ankle. Each touch sent a pinging sizzle shooting from the spot up to his knee. Mako tucked in the loose ends, put the foot down, and took Thresher's other foot, starting the process again. Thresher shook, all of it too much. He wanted to kick Mako, make him let go, because if he touched, *oh my god*, touched him one more time he was sure he would come out of his skin.

"There," Mako said, lowering the foot. "Now the boots won't hurt you. Saw you limping yesterday."

Thresher swallowed the lump that the touches had built in his chest. "Thank you," he whispered, voice gravel-rough.

Mako nodded, stood, and kicked the dead embers. Thresher pulled his new boots on, suddenly snug and comfortable, and laced them up tight. They were black and mud-spattered, heavy and wide. He stood and slipped the coat off the hook, shrugging it over his shoulders. It creaked as he moved his arms, but warmth encompassed him. He buttoned up the front and slipped his hands into the still-damp pockets. He felt like he lived on top of the world. He was dressed. He had things that were his own.

He pursed his lip and shuffled closer to Mako, noting Mako's leather jacket had a wide stain across the back shoulders. He reached out and brushed his hand across it. The leather felt soft, creased from wear. Mako jerked away.

"We have to go our separate ways today," Mako said.

Thresher narrowed his eyes. He may be terrified and helpless, but he had a stubborn streak a mile wide. He wasn't going to be cast off because he didn't know a few things. He would learn, become just as smart navigating the outside as Mako, if only Mako would give him the chance.

Mako glared back at him, as if sensing a brewing fight. Thresher loomed over Mako.

"It's just like you Bruykleeners to push your luck," Mako hissed.

"I'm smart," Thresher said, getting closer and making Mako tilt his head up so they didn't lose eye contact. "I'm a fast learner, but I won't survive one day here without you."

"This," Mako gestured between him and Thresher, "isn't going to work."

"Why?" Thresher demanded, trying to use a combination of Facility-perfected strength and submissiveness to appeal to Mako.

Mako threw his head back in a guffaw. "Because I'm Manahatta. You're Bruykleen. We're at war."

"I'm not," Thresher breathed, thinking that Mako smelled like earth and burnt sugar. "I don't know what that means."

"It means that your tribe is killing my tribe."

"I'm not a part of any tribe. I'll be Manahatta with you."

"It's not something you can become. It's how you're born."

"We're the same species," Thresher said quickly. "We're both human."

Mako hesitated, eyes sliding away. He sucked a corner of his mouth in and Thresher could see the white edge of his teeth.

"I was born in a test tube," Thresher said, leaning closer, sensing victory. "I wasn't in a prison. I was an experiment in the Facility where they did tests on me, but I escaped. I'm here, but I don't know what to do." He gave in to the taste of bravery, the words coming easier and faster now. "I don't have anyone else. I've never *been* anywhere before. I don't even know how to tie my own shoes. I've never even *had* shoes."

Mako let out a harsh breath and still wouldn't look at Thresher. A muscle in his jaw clenched. Thresher wondered if he could box him in any more, just shove him up against the cracked concrete and force him to agree, but that was what got him confined to the isolation chamber in the first place, arms forced together behind his back with chains around his throat. Force only worked up to a certain point before it left you all alone.

"A facility, you say?" Mako asked. His freckles had a toffee-colored tone.

"Yes," Thresher whispered.

"You better back the fuck off," Mako said.

Thresher took three quick steps back until the ground seemed to yawn between them. Thresher wanted to moan. This was one of the hardest experiments he'd ever conducted—one of conviction. Those few feet felt like a precipice, and he was begging the only way he knew how: *please don't leave me out here in this big bad world all by myself.* If this was human emotion, it far exceeded the subjective conscious experience characterized primarily by psychophysiological expressions, biological reactions, and mental states. If all this knotted, sickening throw-up waiting was just a cocktail of dopamine, serotonin, cortisol, and noradrenaline, he didn't know how he could keep drinking it and call it living.

He thought about getting down on his knees, crawling back to the Promised Land, and letting them strap him down and stick the needle into his neck because he'd been outside and it was nothing worth writing home about.

Mako shifted from foot to foot. He gave Thresher the once-over with hard eyes and jaw jutted out. "Tell me about the facility."

Thresher wanted to. He wanted to tell him everything, but he barely had enough information to make him worthwhile. "Take me with you and maybe I will," he countered, proud that his voice didn't shake like he did on the inside.

"You might be lying." Mako jabbed a finger at him. "It would be just like a Bruykleen man to lie like that. Are you trying to find out where the safe house is? I promise you, I'll do a lot of bad things to anyone who fucks with this meet. I sacrificed too much to lose it on starving driftwood like you."

"Please," Thresher said. "I can...take you to the Facility. I can show it to you. I promise I'm not lying and I'm not Bruykleen." The word felt strange in his mouth. The terminology bewildered him without any background to connect it to. The Promised Land had held round robin information sessions about savage, outside customs and cruel men, but nothing of *this*, nothing of civilization and cultural distrust. Were Bruykleeners different due to allopatric speciation? It made sense. All that water.

Mako tucked his pointed finger in against the others, making a solid fist. "I'll take you as far as I want to take you. Take you to Mama Milagros. See what *she* thinks of you."

Thresher felt loose inside. Rattled. Too much talking had rendered him into this trembling thing. He wanted to lay his head down and rest because he wasn't used to arguments he could win, discussions that demanded he keep up and participate instead of shoving a gag in his mouth to shut up.

"I hope that's not a synonym for desertion," he said instead.

"You're damn lucky I've got places to be. I can't spend time fighting with you."

"I'd only follow you." Thresher tried to smile. "Where are we going?"

"Deeper into Bruykleen land," Mako snarled, but his lip curved into a grin as if against his will. "We should really find you some pants."

6

Thresher didn't expect that finding pants meant looting more dead.

The sun filtered through streaky clouds without any warmth. He kept a close observation on Mako's rituals: backpack hoisted and satchel strapped down tight. Ankles flexed. Leather jacket zipped up, hiding his chin deep inside the collar's ratty sheepskin lining. He motioned for Thresher to follow, but it didn't matter when Thresher kept in Mako's personal space, terrified of Mama Milagros, wondering how real the inside joke for abandonment might be.

Thresher loved his long legs, but refused to use their length, walking in a shuffling gait. The farther they walked, the more disoriented he felt. He didn't know north from south. Soon enough, he stepped on Mako's heel. "Sorry." His voice trembled with shame. Any misstep might make Mako leave. "I'll be more careful."

His stomach grumbled. Back in the Promised Land, it would have been time for lunch. Thresher's teeth caught the edge of his lip. His face burned.

"Got a talker there," Mako said.

Sometimes, Thresher was at a loss of what to say back, but he tried. "Who are we meeting in this country?"

"Slavers," Mako said as he turned away. Thresher went cold from shock. Had Mako said such a thing to scare him off? Was it truth? Thresher didn't understand when his trust in this outsider had become so strong, but the land was empty and he knew he could die in it alone or survive in it with Mako. He forced his feet to walk.

Mako kept to the reeds where roots, glass bottles, and acres of cardboard held the ground together. His hazel gaze scanned the beach until he whooped and strode wide into the mud toward a stick figure angling out of the earth.

Thresher followed, just this side of too close, and almost gagged on the smell.

"Ripe," Mako said, leaning down. "Not much here. Not much time to build a scaffold, either."

"A what?"

"A scaffold. The soil became too sour for burials, so we adopted the tradition of lifting the deceased on scaffolds from those who joined our tribe after the volcano blew." His finger poked the bloated stomach, which squished and emitted a wet sound like water being squeezed from a plastic bag.

"I'm not wearing anything of his," Thresher said, backing up a step.

"Queasy stomach, huh?"

"What kind of dead man's clothes do *you* have on?"

Mako shot him a full-blown grin as he drew three mud-lines from the corpse's eyes to the hairline. "Stop being such a baby."

Thresher liked this talk, this back and forth banter that kept him on his toes. He rehearsed all types of responses in his head after they left the dead to its decomposing. He studied Mako like he studied his books. Mako liked quick responses that made him unable to hold back a smile.

"There's one," Thresher said, when he noticed a break in the wrack line. A long bumpy body face down in the algae.

"Nice catch," Mako said, winding his way down the bank.

The body was female with long sun-bleached hair braided with salt and sand. Mako looked her over, then eyed Thresher's legs. He patted the body down, slipped a braided leather bracelet from her bony wrist, and stripped her shift dress off. Drew the three lines. The woman's back looked sickly white in the yellowed light. Mako tugged on the cotton, testing it, before wringing out the water.

"For you to...cover up," he said to Thresher's frown. "Are you gonna bitch about it?"

"She doesn't smell," Thresher said and immediately hated himself. He thought about the complete mess he used to be in his restraints. The way he submitted, became a shadow, and how when he saw one of his fellow experiments have a fatal seizure, he'd cried. It was the blood that moved him to tears, that and the experiment's stubbed tongue chopped off by his teeth.

Mako handed him the shift and quirked an eyebrow. "You okay?"

Thresher ripped the material and wrapped it around his hips. He crossed his arms and wouldn't look at Mako.

"What, she too pretty for you or something?" Mako asked, standing. His eyes drifted to the sky. He was always checking the sun. Thresher sidled up to him as close as before, but didn't respond. He was done talking for the day.

Somewhere along the way and hours later, Thresher lost sight of the ocean.

Submerged in his thoughts, it became automatic to follow the trail left by Mako's footprints. When he came out of the half-remembered flash of laughing with another experiment—how the grooves of her white teeth gleamed—he glanced up to find the quicksand beach had transformed into pavement.

Each step vibrated up his sore feet to his inner thighs. Blisters roared hot and irritated. He needed to take his shoes off, stretch, and bend his toes. The sun sunk low over his head, another day dead and almost gone. The air smelled drier and sharper. He realized he was parched.

Big block houses of brown stone or brick were stacked like books on top of each other all the way into the sky. Metal grates guarded shuttered or shattered windows. Glass glittered on cracked asphalt. Sprouts of grass and moss crept between the crevices to reclaim the land. The place felt dirty, used, as if a well-worn grime had polished up to a good patina and somehow that made the grime edgy and good, even if there were old spots of gum stuck to the ground and scuffed skid marks, but it didn't make the place trashy, oh no, it gave it character.

He saw big, bold statements proclaiming brands he didn't recognize and pieced together the meaning of other ripped signs. Advertisements told him he could lose weight, that he shouldn't do meth, that smoking was bad for him with happy half-smiles melted from acid rain, spattered with bird urea, and faded from exposure.

He felt surprisingly strong in this modern era. This, after all, was a world he was used to: a world of concrete boxes meant to be homes, encouraging slogans telling him how to live, and names he had never heard of before, but took for granted, because they knew more. It felt different from being out in the open with nature pressing in on him, reminding him how much of an abject failure he would be if she showed her wrath, how fast she could put him down with her winds and rain and starvation.

Sticking close to Mako still remained Thresher's best policy and, luckily, Mako quit snapping every time they tripped over each other. Soon enough, it felt as if Mako hefted Thresher's shadow like another backpack and picked up his pace. The looming buildings fell away to become smaller, intricate houses with faded paint, white shingles, and small squared-off gardens, as if having a green thumb used to be cherished. A good reminder of how the elements could tear you apart. Thresher smirked at the desiccated yards and resisted pointing a finger at its dolled-up docility to say, *I know what you're hiding. I know what you are, sneaky nature, just biding your time. You know you can take us down without a second thought.*

He wanted to leave, but Mako had stopped. He squinted at a black-shingled roof as if trying to conjugate the verbs of a new language.

Thresher stood shoulder to shoulder with Mako, struck with a terrible thought that this was Mama Milagros's home. Their time had ended so quickly. He should have bargained for more. So stupid to assume it meant they would be together for longer than a day.

Mako eyed the sun. Thresher wanted to say something, but ever since they raided the woman on the beach, he couldn't bear to put words together. They made him callous.

Earlier, Mako had jostled for entertainment, telling stories that started out interesting, like when he was a kid he scaled to the top of a tower built like a rocket, walked all the way up to the top of an empire state, and with eyes to the sky and the world a dark smear below him, knew he was king of the earth. "Don't you want to know what I saw up there?" Mako prodded.

Thresher didn't answer, shame still a rock in his throat.

"Ruining my best story here," Mako said. Then the tales got harsher, *meaner*, as if Thresher's silence had become Mako's challenge. Thresher tuned him out, transformed him into background noise because there were only so many times he could hear: *how you Bruykleeners sure screwed up. Think you can attack us by boat? We're a fucking island, a fucking rock. Nothing can touch us and we beat you back, you son of a bitch.*

Whether Mako ran out of steam, realized he had overstepped his bounds, or finally got it through his stubborn head that Thresher didn't care, he shut up. Thresher didn't mind the silence. He was used to it, but he wondered how Mako, a man who craved interaction, got along. He studied the sky, too, wondering what they were looking at.

"This has to be it," Mako said, his voice scratchy from disuse. He shut his eyes. The lines on his face sharpened and his energy stilled, as if morphing into his predator namesake. "If you plan on sticking with me, you have to be absolutely silent when we go inside. You make one peep, we're fucking done."

Thresher's brain buzzed with white noise at the request. He nodded, and if his words had been hard to get out before, now it was near impossible. This was an unexpected test he didn't want to fail. He followed Mako up the three steps to the porch. Mako pulled gently on the screen door, but it came off its hinges. He put it to the side and opened the sturdier door behind it.

It was the first time Thresher had seen Mako skittish. Mako paused on the threshold as if the next step would define the rest of his life. Thresher glanced over him to see a hallway with rooms branching off the sides. It looked like a real home, where people cooked meals and sat together at a table, and asked about their day. There would be a dog. Every story he read about homes like this had a dog.

Mako eased inside, strung tight as a drum. Thresher followed, suddenly yearning to claim his independence and explore. It was nothing like a cell, or a reading room, or a physical therapy room. It had wallpaper, wallpaper that curled off the plaster, sure, but *wallpaper*.

"Shut the door behind you," Mako whispered. "Carefully."

Thresher obeyed. Mako crept past the first room, while Thresher peered at an overturned couch with the stuffing rooted with mice and dried feces. It smelled musty. Crumpled lamps with brittle skeleton wires and smashed light bulbs tipped towards the floor.

Mako stopped at the last room before the hallway opened up into what Thresher assumed was the kitchen. He made a sound in the back of his throat, then said, "I know you boys love your deals, but I sure am glad you decided to keep this one."

Peeking over Mako's shoulder, Thresher saw two men. One pulled the tattered remains of shades over the broken window. The other circled behind them, closed the door, and stood in front of it, trapping them inside. Pastel paint flaked off the wall in discs, the numerous coats forming a colored timeline.

Thresher tried to still the telltale signs of panic. This felt too much like the Facility, without the sterility and the too-washed walls, but the feeling of danger lingered, as if at any moment, he would be wrestled to the ground and put in containment. He couldn't get any closer to Mako, who stood tall with his bow legs at a stance and said in one of the strongest voices Thresher had ever heard, "What do you have for me?"

The man near the window sneered. "What I got for you depends on how much you've got for me."

Mako pulled a pouch out of his coat pocket and shook it, clinking the shells. Thresher knew the bag held many purple-white smoothed coins like the ones they found on the beach corpse. "I'm paying for everything, Wadi." He threw the bag on the floor.

Wadi stared at the bag but didn't pick it up. Thresher wondered if it was a sign of trust between them. "You must be fucking desperate," Wadi said. "If the Bruykleeners knew we'd be here—tribe-to-tribe meeting in *their* safe house on *their* land—we'd be strung up like *that.*" He snapped his fingers.

Thresher shifted to the side, his back against the wall, keeping an eye on the man guarding the door and protecting Mako's blind spot.

"It's saying something that the only place we can be truthful with each other is in a place where we both have a good chance of being killed. But I'm not here for what-ifs," Mako said. "I'm here to understand what's already happened."

"Not sure how much I remember," Wadi said, pacing in front of the window. The window shade let in enough light for Thresher to make out the long scar disfiguring his upper lip.

"Let me refresh your memory," Mako said. "Two years ago, you—Reckowacky-Queens tribe that you are—poached two Manahatta. A man and a woman."

"Two years is a long time," Wadi said, spreading his hands. "My record-keeping ain't that good."

Mako shot him a withering look. "I don't think you'd forget this transaction. At least, that's what the South Woodlanders say."

Wadi paled, but Thresher admired the way he didn't fold. While Mako hadn't moved, the intensity vibrating from him sharpened by the minute until Thresher wanted to fall to his knees and expose his neck, just to ease the pressure.

"I take the commissions I'm given. This isn't exactly an easy way of life, but it looks like you've taken to it. Maybe you can *trade* me for the information you want instead." Wadi stepped up to Thresher, gripped his wrist, and ran his thumb over the soft inside. "Finely marked too," he said.

Thresher wanted to wrench his arm away, wished the heat radiating from Wadi didn't make him feel so ill. Maybe this was why Mako brought him along, as collateral to be sold to this man. He dug deep for control, held onto the thought of the experiment he'd been on the beach who had no one, and somehow didn't break the man's jaw.

Mako pushed Wadi's shoulder and inserted himself between them. Thresher wanted to rest his forehead on Mako's shoulder in relief. Tested so far, he hadn't broken his promise.

"Two Manahattas," Mako said. Each syllable had a bite.

Wadi backed away, but the hard gleam remained in his eyes. "Sold them down south. Surely you gathered that already."

"Oh, I gathered that," Mako said, stepping into Wadi's space. "I chased that hint down the dark coast and came out the other side fighting a war that wasn't mine. I found out you sold my best friend as a warrior-slave. Do you know what happened to him?" Mako held up two fingers and ticked them off. "Dead, or missing. Either way, he can't be found."

"You know how it works," Wadi said, a whine to his tone. "Commissions are executed based on need. The Woodlands needed soldiers. That's what we sold them. I didn't play favorites or take where there wasn't fat to skin, you see? For your friend, sounds like wrong place, wrong time."

"What about the woman, then?"

"Women fight the war too."

"Not her. There was nothing on her. Where did she go? You sold her, and by the trinity, it sure wasn't to the Woodlands."

Wadi didn't look nervous anymore. He looked downright scared.

"You know how the Woodlands are, Wadi. I got really good at getting what I needed. There's a lot about the tutelage of torture that can shape a man. And when *I* got good at it," Mako stood face to face with Wadi, "I mean, really good at it, I found out that yeah, Tarek had been sold down to the Woodlands, but he'd also been sold alone. Which gets me thinking, as I sometimes do when I'm agitated about a situation like this one, where could the Manahatta girl possibly have gone?"

"Look," Wadi said, putting his hands up. "I don't know where she ended up. All's I know is sometimes we get wind that the Promised Land is looking for women, very specific women, we're talking exact tribes, even—"

"What the trinity is the Promised Land?"

"I don't know." The man gasped, as if the words couldn't be spoken fast enough. "Whenever we get commissions like that, it's good. I'm not talking real nature-crafted shell-coins. I'm talking pay in goods that don't exist anymore. It's not often, but it's always worth it."

The danger in the air twisted. Thresher knew that at the beginning of this meeting, Mako sensed prey was near, but now he tasted blood—and it drove him crazy.

"Where is the Promised Land?" Mako said, his teeth creaking against each other.

"I...I don't know. We traded the girl to the Wallabouts to bypass the treaty with the Enders. There was a contact—*I don't know who she was, man*—she was new, young, but vetted. Scars on her wrists."

"When was the last time they made contact? When was the last commission?"

"It's been two years, at least. There hasn't been one since your girl."

Mako took a big step back. Wadi released all the air from his lungs. The wall dug into Thresher's shoulder, but he didn't have to clamp his lips shut anymore. His words had shriveled.

"Get out of here, Wadi," Mako said.

"Deal still holds." Wadi had to say it twice. "My people have ensured this place is safe for the night, but once the Bruykleeners learn it's been compromised, they'll trash it. Kill anyone they find. Anything remaining is free game."

"Got it."

"You don't follow me," Wadi said.

"And you stay the fuck out of my way."

Wadi nodded and inched for the door. He fled with his companion. Mako paced the room, hands on his hips, before smashing his fist into the wall with a roar. Colored paint rained down. Plaster dented under Mako's boot. He kicked the wall as if he planned to take the whole house down. Thresher wished he could disappear, yet he felt desperately invested in watching Mako fall apart. He'd never seen anyone physically take their rage out on anything before being subdued. It must have lasted only seconds, but it felt so much longer.

"I should've killed him," Mako said. "I should've, right? That's what I should've done." He turned to Thresher, expecting an answer.

Thresher remembered his promise, now transformed into a blessing. He wasn't supposed to talk inside the house.

He imagined his face under Mako's boot, his ribs cracking under Mako's fists, Mako demanding to know who, what, and where. Fear, teetering on terror, seeped out of him, but in the midst of it, realization of his value felt pure and horrible. Mako didn't know that the Promised Land and the Facility were the same thing, but Thresher did.

Mako teased his lips with his teeth. Thresher dreaded Mako's opened mouth, but instead of asking questions, Mako said, "You did good. This place has hardly been picked over. Let's see what we can find."

7

Whatever mask Mako wore during his meeting with Wadi disappeared as they looted the house. Guilt twisted Thresher's stomach. Some sense of loyalty urged him to tell Mako about the Facility, but at the same time, it sounded like the worst discussion he could ever have. At first, he clung to his promise of silence, but Mako had said it—*he'd done well*—and Thresher hoped that that praise made Mako's previous order null.

"Why...didn't you take Wadi up on his offer?" Thresher asked. In a room that might have once been a study, he ran his hand over a desk ruined with claw scratches and rounded stains from a wet glass that ruined the lacquer. "For a moment, I wondered if you'd sell me." It felt foreign, referring to himself as something that could be bought and sold. He didn't quite understand, only recalled the way Wadi had stroked his wrist.

"Slave trade isn't my thing. I've seen enough of it to make me sick." Mako reverently took a blue blanket draped over the back of a rocking chair and unfolded it to see the design. Some kind of blue and white stitched angel, palms together in prayer and a halo over a nondescript face. He refolded it into a tight square and stuffed it in his satchel.

"Then, why have you been so kind to me?" Thresher asked. "Why help me if you thought I was your enemy?"

Mako tipped his head back and sighed. "You know when the volcano blew and everyone started dying? The tribes with blood-lines originating on this continent came together. My ancestors faced extinction before, but this was a new wave that affected not just us, but *everyone*. We knew we'd have to come together, no matter what tribe we were from. Everyone else put stock in the government, but that institution had never been trustworthy, so it wasn't a surprise when it collapsed. It left people lost, starving, and isolated from the rest of the world. This was before I was born, you know. I'm just repeating history."

Mako rubbed a hand through his hair, making it stand up even more, and grimaced when he saw Thresher's overwhelmed face. "People soon came to us and relied on the associated governmental tribes on Manahatta for guidance and help. The death toll was so high, it was cruel to turn anyone away, even if it was just so they could die from environmental causes among fellow humans. It didn't matter who we were, just as long as they weren't alone."

"Like radiation?" Thresher whispered. He remembered that particular experiment. Thick tumors bulging through skin.

"Sure. Like radiation. It wasn't long before there weren't enough people left to maintain cities or states or tribes on the island. Those who remained came together under the blended tribal banner to reclaim the island as Manahatta. We were tiny, but we were alive. We're from all over: Lenape, Irish, Choctaw…"

Thresher's brow furrowed. The names flowed over him as he grasped for something recognizable. He didn't know about the volcano, didn't know about what happened on the outside, only that it had become a land of death and disease. He imagined an endless human tally whittled down to a sparse handful and clung to his original question as a grounding point. "But why help me?"

Mako paused. "Maybe you were cast out as a sacrifice, maybe you were an escapee, but you reminded me of what it was like when I first arrived in the Woodlands, ready to do anything but knowing it might ultimately kill you. You were close to death. I helped you because I have people dear to me that are lost, and if they are alone, starving on the beach, I hope someone would help them."

"Like your friend."

"Yes. Tarek." Mako swallowed hard. "Wherever he may be."

Thresher had planned to be on guard, but any plan regarding Mako never seemed to work. "I'm on your side," he said, hating that he had to keep this secret to ensure his future usefulness.

"Forget that," Mako said in a way Thresher knew meant anything but that. "A house that hasn't been looted never happens. Usually everything's already been picked over or isn't good enough to use. Nobody makes anything new these days, it's all hand me downs and thrift shops from here."

To Thresher, everything felt like new.

Mako led him to a smaller room with a white oven spackled in grease and a bulging refrigerator that gave off a dank scent. Mako flung open a cabinet door like a magic box and squeaked when a mouse scurried out of the way. Thresher couldn't help but laugh. While he still believed he was betraying Mako, the last traces of fear *of* Mako peeled away. "Scared of a mouse, huh?" Thresher said, words feeling good again, addictive like the meth and the smoking.

"They're unclean vermin," Mako said, glaring at the empty shelves. He opened another cabinet and cried in triumph, turning to show Thresher the tin cans in his hands. "We're going to feast like kings tonight." Humming, he separated the cans of tuna, mandarin oranges, and pickled beets based on whether the tops were warped or not.

Thresher wasn't paying attention. He opened drawers near the floor and pulled out a boning knife, a can opener, and what looked like a measuring cup.

"Good find," Mako said, cleaning the measuring cup with a hard puff of breath and his finger, then smearing the dust on his pants. The can opener didn't need inspection; its use was too tantamount. Everything useful slipped into the ever-bulging satchel.

Mako tested the blade on his thumb and made a face of approval, his mouth turning down, his eyes widening a touch. "You're gonna want this," he said, handing the knife to Thresher. The black wood had three vertical metal circles on each side and looked like a pencil next to Mako's machete. Thresher thumbed the blade, imitating Mako's expression—that pleased, yet surprised look— feeling the scritch-catch of his pad against the sharpness. He put the knife into his pocket, careful not to snag it. Thresher felt elated, as if Mako somehow transferred this energy straight into his bloodstream like a shot.

Mako was already on his way out, but Thresher paused in front of the refrigerator. It was sticky when he opened the door, like tacky blood or stepping on sugar water. He cringed at the smell. White bugs writhed over blacked bits of indistinguishable *something*. Freed flies aimed for his face like military bombers. Thresher shut the door hard, covering his mouth and nose with his coat sleeve. He inhaled the scent of mud, salt, and sweat that was quickly becoming *his* scent.

He followed Mako into the bedroom. Mako knelt as if in prayer, smoothing his hands along the spring mattress with an awe Thresher had never seen before, as if he wanted to sink into it.

"Watch out for the snake den." Mako nodded at a corner covered in leaves and rumpled clothing. "It's why the pests aren't in this lovely piece of civilization. Evolution knew what the hell it was about when it made snakes. Best animal on the entire planet."

"You really hate mice that much?" Thresher asked, confused. In children's books, mice had big, bright eyes and were considered the perfect animalistic interpretation of a human. "Aren't they cute and friendly?"

"Mice are the slugs of the earth. No. I won't insult slugs because slugs have a purpose. Mice are the lowest dregs, worse than pigeons, worse than *germs*."

"Aren't children supposed to keep them as pets? Because they're good to hug?"

Mako looked horrified. "Only if they want to develop rabies."

Thresher wanted to indulge his smile, wanted to tap this personality quirk of Mako's and see what exactly made it tick.

"Hantavirus, man," Mako muttered as he tore a dresser apart. "Fucking mouse shit gets you sick with hantavirus, and he wants to give 'em goddamn cuddles."

Thresher opened the end table drawer. Inside, he found a pair of wire bifocals and a faded picture of an elderly man poised with a woman in his arms. They both smiled as if proud of the woman's wrinkles and liver spots dotting the husband's balding forehead. Thresher had never seen anyone so old before, never seen a person reach that mystical age over fifty and live to tell the tale. He guessed this couple was in their seventies, all bright and happy in this faded photograph. He folded it carefully and put it in his pocket.

Three books rested in the drawer. Delighted, he pulled them out and rejoiced in the familiar sharp cut pages and tight print with precise numbering in the header. The paperback smelled like dust and cracked glue. One hardback had lost its dust jacket and the other older one was bound in green. He opened it and read the neat brown handwriting on the first page. *To my compass.*

"You're in luck." Mako turned to Thresher holding long blue pants in his hands. "Jeans," he said with a devil-may-care smile, "and slacks. Your huge size too."

He stopped when he saw the books. Thresher cradled them by the spine and supported the backs along his forearm. "What books are those?" Mako demanded with a look of untarnished hope.

"Looks like textbooks," Thresher said.

"What about the paperback?"

"Maybe a romance," Thresher said, skimming through the spider web thin pages.

"All intact?"

The paperback began to fall apart in his hands. The glue was too hard to stick, the pages shedding like the hair of a balding experiment infected with cancer. Oh, how they wanted to cure it. She was the holy grail of experiments, doted on by all the doctors, envied by all the experiments. *Jealous.* Thresher had been so jealous of the attention she was getting when he wasn't supposed to present his disease for years and years, if he presented a disease at all. He felt a sickening shift in his stomach. Infected and no good, *an experiment.* When he looked at Mako, he didn't think experiment, he thought *man.*

"Just the hardbacks," he said softly, far away.

"Thank you, thank you." Mako exchanged the books for the pants. The books went into the backpack. Thresher inspected the long pant legs and the slim cut. He'd never worn anything like this before, blue denim like they wore on ranches and farms, hard-working clothes for hard-working men.

"Try them on," Mako said. "I want to stay here tonight, so we might as well get comfortable."

"With the snakes?" Thresher asked, quelling a tremble in his throat. He didn't want to sleep on the floor with the reptiles, would take his chances with the mice if he could. No one wrote stories about nice snakes.

"I'm not sleeping out there," Mako snapped, cocking a hip and pointing outside. "It will be safer in here."

Thresher took in a deep breath. He didn't want to leave this room in case Mako would escape out the window, leaving this perceived Bruykleen experiment with the pests of the earth. Thresher would have to sleep in the corner, boning knife in hand in case those slithery creatures tried to wrap around his leg, distend a jaw, and make a meal of him.

"There's underwear, too, but that's up to you. I don't like wearing clothes that've been touching another man's junk even if it *was* decades ago." Mako tossed the clothes to him.

Thresher didn't care. He'd been wearing other people's things his whole life and would rather wear the underwear of a sweet man who'd found the elixir of life rather than no underwear at all. Maybe the secret would rub off on him, and he'd live until he was as wrinkled as the man in the picture. He took off his coat and laid it on the bed gently, then tried on the black slacks first and the jeans second.

"Yeah? Here," Mako asked, handing him a blue backpack. "Found this, too."

With a thrill of ownership, Thresher put his black pants in a bundle at the bottom and slung his plastic backpack with mesh padding over his shoulders to test the fit. He tightened the straps. He grinned at Mako, and Mako grinned right back, two comrades against the world, rich on measuring cups, backpacks, and old man boxers. Mako stripped off his satchel, leaned it against the wall, and walked to the adjoining room.

"Oh, sweet god, it exists."

Thresher peered over his shoulder into a bathroom smelling like scat and urine.

"I don't know what I've done to deserve this, but I'm going to do it more often. That, Thresher, is a toilet. An honest to trinity toilet not full to the brim with shit."

Thresher quirked an eyebrow. At the Facility, there had been lots of clean, bleached, and sterile toilets. They even flushed.

Mako started rummaging through the mirrored cabinets, swaying in glee when he pulled out a bottle of hand sanitizer. He pumped the stiff handle until a clear green-beaded ooze spat out. The smell of alcohol, raw and unfiltered, filled the air. Thresher stepped back violently, remembering the sterilizations, the sharp smell of ethanol used to keep tools hygienic, the way he had been cleaned with isopropanol when he tugged on his restraints and hurt himself, the way a guard on a vindictive streak punished him, holding a soaked rag over his nose and mouth until he almost passed out.

Mako breathed it in with bliss and rubbed his hands together. Thresher fought not to split right then. Mako stepped to the front of the door and shot Thresher a look that said fate was having a field day, and this was a time to take what you could and be grateful, be so grateful for it.

"We're going to spend the night here," Mako said, putting his hands on the doorframe and leaning into it. Thresher nodded miserably, wondering how much of this display was true pleasure or a front. "So decide which side of the bed you want, because I want the side closest to the door, but I'll leave that up to you. We'll be the last ones to ever sleep here."

Thresher gaped at him, not understanding, and yet understanding all too well.

"Now if you'll excuse me, I'm going to spend some quality time with this toilet."

As Mako shut the door, Thresher heard him purr, cowboy twang out and proud, "Why hello, darlin'."

8

Thresher was dumb. No, he was unbelievably stupid to think he could do this. The dark had settled into a comfortable night, but he was squished to the edge of the mattress, his body wound so tight his muscles ached. Mako snored and sprawled too close beside him. Thresher could feel his heat like a line of fire where their backs brushed. He wanted to scoot farther away, but there was nowhere left to go.

Mako had thrown a fit after his rendezvous with the toilet when he'd found Thresher making a nest in the living room. Away from Mako, but close enough that Thresher would know if Mako tried to leave. "You want to sleep here?" Mako asked, abject horror written in his crossed arms. Thresher had stood his ground, looked those hazel eyes straight on and said, "I'm not sleeping on the floor with the snakes."

"The bed is big enough for two," Mako said. Thresher had stared at him, not *exactly* sure what that meant. "We can share it," Mako said slower this time, as if he were talking to a lesser experiment, then hurriedly added, "No funny business or anything like that. Just sleep."

Thresher had felt like he was going to come out of his skin just hearing the words, but now that he was actually doing it—sleeping in the same bed with another person—he couldn't get comfortable. He couldn't find a spot that wasn't hogged by Mako, couldn't stop the whispers in his head saying *claustrophobia*. The bed wasn't big enough, even though he had been in worse situations, such as sleeping in a straightjacket on the floor unable to even roll over. He closed his eyes and tried to clear his mind, but the uncomfortable feeling persisted, making his legs twitch as if he couldn't stretch them out the right way. He was cramped in this tiny room with this outsider who had begun whimpering in his sleep.

The sound brought Thresher up short. He went still as he listened to Mako's breathing pick up in short gasps. Thresher knew those sounds: the beginnings of a nightmare taking hold and gripping deep. Mako's leg kicked Thresher's and Thresher turned so he could see Mako's hunched shoulders. Mako released a low-pitched moan, like he was desperately trying to keep his pain inside and secret. Thresher's heart twisted, wanting to mother Mako through these dark dreams that he had walked countless times in his own mind. This man had fed him, shared cans of food with him. He could still feel the fish and fruit rolling on his tongue and mixing in his stomach.

Sharing. He had trouble understanding it, this give and take, this parting of bread. It had always been *steal* for him, borrowing items before they were viciously taken away or forever removed. But here, on the outside, Mako had given him things, shown him how to wrap his feet with cloth, what it was like to share a meal, share a bed. Thresher was no stranger to nightmares. He knew how to deal with them. Maybe this was something he could do for Mako.

Thresher reached out and laid a careful hand on Mako's leather clad back. Even in sleep, Mako refused to remove his jacket, zipping it up tight and snuggling his chin and mouth inside the sheepskin. Mako mewled, a harsh half-cry before rolling onto his back, eyes wide-awake and wild. "Fuck, *fuck.*" He choked on the yell. "I can't be, *I can't be.*"

Tears gathered in the corners of his eyes. Thresher felt a stab of terror as Mako ripped the zipper of his coat down in one violent tug. He gripped the sweater underneath, pulling the hem up to expose the long expanse of his belly.

"Oh my god, oh my god, I can't be, I can't be." He ran his hand over his stomach as if reassuring himself that he was whole.

Thresher propped up on his elbow and put a soothing hand on Mako's shoulder, uttering small nonsense words that seemed to help, something along the lines of *it's okay, don't worry, it will be alright,* because that's what people said in books when their friends were in distress. Mimic and survive.

"I can't be pregnant," Mako sobbed. "I can't be pregnant."

Thresher didn't understand. He studied Mako's stomach as Mako frantically smoothed his palms over the flatness until the skin turned red. White scars marred the flesh and shiny stretch marks wrapped along his hips below his navel.

"You're not pregnant," Thresher said, confused. He'd heard rumors of failed experiments like that, of genetic rewiring that had never worked. Mako was an outsider, and there was no way nature could accomplish what a team of highly advanced scientists with equipment light years ahead of the status quo couldn't. "Shhh," he soothed, laying his hand over Mako's frantic one. "You're not pregnant."

"I don't want it inside me," Mako whispered as he stared at his body. "It's inside me. Get it out, get it out."

"Feel this? It's flat. Nothing's growing. You're a man and males do not get pregnant," Thresher said.

Except for seahorses, he amended in his head. But that didn't seem to be a good aside to mention, at least not right now.

And sea dragons. And pipefish. Maybe there were more male pregnancies floating around than he thought.

As Mako made small desperate noises, Thresher spread his hand wide on the man's stomach, feeling the jump of abdomen muscles and the curl of dark hair slicing through the stretch marks and scars. "Nothing is there." A strange feeling came over him, a hint of authority. "Do you hear me? Mako, look at me."

Mako's hazel eyes snapped to Thresher's, so large in the glow of the moon.

"You aren't pregnant. You're a male. Male humans are not anatomically equipped to give birth or incubate an egg."

Mako's chest heaved and his eyes skittered back and forth between Thresher's. He drew in a shaky breath and let a stuttering one out.

"It's just a dream," Thresher said.

"I could feel it. They put something inside me. Filled me up with this creature. It was my baby. They said I couldn't keep it. I didn't want to, but then I kind of did, but it was going to kill me."

Thresher realized he was carding his hand through Mako's hair.

"And I wanted it but I didn't, but they forced it inside me with all these tubes, and I had this awful feeling. It was like I was full and too big for my skin."

Thresher realized how close he was to Mako and how the claustrophobia had floated away, *wiped* away, and now the heat was a good heat, a *we're alone against the world and there's just us here* kind of heat. He leaned into it, abashed at his boldness, but too addicted to the way he tingled everywhere he touched Mako. Anywhere he was allowed to touch, like this was an experience no one else had, even though he knew people touched all the time. Mothers gave kisses to their children. Grandfathers hugged their grandchildren. Friends locked arms and got through the world together that way. Bound by touch.

"And you're a fucking liar because seahorses can get pregnant. Some kind of help you are in a crisis," Mako snapped, a blush sweeping up his cheeks. "I'm thinking I'm infected with a parasite and you're handing out flawed scientific facts."

"You thought you were actually pregnant with a baby," Thresher corrected. "You even expressed maternal instinct."

Mako's eyes shuttered. Thresher felt a gut stabbing pain of regret. He wished he could lasso the words and wrangle them back. Mako pulled his shirt down and zipped his jacket up to his chin.

"It was just a fucking dream," he muttered, rolling away and putting his back to Thresher. "Just a stupid dream. Let's forget this ever happened, okay?"

Thresher didn't know what to say. He never wanted to forget this moment for the rest of his life. It was too full of intensity, the way he felt closer to Mako than he had with anyone else. He had experienced a whirlwind of emotions in the span of fifteen minutes: panic, worry, consolation, reassurance, anger, and silence. He wanted to poke Mako, make him turn over and talk, make him tell him about the dream and what it meant and explain that he wanted to know it all. That Mako was the most interesting thing Thresher had ever met.

Instead, Thresher curled as close as he could to Mako's back without instigating rage, and listened to Mako's breathing slow and deepen, selfishly wishing for another nightmare so he could have an excuse to satisfy this sudden flesh-hunger and be closer to that heat again.

9

Bruykleen land made Mako's skin crawl. Always had. Whatever bad luck or curse that drew Mako back to these enemy tribal lands time and time again had fucking *vigilance.* This place made him lose control. At least when he woke on the cusp of a second nightmare—clinging to him like the Woodlands' humidity—he hadn't cried out like before, convinced something grew inside him. This dream was full of panic, sure, but it was also familiar.

His machete slicing through the air. Flattened land bearing the scars from hurricanes and storms. Wicked laughter radiating from camouflaged shacks. Haphazard swamp battlefields where Woodlanders fought over clean water, free from the slick rainbows leaking from shipwrecked oil tankers. Fireflies and glow worms illuminating the pale green witch's hair dangling from sacred oaks.

The way he dragged those who might've known something—anything—of those who'd been stolen and lost. How he'd strung up those kidnappers and warriors and slick wordsmiths who spoke in lies and bargained hard for truth, how he used the potions and talismans from the women of lore and shaking bones to see his victims as wood, dolls, and fossils with a story to tell instead of flesh and blood with information to hide before he extracted what he needed from them.

Thank the trinity Thresher didn't wake as Mako eased out of the bed. He couldn't stand another episode of mothering from the Bruykleener...or whatever he claimed to be. This facility—whatever the trinity *that* was—sounded like something cooked up in the Woodlands. Mako ran his hand through his short hair, wishing he could make sense of the things he came across—Promised Lands and facilities and slave traders terrified of who knows what—and slipped out of the room.

Curse his foolish heart that prompted him to help Thresher. He had seen far too many Woodland soldiers lost and dying, begging for any kind of help and none that he could give. There was a good chance any one of them could have been Tarek, and Mako hoped that one good deed on his side of the world could cancel out all the bad he'd done down the line. Plus, the idiot had been dining on piss-clams. That alone was enough to say the poor soul wouldn't last.

Easing down the stairs, Mako marveled at the quiet, wondering how fast word of mouth would travel and alert the tribe that he—Mako Saddlerock—had put foot on Bruykleen land before even returning to his own home. He felt an urge to skip visiting Manahatta completely. As much as he yearned to see his family, the Promised Land awaited—whatever that was. Could it be a place up north? To the west? No clues, no hints—nothing to go on but Wadi's contact, who was like dust in the wind. He had nothing but a name. Promised Land.

"Where are you?" he whispered to no one. He ran his hand over his mouth. The future yawned dark and unknowable before him. The night sky began to lighten, the stars blinking out of view, and Mako went outside, sat on the porch out in the open like some daring dumb chicken bobbing out of a Manahatta's coop, and gnawed on the rawhide of a plan. Molding the future into a direction, a goal, a path where he could place his feet and walk upon.

10

There was blood on Nika's jeans now. The dark stain flowed down the inside of her thighs. She looked like she'd pissed herself. Nika smelled metal whenever she moved, but she had a skip in her step because, if at first you don't succeed, try, try again. If you keep on succeeding, don't change a damn thing. There wasn't one reason not to flaunt it—the jeans, the blood, the smell.

The same two pills were missing from her daily drug treatment, but Nika hadn't seen that son of a bitch experiment when she sauntered out of the cafeteria. She went to her physical therapy session where she lifted weights until her muscles ached and burned. She talked to her psychiatrist.

"Subject O has great difficulty conceiving," the doctor said into his tape player.

"That's what happens with outsiders," she said, opening her hands. "There's a lot of death. A lot of sterility."

The doctor looked up from his notes and charts and put a palm flat over the paper to hide it without instigating alarm. "Tell me about your family," he said, face open and waiting.

"What?" They never asked anything like this.

"I want to know about your family. You're from the outside, so you had a mother, a father, siblings perhaps?"

"I don't want to talk about my family."

"Tell me about your mother."

"No."

"She must've been like you, I think."

"Why are you asking me this?"

"Mothers are a critical part of a child's life. I believe one of the issues we have with our grown patients is that they have no family binds to keep them emotionally strong."

"*Now* you're worried about their mental state?" Nika felt her hackles rise; the nape of her neck prickled, an animalistic sense of danger crowding around her.

"Are you feeling emotionally ready to have a baby? Do you feel supported by the faculty and staff?"

"Do not tell me you're giving me a pep talk. You're giving me a pep talk, aren't you?"

"We want you to feel safe. We know how terrifying it can be to suddenly become a mother, but you know you're in good hands. We are all excited and hopeful for this just as much as you are."

"This place is sick. You're all sick and twisted, you know that?"

"Wouldn't your mother be proud of you?"

"That's not what this is about," Nika snarled.

"Don't you think she would be scared for you? Worried about you?"

Nika blinked away the sudden wash of tears. She hated how he could get to her so fast, especially this first time. She felt unbalanced.

"She'd give you advice. Tell you about the fear and the hunger cravings, but she would also tell you how wonderful it felt when they handed you to her the first time. When she got to look into your eyes for the first time."

"My mother gave birth to us in a run-down apartment with a barely competent midwife," Nika snapped. "There wasn't a slew of doctors and there weren't any pain pills. She almost died."

"Birth can be a terrifying experience," the doctor said. "But it can also be very rewarding. Who was the other one?"

"What?"

"You said your mother gave birth to 'us.'"

Shit.

"I meant me. She gave birth to me."

"Do you have a twin?"

"No."

"You must. No one would refer to her own, single birth in the way you did."

Nika remained silent while the doctor leaned into his tape recorder. "Subject O is reported to have a twin." He paused. "Is she fraternal or identical?"

"Who?"

"Your sister."

"Fraternal."

The doctor frowned, but made a note in his report. Nika's breath dried her throat, making it scratchy. She wanted to jiggle her leg and release all this pent-up energy, but couldn't. The psychiatrist would notice. He noticed everything, apparently.

"Were you the younger twin or the older?"

Nika snorted. "Why? It was a matter of seconds."

"Please. We want to understand your history. We think it will help."

"Younger," she spat.

"Do you think your twin would be angry at you for having a baby before she did? Do you think she would resent you?"

Nika almost smiled, sibling glee elating her like laughing gas. So much ammo. She had so much ammo now. "She'd be so pissed. So very angry."

"Why are you laughing? Did I say something funny?"

"No," Nika said, dissolving into giggles.

"I think that's enough for today," the doctor said slowly as Nika leaned over her knees, her giggles ramping to hysterical laughter. It was just too funny.

"We're going to give you a change of clothes," the doctor said, handing her a neatly folded bundle. She accepted it, tears rolling down her eyes, mouth pulled in tight and wide to stop smiling. "Thank you," she said, tucking the clothes under her arm. "I appreciate you watching out for my fashion sense, doc."

II

She tightened the standardized cotton drawstring pants then folded her crusted jeans and ran her hands over the denim's fraying holes before lifting the mattress of her twin bed and hiding them underneath. She shared a room with another female, some asthma-ridden creature, who breathed with mucus-thick gasps and carried a breathing apparatus for when the attacks doubled her over.

Nika suspected an asbestos experiment, maybe concentrated air pollution.

She had the room to herself for once, the silence as light as the dust specks floating in a sunbeam. She basked in it, this moment to think. She shook out the shirt they gave her, some scrub-like material, folded it and stuck it next to her jeans. Her sweater still had wear left in it. She sat on the edge of the bed, feet pointed like a ballerina, and felt the tug in her shin. The two beds barely fit inside the room. If she extended her leg out, she could touch the other one.

She waited for the shaking to start. Whenever she was alone, the whole world seemed to collapse on her as she realized the situation she had gotten herself into—but nothing happened. It was calm before the storm—*acceptance*—and she replayed in her head the moment this whole catastrophe had started.

Stupid decision, really. It was ironic. The reason she'd gone out on her own was because she wanted to have sex, hadn't had a chance to do it yet and she was in her early twenties, still a virgin. She had read something about how a big problem with whales mating in the wild was their inability to find one another in the great big blue. That was how she felt. That was how it was. Between the shaky peace after the tribal wars, finding someone else outside of the tribe was just too hard. Too scary.

Sure, she'd run into Bruykleen kids and Reckowacky-Queens teens, but her hatred over her mother's death crushed any romantic possibilities. She wasn't a star-crossed gal, could never be, especially when she wore her mother's bones—powdered to a fine grain and lovingly poured into a vial—around her neck as a reminder. An odd piece of jewelry she insisted on wearing after her mother died.

Something that had her grandmother tutting in disapproval. Not part of tradition. *Any* tradition, ever—ancient past or apocalyptic future. But it was *hers.*

She'd been playing with boys since she was a child, been flirting with them ever since she woke up and realized she had breasts and a menstrual cycle, been making faces at testosterone farts and disgusting eating habits for forever. They ran in a pack, the five kids in her neighborhood, within a panicked closed-knit community who survived the first tribe war, then the second, and finally set up shop as survivors determined to keep their heads down. The other girl, her best friend Anna-Skye—oh *now* the tears started—had a crush on her brother, but Nika nipped that in the bud quick. Anna-Skye's mother was some kind of residual hippie freak—at least that's what Nika's grandmother said—who liked to shake her finger and say, "I told you this was going to happen. Didn't my sixties war-fighting, tree-hugging, flower-power, great-great-great-great-grandmother tell you this was going to happen?"

Nika didn't quite know what that meant—whether she referred to the country's isolationist agenda before the Western volcano blew, or the tribal wars that decimated the islands. Nika's grandmother always shook her head saying, "Now's not the time for I-told-you-so's. We all have plenty of them."

Anna-Skye hooked up with the other boy in the pack, leaving only one other available male for the only other available female. Tarek. Nika and Tarek. He wanted to go to the rooftop. Nika knew they would make out for a while, and then she'd push him a little more, get him that much more hot and heavy before she'd whisper something naughty in his ear, and there you go: deed done, memory made, experience had. Tarek wouldn't tell because Nika's brother would beat the shit out of him. She bit her lip, wondering if her brother ever had a chance to lose his virginity.

She'd snuck out of the apartment, scaled the drainpipe to the concrete below, and pounded pavement to their meeting spot. She put on some kind of dried-up perfume found on the floor of a store. Mixed with spit, the smell came out just fine. She had on her best jeans and prettiest sweater. She remembered her feet banging on the pavement.

Bang.

It was chilly, autumn almost done. Stars shone with diamond sparkle in the patches she could see between abandoned skyscrapers.

Bang. Bang.

Tarek had been warm. He smelled like purloined cigarettes, although there wasn't anyone to steal cigarettes from, only empty corner stores picked over and falling apart from last year's hurricane.

Bang. Bang. *Bang*.

Her head snapped up and she yelped at the face pressing against the small square of striated glass, nose bent and forehead smooshed. Goddamnit. Goddamn son of a bitch experiment. Knocking—bang bang *bang*—against the door.

She scrubbed her face with her sleeve, smearing the tears across her cheeks. Dried, they sucked out the moisture, leaving her gritty and baked as a desert. Opening the door, she put on her best bitch glare.

The mutation fell into her room and closed the door quickly behind him. He scooted to a corner where he couldn't be seen even if someone looked through the window. "What the hell do you want?" Nika asked, trying to clear her throat.

"Can't be seen together," he said, eyes flickering from her face back to the door. "Experiments and outsiders aren't supposed to talk on their own, you know?"

She did. Talking was reserved for the activity room, the lunchroom, the reading room, where guards and attendees were able to keep close watch. Even her roommate, rarely present as it was when she wasn't gasping for air, refused to speak with her without an orderly present. She didn't know why, especially when most of the experiments here were either brain dead, regressed to four-year-olds, or just plain socially inept. The place was airtight against conspiracy. "'Cause outsiders are contaminated, right?" she said, sarcasm dripping like hot wax.

"Pretty much," he said. He paused and stared at her, eyebrows slanting tightly together. "Are you crying?"

"What the fuck are you doing here?" she snapped back, question for question. She cocked her hip and swept her hair back from her forehead, gouging her fingers along her face to erase any traces of tears.

"You wanna get out of here, yeah?"

She felt as if he'd handed her pure hope—shiny and terrifying—on a silver platter. "Of course," she whispered.

"I know someone who escaped," he said, face lit with zealot belief, eyes glowing with the future. "I think we can do it."

"What do you want from me?" she asked, suspicious as hell, her hackles rising for the second time today.

He held out his hands, placating. "I've never been outside. I don't know how to survive. They tell us stories about how awful it is out there—about cannibals and zero genetic diversity—how you don't survive a second without knowing your way around. You do. You know and I want out."

"Is that why you've been fucking with my pills?"

"Had to get your attention one way or another."

"Could've introduced yourself."

He looked blankly at her. "And said what? Hey, you want to be friends?"

She felt at a loss. "Yes?"

"Now I know this plan really isn't going to work," he said, sounding so mournful.

"What's that supposed to mean?"

"Only that I've got outrageous expectations and a low threshold for bullshit. We gotta go now." He took a deep breath and grabbed her elbow tightly.

She stared into his eyes, pale blue, and then down to his grip on her. She raised an eyebrow, but he didn't let go. "Took a lot of courage to manhandle you," he said, his voice somewhere between exhilaration and fear.

"Never been touched by an experiment before," she said. "Unless you count when you pushed me."

"Am I going to get cancer now?"

"You can't get cancer from touching someone, you idiot."

He flashed her a smile still nervous around the edges, opened the door, and pulled her next to him. She shivered as his hand dropped clumsily to hold hers. "Keep close," he said.

"Why?" She should pull away. While he might not catch anything from her, who knew what kind of crap he had running through his body, what kind of engineered germs he'd been exposed to in the name of the Promised Land's progress. Curiosity ran through her veins like a sickness. She decided to listen to it. Couldn't hurt. She wasn't doing anything else, anyway. It felt nice actually; unsolicited, basic human contact.

Out in the empty hallway, dull electric lights flickered beside mounted candles, illuminating the white walls and cracked tiled floors. The experiment pulled her along, leaning down to whisper in her ear. "I've been watching you. I saw you when they first brought you here."

A thrill ran down Nika's spine. Her toes curled painfully against the floor.

"Don't get a lot of outsiders in the Facility. They brought one in, maybe a few weeks before you got here. After the first round of testing she made rope out of her clothes and sheets and hanged herself."

Nika shrugged. She'd thought about it a few times herself. Carelessness ran rampant here, the tools of a suicide comically laid out all over the place.

"Never seen something like that before. Never even *heard* of anything like that happening. Ever."

Experiments weren't exactly known for their resourcefulness.

They walked out of the dormitory into a stairway and descended three flights before the experiment guided her into another hallway. A large array of experiments clamored against the walls, drew in their drool, and were herded to their rooms by attendees. Her companion—the mutation, she corrected herself—parted his lips in a wide grin and he waved at one of them like they were good friends.

"You think now's a good time for a walk through?" The attendee sneered at them, his face red as he tried to soothe a newly-free experiment. "This is unacceptable, *reportable*. I don't care who your doctor is—you're too damned bold."

"Looks like you've got more to worry about than little old me," the mutation said.

"Trinity," Nika breathed. This mutation had a death wish. Terror washed over her and she clutched his hand tighter. He made a surprised sound. She turned her face into his shoulder when one of the experiments started to seize on the floor.

"I've always wanted out, you know?" he said, maneuvering her around the twitching boy and away from the attendee. "Heard stories, of course, all the propaganda about radiation and tumors you'll get from stepping outside. They told us to stay away from you because you had the plague."

"Glad to know I'm a topic of conversation," Nika muttered, sidestepping a hunchbacked experiment clawing at her ankle. Glancing behind her, she watched the attendee wrestle his charge into a room and then motion his colleague over, bending low to whisper into her ear. The woman caught eyes with Nika and for a brief moment, a heavy lump of ice formed in Nika's stomach.

"It didn't scare me," the mutation continued, not even fazed. "It made me feel alive, learning how you survive out there. I had all these questions about what you eat, what you wear, why you don't abandon the place entirely and find someplace new."

Nika bristled at the assumptions. They weren't refugees. It was their land—land they'd been living on for generations. You don't just give up the home your ancestors walked on, the grid streets and valleys of familiar places with familiar names. She wouldn't know where to go anyway. Wanderlust belonged to her brother.

"Wanted to be like you. Wanted to get outside more than anything in the whole world. Kept me up at night, dreaming about it."

"It's better than here, that's for sure."

"I talked to the other outsider, just briefly before she..." He swallowed hard.

"Killed herself," Nika supplied. "If you can't say it, you can't do it."

The experiment looked at her in pure horror and yanked her closer to him, stumbling to an unsteady halt against the wall. "Don't you say it then," he hissed into her face. "Don't even think it."

"Hey, break it up you two. No outside interrelations," a third orderly snapped at them, dragging two snarling experiments away from each other.

Nika took a big step back and watched the experiment's eyes widen. He reached out to her. She came back within his orbit, but shook off his seeking hand. They stood awkwardly in front of each other, looking at the hallway's chaos instead of each other. "What's happening here?" Nika finally asked. She'd never seen such pandemonium or the orderlies so outnumbered.

"This is the mentally damaged ward," he said. "It's after their bedtime, so I opened all the doors and turned on the lights."

"Well aren't you a rebel," Nika said in appreciation, earning her a broad smile. She regarded the experiment with a keener eye, from his dark curly hair to the long fan of his pale feet. If he had the nerve and smarts to figure out how to steal her pills *and* cause a scene like this, he might not be so bad to have around. He reached for her hand again and she let him take it. He pulled her further down the hallway. Nika swallowed hard. Behind them, the three attendants had clumped together, shoulders hunched, talking intently. "Hey," one of them shouted down the hall. "Don't move, X."

"Been studying you," the experiment said, softer, ignoring the authorities. "Trying to learn how you outsiders interact."

She thought back to their first encounter, his in-your-face attitude, the way he shoved her back.

"Copied the way you talked. Need to sound natural when I'm outside."

She replayed their conversation, his questions bold against hers, his straightforwardness, the bulldog taunts. *Pistol for a mouth,* her mama said. *Got it from you,* her father said.

"What else do you know about me?"

"I changed your dosage. They were giving you hormones and amped up vitamins. Prenatal." He glanced over his shoulder, his mouth pursing in dissatisfaction. The attendants broke from their conversation, pushing the confused experiments out of their way and into rooms, making their way towards the two of them.

Nika snorted. "Figures."

"I don't know your name."

"This tattoo doesn't do it for you?" She waved her wrist in his face.

"I want to know your real name," he said, still leading her down the hallway. He glanced back again. The orderlies were closer than ever, a gleam in their eye that *wanted to teach a lesson.*

"Nika," she said, softly. "What's yours?"

"Don't have one. I like Bartholomew."

"By the trinity, no."

"It's regal," he said, picking up their pace.

"It's old," she said and yanked on his arm. They were nearly at the end of the hallway. The experiment looked over his shoulder again. His cheek indented as he sucked on the inside of it. "Just keep walking, okay?" he said.

"What?"

"I'm going to let go of your hand. Go out and up the stairs, *four flights,* walk to the end of the hallway, and go down one flight. Should bring you back to your room."

"What are you going to do?" she asked.

He smiled. "Just keep walking."

He let go and careened into the wall, slamming his face up against it like his head was too heavy. The rest of his body leaned away from it. Startled, Nika watched instead of walked, as he mouthed at the white wall, drooling on it like the rest of the mutations.

Two orderlies grabbed him immediately. Nika lurched into a sidestep. The experiment thrashed in an attendant's arms, flinging wild punches. One of the orderlies hit his jaw. The experiment spit blood at them.

"You can't stop me!" he cried out. "I'm insane! I'm out of control! I might do something crazy!"

Nika walked backwards, head down, her eyes still trained on the scene. She never noticed before how *young* the orderlies looked. It took both of them to contain the mutation.

"You'll never make me submit." He gasped as the orderlies pinned his arms and dragged him away. His bared teeth shone with blood as he reared up to escape. A punch to the gut had him gagging. She could see his wide eyes telling her to *go* before a needle was shoved into his neck. He wrenched to the side, dragging the hole wider, but the sedative worked fast and he sagged. A female orderly rushed forward with a straightjacket and manhandled him into it, buckles tightening across his back.

Nika swallowed hard, not sure what to do, but there wasn't much left to see, and she had four flights to climb. She punched the door open and scampered up the first flight before encountering another group of attendants rushing down to help control the commotion.

Nika froze on the stairwell. The attendants stared at her like a wild animal freed from its cage, both stuck in a standoff, before one made a move for her arms. She kicked out, rushed back down the steps, but they had her by the hair, by the arm. She twisted. There was a pinch in her neck.

Walk, the experiment had told her, but she was an idiot, always staying behind to catch one last look, always reading the last page of a book first because she couldn't stand not knowing what happened. *Walk now*, he had said. He would have walked her out himself if he could have. What a gentleman. She tossed her head back, a laugh caught in her throat. Bartholomew? She would call him Walker, if anything.

N ika had never been in a straightjacket before.

In all her time, she had never been restrained and abandoned like this, as if she had to be dealt with like a temperamental hog familiar with the smell of slaughter. Her mouth was tacky and stale from the sedative easing out of her system. Every joint in her body ached. She hadn't opened her eyes yet, but she could feel the canvas tug when she moved her arms, elbows numb from lying on a stone-cold floor. She rubbed the sides of her fingers together, grateful for some kind of contact, no matter how slight.

Her eyes gummed together but she forced them open, taking in the blank cell made of stone and concrete with a windowless door. She wasn't chained. She wrestled to sit upright, her torso a useless ball, her legs scraping against the stone seeking purchase. Finally, out of breath, she leaned against the wall, tilted her head to look up at the ceiling, and wished to the trinity someone would get her out of this thing. So confined, so useless—but that's the point, she thought. That's the point of it.

The thought left her hollow-bellied. She swallowed, trying to conjure up saliva to wet her mouth. She realized she had been privileged despite the experimental pregnancies. She had it good, never went hungry or thirsty, and even if she was dirty, it was better than this. Things got put into perspective real quick when she lost the use of her arms.

She hadn't felt like this since her capture. It had happened so quickly. She fell right into the trap laid for the unsuspecting. Tarek had tumbled down the stairs. The last thing she saw was his motion-less body before a sack went over her head. Needle in the neck and it was lights out until she woke up with tears coating her lashes and fear binding her like iron. Her mind replayed a mix of senses: the heat of Tarek's mouth on hers, the rare smell of her grandmother's coffee cake, and the uncomfortable wet between her legs that at first had been sexy as hell and now just made her itch.

She could smell the stench of ashy fire kindled from wet wood. She heard the harsh mucus-lined laughter from lifelong smokers in the distance. Being kidnapped by poachers had the same impact as if she'd been struck by lightning: she had always been warned about it but considered it something that happened to other poor souls, never to her. She lifted her head, groggy. She felt the vial of her mother's bones thump against her chest. She snapped it off with bound hands—the chain was tarnished shit—and worked the vial into the bark of the log she had been thrown next to. Landmark. Her one breadcrumb.

It broke her heart to leave her mother there. She whispered farewells full of hope and forgiveness. Her brother always made fun of her for talking to their mother who was nothing more than dust. He even chastised her for not burying the bones, but Nika always felt her mother surrounding her. Her mother wouldn't leave Nika alone in this world. The bones would let anyone looking for Nika know they were on the right path.

Jingled scratches outside her door brought Nika back to the present. She felt half-lit with a mixture of terror and salvation. Time crept by, but it wasn't long before the door opened inward revealing her psychiatrist, his hands folded over his manila folders like a saint come to lay prayers at her bound feet. He wore his white coat, but he was disheveled and looked half asleep. Disapproval made his lips smaller, his eyes narrower, his cheeks sharper. The pit in her stomach spread. She had been caught being bad, very bad, and it was time for punishment.

An orderly followed him into the room carrying a straight-backed metal chair. He set it some distance away from her—like she could do anything—and her psychiatrist settled on it, his legs straight and together. The orderly nodded and stood against the wall. The psychiatrist rubbed the bridge of his nose, his palms baby pink compared to the dark brown of his skin. He shifted and sniffed, his broad nostrils flaring in distaste. He regarded her for a moment, observing the way she tugged uselessly with her arms. She wanted to shake, coming out of her skin here, and every muscle ached to stretch to a painful point.

"How is this arrangement working for you?" he asked. "Does it suit you?"

Nika shook her head.

"Do you like being treated as an equal?" he said. Nika realized just how angry he was. Fury made his black eyes burn. "Do you enjoy being like the rest of them? Shackled like a cow?"

Nika wanted to let out a moan, but she bit the inside of her cheek to keep it inside.

"Now this is how our session is going to go," he said. "You're going to answer my questions, each and every one truthfully. If you don't—and I won't be able to tell, but honestly, you're not that good of a liar—I'll let my friend here," he nodded to the orderly, "make you feel even more at home. Treat you just like one of the family. Make sure you feel like you're not human, just a test tube baby like the rest of them out there."

Nika breathed slow and steady out her nose, trying to stop her leg from jimmy jiggling all over the place.

"My first questions are easy ones. What were you doing out so late and why were you in that particular ward?"

Nika swallowed. "I needed to get out of my room."

"Why?"

"Too claustrophobic," she said, wanting to glance at the orderly, but sticking to her guns and staring straight at her psychiatrist.

His eyes flickered back and forth between hers. She wasn't lying, not really, she *did* feel claustrophobic most of the time. She felt like she was inside another cage, dropped into a chasm of emotional ties and mental agony with only one pinpoint of light at the top where he could throw stones at her until she broke.

"And?" he prodded.

"Heard the commotion. Went to investigate."

"Some of the orderlies said they saw you with another experiment who seemed to be leading you somewhere. That you were touching."

"I met him in the corridor. They're all crazy in that wing, aren't they?"

"What did he tell you?"

"All sorts of gibberish."

Her psychiatrist snorted. "Like?"

"Kept babbling about how I was contaminated, how I shouldn't be there. Is that what you tell those experiments, that us outsiders are full of radiation and shit? You know you're just as much of an outsider as I am, don't you, doc?"

The psychiatrist's mouth curved in a momentary smile. She felt colder now, not sure if he was happy to recognize her usual banter or if he knew what she really had been up to. Walker did tell her those things. It wasn't a lie.

"Did he scare you?" the doctor asked.

She laughed. This one she could answer without any slides. "To hell and back."

"We don't like you being contaminated by them either. There's a reason for telling the experiments you're dangerous. They could hurt you."

"He didn't seem *that* concerned with me," she said.

"I want to know about your mother."

That caught her off guard. "What?"

"What was she like?"

"She wouldn't put up with this shit that's for sure," Nika said.

"Was she like you? What did you call yourself? Whiskey? Asked if I liked the way you burned going down?"

"Yes, she was just like me," Nika said, sullen.

Her psychiatrist nodded to the orderly who approached her with his big hands spread wide. Nika scrambled as best as she could to get away and banged her head against the wall for her trouble. Something stiff and unyielding settled against her throat and cradled her chin. She heard straps cinching into buckles. When the orderly backed away, she couldn't move her neck. Panic cradled her like the collar. She could feel it each time she swallowed. She rolled her body, tried to kick her legs out, but it cut into her trachea. She couldn't fucking breathe.

Vaguely she heard the psychiatrist whispering her through it, telling her to be calm if she didn't want to be treated even more like an experiment. She willed her heart to stand still, fought through the drug haze of natural adrenaline to hear the next question.

"Now," the psychiatrist said. "You're not like your mother at all. Your mother wanted to have children. After today's little display, it looks like you don't. Is that true?"

Nika realized this was a question she had to answer, right or wrong. She couldn't stop watching the orderly, her eyes so wide they might pop out. "No, I don't. Not this way."

The orderly bent behind her. She felt a thick chain attach to the collar with a clink. He tightened the chain until she was flush against the wall. They couldn't do this to her. She was a person for the trinity's sake, not a fucking dog.

"What about your twin?" the doctor asked. "Does she want to have children?"

Again with the *she*. Nika wouldn't correct her psychiatrist. "I don't know. Maybe? We never talked about it."

The orderly made a move toward her and Nika began to cry, wriggling and fighting as much as she could, but she'd never been strong like she should. All she wanted was to answer him right, tell him what he wanted to know.

"Why don't you want to have children?" The psychiatrist asked, motioning the orderly away with a slight nod.

"The way you do it, it's not natural," she gasped.

"You would rather have a man in the lab impregnate you?"

"No, no, that's not what I meant—"

"Because that can be arranged. After all, you want to be treated like an experiment."

"No, I don't, I don't. Please get me out of this, please let me go."

"You want me to treat you like you don't have any emotions or higher-level thinking, experience, or past history. Is that how you want to be treated? Like you were born in a tube?"

"No." Nika moaned. "I don't want it. Please get me out of this, by the trinity I'll be good, I promise."

"Do you want to have children?"

"Yes, I really do, I really, really do."

The orderly secured a wide belt around her knees, locking them together. Nika screamed, kicking her legs as much as possible without cutting off her air. Blackout rings gathered behind her eyes. Higher level thinking? She couldn't process past the panic trembling in her bloodstream.

"Do you?" The psychiatrist sighed. "I don't like this. You may not believe that, but you have to learn that you're different. We treat you differently because this is a research facility. We're learning about the impact of diseases and environmental disasters that have wrecked our world. Those experiments in the ward you decided to visit? They're mice. Mice in a cage with the lifespan of a finger snap. They can be regenerated and multiplied, reborn by the dozens with each environmental factor attributed for. Those of you who were lost in the world, stumbling with nowhere to go, are like endangered monkeys. We don't want to harm you. You're more precious than a hundred mice. You're human. Let me treat you like one. Would you like that?"

"Yes." Nika sobbed as the orderly strapped her ankles together. "Please, I'm a human. I'm different, I'm better. I want to have children. I want to help you."

"That's a good girl," the doctor said. "That's what I like to hear. Now tell me what happened to your mother."

"She died." Nika coughed, her heart razor hot from the pain inside her. She never talked about this. Ever. "She was killed in a tribe war."

"Between?"

"Manahatta and Bruykleen. We were hiding on their land. They had rights. They clubbed her down."

"Do you want to be clubbed down like an animal? Like what those people did to your mother? Put her down like a dirty rat?"

Nika screamed just before her whole world turned red. She thrashed like a worm. He had no right to talk about her mother like that. Her mother, whom she left sticking out of a log in the middle of a godforsaken nowhere, who was nothing but a thimbleful of dust. The mother she couldn't bring herself to bury as tradition demanded, whom she dishonored and abandoned.

The psychiatrist leaned back in his chair, a soft sheen of compassion highlighting his dark eyes. He had the gall to even speak about her mother and then feel sorry about it?

"You don't have to be strong," he said. "She was probably protecting you."

"Fuck you, you worthless piece of shit. She was better than you, better than all of you. You're nothing but a putrid disease, a stupid boy playing scientist because he can't get out from under his daddy issues to grow up and learn what it's like to be a real man."

"Be careful or I'll put a head strap on you."

Mucus and spittle coated her mouth. She was five again, spit and snot on her upper lip that her mama wiped away and she cleaned all the things that made Nika less than human, taught her with actions how to be a woman. A good mother.

"You know what the strongest instinct in the world is? A mother's instinct. She'll do anything for her young. Drive off threats. Sacrifice herself. Kill. I think that's why you're fighting us. Your mindset is that we're the bad ones. That we want to hurt your young. We don't. You're safe here. You can have a child and it will grow up beautiful and intelligent. But I can't give you these things—things like freedom— without some indication that you want to be human. You have to act humanly. Can you do that? Can you be strong like your mother?"

"Yes," Nika sobbed. "Yes, I can, just get me out of this, for the love of all that is holy, the trinity, anything, get me the fuck out of this."

"We're going to take you to the lab," the doctor said, standing. "It's time to give it the old college try again."

13

Nika wasn't sure if she woke voluntarily or maybe her brain had finally had enough of comatose blankness. She knew time had passed by the color of her bruises. She hadn't talked to her psychiatrist—even when he pressured her—instead falling back into the cool, gray mist where she didn't have to think about the future, the past, or even the present.

All of her pills were back, even an extra new one. She swallowed them easily, wondering how hard it would be to choke on them. She replayed Walker's story about the other outsider who found herself in this hellhole. Suicide sounded like relief, a balm to an aching world that would only get worse for wear. She knew her psychiatrist was worried, having pushed her like he did. She felt cracked open at the ribs, needing only a few well-meant prods to spill her guts about what truly mattered: her brother's smile, the discovery of flowers growing between the long lines of concrete cracks, the gutter smell of the river. Even full of mercury and sewage, she still sensed that water could be purifying. Could still look beautiful when the sun hit the waves, green like the highlight of her twin's eyes—her own eyes—and she missed him so much it twisted like a knife inside.

The door to her bedroom opened and the room filled with the rubber sole slide of doctor's shoes. She felt a hand on her arm.

"I have a question for you." Her psychiatrist knelt before her. He shuffled a long, perforated paper and she peeked at the sequence of ATCG and multi-colored histograms. "A rudimentary DNA analysis indicates your genetics contain a high proportion of Native American alignment..." He licked his lips. "...which is unique. It leads me to wonder about the composition of your tribe. Manahatta, did you say?"

She wished she could recover that spitfire girl who fought with every ounce of available willpower. She wasn't broken, but she put up a whimpering resistance. "Isn't it in my file?"

"The other...limited outsider females we've worked with haven't yielded this kind of genetic profile." He continued as if he hadn't heard her. "We're only just starting to understand and map the human populations surviving successfully outside of the Facility's controlled environment. Your insight would prove useful in the future."

Nika shook her head, her thoughts reaching through the mist of her coping instinct to retrieve the tale of the end of the world, told to her as often as its beginning. "You once told me that great scientific minds came here, after the volcano, to change the world. Your great-grand-something survived to make this." She gestured wildly around her. "My *unique genetic profile* is made of a lineage who survived the end of the world once before. We came together because of a genocide that couldn't be forgotten. We banded together again when the volcano turned the earth to ash. We survived because our stories, our way of life—old and new—will outlive the ink and charts of your Promised Land. We are not unique in this world. We are the strength in it."

Her psychiatrist pursed his lips and Nika winced, knowing she'd crossed the line of disrespect. A shiver of fear made her numb. She heard the door behind her open again. Two doctors led her back to the lab, strapped her down with a familiar tightness that almost started to feel good, and stopped her from floating away into the misty gray. Her feet slid into the cold metal stirrups, her legs cockeyed at a wide angle, and she watched as people knelt between her legs. If nobody touched her down there for the rest of her life, it still wouldn't be long enough.

She thought about being full of some man's spunk and felt so dirty. Shame rose in her chest. Her body might betray her and obey its time-honored duty to procreate. What would her brother say if he saw her in such a state, spread wide and impaled on tubes? She wouldn't love this baby—couldn't—because it was forced on her, wasn't something she wanted. It was rape wasn't it? Even though she couldn't fight it?

Her mind blanked at the word. She looked up into the bright lights, the smell of ethanol strong today, and blinked hard to clear her vision. The procedure complete, silence surrounded her when normally she'd be hearing the soft coos of the doctors' encouragements. The doors opened and closed, her bed being pushed somewhere new. Dread gripped her heart. What did they have planned for her now?

She didn't understand what was happening above her. She didn't understand what Walker was doing there with a white doctor's coat over his shoulders and black-framed glasses perched on his nose. He peered over her. She could see his blue eyes stained with tealeaf brown and his long hair curled around his neck. One side of his mouth twitched in a smile. Before she could speak, he put a soaked rag over her nose. Pungent. Chloroform? She inhaled the chemical deep into her lungs like a drag from a good cigarette where the nicotine rush came instantly, and watched the gray blink out to black.

14

Thresher woke in a cold, empty bed. He ran his hand down the indent in the mattress, imagining Mako's defensive hunch, the cadence of his breath, and the time it took Thresher to fall asleep after Mako's dream.

His brain, too quick to revel in regret, dumped panic into his bloodstream. Thresher snapped upright, looking for Mako's bag against the wall. Gone.

Thresher scrambled to his feet and snatched his backpack—so beloved the night before, but now a hateful sign of independence—and ran out the door. He thundered into the kitchen, his stomach rolling in knots like he'd eaten a piss-clam all over again. Sprinting into the living room, he clocked the side of the couch with his hip and hissed at the sudden throb. Disturbed mice chattered. Frantic, he looked out the window and everything froze inside him when he saw a familiar shape sitting on the porch.

He never realized how his anger pinpricked through him in waves. The resurrected screen door bounced off the wall and clattered onto the porch when he slammed it open. "Is this a joke to you?" He hissed at Mako's back. "Me waking up and thinking you're long gone?"

Mako was silent as he simply scooted from the middle of the porch to the side. Thresher didn't want to sit beside him. He wanted to yell his fear and make imaginary neighbors stop in their tracks. He wanted to cause a domestic dispute.

But wild anger could be subdued, leaving nothing but scattered ashes. Experiments weren't allowed to act out; experiments weren't people. He plopped beside Mako, propped his legs on the step, folded his arms on top of his kneecaps, and *huffed*.

He watched the bright new morning in silence. The buildings cast long shadows over the pavement, and breathy breezes made the browned lawn rustle like too-stiff cotton. The blue sky swallowed up his panic, and he realized how much his loneliness had faded. He shuddered and thought he was transforming, becoming good at not only blending in with the shadows but blending in with this world.

He might be blending in so well that no one will notice him. Wadi's threat—or offer, if considered from Mako's perspective—to buy him still haunted him. He couldn't imagine the consequences, but the Facility—even the rebellious woman doctor he followed blindly into his own kidnapping, who left him on the outside—issued warnings of what outsiders could do to each other, and he believed Wadi capable of every single one.

His throat tightened at the memory of his last night at the Facility. He would never know if he was chosen or if it had been right place right time. Either way, he knew she didn't care if he lived or died. It was the act of freeing him that was important. He still remembered her parting words as she drove him to the middle of nowhere and shoved him out the passenger door. Her soprano voice, the sharp syllables cut off by her teeth, the strength of her conviction.

He wouldn't look at Mako. He just wouldn't.

But Mako sighed, earning back Thresher's attention. "Not going to just up and leave you." He looked subdued and tired. "Like you could even figure out east from west. I keep my word, alright?"

The claws around Thresher's heart unclenched. He exhaled hard, still feeling hurt but grateful for the relief. He wondered what else he might find in this world that seemed as if he and Mako were the only ones scavenging for humanity in humanity's rubble. "You snore," he said, instead.

Mako looked scandalized. "I do not."

Thresher bobbed his head in a nod. "All night. Couldn't sleep a wink."

"*You* snore," Mako said.

"Deflection." Thresher waved a finger in front of Mako's face. His reward was a half-hearted grin, nothing lively like Mako's usual dazzling smiles, but Thresher decided he'd take it anyway.

"In a couple hours, this house won't have a purpose," Mako said. "We'll be the last ones to use it. I made it unsafe after that meet yesterday."

"Not that nice anyway," Thresher said.

"I'm sorry about that—when Wadi grabbed you. I thought I'd be there alone and figured being separated would be more dangerous than being together."

"Thank you," Thresher said.

"I wanted to ask you about that facility you said you were from." Mako paused, as if trying to gather courage. "Is it…a bad place?"

The question was a stain, something that couldn't be undone. Thresher noticed the deep purple bruises under Mako's eyes, the way his mouth crimped at the corners, a sickly pallor hanging onto his tawny skin. "Yeah," Thresher said, surprised that the answer came so easily. He suspected that Mako was pumping him for information, that he was on the verge of putting two and two together.

"Fucked you up good?" Mako asked desperately. "Like, it's a miracle you got out?"

Thresher's eyebrows drew together. It suddenly hit him that he didn't know Mako, not really. He'd been building this camaraderie with him for days, but what if it was only one-sided? What if Mako knew what mask to wear to get the most out of his prey and switched from hard-ass for Wadi to compassionate for Thresher? "It's different for everyone," Thresher said. "It was bad for me."

Mako looked away, but Thresher continued to study the way his jaw clenched and his eyes welled up with tears. Mako rocked back and forth with quick violence that would keep a baby awake more than soothe it. His mouth parted and a twisted sigh edged past his lips, like he was holding something down and it was fighting hard to get out.

"Do a lot of people *escape*, like you?" Mako asked, voice reedy.

"I don't know of anyone who has." Thresher was a harbinger of bad news, handing off messages of woe without fully understanding the consequences. He remembered what Mako had said about his nightmare, a dream that resembled a Facility experiment, and wondered if the tubes and machines scared Mako as much as the outside frightened Thresher. Perhaps Mako didn't have the means to understand it.

"How did *you* get out?" A tear slipped past Mako's dam, sliding down his cheek.

"A woman helped me," Thresher said, recalling her mousy brown hair, the way her nose had a slight upturn. If she didn't have such steel in her eyes and determination cracking her teeth, he would've said she was cute as a button. "I knew her from the tests. She observed many of my procedures."

"Procedures?" Mako looked baffled.

"I'm an experiment," Thresher admitted, hollow-bellied at the truth. He hated the way it stripped him down to his essentials. "They did tests on me. They're trying to figure out how life forms react to different environmental stimulation when exposed during certain times of the life cycle. Something like *in vitro* toxicology."

"Fucking human experiments."

Thresher winced. While Mako sounded flabbergasted, Thresher had heard that sentence a million times before. Human experiment. Test tube baby. *Abomination.*

"Do…they do tests on everyone?" Mako asked.

"Everyone *is* a test."

"What was your test? Your…stimulation?"

"I don't know. We weren't *supposed* to know. Only the doctors knew." Thresher suspected his was pure genetic manipulation, but he wouldn't say that out loud.

"How'd this chick break you out?"

Thresher despaired that the conversation had evolved into a question-answer module. The truth wanted to force past the lump in his throat and spill onto the ground, to *let Mako see what you're made of and watch how fast he runs.*

"I don't know," Thresher said, his voice small. "I'd seen her before but never thought anything was amiss. She watched behind the glass, read my charts, and only participated once in an actual analysis."

Now that he thought about it, he remembered the exact exam. Repetition and memory tasks. Questions about what kinds of images he saw in inkblots. Thresher didn't see much. At that point, he didn't *know* much, but she seemed pleased all the same. She wore black pumps and insisted he be uncuffed during their session. Thresher hadn't been violent then, hadn't had any outbursts, hadn't broken anyone's jaw, yet. She told him he was smart, smarter than a lot of experiments, that he had great potential.

"I got in trouble a lot," Thresher continued. "Got mad. Hurt some people. Wanted to do my *own* tests. Kept breaking theories in the attempt to formulate an unbeatable hypothesis about what being a human amounted to. Ultimately, they locked me away because I was a danger to them and myself."

When he said it out loud, it sounded so awful. So out of control. In reality, it had been methodical. His own experiments. So this is what a broken nose looks like. These are the stakes when I fight the guard. This is how long I'm in isolation for tipping over the bookcases.

It got even more technical than that. This is what fury feels like. That is what pain, devastation, disbelief look like. It wasn't a test to see what he could get away with or an emotional outlet. It was to observe emotion.

"Bar fighter," Mako said with a laugh.

Thresher didn't know what that was, but it seemed to be a point of pride. "I was half out of my mind on anti-psychotics, all straight jacketed up in the isolation cell. She opened the door and undid my binds. I thought the punishment was over, that I was going back to my room."

"Paid your penance," Mako whispered.

Thresher liked that, *penance*, like he had done something wrong, but it was a wrong good enough to be forgiven. The woman smelled like ethanol and lavender. She didn't speak, simply manhandled and punched him when he wouldn't obey, her arm steady around him. He stumbled when the fresh air cut into his lungs. Blinking into the midnight darkness, astounded at the sublimity of the sky, he suddenly knew what a god's presence felt like. His mind offered up the factoid: *that's the Milky Way.*

"She shoved my legs in a vehicle. I could feel the engine rumble," Thresher said. "I don't know how long we traveled, but long enough that the wind numbed my face."

"She had a car?" Mako asked as if the word *car* should be on par with *god*. "Gasoline to make it run?"

"I don't know."

"That's impossible."

"She said she'd been sneaking select experiments out over the course of a decade because she hated the state of the country. Said a god sent down a plague to rid us of our wrongs, but we studied it instead—studied sin. She never released her escapees the same way twice, she always had an alibi, and I was a smart experiment. I could make it on my own. She had faith."

Her hands had gripped the steering wheel so tight her knuckles were white. She had thin bobby pins that weren't the color of her hair dangling from her wind-whipped bun.

"She dumped me on the side of the road. Just opened up the door, shoved me out, and drove off. 'Godspeed,' she said."

"An honest-to-trinity practitioner. Those are few and far between."

"But *you* swear on the trinity." He knew enough to make that connection.

Mako grimaced. "I use it more as an emphasis. It means something completely different now. There isn't any of that old holy one-God belief behind it. How long were you out there?"

Thresher shrugged. "Don't know how long it took the drugs to wear off."

Mako traced the outline of his mouth with his index finger and thumb. Scruff lined his jaw. "Good thing I found you."

Thresher bristled at that. He didn't like feeling useless, like someone who could be told *godspeed* and good riddance all at once. He hadn't been put on this earth just to be saved.

"You know of any trusted folks in that facility? Maybe even find your way back to it?" Mako asked too quickly.

Thresher had had enough. Too many questions. Too much *knowing*. Mako's play was good—putting impossible cars and Wadi's mention of the magical together and trying to get Thresher to verify his suspicions. No. He was too scared of what Mako might do if he knew the Promised Land was the Facility. "Your turn," Thresher said, irritated. "You tell me something if you want to know more from me."

Mako's mouth pinched and he huffed, but he didn't push. Thresher felt a swell of pride in his social skills. He now knew when to hold his hand close, knew when someone had an angle.

"I'm thinking it's time for us to get a move on," Mako said with a gruff edge to his furious undertone. "Burning daylight as it is." He stood and stretched.

"Sure you don't want to use the toilet before you go?" Thresher asked, reckless and angry, suddenly wanting to conduct a new experiment on Mako that would make him just as pissed off. He saw the questions burning in Mako's eyes, but Mako didn't want to tell him anything, didn't *trust* him to tell him anything? Because he was an experiment, abandoned on the side of the road, out of his mind? He had his pride. "We had hundreds of them at the Facility. Polished, clean ones with flushing water. Not filled to the gills with shit. Every. Single. One."

He stood, strapped his backpack down tight, and walked away. Didn't matter which direction. Only the smug warmth chasing away the crushed feeling in his chest mattered, made richer by Mako's fading curses as he tried to catch up.

15

Mako's hand dug into Thresher's shoulder, strong like Thresher imagined penance would feel, and forced them to stop. Thresher pushed back into the touch, glad their earlier tiff fell to the wayside. Reconciliation was better than walking in off-put silence where buildings rose and fell in urban waves of claustrophobic high-rises and small patches of domesticity. Where his stomach was a knotted fist under his ribs and his tongue felt thick and clumsy. Where the dust and quiet remained the same.

Mako's hazel eyes darted along the brick walls. Thresher followed his line of sight and noticed white slashes in the shape of arrows.

"There's a market close by," Mako whispered, his mouth close to Thresher's ear. His breath held a hint of sweet ketosis.

"Is that bad?" The hairs prickled on the nape of his neck and he suppressed a shiver. These bare touches kept him balanced on a tightrope—terrified to misstep but eager for the rush, yearning for more.

"Not usually," Mako said. "Been some incidents, though, and we aren't exactly welcome in Bruykleen. Keep your stuff close."

Thresher did shiver then—*he owned stuff*—and his hands gripped his backpack straps, his blue jeans snug on his hips, his red jacket warm. He wouldn't let anyone strip him down again.

The white slashes led into a deserted alleyway. Over Mako's head, Thresher saw a green tarp held upright by mismatched poles and pipes stretched like a carnival tent. A young face peered around a booth, his long arm waving them over. "Nothing to be afraid of, gentlemen! Everything's for sale!"

As they approached, the boy walked around the table and sat on it, crossing his legs and thrusting out his chest. Mako raised an eyebrow, but Thresher, shocked and amazed, couldn't stop staring.

"See something you like?" The boy smiled.

Startled, Thresher took a step back and immediately looked down at the displayed wares: a tarnished silver locket, an impeccable hairbrush, and a pair of heels.

The boy's smile widened, showing off browning teeth, as he played with his necklace, running the chain over his fingers and fiddling with the pendent. Shoulder to shoulder with Mako, Thresher felt every muscle in Mako's body tighten. A powerful gust of tension wrapped around his gut and tied it off like a tourniquet.

"Where did you get this?" Mako demanded, shoving the kid and grabbing the chain, suspending the vial pendent between them.

"It's cocaine, man," the kid said with a toothy grin. "Makes you feel good. You wanna feel good?"

Mako transformed with rage—not red-hot rage that Thresher knew—but a fury that drained the color from his face, his freckles standing out in stark relief. Thresher wasn't sure what to do. Fighting meant dominance.

"I'm going to ask again before I push your teeth in. Where did you get this?" Mako asked.

"What's it matter to you?" The kid snarled, all joviality gone as he realized Mako wasn't playing the game. "You can't have it, man, it's mine. Nothing like this is left in the whole world."

Mako snapped the chain in one violent pull. The kid cried out as the chain scored his tanned skin. Holding the pendent in his fist, Mako shook it in front of the boy's face. "This is my fucking mother," he roared. "You're sniffing my mother's ashes and getting *high* on the placebo effect."

"No, no, man. I'm not, it's a drug, like coke, I swear."

"You telling me I don't know what my own mother looks like?"

"It's a bunch of powder!"

"That's what bones look like, you two-faced *sonovabitch* bastard of a whore!"

The kid screamed in a language Thresher didn't understand, loud and harsh. A cold rush encompassed Thresher's body as his mind laid out the facts: Mako's tribe had once been in a vicious war with the Bruykleeners, and now the two of them were crossing into enemy territory. The footsteps behind him didn't come as a surprise. Neither did the unknown voice, snarling, "What the fuck do you think you're doing?"

Thresher nearly dropped to the ground. He'd heard that sentence a hundred times from Facility cliques and guards wondering why he wasn't paying them heed. He pivoted and saw two men and a woman emerge out of an alleyway shadow. Broad-faced and tall with a black-dotted pattern tattooed on their dark faces, they looked much different from Mako. Allopatric speciation will do that, Thresher's mind babbled. Will bring out certain genetic traits due to isolation. It's a slow process to a new species. At the woman's feet, a third pale

been a calculated move, and he'd ended up an outsider's pet like this so-called freed experiment?

The woman dropped the leash. "I'm sick of Manahatta shit walking my streets." She drew a long blade and advanced on Mako.

"I seek safe passage, that's all," Mako said, but Thresher heard the trembling heat making the statement a lie. Mako wanted the violence.

"Then you shouldn't have slung such words," Soul-Dago said, creeping to Mako. "I didn't think I'd test my strength against you so soon."

"Can't wait to be under my foot, huh? You like it so much, maybe you should be the dog." Mako wrenched his arm from Thresher.

"What a picture," Soul-Dago purred.

Mako shed his bags, his hands in fists. Panic threatened to consume Thresher, but he mimicked and threw his backpack down as the second, silent Bruykleen male came for him with the same gleam in his black eyes that Thresher used to spot in the guards' when they wanted to experiment with cruelty. His blood roared like a tidal rush. The rhythm pounded in his temples. The world slowed to razor sharpness. When the Bruykleener swung at him, Thresher remembered to use his height and fight back.

His fist cracking the man's jaw felt good despite the pain of impact. A stomach punch left him in breathless agony. Panic overtook him as he realized his previous fights had been nothing but squabbles. He thrashed, defending chaotically, as the Bruykleener drove him to the ground. His world turned upside down when his head cracked on the concrete. He scrambled for his knife in his pocket, the blade biting through his coat, as the Bruykleener grabbed his wrists. Thresher bucked as cloth tore and he swung wide, slashing the blade across the man's face. Blood felt hot on his fingers as he dug them into the Bruykleener's new wound. As the Bruykleener bore down on him, Thresher jammed the knife into the man's throat.

The Bruykleener gurgled and clutched his neck, surprise on his face. Thresher felt the same. He stumbled to his feet, his breath wheezing, and tried to get past the ringing in his ears and the wobble in his vision. Looking at his hands, he saw a delicate infrastructure of bones capable of dousing life.

Dazed, he turned to see Mako deliver two sharp blows to Soul-Dago's temples, sending him to the ground. Mako dove for his fallen machete, only to have the woman's boot catch him in the chin as they both scrambled for the blade. Mako yanked it away and jammed it into her chest, jacking it back out and stabbing her again until she crashed to her knees with a gasp. Thresher heard the death gurgle a second time. The concrete drank their blood.

Thresher's opponent crawled away, gasping. Thresher didn't know it could take so long for someone to bleed out.

The dog-human screamed in a language Thresher assumed was Bruykleen-specific.

Soul-Dago shook his head as if coming out of a dream. Emitting a war cry, he charged Mako. Thresher caught a brief flash of panic crossing Mako's face, and shut his eyes, but it didn't save him from hearing Mako shout as Soul-Dago crashed into him, sending them skidding on the ground. Mako threw Soul-Dago off, but Soul-Dago grabbed a handful of Mako's hair and bounced Mako's face off the concrete. Mako's elbow shot back and caught Soul-Dago in the stomach, and then he twisted, his fist colliding with Soul-Dago's temple in the same place as before. Soul-Dago swayed. Mako staggered to his feet, wrapped an arm around his neck, held him there until Soul-Dago went limp. Thresher waited for Mako's machete to slide across Soul-Dago's throat and hoped that this time, the bleed-out would be quick.

Thresher didn't know when he started to cry. He didn't know how long he'd been on his knees, fighting the urge to be sick. Once, he wanted to know emotion. He wanted to experience the purity of rage, but realized instead why the Facility deemed the outside so dangerous. This wasn't the contained outbursts of captives—it was the true survival instincts of predator and prey.

When the overlooked kid jumped on Mako's back, Thresher saw the imminent future. Mako would murder the boy without a second thought. The tribal wars must have been just like this. Sticky with the blood and battle rage of a street fight.

Thresher leapt up and ran for Mako as Mako slung the kid over his shoulder and thumped him down beside an unconscious Soul-Dago. Thresher grabbed Mako's shoulders and wrenched him back, terrified of the wild, unpredictable man yearning to be bloodied like his knife. Thresher could taste the kid's fear and knew the boy must feel small, with Thresher pushing past six feet and Mako's fury as tall as the heavens. Mako shrugged Thresher off and got into the kid's face. "Now, tell me. Where did you get this pendant?"

"I found it," the kid stammered, perhaps realizing that he had just pissed off a dangerous man and boy, didn't life look pretty good right about now?

"I'm gonna need more than that." Blood dripped down Mako's face.

"Some Ender found it outside of Amagansett. Thought it was some leftover drug drop from the old days. Please, please don't kill me."

"When?"

"Months ago! I've had it forever!"

"What about this Facility? This Promised Land?" Mako pointed his blade at the cowering dog-human.

"He...he's been with us for *years*," the kid said. "They found him gnawing his own arm. He's *crazy*. He told stories about this place that could do *magic*, but there ain't nothing but sand and sea and the Ender tribe further out. There's nothing *there*."

The dog-human crawled over to his former mistress. His howl terrified Thresher, making him wonder at the brutal lines drawn between human, experiment, and animal.

Thresher pulled Mako back from the child, his fingers digging into Mako's shoulders. The boy sagged in relief. Mako fixed him a death glare. "Best run home to your mama, boy. You're playing with the big dogs here."

16

Thresher bullied Mako away. The two of them grabbed their things and rounded a corner, losing sight of the dead tribesmen as they ducked through a break in the rusted fence surrounding a field, complete with the skeleton of playground equipment and broken swings. The image of the boy propped up on one elbow reaching for the dog-experiment as if seeking comfort would stay with him long after, he knew.

Mako shoved Thresher off him. "That little shit. Snorting my mother? Fucking thinks he's high?"

Thresher let out a shaky breath and tried not to stare at the blood on his hands. He couldn't go to pieces, especially when nothing felt stable, so he motioned to the vial with his jaw. "What is that?"

"It's my mother's bones." The vial rolled in Mako's palm. "This belongs to my sister."

"You have a sister?"

Mako took in an unsteady breath. "Yeah, I do."

Thresher gripped his bicep, terrified Mako might topple over. Warning bells sounded in his head as he replayed the crunch of Mako's head connecting with the concrete. Mako laughed and swayed. "I sounded like my father, just then."

"Maybe we should sit down?"

"Never thought something like that would come out of my mouth. Playing with the big dogs. I can't believe I said that."

"We should sit down."

"We can't, unless we plan on becoming Bruykleener slaves. We need to get out of here." Mako sagged against him. Thresher took all his weight, thinking *concussion*. He didn't know where to go, what to do, but the closest thing to safety was a deteriorating building in front of them, still held up by worn granite pillars. They stumbled up the building's wide steps and slipped inside. Mako collapsed in a shadowed corner. Thresher towered over him, hands on his hips, absolutely out of his depth taking care of someone else. He monitored the outside through a broken window, terrified of new Bruykleen forces. He didn't know how long they remained like that, Mako shaking so hard Thresher was sure he'd moved from laughing to crying.

"You wanna tell me what that was all about?" Thresher hissed, nicking his tongue with his teeth. Copper coated one side of his mouth. The Bruykleener dying among the silent homes, gagging on his own blood, filled his mind. Suddenly, he felt like he should sit, but that wouldn't be *strong*.

Mako's blotchy face snapped up to him, his lip curling in distain. "Don't want to fucking talk about it. You're the one that has to do the talking."

Thresher: like the granite pillars, eroded but still standing. He bent down so he could look into Mako's face. "I just killed a man for you."

"To save your own skin." Blood crusted around Mako's nose. Road rash tore up his cheeks.

"For you."

Mako's smile wasn't pretty.

"I didn't lie, I didn't…know how to tell you."

"Try this: 'Gee, Mako, that Promised Land you've been looking for? I can take you there.' We would've gotten off to a great start."

"How was I supposed to know you wouldn't leave me as soon as you could? Kill me? Torture me? How was I supposed to trust you when I don't know anything about you?"

Mako wiped his nose with the back of his hand and stared at the bloody smear as if he couldn't remember how he'd gotten hurt.

"If I had told you, you wouldn't have helped me survive. I needed to survive," Thresher said sounding desperate. The minutes seemed endless. He couldn't handle silence.

Maybe Mako was biding time for the Bruykleeners to catch up with them, but Mako had to know Thresher couldn't be sold or traded, now. He was worth too much.

"I think you have a concussion," Thresher said.

"I'm fine," Mako said. He turned to the side and promptly threw up.

"You sure look fine," Thresher snapped, feeling the pinprick of rage race through his blood again. He itched to shake Mako senseless, knock him down, make him think about Thresher just like Thresher thought about him.

"Good. Cause I am," Mako said.

Thresher reared up, ran his hands through his hair. Frustration jailed him with thoughts that grew wilder with each passing moment. He was grateful, he truly was, but it wasn't fair when he was willing to spill his guts for a man he barely knew while Mako wouldn't explain why his mother was some kid's cocaine. That Bruykleen boy got more information out of Mako than Thresher ever had.

"We need to get off Bruykleen land," Mako said. "Is anyone coming?"

Thresher glanced outside. "No, but can you stand?"

Mako rolled and gasped, leaned back hard enough to smack his head on the wall. "Everything's all splotchy," he said. His head rolled and he lost consciousness.

"Mako?" Fear built in Thresher's belly as he sat beside the outsider. His stained hands twitched. If the Bruykleeners found them, they wouldn't stand a chance. Thresher would be shackled like the dog-experiment, doing anything yet again to survive.

He shook Mako, but Mako flopped uselessly. Thresher put his ear close to Mako's mouth and nearly collapsed in relief when he heard Mako's erratic breathing. Thresher pushed them both farther into the shadows, hoping to make them small, and stemmed panic by recalling his favorite stories. About how easy it was for characters to expose themselves in text, and with an uttered word of acceptance or love, take the other character as their soul mate, who knew each other better than they knew themselves.

Mako wasn't like that. Hard-edged and standoffish, Thresher had to pry off Mako's many masks to get to his core. Thresher wished he knew how to stop pretending he was an equal in this cross-island road trip. If Mako was taken prisoner, Thresher bet he wouldn't be taken alive.

He suddenly wanted to speak with the woman who'd freed him, demand to know why she'd done this to him. Was this some new, immersive test? What was his true purpose as an experiment? As a human?

Out of his peripheral vision, he saw Mako list to the side, head on an inevitable path to rest on Thresher's shoulder. Mako's eyelids fluttered and his temple landed on the sharp point of the coat's epaulet.

Touch made Thresher crazy. It made him feel like Mako wanted Thresher in his world, like Thresher belonged there. Despair clutched his heart. He hoped Mako knew he wasn't there to trick or capture him, but even so, he mulled over the mere power he held as he had steered Mako away from the boy by firm pressure of palm to pointed shoulder blade. He replayed Mako cradling his foot, and he sank into the memory instead of trying to suppress it, learned the force of it, and wondered what he would do if someone tried to influence him through touch. He wondered if he'd already passed the first step of integration into Mako's world by killing Mako's enemies. What ghastly data.

Out of the corner of his eye, he watched Mako's hand tighten into a fist around his mother's bones. Soft warmth bled into Thresher's side. His back ached, but he didn't move, and kept watch for danger, trying not to replay the past when Mako sliced a woman's chest to ribbons.

He never had friends in the Facility. He hadn't known he was going out of his mind from loneliness until now. He'd loved his mental health days where he could talk about whatever he wanted, but mostly he didn't know how to begin and they sat in silence until the psychiatrist prodded him with a question. He loved being praised, loved being asked about his well-being, wanted to tell them every-thing he'd learned, seen, and heard.

That happened before the anger welled up inside him, a never-en-ding need to know what it meant to experience emotion. He felt like he was coming out of his skin half the time, surrounded by blubbe-ring imbeciles that he adored like brothers yet wanted to put down just as fast. He felt alive when he threw fits and thrummed with an energy he never experienced when he'd been obedient.

He felt intimacy once, when an experiment shaking from her disease boldly pulled him behind a bookcase and plastered her lips on his. He'd never talked to her before. The kiss tingled from his toes to her tongue in his mouth, the taste of mothballs and candy-coated medication flowing between them, and he trembled with the sudden force of it. *This is what it's like to live.* He pressed into her, wanting more, but she knew how fast kisses needed to be without getting caught and broke free with a wanton smile and a caress on his cheek. He felt that touch for weeks afterward, and as hard as he looked for her again, he never saw her. Figured she died like all the others, her dissected body studied, her organs harvested for further testing and donation.

Mako snuffled against his shoulder. He blinked, looked up at Thresher—hair mussed, wide-eyed disorientation—before jerking straight up. "Sorry," he croaked. "Where...where are we?"

Thresher didn't say anything, but he felt Mako's gaze, as if Mako waited for Thresher to bark at him. Thresher was done with that. Being bound by this human interaction fulfilled a hunger he didn't know he needed—even if it involved death and fear. He would take it any which way before Mako left him, either by shoving him out of a vehicle driving at high speeds or through a kiss that briefly opened his world before slamming it shut. He would make the sacrifices and deal with the consequences of betraying the Facility until he died. On the outside, it wouldn't be long.

Mako scrubbed his face and hissed in pain. Always on the move this Mako shark, couldn't stay still until his body collapsed.

"Stop," Thresher whispered. "You're hurt."

"Let me orient myself." Mako rifled through his backpack pulling out a can and the can opener. Opening the can on his knees, Mako squeezed the metal top down, and turned it upside down to drain the juice. The sharp smell of fish overpowered the vomit. Thresher's stomach made an embarrassing groan. Mako pried back the top and held the can out to Thresher.

"Do you really think this is a good time for lunch?" Thresher asked.

"Didn't eat this morning," Mako said. "You were in a state about something."

"You're just jealous I got to shit in a real toilet for most of my life," Thresher said, but he couldn't eat with the blood on his hands. Mako paused, then rummaged through his pack again, bringing out a flask. Thresher remembered how to do this, and held his hands under the lip as Mako splashed water over his skin. The blood washed away easier than he thought.

The pink meat folded under his fingers and shredded under his tongue. A metallic hint mingled with the taste. He wondered if this meal ritual was Mako's touchstone, a way to blaze through the fog of brain trauma. Either way, he was selfishly pleased it held off questions.

"Maybe a little," Mako said. "I need a moment. Everything feels hazy." Two fingers rooted inside the can, and he held his fish covered appendages to the light, like he could read omens from them. He sucked the meat off with blasphemous sounds. Thresher stared at him, hoping that his face conveyed: *Is that how you plan to get out of telling me about your sister? Acting like a bitch in heat? For tuna?*

Mako's sounds quieted to mere slurps of delight.

"Concussions will do that." Thresher licked the inside of the can and wiped his hands on his jeans. Mako tracked him like a quiet hunter. Thresher figured they could keep ignoring the obvious conversation they needed to have. He stood, feeling good and full. Hopeful. "I kept watch. Didn't see anything."

Mako didn't miss a beat. "Doesn't mean they aren't coming."

17

We've got maybe a few hours before Soul-Dago starts hunting us. We need to get somewhere safe," Mako said, guiding them out of the house and back to the road. Dried blood covered the side of his face, similar to Soul-Dago's war paint.

"Why didn't you kill him like the others?" Thresher asked, but his attention focused on Mako's fist shoved in his pocket, most likely holding tightly onto his mother. Thresher wondered at the miracle of parents, how they could lay claim to the children they put so much energy and care into. What would Mako's mother think of her son who flagged through the hours buried under an invisible weight, who saved and killed without rhyme or reason? When she held him as a baby in her arms, could she fathom what he might become?

Thresher wasn't in the dream business. He knew no one laid claim to him. His parents were donated zygotes, a petri dish, and a plastic womb incubator that let him swim in chemically balanced amniotic fluid.

He couldn't quite put together why Mako's mother's bones were important, or why they'd been ground up to be worn around his neck. Not for the first time, Thresher felt a cultural loss and groped for a logical explanation when he knew the answer to be spiritual.

"Soul-Dago and I...its complicated. Tell me about the Promised Land," Mako said. He sounded out of breath as they walked up a hill. "About the Facility."

Thresher's throat dried up. He'd started them down this conversational road. Sorrow gripped him, alive and growing, devouring the leftover moments where Mako was ignorant and Thresher was one more soul lost on the coast.

"Tell me or I'll drop you right here," Mako said. "I swear, I'll make you talk."

Thresher realized Mako had taken his silence as refusal, but that wasn't it at all. "I'm trying, it's just..." He simply didn't know how to start, and it terrified him to imagine where it might end. "I told you I'm from the Facility. My sole reason for existing was to overcome the toxicity of the outside—either by becoming resilient to it through genetic manipulation or resistant from ongoing chemical exposure.

Even though I'm not sure what I'm supposed to express or overcome, making a promised land is what the Facility hopes to achieve."

"But there are people out here already. We're living just fine."

"It's not about living—it's about thriving. You can't deny it's difficult to procreate and advance as a society on the outside." Thresher paused as Mako pulled a face. "What?"

"*The outside*. Like its some terrible apocalyptic world. It's not the first time *others* assume they understand a place and people. What exactly does 'the outside' mean?"

"Everything outside of the Facility." Thresher stared at the sky. It never occurred to him he might be as foreign to Mako as Mako was to him. "I don't know everything, but the Promised Land is the Facility's promise for the future. They want to solve the survival problem by integrating experiments with resistant genes into the outside population and transition humans away from being endangered, back to how we were before whatever made the outside so terrible happened."

"And their experiments aren't meshing well with the tribes."

"I don't think they've had the chance to test it very well." Resentment flickered in his heart. Questions fueled a new rage for the Facility. *How expendable are your creations?*

"Which is why they need to steal people. Are you actually attempting to capture me? Take me back there?" Mako locked his wrists together, pretending to be in restraints, and grinned.

Thresher resisted the need to shake Mako senseless and shifted in his boots, feeling the familiar pressure against his heel cutting past the cloth wraps. "Do you think I could?"

Mako's hands dropped. "No."

"I'm not your enemy, Mako."

"I know that." Mako said, softer. "I'm on your side, remember?"

The earth dipped and flattened as they walked further into the broken city, until a hill rose in front of them with a looming gate, a huge testament to mankind with pointed tips and rounded gothic entrances.

Thresher had never seen anything so beautiful, never seen so much effort put into an entryway that didn't frighten but offered a welcoming sublimity that made him want to kneel.

"Hey," Mako called from ahead of him. "Don't let your eyes fall out."

Thresher blinked, still overcome. Dazed, he followed Mako up the path until he stood underneath the gateway. He touched the wind-battered stone. Built to last.

"Hurry up," Mako shouted. "We need to find shelter for the night. Bruykleeners won't follow us in here." Thresher picked up his pace, but it was the meandering walk of the awed. The brownstone houses, cast iron signs, and green grass overwhelmed him. He waited for some authority to smite him, tackle him to the ground, and explain that only real people got to come here, people with something to lose and things already lost. He'd lost nothing in his years of living; he only kept *gaining.*

White marble and granite blocks with curved tops scattered over the grounds like dominos, radiating a quiet energy that chilled him. Peace seeped into his muscles. The quiet explained to him he was simply too loud by living. Unknown memories rolled through the stones like fog, tracing the etched names, and he wondered if that was what it felt like, to be haunted.

Thresher wiped fast and rough at his face, smearing his tears. Angels watched him with leprosy faces, perched on the tombs like birds with too-small wings to carry the true weight of a human stitched to their backs. Thresher marveled at the angels, wanted to know if these were ancient experiments from an age when mistakes were rendered into useless beauty and hands pressed palm to palm in unredeemable prayer. These creatures watched over their makers, as if begging to resurrect them, and how lovely that would be, to believe your maker was a god to keep with you always.

Mako was a malformed spot far away, his hand laying on top of stones that aged the further back they went. Black streaks dripped from nearly erased names and dates. Mako slipped inside a square mausoleum. Thresher wanted to know how much time it took to make these sculptures to the dead. He wanted to tell the corpses shrouded inside they were lucky to be remembered in such a way, so blessed to be cared for when these days people were either beach treasure troves or were carried out in white bags and taken apart for analysis. The cumulative end point was that they had failed in some way or didn't pass some turning point or produce the right data to be worthwhile.

The setting sun cast dim light. Thresher delighted in the dust specks floating inside the beams, the way the gravestones had elongated shadows like teeth. He jogged to catch up and pushed past the mausoleum's double wooden doors—one swinging by its hinges—and buried the tightness in his throat upon seeing the grated glass. Inside the narrow hallway, a moist, motionless cold hibernated.

He backed up, triggered by the close space, the musty scent, the damp that made his bones creak in protest.

"We can hide here," Mako said. "Bruykleeners are too superstitious of the old dead to follow us for now."

Thresher took another step back. His chest felt too tight. His heart thudded in his temples. Cold chains wrapped around his wrists and suffocating canvas enclosing him.

"Are you okay? You look a little spooked."

He could smell ethanol, the embalming fluid putrid in his nostrils. He scratched at his neck, feeling needle pinpricks that would erase the outside. Erase Mako.

What if this wasn't real? Another test to see how well he survived in the wild, released like a bad animal that wasn't worth keeping? Let nature take its course. Let evolution take him out of his misery.

"Look at me."

A hand touched him—some kind of sympathy pat—that would wrench his arm behind his back, put him to the ground, foot to his neck. He punched out, felt a satisfying *thunk* when his fist hit solid flesh, and let the scream of denial rip from him.

"Whoa, whoa, who said violence was acceptable conduct in a cemetery? Respect the dead, *trinity*."

"Don't touch me, don't lay one finger on me, *leave me alone.*" Thresher swung again, and heard a yelp. Felt an arm try to put him in a headlock. He lunged forward, brought that orderly over his shoulder. *Use your height,* he heard before something crashed into his stomach, making him gag, but he was too tall and he grabbed the fist in his stomach, yanked the orderly forward and off his feet. They both crashed into the door. Glass shattered. Twilight invaded his eyesight—*blessed, beautiful*—and he sucked in fresh air, felt the sky twirl above him, the grass smooth underneath him. Someone crushed him, and he catapulted that orderly over his head, using his arms and rabbit kicking.

He heard a thump and an anguished cry. He hyperventilated until dizzy, trembling in aftershock, his mind piecing together where he was. Rising up on one elbow, he looked over his shoulder to see Mako slumped against a gravestone, murmuring soft curses.

Thresher said his name carefully, too afraid.

"You *had* to slam me into a headstone, didn't you? Wanted to bruise the shit out of me, break a few ribs, huh? Well, you're in luck. You smacked my head, you moron. Now, come here and make sure I don't have another concussion."

Thresher got to his knees and crawled to Mako. Struck with short-term amnesia, he could only recall the terror, helplessness, and overwhelming denial that his world wasn't real. His hands shook. Kneeling in front of Mako, he brushed back Mako's short hair, looking for blood. He focused on Mako's moving mouth, but he couldn't hear anything but scraps. "Look into my eyes. My eyes, Thresher."

He traced the pathway of freckles to Mako's blood-crusted nose, then up the bridge and into waiting hazel orbs centered on him. Thresher felt hooked on that look, pinned down, and analyzed deeper than ever before.

"It's okay, it's okay," Mako said, and Thresher realized he was saying, "I'm sorry," like a litany.

Thresher winced at the blossoming red splotch on Mako's jaw, the sign of a good punch that would be colored come morning. Thresher felt weak. His abdominals hurt with every breath, and his arms were shaky, feeling like they had been wrenched from their sockets and unceremoniously relocated. He brought his legs under him, crossed them in front of Mako, just about removed from everything.

"Hey," Mako said. "You okay?"

Thresher swallowed hard. "Yeah. I don't want to go back in there."

"Well," Mako said. "Spending the night in the mausoleum will be safer than out here now that we've pissed off the Bruykleeners."

A wave of exhaustion rattled Thresher and he shook his head. "I'll take my chances."

"You're a pain in the ass, you know that?"

"You can stay in the cell then. I've had my share."

Mako went quiet, ruminating quiet, and Thresher let the loss tumble through him, untethered and free, smashing against his foundation. The night steamrolled over the sky, unbelievably black and masked with blue cloud cover. *I'm not okay,* he thought. *I thought I was, but I'm not.*

Mako laid his hand on Thresher's knee. Thresher bared his teeth, felt them as white matchsticks in the dark. "I'll get my stuff," Mako said, standing and steadying himself with a hand on a gravestone. Thresher didn't see any blood on the marker.

"I'm sorry," Thresher told the earth and the person lying below him. "I'm so sorry."

Sorry for disrupting. For being a nuisance. For not understanding how to act, how to respect, how to be anything but a crazed experiment.

A hand slid over his shoulder and gently removed his backpack. Thresher let the hand guide and reposition him so he lay with the headstone as a headboard. He curled his hands to his chest. Mako unfolded the blanket they found in the house and flapped it so it landed over Thresher like fresh powder. Mako propped his backpack against the gravestone and laid his head on it, facing Thresher. Zipping his coat up to his chin, Mako mimicked Thresher's folded arms. His eyes shone like liquid gloss in the night. The sparse creak of crickets filled the cold air. Not many left, but bugs were resilient, and after bacteria and viruses, they would survive any environmental holocaust. Mako scooted closer, a hairsbreadth of grass like gossamer lining between them.

"So," Mako said roughly.

"No," Thresher said, wrapped in an angel. "I don't want to explain."

There was an audible click as Mako swallowed. "You wanna hear this story or not?"

He palmed his jacket pocket and pulled out the vial, holding it up with two fingers. Thresher studied the glass tube and the chain hook intricately carved with tiny flowers. Yellowed powder sifted from side to side. Thresher thought it incredible how the human body could be so reduced after bearing children and being alive.

Mako forced each word out like loosening a straightjacket, as if he was too used to the tightness and didn't know what it felt like to breathe without gasping. "The first thing you need to understand is that us *outsiders*," and here Mako's lip curled, gently poking fun, "aren't awful, brutal men killing to survive. I know it must seem that way, especially after *before*, but we have families, *land,* to defend. We steal and fight and kill, and might not have the tools of your promised land, but we aren't monsters.

"The day my mother died, my grandmother had been on a wayfare for weeks and hadn't returned." He paused, seeing Thresher's confusion. "It's like a solo journey for the self; healing, revelation, mourning, communing with nature, whatever. My grandmother always said that since our Saddlerock lineage had been around here *long* before anything else, that if we had a problem, the land would help us heal. Clear the mind. Either way, she'd been gone so long, we began to wonder if she was ever coming back."

Mako cleared his throat. "During that time, my mother decided to cross the river to meet a peddler selling seeds in Bruykleen. Seeds are like little pods of hope out here. She wanted to go alone, but you have to keep what you love close, you know? Maybe no one would assault a woman with children. Kids are rare these days. Women have to deliver naturally, it's hard to reach full term." He paused, eyes skittering over Thresher's face as if hoping Thresher would tell him to stop. Thresher stared back, waiting for the next installment of the story.

"We got ambushed, of course. Bruykleeners chased us down. First time I met Soul-Dago, you know. Even then, he was big for his age, watching us from behind the legs of his tribe as my mother faced them down on the concrete plains, holding me in one hand and Nika in the other. I can still hear her shouting that we didn't mean any harm, we're going back to our own tribe, that she had children for the trinity's sake."

Mako closed his eyes briefly and took in a shuddering, deep breath that seemed like it was meant to settle him. "One warrior bashed her head in with a club. She dragged us down with her. She got the warrior, though. He didn't even notice she'd stuck a knife in his stomach. The second time I saw Soul-Dago, he had her blood and brains all over him, learning how to be a Bruykleen warrior. Nika screamed about how she was going to burn them all to the ground, bloody the whole island, they better watch out because there was a new queen in town and they'd just killed her mother. She was only eight."

"Nika's your sister?"

"Twin. It's weird, you know, how different people deal with shock. I didn't panic. I was looking for an escape, counting how many Bruykleeners remained, and Nika's lost her shit, going off on a rampage, making terrifying promises until I was almost scared of her."

Thresher had a hard time imagining another person as vibrant as Mako, a twin no less. Mako shivered and Thresher lifted the blanket. Mako closed the distance and Thresher settled the blanket over them both. Mako's legs burned with body heat against his.

"The tribe was small, but there were enough of them to surround us. If kids are rare then so is new blood, and I thought they were going to enslave us, take us back for breeding, sick shit like that. They probably thought it, too, because they closed in on us. Nika was sobbing over our mother and the whole time I'm thinking how it wasn't worth it, to get a few fabled seeds to grow food. Starvation would be preferable to having our heads bashed in."

Thresher listened, enraptured. Once Mako decided to tell the story, he didn't hold back. Thresher pictured the horror: Bruykleeners circling like sharks, the unidentifiable smear of Nika's face, her hair sun-streaked brunette like Mako's shining in the twilight as she wept. Thresher's eyes felt gritty, like focusing too long and too hard. He licked his lips.

Mako continued. "But that's when Mama Milagros emerged from the shadows dressed like a wraith, spreading her arms like vulture wings. She shrieked some jumbled prayer or curse that scared all of us half to death. I swear, she wasn't human—she looked like a bird-woman with that skull covering her face. I'll never forget how big Soul-Dago's eyes were as the Bruykleeners high-tailed it out of there. Nika and I almost ran, too, but when Mama Milagros took off her mask, she was human again. She ushered us under her cloak and brought us to her dilapidated apartment. She helped us give our mother the sky burial she deserved. Mama Milagros is a little crazy, you see. She believes in all sorts of things like death magic and the transformative energies of the soul."

"You offered her up to the sky?"

"Wrapped her up in leaves and animal skins—and I mean rat skins and pigeon feathers. Built her a platform out of pipes. Let nature take its course. It's hard to bury people, you know. Soil's pure crap, leached of the rich things needed for decomposition. There isn't enough of it to go around. That's why my tribe adopted sky burials. At the time, I knew nothing about Bruykleen beyond the tribal wars. Didn't even know this place existed." He patted the ground behind him. Thresher felt Mako shiver, and he tucked the blanket tighter around them both.

"Are the people here sky burials?" Thresher patted the earth wondering if the haunting he felt came from above and not below.

"No, just regular burials like they did in the old days."

"It feels…"

"Creepy?"

"Solemn," Thresher said.

"I guess. It's just not how we do things anymore." Mako licked his lips. "Nika and I—we were just kids. Didn't know what to do, where to go, had nothing to go back to. Leaving my mother felt like abandoning her. Once she had been dried out and picked clean, Mama Milagros gathered her bones for bleaching and said our mother was a guardian now. Nika believed her. Started carrying the vial around with her. I asked her to stop, to do right by our mother and put her to rest, but she refused. We lived on Bruykleen land with Mama Milagros for over a year until my grandmother collected us. Out of her mind actually, when she found her dirty urchin grandchildren living with this wild woman clear out of Mĕxihco. But they hit it off and my grandmother took all three of us back to Manahatta. Mama Milagros likes her and Mama Milagros doesn't like anyone. Those two old birds haven't left each other since." Mako closed his eyes and frowned. "My head hurts."

Thresher leaned in closer until Mako's breath coated his face between sentences. Tears turned Mako's lashes into spikes, glossy with the nightlight. The knot of worry in Thresher's stomach settled up into the chambers of his heart, letting his blood pump grief into every artery.

"Where's your sister now?" Thresher asked, even though he didn't want to know. He was putting a story together now, a story about a set of twins who lost a father early on and a mother to war. He desperately didn't want to know the ending. He didn't want to know why Mako wandered the cemetery beaches all on his lonesome, didn't want to think that perhaps Mako wasn't fulfilling some youthful gallivanting but was searching for someone he feared might appear on those beaches.

"She used to talk to my mother all the time," Mako choked. "Talked to this stupid vial like my mother could actually hear. Drove me nuts. Couldn't stand it."

"Mako," Thresher breathed, just to say his name.

"Nika disappeared one night. Poof. Gone like magic. I knew there were traps set up to steal tribesmen for slavery or war. I bargained my way into that world to find her, but now I know there's this Promised Land, this Facility, there's no smoke and mirrors anymore. For two years I chased a dead end. Our paths have crossed, Thresher—be it because of Mama Milagros's magic, my mother's guardianship, or pure dumb luck—but because of you, I know where she is."

"She's not," Thresher whispered, wishing it wasn't true. "You don't *know* for certain."

"I've looked *everywhere* for her. It's the only place left. I know your Facility has her," Mako said, on edge now. Determined. "I'm going to find her and I'll need your help."

"I can't," Thresher said. The reality terrified him. "I can't go back there."

"You have to. You have to take me to the Facility."

The stallion near the back flared his big velvet nostrils and twitched his ears. Thresher imagined rubbing his fingers with the grain between the wet, lustrous eyes down the brown nose. The stallion looked like a starburst, light underbelly and dark saddle. A smaller mare stood close by, splotched white and chestnut with a mane raveled into dreadlocks, her soft lips delicately feeling the ground.

Majestic. A wild family bound together out of circumstance and fate. Maybe unity did exist outside of humans—civilizations could rise and fall, but *connection* never faded. Perhaps connection lived beneath his feet, the dead holding hands to create a root system to hold up the tragedy of living. The quiet seeped into him in preparation for the resting of his own bones.

The stallion's ears flattened against his head, and Thresher realized he wasn't alone. Mako sidled up to him, mouth slightly open so Thresher could see slivers of his teeth worn flat. Mako's eyes looked unnaturally green and wide in the sun. His head wound bled freely. Thresher wondered if that was what Mako was doing, flexing his ears back and forth, assessing the danger of staying or going.

"Feral herd," Mako whispered. Their shoulders brushed. "Escaped from Assateague down south and migrated up here, joined the herds that escaped from the Aqueduct and Belmont tracks."

"What's that?" Thresher asked back.

"Horse racing tracks," Mako said. "Before the Yellowstone blew, some century back when there were such things as *empires*, you could win big money betting on how fast one of those beasts could run."

Thresher vaguely knew about gambling and squinted one eye while his brain raced through hundreds of stored factoids. Horse races. A powerful sport where less weight meant speed. These horses had probably been experiments, cooped up in stables where they were petted, cooed over, and tested for endurance. He was so glad they got their freedom, had found other escapees so they wouldn't be lonely.

Mako leaned hard into his side, a pillar of solid warmth. Thresher leaned back. He looked at Mako, not sure what to express, was surprised when he smiled. Mako studied him as if he had never seen him before, as if cataloging each feature. In the back of his mind, Thresher started to count Mako's sun-browned freckles, got lost around twenty, and still felt wiped clean.

"How's your head?" Thresher asked, momentarily breathless.

Mako winced and leaned his head back. "Hurts. I feel like shit. World's starting to spin."

"Sit," Thresher said, feeling like this moment was a gift.

"We don't have time for it."

"Better to rest a moment than have you black out for an hour."

Mako snorted and eased them down, shoulders still together. Thresher wrapped his arms around his knees. Deemed unthreatening, the stallion gnawed at a particular high clump of weeds. Three fillies trotted on stick-thin legs and knobby knees breakable like toothpicks. One snuck closer to them and then turned tail and fled, clumsily prancing around her siblings.

"I'm sorry." Mako paused. "About earlier. Don't know why shit comes outta my mouth the way it does."

Thresher wanted to scrub at the mud stains on his jacket again, but that would be too obvious, too passive-aggressive.

"I'm a jackass," Mako finished.

Spoken like an apology. Thresher smiled. "Yes, you are."

"Just been feeling like I'm coming out of my skin lately. Not an excuse, but there it is."

"Am I making you crazy?" Thresher's stomach quivered at the thought that Mako might say yes, and wished he'd never asked the question.

"Trinity, insecurity is so not attractive."

Thresher laughed, tension easing out of him and he started to enjoy the company, the conversation, the chance to simply *be*.

Mako shot him a grin, like he'd earned his rights to the day. Propped up on his arms, he looked back at the herd. His smile faded. "I know Nika's not dead because I can feel her."

Thresher stilled. Mako was like the fillies—skittish. He didn't want to speak and risk spooking Mako from talking.

"It's a twin thing, you know?"

Thresher didn't, figured that medically only conjoined twins made a twin thing, and sometimes he felt jealous of those people, always with someone who'd known them since birth.

"Like I can feel her. Right here." Mako thumped his heart with a closed fist. "I'm not one for believing in magic like Milagros, but this feeling makes me crazy. I get depressed for no reason, feel like I'm being chased half the time, and once I got terrified of an open field. My recent lapse in judgment included that dream where I was pregnant." He laughed, throwing off the comment as a joke, but Thresher knew the truth, had been there to witness Mako's terror.

"Don't think I'd feel like that if she were dead," Mako finished.

"What are you feeling right now?" Thresher asked.

Mako shook his head, wouldn't look Thresher in the eye, his mouth tight with self-loathing. "Kind of numb, but I know that's her. Like she's there, but not there."

"I mean, what are *you* feeling?"

"I just told you."

"No, *you*, not her."

"Shit, this isn't some hand-holding session. It's the horses, isn't it? Bringing out your soft side. Next thing I know, you'll be telling me you're sensing the magic, like Mama Milagros."

"Maybe I am."

"That's not a compliment."

"Everything can't just be a joke to you."

That shut Mako up quick, but he didn't lean away. "I hate that I feel free when she's scared out of her mind. I feel guilty for feeling *good.*"

Thresher nudged him. "Is she why you get nightmares?"

"Yeah. Takes everything out of me. Being hunted by Bruykleeners doesn't help, either."

Thresher thought about what it meant to be happy. He liked how it felt, being entrusted with Mako's slumber under the graves. Everything had been such a whirlwind—all that fear and dependence—and this openness steadied him like regaining control after a particularly vicious treatment cycle. Thresher made an inarticulate sound deep in his throat and brushed Mako's hair, pet his back.

"What are you doing?" Mako asked, the only indicator of uneasiness was his curled lip showing his canine. "Are you *stroking* me?"

Thresher pulled back. "Sorry," he whispered. His fingers throbbed with heat.

"I mean, what is that about?" Mako's eyes shut as if in pain.

Thresher's hand retreated. He didn't know where to start. He felt small, expressing this. "It's what you're supposed to do, isn't it? When you comfort someone?"

Mako's closed eyes tightened. "Sure. If you're three years old."

"Is it wrong?" Thresher quelled his insides from shaking his outsides, hating that his books were wrong and afraid of what else he believed to be correct.

"No," Mako said, drawing the syllable out. "Just odd. Men don't usually express comfort with overt affection."

"What do men do then? What do people do?"

Mako seemed at a loss for words.

"Is it wrong? To...touch?"

Maybe that's why the Facility regulated touch, restricted it unless you were good and did well. Nothing big, shoulder claps, strong handshakes, and light guidance at his elbow. It hit him like lightning, a strange mixture of aversion, but he always craved it later, wished it could've lasted longer. Right now, he felt lightning crackle in his fingertips, ricocheting up his arm. He should pull away, but he couldn't. If he did, it would end. That was the last thing he wanted.

"No," Mako said, and Thresher wondered if that was the only thing Mako knew how to say. "But you're supposed to be strong enough not to need it."

A hole opened up in Thresher's chest. Mako's words cut him from his preconceived tethers and he floated freely into that yawning chasm. Perhaps it was another experiment, to make him crave something unorthodox in the real world. Let the written word fuel his dreams, and hope he never ripped his bandage off to teach him the truth. "I didn't know," he choked out.

"It's not a rule," Mako said. "It took me off guard. I wasn't expecting it."

"I'm sorry," Thresher whispered, looking at his hand. It felt like it didn't belong to him.

"Don't be. It's okay."

Mako seemed to say that a lot. "I don't understand."

"Remember when I told you I can't keep my mouth shut? Now is one of those times you should take my advice and ignore me."

"I don't want to make you uncomfortable," Thresher said.

"You're not. It's been a long time since I've traveled with anyone. I've forgotten what it's like to be a decent person. Touch isn't a bad thing. We all need it."

"Are you sure?"

"You've never been touched before? Hugged even?"

Thresher couldn't answer. His throat had dried up. His words were too used to wandering free. He shackled them back into silence.

Whatever pain Mako felt passed, and he opened his eyes, gave Thresher a look that said he understood. Hot tears filled Thresher, caught between the horses and this gift, feral with emotions laying him bare.

Mako stood, held a hand to Thresher. "Let's go," he said. "If I black out, you better be there to grab me. I can't smack my head a third time."

"A trinity-worth of head injuries?" Thresher asked as he took Mako's hand.

"Oh, hilarious. You're a keeper."

As he stood, Thresher felt stiff yet fragile with steel in his bones and all his cartilage removed. Numbness spread from his shoulder to his spine. He gripped his muscles and kneaded them. "Stiff."

Mako swayed, appearing sick for a moment, but recovered quickly. "Imagine how stiff you'll be in twenty years. Now that's terrifying."

Thresher mimicked an eyebrow raise and tried not to imagine a far-fetched future where he couldn't possibly be the man he was now.

19

N ika felt like a dust bunny, grimy and gray, floating in the sky among white clouds. Out of place, but ultimately blending in, just like her time at the Facility. Strictly an outsider at first, roaring with independence and lost rights until she faded into a mothball, still a little off color, but normal enough to pass.

A hard crust lined her eyelashes as she pried her eyes open. Blinking to get rid of the film covering her sight, she lay scrunched on a love seat with a—trinity, could that be a *decorative* pillow?—propping her head up and her medical gown tastefully drawn over her knees. She cracked her neck as she sat up, the pops vibrating into her jaw. Her bare feet rubbed against the carpet. Trinity, carpet.

Her mouth felt chemically dry, the insides of her cheeks chapped, and she felt all of four years old, waking up cranky and disoriented from a deep nap. She rested her elbows on her knees and studied the rest of the room. Popcorn ceiling. Walls painted a soothing blue. A sliver of soft light emanating from underneath a half-closed door at the other end of the room. Unlike the blinding overhead lights of the laboratory when Walker's face appeared above her and then it was lights out for her.

She studied the yellow glow like it might reach out and drag her inside. Finally, she stood and skirted the wall to the desk centered between her and the door. She was used to foraging for materials that could become useful in the strangest of situations.

She sifted through piles of papers on the desk, evaluating paperweights as too light to be clubs and thumbing chewed pencils too dull to cleave. Even the desktop had seen better days. Long, jagged scores and scratches chipped the polish. She yanked on the drawer handles on either side of the pushed in chair. Two were locked, but one slid open, and she found a dagger-sharp letter opener with a regal hilt.

The darkness both concealed and exposed her. Her eyes flickered to the light when shadows crossed it, followed by whispers too low to decipher. She shut the drawer carefully. Her tongue probed her cheeks, but she was still dry as a bone. She would kill for a drink of water, literally take a man behind a shed and shoot him. She didn't know thirst could come from her gut in a dehydrated twist, but if anyone was going to survive, it was going to be her, for the love of the trinity.

She crept up to the light, her bravery such a reckless thing, stupid actually, how *brave* brave could be. She should flee, but it might cause alarm. Then there was Walker to consider, that idiotic boy, taken with language and a Western ideal to live big and free even when nothing was free anymore, especially happiness and survival, but we all died in the end and wasn't that the big joke; you never get out of life alive, and if you could, then damn, share the trade secret and save us all.

She couldn't feel her big toe. Her foot ached as if she walked too far on it for too long. She rolled her ankle to shift her weight, resembling a bow-legged stork. The door creaked under her hand as she opened it.

One of those damned doctors, those fucking people who thought they could do inhumane things to her and not face justice, was backed into a big chair with Walker positioned between his legs. A lab coat drooped over Walker's bare shoulders. Broad black-framed glasses peeked around the curve of his ear. His long legs lifted to straddle the doctor, even as the doctor looked at him in complete adoration and brushed a hand up into the curls darkening the back of Walker's pale neck.

"Shouldn't have brought her here," the doctor murmured. "What were you thinking?"

"I thought she might be fun. Wouldn't you like that? Me and her, together."

"Is that what you want?"

"Aren't you getting tired of me? She could spice things up. Wouldn't you like it, letting me have her while you have me?"

"I don't need anyone but you," the doctor whispered. "I don't want anyone but you, but if you do, then I'll consider it, but only for you because..."

"Because I'm yours," Walker interjected smoothly, "and she's mine. But wouldn't it be nice, to do something *different*. I don't know how many others you've had. I thought it might be a good idea, new flesh."

"There's never been anyone but you," the doctor said. "I shouldn't even be with you, God, the things you've had me do could get me suspended, could get me thrown out with all the other outsiders. I've shown you things I *never* should have."

"Why did you do it, then?"

"Because I love you, don't you know that by now? I don't need her. I don't need anyone else. I love you. Loved you since you strolled into my office, can't get enough of you."

"I love you, too," Walker whispered against the doctor's mouth.

"Make her go away then."

"But she makes me happy. Not like you make me happy, but I want to be outside with her. I think it's gorgeous to imagine eating her out and having you inside me while I do it. In the grass. Under the full moon. Doesn't that sound sexy to you?"

"God, yes." The doctor moaned and Walker swiveled his hips.

"You'll have to collar us both though," Walker said. "Make sure your puppy doesn't run away while we go outside."

"Make me do the stupidest things, the craziest things…"

"I'll let you use a leash this time," Walker said. "You can hold it while you're making love to me."

"Jesus."

"'Cause you'll be owning both of us."

"Don't want to own you," the doctor said. "This…is just a game, right?"

"'Course," Walker muttered. He leaned over the doctor and kissed him. Nika heard a drawer rattle open as Walker's hands fiddled for something by touch. Walker pressed the collar into the doctor's hand. The doctor raised it reverently and fit the wide black strip of leather around Walker's throat and buckled it against the nape of his neck.

"You're so beautiful," the doctor whispered.

"Now do her," Walker said, and without looking toward her motioned to Nika with his hand cocked behind him.

She couldn't move, utterly revolted at the scene in front of her, couldn't imagine submitting to something like that, treated like a dog, like a fucking experiment.

"Come here." Walker turned his head briefly towards her. "Just keep walking, okay?" The electric light caught his blue eyes through the lenses, cast them blind against the hazelnut tone in his hair.

She shuddered, realizing trust was the issue here. She'd never had much of it, but she gathered every shred in her haystack, stepped forward, and tried to look demure. The doctor's hands rested on Walker's hips.

This close, Nika could smell the doctor: sweat and chemical burn. He was handsome for a monster, full head of hair, sharp nose and brown eyes full of soul and personality, but weren't they all, driven by ambition, driven to understand. He pressed the collar against her neck with none of the tenderness expressed for Walker. She had to lift her own hair so he could buckle it around her throat. She swallowed, but she was a thing for show now, especially when the doctor reached out and attached a leash to Walker's collar, a short handhold suspended between them. The doctor watched him like he could never imagine being so blessed, holding something so beautiful willingly tethered in his lap. Walker leaned forward and kissed his doctor, soft and full.

"Wish it wasn't like this," the doctor whispered, eyes focused on Walker's crotch. "Wish you could feel it like I do."

"I've got nothing to lose." Walker smiled. "Wish you could feel it like *I* do."

The doctor smiled back brilliantly. Walker unfolded himself from the doctor's lap, adjusted his lab coat, and straightened his borrowed glasses. Nika faded into the backdrop as the doctor took Walker's leash, looped it twice around his closed fist, and pulled Walker close.

The dark hallway was abandoned and quiet with the witching hour. Nika stuck close behind Walker while Walker sauntered beside the doctor, making her wonder what kind of act he was playing. The doctor hurried them through claustrophobic corridors new to Nika and stopped in front of a large steel door. After fumbling with a set of locks, he pushed it open. Fresh air hit Nika like a slap, the kind that circulated with the scent of trees, old water, and mud. Crickets chirped. The moon shone as bright as the sun and just as lovely. Nika wanted to fall to her knees in praise, bring her hands up, thankful that this sight was real.

Nika barely noticed the doctor pulling Walker in for a passionate kiss, shoving the lab coat down Walker's shoulders until it cradled his body. Walker cupped the doctor's face, even as the doctor held Walker's waist and went to work nipping along his jaw and over his collarbone. Walker's eyes caught hers, the glasses snatching the moonlight and reflecting where his eyes should be. Nika wasn't sure she understood, or if she could even know what Walker wanted her to do, but there was a big boulder half-buried in the grass that she could fit in her two hands. Big enough to bash in someone's face.

Walker fingered his coat pocket and slowly removed a rag like a magician, flicked it, and slid it beside the doctor's face as he devoured the doctor's mouth again. Nika dug into the rich dirt, moating around the boulder's rounded edges. Trembling, she unearthed it. Behind the doctor, she saw Walker's eyes open wide as she positioned herself. She was small, but her arms were strong. As Walker replaced his lips with the cloth over the doctor's face, she smashed the boulder against the back of his head. The impact vibrated down her arms. The doctor collapsed with a muffled cry. Blood splattered the rock. Nika stood over him to deliver the final stroke.

Walker shoved her hard. Her hands lost their purchase and the boulder fell from her grip with a thump, embedded back into the earth. Her toes curled reflexively—she wanted to keep all ten piggies, even as they dug into the ground. Her desire for revenge penetrated her thoughts.

Walker knelt beside his paramour and then punched him hard in the temple. The doctor gasped and went limp facedown. Bloodlust leaking out of her, Nika fought back a snarl as Walker turned the doctor's face to the side so he wouldn't suffocate. He stroked the doctor's hair for a moment, laid a tender kiss on his head, and stood, motioning Nika to follow. A set of keys shone brightly in his hands. "I planned it this way," he murmured. "I can get us off the grounds, but we don't have much time."

"Should take his boots," she whispered, fighting the urge to maul him, too. Free of medication, four walls, and sterilization, primitive urges surged in her veins.

"He won't be unconscious for long," Walker said, as if that were a reason not to.

That was okay, Nika decided, to choose pride over survival and deem that she didn't need the monster's cast offs. She was free now. In the wild jungle, she could live through anything.

20

N ika winced as another rumble of thunder rolled over a sky blanketed with heat lightning. Misty rain flattened her chestnut hair into her eyes and obscured her vision. Slicking it back behind her ears, she shuddered with cold. Mud splattered up to her thighs. Sharp rocks, sticks like tripwires, and broken shells bruised her feet. Exhausted from sprints and full-blown running, she realized around the time freedom's exhilaration wore off that she was a concrete girl. Too used to the tall shelters of skyscrapers, loot-worthy shops, and the hard slap of her feet on unyielding asphalt.

Her calves ached as her steps sank into deep sand that sucked like quicksand. She glanced through the low shrubbery and crooked, winding branches of the pine barrens to glimpse an opened expanse of beach. The roar of the ocean, combined with the thunder, vibrated through her ears and shook her brain. Her stomach growled, not to be forgotten, as she took stock of her bodily woes.

"Walker," she cried out, but the thunder swept away her croak. She tilted her head back and let the rain pitter off her front teeth and slither down her throat, coating her mouth with the taste of sea salt and pine sap. "Walker!"

He kept walking, shoulders brooding against the elements. His soaked lab coat stuck to his torso.

"Hey!" she yelled, irritated to the point of fury. Didn't he know his own fucking name?

Startled, he paused and looked over his shoulder. Raindrops streaked his glasses. *Oh. Probably not.*

"I gave you a name," she shouted, catching up to stand in front of him. The steamy clouds drifting from his nose and her mouth mingled together like cigarette smoke. "I named you Walker."

One side of his mouth curled up in distaste. "Why?"

"I don't know, but that's what I'm going to call you."

"What happened to Bartholomew?" he demanded, fiercely defending his homage to the seventeenth century.

"Chopping block," Nika said, bringing her hand down like a guillotine blade.

He looked like he wanted to argue that he controlled the basic rules of his identity, but he was too tired to win this war. "We have to keep moving," he said, instead. "They're searching for us."

"We should've killed that doctor then, if you're worried about being chased."

He severed eye contact and she knew he wasn't ashamed. He had to figure out a good enough answer for her.

"We need to find shelter. I'm not going to be able to keep going unless we get some rest," she said. Her stomach clenched painfully.

He fixated on something past her and nodded, detached. She couldn't figure out if he was either annoyed with her or wanted her to blend into the forest and go away.

"You're going to fall over too," she said.

"We can't stop now."

"Fine," she snapped, too exhausted to argue, but ready to explode with a temper tantrum that would rival any four-year-old.

She walked closer to him, watching his taut back muscles shiver with an odd sense of delightful malice. He wanted to see how the other half of the world lived, the barebones population not incarcerated in a Facility? Cold and rain were the least of their worries.

Riding on the tailcoats of that thought came the sobering one that she had no idea where they were or what tribes occupied this territory. They had no weapons, no means of defense, and she'd be damned if after going through the Facility's hell she would end up with her head bashed in. Her throat tightened at the thought. She clenched her fists to eradicate the memory of hot blood spilling over her hands as she cradled her mother's brain, to still the lingering satisfaction when she felt the crunch and give of Walker's doctor's head.

The rain lightened to a veil of fog. The sky brightened through the canopy with the telltale signs of soft dawn. Panic urged Nika to keep pace with Walker, who, clearly exhausted, never stopped to rest. Itchy patches burned around her ankles and up her calves. She scraped them against passing brush. Hours melted away with the changing landscape, the bright dawn shifting from warm midmorning to hot afternoon as the trees shortened and spread out.

Crevices lined Nika's mouth like the desert. Her skin erupted into blisters. A rash flared on the inside of her thighs where the skin rubbed together. Her mind had become a blank slate a long time ago, focused on lower body functions like putting one foot in front of the other, resisting the empty nausea swirling in her stomach, and wondering how much of the iron tinge in the back of her throat was actually blood. When Walker faltered down the side of a shrub-covered dune, she grabbed his arm, wheeling him around to face her.

Glassy-eyed and fever hot, he twitched under her touch. They careened against each other like two falling pillars. This close to the yellowed sand, Nika made out smoothed chunks of sea glass, neon-colored against the whorled pastels of nature. Walker leaned into her alarmingly, and she stumbled with his weight, watched him mouth unintelligible words, and knew they were minutes away from collapse.

She scanned the wide expanse of the beach. Her eyes burned from strain. The crashing of the white caps filled her ears. Her vision tilted to the side and she shook her head, blinked, and watched as a dune refocused into a rickety, bleached beach house perched precariously on stilts.

"Walker," she gasped, gripping his arm tight. "Look."

His breathing rattled in his lungs as he peered in the direction she pointed. Drool dribbled from his mouth, and he spit forcefully.

"C'mon," she whispered, drawing a mental line from them to the house. Fastest way to get where you needed to go was by a straight line. Even though they painted a wavering path of footprints in the sand, Nika focused on the building like it was the northern star.

The skeletal house looked like nothing more than a pile of carefully constructed, centuries-old driftwood. Terrified, she manhandled Walker up the deteriorated steps. Cracks ran through the wood, large splinters poked out like daggers, and hinges rusted at the entrance's four corners.

Faltering under Walker's weight, Nika crashed to the floor. The whole place swayed with the impact. *A barren tree house*, she thought with a hysterical grin, something she'd always dreamed about as a child. Salt clung to her skin—sweat and sea—while her hair dangled in front of her face in messy ropes. She never wanted to get up again. Walker moaned beside her. She scraped the bottom of her barrel for strength, shakily sat up, and slumped against the wall. Walker knelt on all fours like a shamed dog, a small puddle of bile underneath him.

Getting back on her feet sent pain shooting up her legs, but she did it, and took delusional stock of the room. Two windows, a huge hole in the ceiling, seagull shit, scattered remains of disemboweled crabs, bleached blue claws, a pile of driftwood covered in a blanket, and dried algae. She took the blanket, stiff with white and brown urea, and resisted the urge to crack it in half. The underside remained relatively clean. As she pathetically rapped the blanket against the wall, refuse flaked off and tumbled to the ground.

Nika's legs finally gave out. She gasped and lurched against the wall, leaning forward to clutch Walker's lab coat and pull him to her. Head down, he came to her, his glasses askew and foggy. She sank against the wall, felt the shaking heat of him cradled in her lap. He hid his face in her neck as she draped the blanket over them as well as she could, her toes sticking out.

She patted Walker's head with a motherly urge she'd never known before. She couldn't do more than that. Outside the cracked window, the sky darkened, and white, drifting clouds shifted into wispy whispers. She saw guns and sharks. She blinked and they faded, transformed into winking stars, a reminder of time slipping by as she passed out from hunger, exhaustion, and the glory of successful escape. Walker shifted against her, disturbing the warmth cradled between them, and her whole body was delightfully numb, threatened with pinpricks of returning blood flow.

"We did it," she said. She couldn't stop smiling.

Walker tipped his head up to look at her. "We did."

"Don't know if it will last." Her joy tasted like metal. "Should've killed that doctor. Would've given us more time to escape." Her mind replayed how they crept out of the courtyard, how she lost track of their location as they meandered through hallways until they slipped into a basement corridor, flanked with crumbling old machines and trade goods, and out a set of doors. Locks and chains fell before the might of Walker's keys.

"I couldn't do that," Walker said.

"Why not? He fuck you right? Is that why?"

"It wasn't like that," Walker said, sitting up out of her arms.

"He called you his puppy, didn't he? You liked being his bitch?"

"He didn't do anything I didn't want him to."

"Did you fucking love him?" She felt irrationally furious. He couldn't have it both ways, couldn't *love* both sides when this was a war of monsters and morality.

"Of course I did." Walker sounded both grateful and enraged, as if he thought she finally understood, but that was the kicker, she didn't understand at all.

"After what he did to you?"

"After he loved me? Helped me, fed me, taught me, showed me how to be more than just an experiment? How could I fucking *not* love him?"

"Don't you dare talk like me," she growled. "I'm the one that makes demands in the form of a question. Copycat."

"That's a childish request."

"You didn't love him. You whored yourself out to him to get what you wanted. That's not love. You used him. Hey, don't get me wrong, I applaud you."

"It wasn't like that," he said.

"Then explain it."

He made an exasperated sound. "He was interested in me, just like I was interested in you. He talked to me like a real person, told me what lay beyond the Facility. Becoming lovers was incidental, a secondary part of our relationship. He knew me as deeply as I knew him."

"Then why didn't you stay with him?" Nika asked. "Should've stayed with your perfect love story."

Walker's face dropped. "He showed me how to be more than an experiment, but I was still an experiment. Even so, I couldn't repay his kindness with death."

"That's how the world works," Nika said, astonished at his reaction.

"Not my world," he said. "When I told him my drugs affected my libido, he showed me a way into the kitchen, which gave me the chance to change your dosage. Without him, I wouldn't have been able to pretend to be a doctor and save you from another round of treatment. We wouldn't be here if it weren't for his love for me."

"You're a master manipulator and the worst part is you don't even realize it." She pointed her finger for emphasis. "We should've bashed his head in with a rock."

Walker tilted his head considering her. "He's a good man."

"He hurt you. He put a collar on you."

"Are you going to kill me now that you're free? Do you always discard what you no longer need?"

"No," Nika choked out. "I'm not heartless."

"You sound heartless," Walker said, "and this *is* your world after all."

She bit her lip. Tears rolled over her cheeks without order or command. She tried to rally them back, stem the tide, but she'd spent her last ounce of willpower getting the blanket. "I won't," she whispered, "but you've got to promise me you're not using me like you used him, because then I *will* smash your skull in. We're in this together, aren't we? You got me out for a reason, didn't you?"

"Yes," Walker said, eyelids dropping as his body sagged. "You needed your freedom, and I couldn't survive out here on my own.

See, I'm still at your mercy. Are you going to kill me? Should I be prepared?"

"Shut up," Nika said. "Just shut up. I don't care, as long as we don't get caught and we get some damn sleep."

"Trinity, yes," Walker breathed in her ear. "Is that how you use the term?"

21

Heat woke her, a boiling, sticky blaze. Walker's breath billowed across her skin like steam. She touched his head where it rested on her shoulder and her fingertips came away slick with sweat. She carded her fingers through his hair, fluffing up the wet strands into limp spikes.

"Walker?" She shifted so she could look down at him. "Hey, wake up."

She shook him, but he flopped uselessly against her. She touched his forehead again, hot like fire, and winced as she positioned him— *more like dropped him*—on his back. Kneeling over him, she lifted a fluttering, red-rimmed eyelid and watched as his eye tracked nothing back and forth. Small, violent tremors shook him, and his breath smelled vile. She tapped his cheek lightly, then harder when he didn't respond. "Shit," she whispered.

She'd seen fevers before, trinity, she'd been the queen of the flu when she was small. She recalled being drenched in sweat, yearning for a sip of water, how every muscle ached, and no matter how hot she felt, she wanted a hundred blankets to seal in a bit of that warmth. Sickness moved fast, she knew that, but this was too quick. Drugs, perhaps? Simple withdrawal? Only the trinity knew, but she needed to cool him down fast before his body fried his brain, an unfortunate casualty in warfare against whatever raged inside him.

"Hey." She shook him again. "Can you hear me? You need to help me get you up."

A cough wracked him, and he slid to his side to gag. He heaved up nothing but warm saliva.

He staggered to a halfway sitting position, shaking all the while, and looked at Nika through half-hooded eyelids. "I don't feel good," he said, petulant.

"I can make you feel better," Nika said.

"Hot," Walker said, his mouth downturned into a distinct frown. He scratched his chest, leaving wide, red diagonal crisscrosses across his skin.

"I know." Nika grabbed his wrists. "How does a cold bath sound? Would you like that?"

He nodded and rotated his wrist to hold hers. She uttered a quiet disbelieving laugh as she lifted him to a standing position and he leaned against her—a damned sauna—because yesterday going up the stairs felt like discovering a true savior and now, going down felt like escaping genocide. Wind blew long, skinny clouds like fishing line over the sun, casting shadows and chill. A disjointed wrack line wiggled into the distance. When they crossed over the braided algae full of blue mussels and black-horned egg cases, Nika felt like she'd traitorously crossed over to another *side*.

The ocean water numbed her to the small bones of her feet. She spun Walker around to face her, unbuttoned his laboratory coat, and shoved it down his arms. She removed the spectacles slipping down his nose, tossed them far away from the hungry tide, and splashed forward, falling to her knees. Ocean spray coated her face and smeared her lips. Salt dried out her tongue and a fishy aftertaste flew up the back of her throat into her nose.

She pulled Walker farther into the surf. Sand slipped out from under her with each wave. She encircled him in her arms and cupped water over his shoulders. The rash around her ankles itched the same as from greening jewelry. She rubbed Walker's biceps, the sand on her palms exfoliating his rough, red skin. Waves rolled over them both as she continued to bathe him as the sea salt mist scored her lungs.

She touched his caved in chest. His long legs spread out on either side of her so she sat in between them. The ocean pushed them and she felt weightless, like flying. Her teeth chattered like clacking piano keys, and Walker shook in time with it. His fists clenched and unclenched. Blue slits peered at her, wary and watchful, tracking her as she bathed his neck and rubbed her hands up and down the jutted line of his spine.

"What do you think it's like?" he asked in a shaking voice.

"What?"

"The outside," he said.

"Walker, we are outside."

"Therapy told me it's wrong to wonder, that it's only a pathway into mental instability. Outside is dangerous. Toxic. They'd know. They once sent out a batch of experiments that died. The air will kill you, but I can't stop thinking about it. Can't stop thinking about all the space." He held his arms out wide and shuddered as the cold swept under his armpits.

"We got out. You got me out," Nika said.

"Maybe you're right, about me being a whore. I shouldn't've used my doctor like I did."

"I didn't mean that, trinity, I'm sorry."

He reached out and placed both hands around her neck, spanning his fingers to run lengthwise over her collarbone and up over her shoulders. Against his red veined sclera, his eyes looked like the sky should—full of summer instead of gray with a storm. "Please don't hurt yourself anymore."

"Walker." Her throat constricted. "You're hallucinating."

"Don't have much to be a whore with, though," he said. "Born all wrong."

Nika swallowed hard, because she'd seen it, the small nub barely bigger than her thumb and the bulging pouch that surrounded some sort of hole.

"Never felt wrong," he assured her with a pat, "but I'm scrambled inside."

"What did they do to you?" She couldn't imagine and hoped he wasn't awake when he had been...what, castrated? Mutilated? He didn't look scarred, but the Facility was evil when it came to experiments.

"Water toxicity," he said with a crazy smile, all teeth, completely at ease with his nudity. "Exposed in the fetal stage. Too much estrogen. Didn't develop right. Mmm, that feels good."

Nika's chin wobbled, and she crimped the corners of her mouth in tight, leaning Walker back to dip his head. She ran her hand over his forehead, baptizing him in the natural environmental waste of the outside, in the unnaturally green-tinged water. He sat up on his own, his spine bending alarmingly, and water droplets slid down his face like tears.

She held her breath, startled when a beat later, Walker did the same. She let out the breath slowly and watched his nostrils slenderize as he matched his breathing to hers. "Copycat," she said.

His mouth slivered open and his tongue skirted around the inside of his pale lips. He watched her. Still glazed, she noted. Still feverish, but better. He floated into her lap, laid his head on her shoulder while her arm braced his back against her. Her brown skin looked revitalized compared to the blush of him, and she wondered if this was the first time he'd been exposed to light—not candlelight or electric light, but *sunlight*.

"I'm tired," he whispered.

"Do you feel better?" she asked, melding her hands on his shoulder blades. They felt like outspread wings.

He nodded, and she watched her legs float in front of her, distorted in the wave's reflection, casting prisms of light, dark, and green until she felt blind. The threat of thunder danced over her forearms. The water felt colder, the wind dug deeper, and goosebumps raced from the base of her spine up to cradle her skull, prickling every little hair to attention on its way.

"I don't like death," Walker murmured, folding his arms.

"No one does," she said as the water soaked the ends of her hair and dragged her head back.

"I really don't like it," he said. "It's like all possibility, poof, gone."

"Talking like me again," she said.

"Maybe this is how I talk now."

"You're hallucinating."

"I know you're dead," he said crossly.

"The other outsider is dead. She killed herself. I'm Nika, remember?"

"I don't think I have a name." He made a distressed sound. "I want a name."

"You do, but you don't like it. It's Walker. I named you Walker."

"It's a verb."

"An action verb," she pointed out, and he snorted.

She tested his temperature. Still hot, but not brain-frying hot. She wiggled her toes. Possibility, huh. The possibility of *survival*. She glanced around, taking in the coastline and the short forest behind the dune shack. The possibility of weaving bark into a net, the possibility of using that net to catch fish, if the fish were edible.

As seagulls circled her like vultures, she remembered the bloated bodies in the canals back home, the stench of twisted, black menhaden covered in flies. She bit her lip, fending off the thought of food because it left her both nauseous and desperate. Still, if the birds here survived on the crabs, she could too. She could live off the land. She could do anything, because she didn't like death either, not one little bit. No matter how soothingly death played promising tunes of *simply being done* and *giving up*, she wasn't ready to stop reading music. She barely hit the right notes half the time, but at least she wasn't lost.

She was Nika Saddlerock. She was outside. She was free.

22

When rain drummed through the hole in the roof of the little driftwood house sounding like pursuing footsteps, and ozone reached deep into her lungs like lightning shocks, Nika laid out cleaned, dissected crab shells for collection. Fat raindrops formed small puddles on the smooth carapace. She emptied the flat bowls into Walker's mouth and stroked his neck to help him swallow. Her wet, high-arched footprints covered the wooden floor, sheltered from the roof's opening.

She'd eaten the dried algae lying around the driftwood and devoured gulps of water, gone from wary to uncaring just as long as she felt full inside. She cracked open the leftover crab claws and put whatever she found into her mouth, like a child exploring the shapes of the world through oral fixation. Just before the storm, she caught sight of a speck of a bird, so high up, dropping a crab through the roof's hole. The flailing victim cracked its back on the floor. Nika smashed it open and sliced her fingers on the bright blue shell. The raw, slippery chew plopped into her growling stomach. She looked up into the sky with sharp, feral clarity. The next time a seagull landed close enough, she imagined she would pull the blanket over it like a shroud and beat it against the wall until the blanket stopped moving. Then, she would roast the bird over a fire and feel the warm grease drip over the back of her hands. She slurped back a warm rush of saliva just thinking about it.

Walker shivered on the floor. She had set his glasses close enough so he could spot them, but far enough away that he wouldn't ruin them in a fevered delusion. It figured he'd get ill; he probably hadn't stopped taking whatever drugs *they'd* pumped *him* full of, because he was *so* smart with his plans and his doctor and his mimicking. Her lip curled in a snarl as she sipped another carapace dry, running her tongue along the smooth white inside.

She remembered hunger like this, not as sharp, not as needy, just before she lost her mother. She had split the last of the hard tack with her twin and her mother told them to keep close. She remembered this kind of fear too, *survival terror*, when they were surrounded by Bruykleeners. When she could smell, taste, and see her mother's blood. The sense of petrifying independence before the vulture that turned into Mama Milagros knelt in front of her, her black eyes level to Nika's hazel, beads and feathers tied in her long, graying hair, and offered her a hand. Mama Milagros's home was a dump, but now her dangling ceiling tiles and overgrown fungus corners of the railroad apartment would be paradise.

The rain dwindled to a sprinkle. Nika migrated off her haunches, her belly swollen with drink, over to Walker. Her nose scrunched in distaste at the seagull-shit blanket. The unsanitary stench crawled over her as she settled underneath it and let Walker's heat-trembling body warm her up. Walker shifted, aligning his body behind hers. She swallowed a grumble as he put his arm over her waist. His stale breath beat against her neck. She hoped this wasn't another mirroring trait. She had never been touchy feely to begin with, and especially wasn't now, after everything.

Her mind drifted on the verge of sleep, lulled with the impossibility that Tarek lay behind her, that he might roll over and cover her mouth with his. With a surge of annoyance, she realized she was too aroused to slip under. She hadn't felt this way since she lived in a skyscraper on Manahatta, and she dully knew how to take care of the tight coil refusing to let her rest. Her hand drifted to the cleft between her thighs. Her finger rotated, familiar in its motion, but still foreign because it had been so long. She angled away from Walker as much as she could, awkward that she now had all this space to do this one simple, animalistic need, and she had to do it in front of him, sleeping or not.

Her finger tapped and she pawed down further, seeking moisture, but returned with barely any. She circled and patted, mind carelessly carding through old memories like sifting through dusty boxes, searching for a glimpse of an image to rile her up. A flash of thigh, lips surrounded by stubble, and the warm, wet way she liked to be kissed.

Her brow furrowed. The images gathered like a cupful of prayers, but brought others: the scrape of a razor close to her scalp because lice weren't tolerated, the harsh vibration of ink pounding into her wrist and the back of her neck, the sterilization steam and the way her old clothes came back washed with cheap detergent, marred by an unidentifiable film. Her finger stilled, but this was something to fight, and she lowered her antlers.

Intelligence tests. Card games asking for a sequence of events. Enlarged images of everyday objects with a detail missing. A cartoon picture of blue-handled scissors, and she couldn't see what was wrong with it until the doctor pointed it out. Laid her finger on the crisscrossed blades and said, "The screw is missing." She almost broke down at that point. The ache of missing her grandmother's grin and Mama Milagros's rattling pouches combined with the shared panic, radiating from her twin over what felt like hundreds of miles, boiled down to finding a goddamn screw on a set of child's scissors. And failing at it.

She couldn't move her finger. All stimulation was lost as she relived those first few days. Fear continued to paralyze her. She wasn't *remembering*, she *felt* the poachers exchange her for a bag of goods before they hauled her inside. Snarky, one psychologist called her, but he seemed pleased with her tiptop form. They treated her carefully for the first few weeks, told her all the rules, showed her all the rooms, led her like a privileged guest until her mouth got her in trouble like it always did. Then came the routine physicals, the bloated bags full of saline and broad-spectrum antibiotics, probing and prodding, trinity, the table.

Her finger twitched away. Her hands curled together and she held them near her face, breathing in the sharp tang radiating from that one blasted finger. Walker shifted, his breathing changing, and for one crystallized moment, she knew beyond a shadow of a doubt that Walker was nothing but another Promised Land trick.

"What was the other outsider like?" she asked, hating the wobble in her voice. Usually when she felt this raw and unsure, she talked to her mother's bones. Talking to herself felt too lonely, but now she was on edge, barely clinging to the difference between reality and memory. Nika drew in a shuddering breath and exhaled slowly, leading her control with shaky reins. Maybe he wasn't awake.

"Tall," Walker finally said. "Blonde. I've read about meadowlarks and think her voice must've sounded like that."

Nika snorted, but continued, dumb enough to be in the charging cavalry's front line. "Were they doing the same experiments on her as they did to me?"

"Something similar, yes," Walker whispered.

We're a conservation group, her psychologist explained in the beginning. *We're figuring out a way to cure humanity. We want to understand the impacts human destruction has on the human himself.*

"The focus was to evaluate the outside's toxicity on human genetics, select the best surviving lineage among that group, and gauge whether those grown in the Promised Land would be compatible with the natural population," Walker said.

"You sound like those Facility textbooks," Nika said. Her eyes squeezed closed and she could see her psychologist sitting across from her.

"We were lucky," he said, licking his lips, "that our great grandmothers and grandfathers attended the same conference coming on, oh, a hundred years ago now." He pushed his scratched glasses up his nose and laughed. "You could consider them our ancestors, our narrow gene pool. After the volcano blew halfway across the country, it caused an earthquake that destroyed the water treatment plants and the nearby nuclear reactor. Somehow, they were protected even as brutal storms ripped away clean living. We survived, even when our call for help from the rest of the world was ignored, but how could we blame them? They were in crisis too. Japan swallowed like Atlantis. The great European fires. The water shortage. The political babble. They had nothing to give."

"She told me I was smarter than the rest of the experiments, that I could imagine the outside, where you could walk for miles and never reach the other side of the country. About the way the sky sometimes looked so bright you couldn't recognize it as blue," Walker said.

Walker. The experiment exposed to high levels of estrogen in the womb. Nika's world spun as the Facility's purpose began to make sense. If you create enough strange things in a human, those strange things get passed to the kids, but what if those strange things resisted environmental problems, like sewage or sickness?

In here, we were brought up on the ethics of science and the morality of evolution, but it's against human nature to let our own species go extinct. You evolved to withstand the perils of the outside," her psychiatrist continued. "We evolved, too, but under different conditions. We created this place to rebuild our civilization. It's a shame how the outside has gone to waste. All that culture. All that identity. Can you imagine how long it took us to build the pyramids? Having to relearn that all over again?"

"I don't know, doc." Nika fiddled with the edge of her sweater. "Ants do it all the time and they don't have a problem with it."

"Ants," he snarled. "You're comparing us to ants."

Walker's lips moved against her neck. "I started to feel trapped. I owned a whole life and kept it confined in one place, and no matter what happened, I would never be able to deepen it into something worth living."

"Think of all the cultures spread out around the world. The intricacies and diversification of them. How they evolved specifically for that region. Now, we're reduced to what, three? Four?" Her psychologist gnawed on his pencil.

Obviously he didn't understand tribal wars. Nika told him so.

"Do you know how long it took them to gather this equipment? To build it, fix it? Putting their minds into overdrive to provide us with a facility worthy of recreating a genetically stronger human population? What did your family accomplish? What did your generational line do to be remembered?"

"Where did she come from?" Nika asked, hating the shudder in her voice, like she was on the verge of crying, even if she wasn't, *she wasn't.*

"Somewhere west," Walker said. "She said she didn't have a clan."

Clan, a foreign word for family. That captured outsider must have been blown way off course to end up here. A stab of horror hit her heart as she realized there had been attempts before her, and the Promised Land must've selected them carefully based on their homeland. They wanted a range of outsiders to test if their mutated human lineages could be born. The Facility would reward poachers well—she was likely traded for food, clothes, medicines. "She give you any names?" Nika asked, picking at a sliver in the floorboard. "Anybody to tell?"

"No," Walker said.

That was the saddest part of all, no name, no family, not even a memory to honor. Just another person lost to despair. Nika couldn't blame her. Trinity, if she had been left in the Promised Land without the sense of Mako drilled into her chest, she might have ended it a long time ago too. At least she knew her twin *lived.*

"If something happens to me, you need to find Mako Saddlerock," she said. It was important that *someone* tell him of her demise. Considering their lack of supplies and exposure, death might be along quicker than she thought.

"Who's that?"

"My brother. He'd want to know. If something happened, that is."

"Okay," Walker said, and she felt him mouth her twin's name to memorize it. "I should be better soon. I didn't get my last injection. I think that's what's making me sick."

"Injection?"

"Testosterone, and the like," he said.

"Gotta take better care of yourself."

"You're doing a good job of it for me," he whispered before sleep folded over her like a blanket, heavy with exhaustion and dreams made for the hopeful.

23

The wind, constant and tumultuous, whipped Nika's hair around her face. She spit out the strands caught in her open mouth, squinting as sand burned her eyes. She couldn't feel her toes, much less her fingers, and she marveled in a detached way how her digits obeyed by sight.

The hybrid net of bark strips, pleated algae, and grass spread out in front of her in a wide U-shape. She walked into the ocean up to her waist with one end while rocks held the other end down on the beach. She threw stretches of the net out behind her, each toss accompanied with a curse and prayer. Once back on shore, she hauled in her beach seine and nearly cried out in triumph when she saw the splash of fish fins inside the net.

Her arms and shoulders ached as she padded around the net, picking out long, narrow creatures with big black eyes and tossing them back. Fragile fish floated on the water's surface, dead from shock.

Lo and behold, the treasure of her catch: a big fat striper, scales silver and green with black parallel lines. It thrashed in her arms, wide, wicked mouth snapping, but she stuck her thumb down its gullet. Mud and silt clogged its gill slits. She threw the fish farther up the beach, near her pre-made, unlit fire, where it flopped uselessly, trying to gain momentum to roll back into the ocean.

An escaping blue crab sideways-walked over the sand and Nika smashed her driftwood club onto the large crustacean. She pushed the corpse to the side and herded other snapping crabs, startled into defensive positions, around dirt mounds and suffocating fish, clubbing down three of them. When one scuttling to safety pinched her, she stuck her fish-goopy fingers to her mouth with a yell, then kicked it. It waved its claws at her before slipping under the waves.

Dragging her kill back to the net, she hissed at the circling seagulls that landed next to her. She tossed smaller dead fish to the birds and found a larger flat fish, all brown and mottled with two eyes on top. She grabbed the tail and yanked it out of the muck.

Tossing the net ends away from her, finally *done*, she hauled her catch to the fire pit. Driftwood crisscrossed in a star pattern with twigs, bark, and brush piled underneath. Striking two rocks to get a spark didn't work after countless tries, so she rubbed two sticks together and prayed for friction. Please, for the love of *trinity*, one simple spark.

A flare caught, held, and fed hungrily on her offering. Her cupped hands protected it until it thrived. She toed the crabs into the embers and watched them transform red. The striper slicked her knees with clear ooze as she pulled it onto her lap. She tried to stab its belly with a rock she had split into an off-kilter arrowhead. The scales puckered inward before giving way with a slight pop, exposing white flesh and pink organs.

Her fingers scooped out the innards and she laid the mangled flesh on a smooth rock. Small oblong parasites wiggled out of the striper's mouth and gills. Nika picked one up and watched it contract, its microscopic legs pin-wheeling helplessly. She tossed it away.

The white-capped waves rolled higher with the urging wind, crashing on the beach like grasping hands. She buried her feet in the bend of her knees, seeking warmth. To her right, the sun sank behind a cloud cluster, spilling golden yellow, tropical orange, and pink shades across the west. To her left, the twilight stretched out as a conquering hero. The moon, that pale rider, sat opposite the falling sun. Caught between the fade of sunlight and rise of night, Nika felt suspended on the turning globe, centered by her body's needs: burning for calories, ill on dehydration, shuddering with sunstroke. She thought of a dangerously thin Walker, shaking off the last of his withdrawal and atrophying before her eyes. She'd counted his bones in the middle of the night as he slumbered, ticked off all 206, and used his ribs as a touchstone when she got lost in her flashbacks. When it stopped helping and the terror and hunger pushed her to the edge, she came out here to hunt and gather.

"Hey there, little lady."

Her head snapped up, holy trinity, she could have broken her neck with how fast she looked up at the newcomer. Damn her tunnel-vision. She was smarter than that. She crab-crawled back, breathing in small hitches of despair at abandoning her meal. The newcomer held his hands up, palm out, and pasted on a reassuring smile. "Don't worry," he said. "I know what you're thinking, but I'm not contagious or dangerous. You're safe." He sat cross-legged across from her and tipped the brim of his hat with a crooked finger so she could see the chocolate brown gleam of his iris.

Nika laughed in his face. Contagious? Dangerous? *Safe?* She had escaped the sterile walls of confinement to face starvation and exposure, and now an outsider claimed she was safe? The situation kept getting better and better. "You sound like you think I'm an experiment."

The newcomer raised a blond eyebrow. "You…believe you're an outsider?"

"I know who I am." The thought had been sitting in the back of her mind for a while now, a fear secondary to being re-captured by the Facility. After all, the last time she trespassed on tribal lands, her mother had been killed. "Where do you hail from?"

"I've heard about the crazy in you experiments, but this is new." He rolled up his coat sleeve so she could see his tanned wrist sans tattoo. "See? I'm all organic. Show me yours." He motioned to her arm.

Terror slid into her bones and she turned her wrist away. "I'm not an experiment."

"You look a little worse for wear," the newcomer said, leaning forward to study her feast. "But that's quite a meal you've got."

Nika snarled a warning.

He made a harmless gesture. "Don't stop on my account."

Without knowing what to do, but knowing for certain if she didn't eat she would collapse, she scuttled back and positioned all of her meat on her side of the fire. She angled a wide stick into the sand over the hottest part and placed the meat strips down the line. She picked up the flat fish, eyes dull and smelling rancid, unsure how to gut it.

"Here, let me," the newcomer said gently, holding a knife out flat in his hand. Bone handle, she saw, bone blade perhaps. Tears pressed against her eyes. He talked to her like she talked to Walker sometimes, like he didn't know any better because he wasn't of the world. She handed him the fish and finally understood defeat.

He placed the fish on his knee. "Watch. I'll show you how." The blade slid against the gills. "Cut deep, but don't hit the bone." He made an expert cut and drew a lateral line down to the fish's tail. "Fluke's good meat," he said, flashing a close-lipped smile. "You'll want to use the spine as a guidepost to fillet it properly."

He dragged his lower lip between his bold teeth. A sandy beard covered his face. She watched silently, taking note of the way he turned the knife and thumbed back the flesh to reveal the meat underneath. Gentle sawing parted the scaled skin and he handed both to her as he flipped the fish to do the underbelly.

She laid the fish on another stick and smelled the roasting char on the striper. She couldn't break bread with this man. Half needed to be reserved for Walker, but how could she get away without this man following, asking questions, hurting her? She poked the crabs out of the fire. The shells pulsed with heat like a breathing ember.

"I'm Milo," he said, finishing the second fillet and handing her the prize, "and you're on the farthest east of the islands. Not much land left between here and the open ocean."

Farther than she'd thought. "Your tribe?" she asked, amused at his soft talk, like she was a spooked horse.

He seemed taken aback. "The End."

She nodded, and he seemed surprised at her reaction. Nika knew little of the Enders, only that their tribe of mishmash people had banded together at the end of this long island and taken a name derived from an old nickname for the area. "I can't share this meal with you," she said finally.

"That's fine." Now he sounded uncertain. "Not hungry, anyway. Do you want me to do the last fish for you?"

She handed it to him, then took the first striper fillet and dropped it, hot and sizzling, on her tongue. Her mouth burned from taste buds to the back of her throat, but she closed her eyes in relish. She spit bones out like cherry stems and threw them in the fire where they glowed translucent. She devoured a second fillet, positive that a few bones went down the chute, too, but she didn't care when she felt fuller by the second.

Milo tossed the fish guts away and a flock of birds attacked it. He wiped his hands on his pants, some kind of canvas reinforced with patches at the knees, but for the most part a solid and beautiful tan. Her heart caught in her throat thinking about the time she spilled the mulch of handmade paper all over her brother's beloved leather coat. Stained the back good and dark. He wouldn't talk to her for days, constantly buffing the leather with fat.

"A lot of people are looking for you," Milo said, breaking the silence cleanly. "You're a good actress, did your research, but you still don't fit. I'm sorry, but I have to take you back."

Nika glared at him. "I didn't peg you for a bloodthirsty Bruykleener, or even a slaver from the Reckowacky, but maybe it's the Enders prerogative to lick the boots of the Promised Land."

Milo looked stunned. "Who taught you that pretty talk, huh?"

"I told you," she said, inching her chin up higher, daring him to laugh or scoff. "I'm an outsider. I'm Manahatta."

Scuffles in the sand made her look up to see five tribesmen following her old footsteps to the fire. She rose to her knees. Milo tutted softly and she sank back down. Two men steered Walker by his winged elbows and he stumbled, his hands bound behind his back. Two other males and a woman stuck close behind. Black circles deepened under Walker's eyes. The flames lit him up like a haunting. Terror boiled her bloodstream. The Enders kicked Walker to his knees beside Nika and swiftly untied him. He trembled, jaw clenched, and rubbed his wrists. Nika caught his eye, read that he hadn't been roughed up, and even though they faced trouble, he had her back.

She studied the End tribe with tight lips. The group's elder shot her a narrowed glare before sitting knee to knee next to Milo, the two of them visual polar opposites. He pushed his straight black hair behind his shoulder. Wide streaks of silver stemmed from his scalp. His gnarled, reddish-brown hands patted his trousers then up to his coat's breast pockets absentmindedly.

"Should kill 'em off," he muttered to Milo. "That's what we would've done in the old days."

"We don't get paid for corpses." Milo sighed and pulled a pouch from his pocket. "You gave this to me for safe keeping, remember?"

The elder held out his hand. A tarnished silver ring encircled his ring finger.

"Do you remember, Jake?" Milo prodded.

"Likely stole it from me." Jake snapped his fingers. "Always been a thief, pup."

Milo handed him the pouch. Jake pulled out a black book from his side satchel and flipped the worn leather cover open. Pages had been raggedly torn from the spine. Licking his thumb and index finger, Jake tore a horizontal strip. He shut the book with a hollow thump and laid the paper over his knee. Words in crowded black type were smeared with fingerprints, and Nika realized as Jake opened the pouch and pinched tobacco between his licked fingers, that he was rolling a cigarette with Bible pages. He sprinkled the green along the paper strip, tucked the edges in tight, and sealed it with a lick—sloppy like a hound—and hung the smoothed tube at the corner of his mouth. He lit it with a smoldering stick pulled from the fire, breathing in smoke made from burning the words of a god.

Nika spared a glance at Walker and saw him fixated on the fish charring on the stakes. Slowly, she took the food out of the flames and laid it on a rock to cool, urging Walker with her shoulder. He hissed as small bubbles of grease boiled the back of his hands, but he stuffed the white flesh into his mouth. He devoured the other fillets, keeping his mouth open, breathing cool air over his scorched tongue. Nika cracked into the crab. If the Enders planned to kill them, she would have one last meal.

"Here," Jake said and passed the burning cigarette to Milo. Milo scrunched his face up in distaste, but accepted the offering by taking a quick drag. "I want to know what these whippersnappers think they're doing, hiding out in our shack, using up all the wood like they own the place."

"You need driftwood reimbursement?" Nika shot back. "Walk down the beach."

"They claim to be Manahatta," Milo said.

"Well ain't that a joke," Jake said. Smoke drifted out his nose. "Look to be experiments to me. Tattoos don't lie, but their mouths sure do."

"Doesn't matter where they came from," one of the younger dogs said from behind the leaders. His auburn hair spiked up from sweat. A dangerous gleam lit his eyes. "They'd probably sell everything they got for another minute with that fire."

"Enough, Tobey," Milo said over his shoulder.

Tobey spread his stance and crossed his arms. "Pretty one over there." He leered at Nika.

"You're such a pig," the End girl scolded. "Keep it in your pants."

"I don't have to listen to anything you say, Maggie Mae. I'd call you a cock tease but I already know you've no fucking idea what a cock is."

"*Shut up, Tobey,*" Maggie shouted, hands on her slender hips. Loose, dark curls bobbed around her shoulders, streaked with an early show of elderly white. She had the same russet-brown skin as Jake.

"Why don't you keep quiet like you usually do? Didn't know you had a mind to make an opinion, much less a sentence."

"Fuck off," one of the other males said, stepping in front of Maggie.

"That's right, Maggie Mae. Let Buck fight for you. That's all you do, isn't it? Fight her fights. Not gonna get you anywhere."

"*Shut up,*" Buck yelled, lunging at Tobey. A yelp followed by a jaw-shattering crack came next and sand kicked up against Jake's back as the two fumbled down the bank.

Jake sighed. Milo raised an eyebrow and said, "Not so intimidating now, are we?"

Nika couldn't help but laugh. What was the old saying? Boys will be boys? Nothing entitled them to act like *that*.

"Don't cry, Maggie," the last male said, putting his hand on her shoulder and dragging her into a one-armed hug. "Let's sit down." He smiled at Nika over Maggie's head, as if they shared camaraderie. The flames lit up the russet and blonde tones of his hair, but nothing could match his whiskey eyes. He looked toward Milo, who gave a small nod. The two of then sank into the sand, close enough to their elders to be respectful and near enough to the crowded fire to stay warm.

"Thanks, Beau," Maggie said. Her small face flushed with shame as she wiped her eyes. Beau patted her back. "Sorry," she whispered, more to herself than anyone else.

"I'm glad you've grown out of all that," Jake huffed, pointing his thumb over his shoulder and nudging Milo. "But you," he pointed at Beau, "better not let those pups get away with too much. You're still young enough to be stupid."

"I'm saving up my fights," Beau said, plunging his hands inside his patched puffed coat. Nika couldn't keep her eyes off it, bright orange and probably stuffed with feathers. Trinity, she could imagine the warmth.

Jake snorted, but Milo nodded in approval and stretched his hand out before making a tight fist. "I broke my hand once," he said. "All over a stupid bottle of oil. I feel that fight every day."

"Why don't we keep unloading on these experiments," Jake offered. "Want to take them home with us? Let them nest before they stab us in the back?"

"No, Jake," Milo said.

"No, Jake," Beau whispered. Maggie Mae mouthed the words.

"We wouldn't do that," Walker said, sounding eager. "I'm the experiment, but Nika isn't. Please don't hurt her. You can let her go."

"*Trinity,*" Nika exclaimed.

"Chivalry really isn't dead," Jake said. He pulled his Bible out, ripped another strip, and rolled a second cigarette.

"You're starved as it is," Milo said. "No clothes, no food, no water. Don't think you'll last long. This isn't a concrete jungle, sweetheart, we've got wolves in our forests."

Nika couldn't argue with that. She gauged the distance between her and the trees, wondering how fast they could get lost in the brush and how quick the Enders could run. She watched the two fighting boys shuffle back to the fire; black-haired Buck cradling his head while Tobey nursed a black eye. They slumped on the other side of Milo, leaning heavily into each other. Must not have been that bad of a fight,

Nika thought. No one had to separate them. Still meant there were two extra bodies to pursue them.

"Here's the rub," Jake said. "We've got an unofficial treaty with the Promised Land folks. The treaty pretty much reads as—"

"Don't fuck with us, we won't fuck with you," Milo finished, sharing Jake's offered cigarette without a hitch in his speech.

"We can't turn a blind eye when the Promised Land sets a bounty. We mean to fill it."

"Do you know what they're doing to people in there?" Nika said, jumping to her knees, her hands clenched into fists. "Do you know that they're experimenting on people grown like a damned crop? They tried to make me have an experiment's baby to see if we were compatible. *Compatible.*"

Maggie shuddered. Nika looked straight at her, put all that intensity into the space between them, and pointed a finger at her. "That's rape."

Beau shifted uneasily. Nika met Jake's glare. The unpleasant feeling in her chest told her he didn't believe her, not one lick. "I was poached by slavers from my family in Manahatta and traded to the Promised Land. I wasn't the only one. Before me, there was a girl from a clan." Nika let the foreign word ring. They'd understand. "They did the same thing to her and she hanged herself. Now, you're telling me you're in the flesh business too? How long before they start looking toward your women as a test variable? How long before your treaty isn't worth shit?"

She didn't know she could sound that scary.

Jake's gnarled hands tightened on his knees. Milo, the second in command, waited for judgment. Nika wanted to talk, bargain, and curse, but she held back, balanced on this edge of justice she didn't understand. What was the use of getting this man's trust when in a few short strides she could be swallowed by the darkness and go any which way she wanted? She didn't need to rely on these people with their hotheaded boys and their scared little girl. They were just a tribe after all. She suddenly yearned for that unity acutely.

"I'm not going back," she said, glancing down. Walker's confused blue eyes couldn't compete with her horror of the straightjacket or the suffocating pressure of the collar around her throat. The sand skidded under her as she leapt to her feet. She couldn't wait, or play this true or false game. Fleeting guilt crushed her, but it didn't stop her flight toward the dunes. There was her twin and grandmothers to think of.

Jake's commands echoed behind her and her name wrenched as a cry from Walker's mouth. Her breath tasted like hot iron, but running miles during her exercise hour at the Facility helped her fly to freedom. The pursuing footsteps sounded too close. She dove into the shadows of the tree line and tripped over a log. Branches slapped at her face as the Enders snapped orders—she could tell by their curt tones—but she'd given them fair warning: *she wasn't going back.*

She skidded down a narrow deer path but was suddenly airborne as her legs gave out from under her. Her calf muscles spasmed and wouldn't obey, clenched so tight she felt contorted. Tears streaked her face. She dragged herself into a small hole sheltered by a decaying log and threw handfuls of dirt and grass over her body. Through a crack in the log, she saw the beach and the glow of her fire. Her breathing roared in her ears. Milo stepped up to the edge of the dunes and held up a torch. The orange light flickered over her and she ducked, terrified he could see her eyes reflect the glow. Tobey dragged Walker into the light, his hand clenched in the experiment's hair forcing his neck back. Walker clutched at Tobey's hand, his face transformed in agony. "Think you can leave your friend so easily?" Tobey yelled. "Are all so-called Manahattas this disloyal?"

Nika's stomach plummeted seeing the glee on Tobey's face. He grabbed the stick from Milo and blew out the flame lighting the top, making the remaining ember pulse. "He might be going back to the Promised Land, but he doesn't have to go back the same. It's hard out here, even harder when you can't see." He edged the stick closer to Walker's eyes. Walker screamed and Nika stifled a sob. She couldn't go back, but her disgrace tore at her heart. Walker had trusted her and she abandoned him. She was sacrificing the one person who helped her escape, the only good thing that came from the Promised Land.

Closing her eyes, she swallowed hard, finding her voice. "Don't!" she shouted. "I'm coming out!" Trying to stand, she collapsed and dragged herself over the ground. Shakily leaning against a tree until her legs held her weight, she stumbled back onshore, hating every moment, hating herself, hating Walker for making this decision for her. As soon as she entered the light, the Enders surrounded her and grabbed her arms. Her head hung down. The stick sizzled in the sand. Yanked toward the fire, she gazed at Walker. She had to see her betrayal in all its colors. Tears glazed his eyes and she accepted the pain, let it wash over her and realized how awful she could be.

"Maggie Mae," Jake said and the girl jumped. "You have clothes stashed up, don't you?"

"Not many," Maggie said.

"Why don't you try to find some things that will fit our new guests. In exchange, you can learn some lessons about *pluck* from Miss Manahatta."

"Yessir," she said, and reluctantly began rifling through her bag. She pulled out a wrinkled bundle and brought it to where Walker and Nika stood.

The Enders surrounded Nika, keeping her prisoner within the circle. Curling her lip, she accepted the clothes from Maggie and stripped in defiance. The remaining light played on her gooseflesh skin. She hadn't paid much attention to the state of her body, and she despised that the Enders didn't either—even ruddy Tobey looked away. Her legs shook as she tore off the ripped Facility scrubs, yanked on a pair of gray pants, and shimmied into a skirt thick like wool with a ragged hem. A long-sleeved shirt covered her, paired with an oversized fleece jacket. It must have been blue back in the day, but stains had worked their way permanently into the fabric. Happiness radiated from her newly moccasin-clad feet.

"Here, let me," Maggie insisted, even as Nika snarled at her. Maggie wrapped strips of recovered cloth around Nika's hands and up her forearms like gauntlets. She relaxed when the tattoos disappeared from view.

Warmth began to build. She stroked the edge of her skirt. She was finally safe from the elements.

When she was done, she saw that Walker was outfitted as well. His pants molded to his thighs, and a woven sweater with patched elbows hugged his torso. A long cloak wrapped around his shoulders. He couldn't stop fingering the cloth, as if he couldn't believe it was his. Nika looked at it with longing.

She didn't understand why the End treated their prisoners this way.

Beau and Buck led her back to the fire and put pressure on her shoulders, bidding her to sit. Rope bound her hands in front of her. As Walker was being tied, she tried to catch his eye to impart a glance of apology, but he refused to look her way. Deep inside, she screamed at herself for not running faster. Thought versus action. How different hers ended up being. She had broken their bond ruthlessly.

Jake folded a third cigarette. Milo snatched the pouch out of his hands. "You're on your last one, old man."

"Don't need you to ration what's mine," Jake growled.

"Looking out for your health," Milo said, tucking the pouch away and sliding his shoulder up against Jake's.

"Think it's time?" Jake said. "The mother of monsters said two sharks were coming for me. Perhaps it's these two?"

"I hope so," Milo said. "Maybe her prophecy will die after we give the Promised Land their flesh."

Nika wanted to weep. She curled up in a ball and hid her face behind her hands, waiting for terror where there was only oblivion.

24

The table waited for her.

The overhead lights were off, but the darkness horrified her more. It would be worse in the dark. The audience stood in the shadows, their faces hidden behind masks, and Nika willingly walked forward, laid down, and spread her arms out. No fight left. *Submission.* The open restraints remained lax, until suddenly, it wasn't a dream anymore. Her eyes shot open, and she was *there*, her air flow cut off, her legs thrashing, Tarek's love still hot on her skin, and she screamed, knowing it would only bring a gag to her lips faster.

The doctor above her called her name, pleaded with her again, told her to wake up, it was just a dream, wake up...

She shot up and into Walker's arms. He whispered her name frantically, and she clutched at him, digging her nails into his sides as she tried to stop hyperventilating. Her eyes roved wild in their sockets. She didn't know where she was; she could have sworn she was back at the Facility, how did she get here, on the—

Outside.

"What's wrong with her?"

The dying fire highlighted the concerned and solemn faces of the End tribe. Raw throated, she outspread her hands which cast shadows. A length of rope burned brightly in the firelight, curling out of the ring like a snake. Her bonds.

"Nothing," Walker snapped. "Nothing's wrong with her."

Milo shook his head at Buck and then leaned over to whisper to Jake. "Girl doesn't have blue eyes. All experiments have blue eyes, don't they?"

"You're safe, you're okay, I promise." Walker stroked her head and she breathed in his scent, leaned back just enough to see the bruise blossoming on his chin in the shape of her fist.

"I'm sorry," she said and put a hand over her mouth, aghast at what she had done and then some.

"It's okay," he said, pulling her back into a hug. "I like to be marked."

She closed her eyes, trying to figure out reality, and focused on the End voices.

"They're not like the other experiments," Milo said, grabbing Jake's shoulder. Conversing so close, they appeared like the sun and moon she'd seen earlier that day: Milo's sandy beard bright in the firelight and Jake's burning eyes framed by his silver-black hair.

The elder snarled. "They were probably released on purpose. Promised Land always thinks we'll take care of their cast-offs."

"The other ones were like children. This is different. If they're telling the truth, Jake, if she *is* Manahatta…"

"Tova *did* say the bounty was only for one. A male. Not two."

"Maybe we should go back, get an updated report. Maybe she had it wrong. Maybe we *heard* it wrong."

Jake snorted.

"Someone has to be wrong, Jake."

"If she's Manahatta—" Jake took a deep breath. "If she is, we've got a big problem on our hands."

Milo nodded as he broke from Jake, walked toward Nika, and passed her a bladder full of purified water. She drank deeply. Walker wrapped her in his cloak, and she nestled her head on the cold sand. It radiated freezing air, but with his body snug against hers and the blessed cloak covering them, she fell into a dreamless sleep.

25

With the cemetery behind them, gutted and crumbling buildings rose on either side of the mud and concrete pathway they followed. Thresher knew the ocean was close by the moist smell in the air. Mako couldn't keep his eyes off the sun, his brows drawing together in displeasure. "We're losing time," he murmured and, as if to slake his worry, delved into his satchel, then brandished jerky like a saber. He handed two strips to Thresher.

"If the piss-clams are unhealthy, how can this be better?" Thresher asked. The scent of salt triggered a hungry growl from his stomach.

"I've been eating fish for months and haven't gotten sick yet. Maybe I'm chock full of toxins, but thank the trinity, I'm still kicking."

"What does that mean?" Thresher asked, his mouth full of food. "The trinity?"

Mako looked at him blankly, his pace slowing for a brief moment. "I suppose you wouldn't know. The trinity's a sacred triangle made from two souls—your heart and your blood—held up by the essence of who you are." His thumbs and forefingers met to illustrate the shape. "It used to represent the old religion of the father, son, and holy spirit, but those words don't mean much anymore. I'm not religious. I use the term to emphasize what I'm...feeling."

"What you're *feeling*, huh?" Thresher shot him a sly smile.

Mako gave him a withering look. "Cultures change across islands. Bruykleeners don't hold the same traditions as Manahattas. They didn't even know about sky-burials until they saw us do it. I'd bet my boots the tribes further east are even stranger. It all boils down to who your community was—who you got stuck with—when the volcano blew."

"What do the Bruykleeners believe in?" Thresher said, thinking of Soul-Dago's painted face.

"Never took time to ask," Mako said. "What about you? Did the Promised Land preach that old religion?"

Thresher thought back, but religion was always science: the beauty of evolution, the elegance of genetic drift, the worship of selectivity. "Nothing like *that*. Nothing to swear by."

"Any stories?"

Thresher squinted, trying to understand, but an oral tradition didn't exist in the Promised Land. "Any myths came from books."

He recalled the reading room, the shelves stuffed with paperbacks and beaten hardcovers, pages watermarked with mistreatment. There had been another library, one filled with catalogued magazines kept impeccably clean, the glossy pages marked with notes. The bibles of the scientific community he'd grown up in. "Can you tell me a story?" he said, suddenly wanting to experience that Manahatta custom. "I've never heard one *told* before."

Mako blushed, making Thresher wonder about the implications of his request. "Ah, sure. My grandmother tells them far better, and they're all older than any building you'll see here. She used to say that the old stories almost died out long ago, and many had been lost before that, but the remembered ones have transformed with the many different tongues that called Manahatta home after the volcano blew. My favorite one is about a young man who played music for a monster who lived under a bridge."

Maybe it was the way Mako's voice deepened into a hypnotic lull or the way the tale became flavored with little Mako-intricacies that made it easier for Thresher to picture the tale of the Man the Monster Cannot Hold. Either way, he was enthralled. Enchanted by the boy who played songs for the bridge monster; the boy who attracted the attention of those who wished to make a marriage bond with him. Yet, the boy loved no one. He couldn't be persuaded away from the riverbank. Soon, the tribal leaders discovered the monster's infatuation with the boy, and the curse on him to never stop playing. Upon lifting the curse, the boy perished. Grieving, the tribe gifted him to the water and back to the monster, where he sank to the bottom. The monster recovered her human beloved and gave him part of her trinity—the heart—to resurrect him. Six days later, the boy emerged from the water as a man and returned home, where he became a revered elder, for he now had the power to speak with creatures from all walks of life. The monster departed, maybe homesick for her homeland, perhaps to the underworld, but that was another tale.

"We all come home in the end," Mako whispered. "Whether we want to or not."

An electric path lit goosebumps up Thresher's back. He mulled over *homesick*, sucking his lower lip against his teeth until the soft flesh was imprinted with the shapes, like small gravestones. He wiggled his toes, wondering if they would ever compel him to go back to the Facility. His heart blanched at the thought.

"Not far now," Mako said, pointing to the glimmer of water emerging from between the buildings and beyond it, the tip of another rounded island. "We're almost home."

A surge of relief and giddiness that he was included in Mako's *home* surpassed his fear of Facility homesickness. Mako never slowed, even with his injuries, as he maneuvered them through winding concrete trails, but Thresher learned how to use his stride, pleased he could outpace Mako if he put his mind to it. Thresher straightened his shoulders, feeling the story replay through his mind, bringing back memories of another boy who couldn't love.

That boy, from Thresher's social growth sessions, was Subject A. Thresher didn't know what it was, but that experiment got under his skin. He couldn't put his finger on why. Haunted him like a ghost. Annoyed him like a blood-sucking tick. Used to say the ugliest things to him. Thresher never responded, but the taunts kept him up all night until the orderly announced a new day had bloomed.

Exhaustion burned his eyes and filled his mind with cotton blankness. Thresher had been useless at sessions, unreceptive to treatment, resistant during therapy. He couldn't get it out of his brain—those whispered words.

"What's gotten into you today?" his psychologist asked. "I've never seen you so distracted. Is it the new drugs?"

He blinked and scratched his forearm. She frowned and made a note. "I'm requesting they take you off," she said. "I don't like who you've turned into."

How could he tell her he didn't feel *safe* when he'd never felt *unsafe* before?

"It's not your fault, but your behavior is worrisome. I'll have you monitored, you understand." She dismissed him.

That didn't scare him. He was a good experiment compared to others, unlike *that boy*. The orderlies put him in the activity room and completely ignored their new orders.

Subject A sat in front of a half-finished puzzle. He patted a piece against his lips, as if pondering where to put it. Subject T slid into the chair opposite, determined to connect and understand the hatred this experiment had for him. He placed a faded blue piece in the corner. Subject A asked if Subject T was in a blind study. Subject T said yes. The experiment asked if maybe he'd like to experience a true blind study. Maybe he'd like to never see again?

Subject T's mouth dropped open. Violent patients existed of course—how could they not when their tribe was enclosed in an ancient mental institution research center, their land walled with barbed, looping hangman nooses, their elders controlling every nuance of every second? Restlessness was contained with expired, pilfered medication or concocted in a fading laboratory.

Yet, the threat calmed him as if someone had dosed him with such a drug. He looked the experiment up and down, watched the boy rub the puzzle piece against his mouth, plumping out his lower lip and showing the wet gleam underneath.

"I'm going to pluck out your eyes," the boy said. "You're so *weak*."

Subject T's hand curled, his knuckles jutting out like mountains, and while that boy was running his mouth, Subject T took his landscaped fist and slammed it into the experiment's nose. He never realized how big he was until then, delighted in the *newness* permeating his world. The boy's nose crumpled. Subject T heard the clacking of loose teeth. He was the rock that knocked the great bird right out of the sky.

That had been the first time he'd taken a strange road into the new land of violence. Wrestled away, then, contained, stuck with a needle, but he didn't blame the orderlies for their oversight. They were nothing but kids, the scientists' children working to learn how to serve their world. He knew it was their rite of passage to handle the people their parents had grown.

Bound. Groggy. Put somewhere dark. Howling against his gag. Still, elation ignited deep in his chest, an open wanting he couldn't douse.

A hand grasped his shoulder, yanking him down into a hunch against a concrete slab jutting out of the earth. *"Thresher, get down."*

The memory shattered. Subject T—no, Thresher, his name was Thresher—took a shuddering breath and realized a fine sheen of cold sweat coated his face. He braced against the rock that must've fallen from one of the buildings. Mako shielded him, peeking over the top into the distance.

"Look." Mako's mouth was a thin line. A shimmer of gray smoke rose into the sky. "That's where the canoes are stashed, but someone's already there."

"Bruykleeners?"

"Who else could it be? They must've known we'd be headed this way." Mako's hand balled into a fist. "There's not another way across."

Thresher stared past the concrete edge to see waves. It was like he had been brought back to where he had begun. A choked cry caught in his throat—*always going to end up home*—but he shoved it down.

"Thresher, are you alright?"

The touch on his shoulder tightened.

"Hey, man, look at me."

The intense recollection of his Facility violence mingled with the sensation of taking a life on the outside. Perhaps thriving on the outside was the Facility's experiment for him, but the need to know *why* he had been chosen and released burned through his doubts. The only way he would discover that answer was to survive the path that lay before him, but he refused to make it a path of death and blood. Thresher closed his eyes, mentally repeating his Mako-given name until Subject T was scrubbed away. He wasn't weak anymore. He wasn't an *experiment* anymore. "I'm okay. I'll stand by you."

"Follow my lead," Mako said, still looking concerned. "Stay low. We might be able to sneak around them. Be careful."

"You worried?"

Mako flashed him a grin. "I've seen you slit a man's throat. I'm worried for them." He trekked past the concrete slab down the mud flats, sticking to places with cover. Thresher followed in his waterlogged footprints, stepping on skeleton reeds growing in thick patches. Thresher stared hard at the island across the wide channel. Concrete buildings, weathered and decayed on one side, reached into the sky. More jagged squares. He counted them in his mind: teeth, graves, and skyscrapers.

Mako held out a hand, and Thresher halted, gazing through the brush they hid behind to see two women sitting around a cook fire. Dressed in rags the color of the mud, the first woman sported matted dreadlocks and a set of goggles obscured half her face. A long knife hung from her waist. She spoke to her companion, and their laughter colored the air with affection. Mako drew his machete, the blade hungry and sharp. His eyes fixed on the wooden canoe tied next to their fire, his body tight as if already scenting blood. "They don't look Bruykleen," Thresher whispered. Not ebony-dark like Soul-Dago. He heard Mako's voice echo in his head: *Cultures change across islands.*

Mako licked his lips. "Can't tell. Either way, they have our canoe and we can't wait around for Soul-Dago to catch up to us." He tapped the blade against his leg. "Sun is too low."

"Should we negotiate?"

"We go in, knock them out, and get out. Why would they be squatting here anyway? Scouting party? Thinking about raiding my homeland?"

Dread twisted Thresher's stomach. These women didn't understand that Mako slit throats and housed a love of chaos in his trinity triangle that made it *practical* to spill blood. They had nothing—only the ragged clothes on their backs. One of them coughed violently. The woman with goggles handed her a cup. What if they were lost ones, like Nika or him? What if they wanted nothing more than to survive?

Mako's instinct might be to kill, but these people might not even be Bruykleen. Thresher didn't want to kill without knowing why. He stepped away from their cover.

"Where are you going?" Mako hissed, and Thresher felt Mako's hand swipe against his back, trying to grab his coat to drag him back to safety.

"Trust me," Thresher said. "We can talk to them first."

"They'll kill you."

"If we've outrun the main Bruykleen tribe, how would they know we're enemies?"

"First instinct of any tribesman is to fight!"

Thresher smiled at him. Thought about connection. "You didn't fight me when you found me. Watch my back."

"Thresher, no—"

Mako lunged at him again, but Thresher sidestepped farther into the open and walked down the slight embankment with his hands raised. He felt fear, but also belief. He didn't want another tribesman's blood on his hands. This land was slowly becoming a part of him, but he wanted it all—the rough, unexpected kindness alongside the brutality.

"I come in peace," Thresher said loudly, pleased he could use a line from his books, and lied. "I've already parlayed with the Bruykleeners and have safe passage out. I'm not here to fight."

The two women scrambled around the cook fire. The one with the goggles drew her blade. The other pointed something dull and black at Thresher. "This gun isn't for show. It works. I'll blow your brains out," she said.

Thresher stopped feet from their fire and inhaled the scent of burned wood. "Please, I don't want any violence. I have need of the canoe. You're going one way, I'm going another. No reason why this should end badly. We can work together."

"Get on your knees," the other woman demanded. She pulled down the rag that covered her mouth. *"We* need the canoe." He couldn't help but notice the deep lines around her mouth that led up to her green eyes. An array of sores covered her chin, and the smell radiating from her made Thresher shrink. *Sickness.*

He closed his eyes as he knelt, feeling the cold mud sink through his jeans. The weapon clicked and the cold touch of the barrel rested against his forehead. The breathing of the goggled woman sounded ragged like a whine. "Where are you headed?" she asked.

Thresher jutted his jaw in the direction of the island across the water. "Manahatta."

The women spoke in an unknown language. He caught a handful of words, but most of it sounded like inverted common tongue. "Can you guarantee safe passage across your island?" the woman in front of him asked, her voice growling, as if it had been ruined at one point. She dug the barrel into his skull.

Thresher winced, hating the grinding sound. "Are you Bruykleen?" he asked.

The goggled woman crossed her arms, the wide knife tapping against her elbow. "We're Shinnecoes."

The name meant nothing to him. "Is your tribe only two people?" The rules of the outside oscillated so much, he couldn't keep anything straight. He wondered if he and Mako could be considered a tribe. If he applied the tribal idea to the Facility's rules, there would be the external environmentally tested, the *in utero* environmentally tested, the genetically manipulated, the accidents, the crazed…

The gun trembled. "Our tribe is dead."

"Disease?" Thresher asked, a secondary fear leaking into his voice. These women looked rough. The Facility had been right. Plague saturated the air, radiation caught him from all sides, bacteria festered in the water. He swallowed hard, remembering the jolt of a booster shot. Maybe his hallucinations and illness on the beach weren't only drug withdrawal.

The Shinnecoes conversed in their language until the woman with the knife trailed off and peered closely at Thresher. She grabbed his wrist, swiping her thumb over his tattoo. She laughed outright, and held it up. "You worry about disease, but you wouldn't understand, being blue-eyed and Facility protected." She threw his hand down.

Thresher's mouth went dry. Words clogged his throat.

"His promises are useless," said the one with the gun. "He's using us." Her eyes hardened. The woman with the knife stepped back, and Thresher's throat closed with terrified panic. Any human connection he had created with them withered. He breathed out a *no* as the woman clenched the gun, but her arm jerked hard to the left, a knife sticking out of her elbow. Her scream was the final thing Thresher heard before fire exploded from the barrel. Hot specks peppered his face. The world went silent except for a loud ringing in both of his ears. Something whizzed by him.

Mako lunged between the gun and Thresher, his machete raised high. The blade sliced through her forearm. Thresher slid to the side as the woman's arm landed in the mud beside him, the hand still gripping the gun. The machete sliced upward across the woman's throat, nearly severing her head from her neck. Blood splattered up Mako's throat, his mouth open in a scream Thresher couldn't hear.

The woman with the goggles backed away, tears streaming down her face as she raised her own knife to fight. Thresher screamed for Mako to stop, but he couldn't hear himself except for a high-pitched whine. Mako charged the Shinnecoe. Their knives clashed soundlessly. Thresher wrestled the gun from the amputated arm, peeling back the twitching fingers, prepared to create another explosion of fire to make them stop. Mako couldn't kill her. She knew about the Facility. These Shinnecoes knew more than the Bruykleeners. They might know something about Nika.

An arrow slammed into the mud next to his hand as he freed the gun. More fell from the sky. Mako's head snapped up to the slopes while the Shinnecoe woman's eyes widened. She bolted for the canoe. Mako ran for Thresher, grabbed his arm, and hauled him under his shoulder to protect him from the arrows. They slid for cover against an asphalt slab sticking out of the surf.

He couldn't help remembering how the waves had knocked him to his feet the first time, how cold and unforgiving it could be. Arrows thudded against their protective blacktop. Mako's mouth worked soundlessly, but Thresher couldn't understand what he was saying. Mako yanked the gun from Thresher's hands and aimed for the Shinnecoe hiding by the canoe.

Thresher yelled and wrenched Mako's arm. Another muted bang exploded from the gun, again missing its target. The Shinnecoe woman ducked. Mako turned on Thresher, fury hot in his eyes. Thresher couldn't hear himself, but he knew how to form words, and screamed, *"She knows about the Facility."*

Mako bared his teeth, a feral smile of approval, and took Thresher's hand. Thresher slipped as they ran out into the onslaught of arrows, bolting straight for the canoe. The Bruykleener war party emerged from the hills, running with weapons held high, masks covering their faces. Thresher heard their war call, the sound similar to the one the Bruykleener boy had shouted.

The Shinnecoe struggled to push the canoe into the water, but an arrow slammed into her leg. The canoe tip waved wildly back and forth. Mako lunged for the boat and managed to steady one side, then he and the woman ran it into the waves. The Shinnecoe met Thresher's eyes. Suddenly, they were in this together.

She leapt into the boat, staying low. Thresher didn't like the idea of so much water in the first place. He especially didn't like it when it looked so deep and angry. His mind reeled, desperately trying to figure out how to get into the boat without capsizing it.

"Pick up your feet," Mako screamed. "You don't want to be left on this side of the shore."

Thresher heard that. He glared at Mako, glared at the canoe, then glared at the water for good measure. He hoped Mako understood that Thresher was a threat, a dangerous person, and if anything tried to mess with him, he'd hurt it. Thresher hitched one leg up and over. The contraption swayed, and he fell into it. Another set of arrows thudded into the water where he had just stood.

Mako pushed the boat farther out and jumped in behind him. Too much weight in the back made the canoe sag. Water flooded over the sides. Mako hollered and pointed to the front. Thresher cater-pillar-crawled forward, fighting with the Shinnecoe for space as she followed. The canoe swayed again, and Thresher peered behind him, past the woman, to see a swimming Bruykleener warrior scramble for a handhold on the back. Her knife flashed in the light, close enough to plunge into Mako's side.

"Mako, behind you!" Thresher yelled.

Mako slammed a greatly battered and discolored oar into the warrior's face. He plunged the oar into the water, and with a long stroke, catapulted them out, heading for the island across the way.

"Get down!" Mako cried as another volley of arrows thudded around them. The Shinnecoe collapsed on top of Thresher, her weight suffocating, her wide eyes staring down at him. Two arrows stuck out of her back. Bloodied saliva dripped from her open mouth. Thresher bucked, but her body pressed on his as more arrows thumped into her. Thresher cringed under his human shield. Her spit dripped into his mouth and he gagged, tasted iron and something foul. He wasn't sure if it would be better to die from impalement or from whatever disease had caused the sores around her lips.

Thresher rolled the dead woman off him, scrambled to hang his head over the side, and promptly vomited. The water swirled the half-digested fish jerky away, sending up a stench that made him retch again.

Mako stood and screamed in joy back to the warriors waiting on the bank. "Take that, you bastards! We made it! We're safe!"

Thresher didn't believe him one bit. Mako was a filthy liar, and it had been proven on more than one occasion. Mako could take them someplace where his life wouldn't be in danger, if he would just stop *laughing*. Mako plopped down hard with a grunt, pitching the canoe as another wave crashed over the tip.

Thresher suddenly hated the water more than anything. People evolved from the water, not the other way around. He didn't have fins, he didn't even have goddamn gills, and there was no logical reason to carve a piece of wood as a means of transportation or escape. There were great monsters in the deep—huge streamlined creatures full of teeth—and Mako wanted to play a game of catch-me-if-you-can with the rulers of it.

Thresher sat back, hung his head, and noticed the gun sitting on the bottom of the canoe. He picked it up, ran his hand over the metal, and imagined he could feel the heat from the shots. He released a heavy breath and had the sudden urge to purge his insides again. He felt tainted.

"Shit," Mako said. "I think I've been hit."

Thresher had the strangest sensation of floating as he scrambled to Mako's side. An arrow protruded out of Mako's shoulder. Blood seeped around it. "I...I don't know what to do," Thresher said, laying the gun next to him, out of Mako's sight.

"Break off the shaft," Mako said, gritting his teeth. "Leave the head in. I can make it home. We're close enough."

Thresher reached up, his hands quivering, and snapped the wood in half. Mako gasped and curled over. "My whole arm is numb," he panted. Thresher imagined the arrowhead slicing through the tendons and cartilage like thread and wondered if the wound would be crippling. The thoughts amplified in his brain until he had to look up at the sky to not be sick. Mako's blood painted his fingers.

"Your coat," he said, instead.

"It better not be ruined," Mako snarled, a high rasp to his tone.

"At least it didn't go all the way through the shoulder," Thresher said.

"Might've been cleaner."

"Would've really ruined your coat."

Mako's laugh sounded like a wheeze, but at least he was laughing. "She dead?" He inclined his chin at the Shinnecoe.

"Yes," Thresher whispered.

"Get her knife. Throw her over."

Thresher shook his head, wondered if he would ever be shocked again. "Would you do the same to me if I were dead?"

"I get it. I'm being callous."

"You might have to, you know. Her blood got in my mouth. I might be infected."

He hated the smile playing on Mako's lips. "Where's the gun?"

Thresher laid his hand on top of it. "I have it."

Mako snapped his fingers, expecting Thresher to give it up.

Thresher shook his head, remember the crazed mask Mako wore when Thresher had ruined his gunshot. "I'm keeping it."

Mako's hand closed but his voice was uncommonly gentle. "Why?"

Thresher sighed. "You're…terrifying when you fight. You nearly killed that woman without knowing what she had to offer the world."

"She would've let you die."

Thresher realized that was the line for Mako, the decision to kill or be killed. He didn't want to say he feared Mako, because that wasn't it. Mako's ruthlessness belonged here, but Thresher didn't have that kind of *thirst* in him. He remembered the Facility boy, how even though Subject A had been cruel, Thresher had first made the step to connect before fighting back. He always would. It was too easy to point and shoot. "Probably," Thresher said, "but if the Facility has taught me anything, it's that we all have something to offer, whether it's in the genes or our constitution. You would've slain that woman whether she threatened me or not. You'll destroy anything in your way, and I won't give you this instrument to do it."

"Hainted."

"Excuse me?"

"That's what the Woodlanders call what you're describing. A haint. A ghost. Possessed. Bloodthirsty. What you see in me is something I wouldn't want to show anyone. Not even Nika."

"I'm not scared of you," Thresher said.

"But you're on your guard."

"I understand you want to find the Facility. And I want to understand why I was released, but you have to trust me. I won't last without you. You know that."

"You're more capable than you give yourself credit for." Mako sighed and held Thresher's gaze. "It makes things easier, you know. Having someone with you. Keep the gun. Flip the switch on the side. It's a safety feature."

Thresher didn't know what to do with all that attention, those hazel eyes zeroing in on him, but he tabbed the crusted knob to the side and let Mako walk him through the mechanics. One bullet remained in the chamber.

The canoe scraped against the rocky bank. Mako climbed out and offered a hand to Thresher. Getting out looked just as terrifying as getting in, only this time, submerged algae-covered rocks waited to slip him up. Thresher bared his teeth and gripped Mako's hand. The canoe pitched, but Thresher scrambled out. They jerked the canoe onshore and nestled it between two boulders, tying a thick fraying rope to a tree with a scoliosis spine rising out of the rubble.

Together, they lifted the dead Shinnecoe woman and placed her beneath the tree. Thresher memorized her. She was the last of her kind. He leaned down, dipped his hand in the mud, and drew three lines from her eyes to her hair.

"Here," Mako said, handing the Shinnecoe's knife to him. "You'll get more use out of this."

The hilt felt heavy. Scratches and dents marred the blade. In the reflection, Thresher imagined he saw the skull of the man he'd killed once upon a time staring at him out of dark sockets.

As they walked the broken road, buildings blocked the yellow smear of the sky, giving Thresher the eerie sense of perpetual dusk. Even wounded, Mako sped past crisscrossing streets and endlessly long avenues. Claustrophobia settled in the back of Thresher's head as the world narrowed to a grid and extended endlessly upwards. His heart leapt into his throat when the flash of a fleeing deer's flank disappeared around a corner.

With his eyes to the skies, Mako didn't seem to care. His excitement soothed the fear pitting Thresher's belly. "I never thought I'd be saying this, but it feels good to be home." Mako's lips parted into a young and indestructible smile.

Contagious, that's what Mako was, some kind of infection that wreaked havoc in Thresher's bloodstream. Tied his stomach up in knots, gave him high blood pressure, caused his brain to hallucinate on smiles that felt never-ending.

"I almost died up there." Mako pointed to a deteriorating building. Thresher squinted to see the shadows of collapsed beams crossing glassless windows. "Game was, the ground was lava, and if you fell, you burned. A monster tried to grab your feet and drag you down. I got cornered on a thin beam high up and lost my balance, crash-landed through the floor to the next level. Broke my arm. And you wanna know the worst part of it? Nika won. She always won."

Imagination ran in different ways because Thresher would never use his to create such a horrific scenario, but now the conjured scene played out vividly: so easily broken, this small Mako-boy, gap-toothed grin and mischievous chubby face.

As they turned onto a wide street, Mako bolted up five flattened steps of a building on the corner and paused on the stoop in front of a sturdy, wooden door. Shiny, unlike the other ramshackle doors— cared for, sanded down, and finished. Mako lifted his knuckles to rap on it when the door swung open.

A tall woman with wide hips filled the doorway. Brimming tears of joy coated her eyelashes. "Oh, my boy," she whispered in a strong, but aging voice and fit craggy hands around Mako's face, as if memorizing the contours of a visage lost to exploration. "Heard you coming from miles away. Could feel in my bones that you were coming home."

"I take it you missed me, then?" Mako answered, his voice thick in a way Thresher had never heard before.

"I'm saying I could hear your lead foot clomping all the way here," the woman said. Her grin echoed Mako's wide, familiar one. Her hands migrated from his face to his shoulders, touching the coat's bloodstained rip. "Mako, are you hurt?"

"Arrow to the shoulder. It's nothing, Gran."

"Even your face looks awful." She pulled him into an embrace, nestling her graying head on his chest. Thresher felt something thick in his chest, too, an unknown melancholia flavored happiness.

"Gran, I gotta introduce you," Mako said into his grandmother's hair. The woman lifted her head and glanced over Mako's shoulder at Thresher. Her affection had tendrils, and Thresher felt them tentatively reach him, and retreat to verify her verdict. "This is Thresher," Mako said, turning around. "He's a friend of mine. This is my grandmother, Gela."

"Hello there, sweetie," Gela said, sounding exasperated, like Mako picked up strays all the time. The light illuminated her dark golden-brown skin until she seemed to glow.

Thresher's palms began to sweat and he thumbed through his memories, searching for some semblance of a proper greeting. "Hello," he stammered.

"You been keeping my Mako company?"

"Yes," Thresher whispered, feeling very lost-and-found. Worn, but still re-sellable.

"Letting him get bashed in the head and stabbed in the back?"

Thresher gulped. His fingers twisted together until they hurt.

"Don't pester him," Mako said.

She smacked his shoulder and Mako huffed in pain. "Don't be telling me what I can and cannot do. You sound like Milagros."

"Where is the old *bruja*?" Mischief coated Mako's tone and Thresher knew Mako would never call Mama Milagros that to her face.

"Upstairs. Just because you decided to grace us with your presence doesn't mean the garden stops being tended to. Come upstairs, let's fix that shoulder."

Mako dropped a kiss on top of her head and threw a pleased look at Thresher as they entered the building.

Thresher stepped over the threshold and felt like he'd fallen into a dream. A narrow hallway led to an even narrower staircase. On either side of him, fenced off with wide beams and sundry pieces of wood, milled animals. A ceramic bathtub full of water sat near an open window and beams of sunlight illuminated the large pen. Ragged indents along the wall made it appear as if the habitat used to be full of dividing walls. In the corner sat a pile of graying hay and vibrant green weeds. Thresher clapped his hands in glee. He had a compulsive need to climb through the wooden slats and place his hand on the black and white nose of the gentle cow. A clump of long grass stuck out from the cow's sideways mastication. Her glossy eyes studied the newcomers with disinterested kindness.

"Do you wanna see her?" Mako asked as Gela prodded his shoulder.

Thresher realized he was leaning over the beam towards the cow. "Can we?" he asked, breathless.

"Of course," Mako said, his voice deep and smoothing, as if taking pleasure in showing off the tender marvels of his home. As he wiggled one of the hinged slats up, the bottom door swung inward. Dirt clods covered the floor. The cow remained still, curious now as Mako approached without fear.

Thresher hung back, suddenly shy, and took a deep breath scented with manure.

Mako slid his hand along the cow's side and held a hand under her nose, letting her smell him. Thresher shuffled closer, nervous about being rejected due to the basic elements of his body. This wasn't a feral herd of horses. This was the closest he'd been to an animal that wasn't human. The cow loomed over him like a deity. Her cellulose crunch filled the immediate air with the scent of broken stems. Thresher raised a hesitant hand to her cheek. She back-stepped. Crushed, he curled his hand against his chest.

Mako gave him an indulgent smile before taking Thresher's hand and placing his palm on her neck. The muscles contracted as she chewed. A white beam of light reflected off her silky hide. Thresher petted her in small contained strokes, terrified of spooking her.

"Gran," Mako said softly, favoring his shoulder. "You asked where I've been. I tracked Tarek and Nika to the Woodlands. They were been poached."

"Mako Saddlerock, you went to the Woodlands?" Gela hissed. "You could've been maimed, captured, killed. Do you know what they do to people down there?"

"I wasn't," Mako said, but by his tone Thresher could tell he lied. "Point is, I couldn't find Tarek. Mighta' escaped or been killed, I don't know, but I finally caught wind that Nika wasn't sold south. She was traded up here. The Reckowacky poachers sold her to someplace called the Promised Land. She's been under our noses this entire time."

"*Trinity, Mako.*"

Thresher couldn't spare her a glance, engrossed as he was with his connection with the cow and imagining how loved she must feel to have all these hands seek her out on a daily basis. Still, he heard choked despair in Gela's voice. He realized why Mako had stepped into the pen. Gela would stifle her rage to keep the cow calm, and she couldn't hurt Mako from that far away.

"Thresher is from the Promised Land, Gran. He's not like us. He used to be an experiment, a prisoner, but he's going to take me there. Take me to Nika."

"Experiments?" Gela asked in disbelief. "How do you know these contacts aren't tricking you, leading you somewhere that's beneficial to them? This is just like when you first made the pact with Soul-Dago. Now you tell me that I lost you for two years on a quest to the Woodlands, Mako, *the Woodlands.*"

"They wouldn't dare lie to me."

"Did you take up the knife like those Woodland haints? Those possessed monsters? I've heard stories of the torture they do down there. They send children to war, and you tell me even *they* wouldn't cross you? What kind of man have you become?" Horror laced the edges of her words. She rubbed at Mako's blood on her fingers. Mako didn't respond.

A pastoral brightness blossomed in Thresher's chest. He felt like he could pet this animal for the rest of his life and never question his choice. Hypnotic, like all his worries had been stoppered. Perhaps, if he played his cards right, the cow would come to him seeking attention instead.

"Nika's alive," Mako whispered. "She could be hurt. In trouble. She needs me."

"She could be dead," Gela said, sharp as a whip, as if intending to cut and bleed, bring this boy to his knees.

"*I would know.*"

"And what tribes would you cross to find her?" Gela demanded. "If you invade Bruykleen and Reckowacky, plus all the other tribal lands in between, you'll be the dead one. You know what happened to your mama. You think I can go through that again? Before I left, I told her not to go, but she was like you, stupid as a brick."

"I was already in Bruykleen," Mako said, hot and affronted. He stabbed a thumb at Thresher. "Where do you think I found him? Where do you think I found this?" He reached into his pocket. The small vial swung from the broken chain between his fingers.

"Is that how you got hurt?" Gela said, shaking her head, refusing to look at the crushed bones as if they were cursed. "You're an idiot with an unstable trinity. Too much heart, not enough brain."

"I am not—"

"A foolish boy with a death wish. I should've raised you better, made you respect your elders like the other families, instead of letting your hotheaded ways steer your life. Maybe then you'd listen instead of rushing headlong into a death stupid enough for this cow."

"I came home to prove I was alive, to show you I hadn't given up. I came with good news, I do respect—"

Thresher couldn't spare them a glance, too preoccupied with being so close to such a trusting, beautiful creature. His fingers stroked with the smooth grain of her hide. The cow twitched her tail in a lazy circle.

"Not from where I'm standing. You don't listen. You do whatever you want, never mind the consequences. Don't you know how worried I've been? How convinced I was that I would bury you, too? No one else to keep our line alive after you gave up everything when she disappeared."

"That's not true!"

"Isn't it?" Gela asked, hands on her hips, head angled like a butting ram.

"You didn't care about her," Mako snarled, the shark emerging nasty with fury. "She wasn't gone a month and you'd already forgotten her. But that's what you do, Gran. You didn't mourn Mama, and you certainly washed your hands of Nika."

Thresher felt the peace drain from the room. The cow moaned and shifted away. His fear felt like a second heart.

"That's low, Mako." Tears streamed down Gela's face, but she held her head high. "So soon, you've broken my heart. Let yourself out. I'll remember this conversation as your final goodbye." She turned and walked away, down the hall.

A wash of pure anger burned through Thresher. Mako should've been at home, caring for what was left of the love he had, instead of spitting ugly words into his grandmother's face. Thresher knew firsthand the dangers of the outside. If Soul-Dago had been a fraction faster, he wouldn't have given Mako the same mercy. "Why did you say that?" he whispered.

Mako stared at him, hardened, only the lines around his mouth belying his sorrow. "She should understand. It's her granddaughter."

"Did you ever think I don't want to take you to the Facility? That I'm too scared? Did you ever ask?" In his fear, he imagined all sorts of what-ifs. Mako, head bludgeoned and bleeding out on the side of the road. Mako, drowned, floating and bloated. Mako, captured and put into the Facility, tattoos written on his wrist and ankles, straightjacketed and all his fire quenched. Gela, waiting at home, her hope hung on Thresher, who was supposed to keep an eye on Mako, who failed.

"We have to find Nika," Mako said. "She's out there, alone, terrified. I didn't come home to carry on the Saddlerock lineage. I came home to heal all sides of my trinity with my family, before saying my goodbyes."

"I've seen experiments behave better than the way you talked to your grandmother," Thresher said. "She loves you. She's lost too much already. Do you have any idea what that means?"

"This isn't a democracy," Mako said.

"Looks to be a matriarchy," Thresher said, leaving the pen and blindly following where Gela went, in disbelief at the force of his emotions. On the outside, they grew stronger every day.

Gela hadn't gotten far. She sobbed silently on the first stair. Thresher bent and touched her arm. "That's where we keep the chickens," she said, pointing to the coop on the other side of the hallway. Grief made her hiccup. Mottled birds pecked the ground and meandered in and out of a large box, painted an uneven red. Thresher knew this tactic, had witnessed it personally with Mako. Bait and switch. The lie of *everything's fine*. He wrangled his wild, unpredictable feelings back into their boxes. He had to be strong.

"This building has been the Saddlerock's since before the tribal wars. It's taken some hits, but we're above the flood line." Gela wiped her eyes. "My family has lived on this island since before the volcano blew."

Mako came up behind them, his hand stuffed in his pockets. Thresher was pleased to note he looked ashamed, a feeling that intensified when Gela stood, looped her arm through Thresher's, and leaned against him.

"Don't ignore me," Mako said.

"Tomorrow, when we take the cow out, I'll show you around the neighborhood, meet the families," Gela said to Thresher and led him up the steep stairs.

"This is a coup. A silent-treatment passive-aggressive coup," Mako said. Gela tightened her grip on Thresher's arm.

Fifth floor, seventh floor, tenth floor, so many floors Thresher's thighs ached. When Gela pushed open a door, he sent up a litany of thank yous that they had reached their destination.

Cooking warmth hit his face, and he savored the scents of fresh baked bread, dusky smoke, and drying herbs. Floral. Botany had never been a strong interest of his. He couldn't name one of the hundred plant smells assaulting him.

Gela looked as proud as her chickens, and ushered Thresher into a wooden chair. His thighs signed in relief, but his feet throbbed. He stuck his legs out under the table covered in a crocheted tablecloth. Mako sat across from him, scowling.

"Here you go, sweetie," Gela said, setting a cracked cup in front of Thresher and pouring sloppy, white liquid to the brim. Her eyes were still puffed and red, but her voice sounded stronger. Thresher brought the cup carefully to his lips.

Traitor, Mako mouthed as the warm cream flooded Thresher's tongue, tasting like fresh grass. Thresher cocked an eyebrow as he took another drink. Mako winced as he removed his bags and coat, pushing his layers up and over his wounded shoulder. His fingers alternated drumming on the table and picking at the crochet. *Rough and tumble energy,* Thresher thought fondly.

A brick fireplace housed reddened coals, casting a flickering orange glow on the superfluous carvings, darkened by decades of ash and smoke. Wrapped blocks sat on a ledge above the coals. Shelves held cups and saucers, while herb bundles and drying flowers hung upside down from ceiling hooks. A battered pink couch and matching chair sat close together. Long wide windows dirtied by dried raindrops and bird urea presented an enormous view of the island. Thresher itched to be closer to it, but wondered what the pit in his stomach would feel like when he got nearer to that open sky.

Chalk symbols covered the faded wallpaper. A statue of a skeleton draped in a lace cloak loomed in the center of an altar, her arms outstretched in welcome. Daffodils decorated the cloak's hem, matching the small petals under her black eyes. Pale candle studs surrounded her. The hallucination of the bony lady on the beach beckoning to him cascaded through Thresher's mind as Gela set cloth wrappings and a surgeon's tools on the table.

"Your home is beautiful," Thresher said, sounding far away. Gela smiled brightly and reached out to pat his arm, jolting him out of his dream-memory. Steam curled from the surface of a bowl full of hot water as she dipped a pair of long tweezers into it. "I thought you were the instigator of Mako's craziness," she said. "Now, I see you're the voice of reason."

Mako shook his head at Thresher in slow, barely perceived back and forth motions, as if he still couldn't quite believe how things had turned on him so fast. Thresher licked his lips, cleaning the creamy layer with one languid swipe.

Mako grunted in pain as Gela wiggled the tweezers into his shoulder. Carefully, she eased out the wide arrowhead, slick with blood, and plopped it into the bowl. Within Gela's hands, the bone needle and thread danced on Mako's skin, creating a neat row of pale stitches. Thresher breathed deeply as she crushed herbs and leaves between her palms, rubbing the juice on the puckered wound, before wrapping it tightly with bandages.

Her finale was to lay a kiss on Mako's head. Closing his eyes, he accepted it, seemingly putting off the fight until later. "I love you," Gela whispered into Mako's hair.

"I love you, too," Mako said. Thresher wondered if proclamations of affection were easier than displays and filed the question away for later exploration. His tongue felt oddly numb in his mouth.

Thresher peeled off his coat and flexed, relieved of the constriction. Gela tittered. "I'm gonna fix that for you," she said, reaching over the table and snagging Thresher's coat.

Thresher almost made a grab for it, his *mine* proclamation clipped off by his teeth as Gela inspected it. "Too tight," she said, smiling at his distress. "Don't worry, I'll have it fitting you like a glove by the end of the night."

Mako reached into his satchel as Gela spread Thresher's coat open on the table and felt the stitches in the lining.

"They give this to you at the Promised Land?" Gela asked off-handedly as Mako emptied the books on the table with muted thumps.

Thresher shook his head. "Took it off the beach."

Gela made a face. "Dead men's clothes. Shouldn't be bringing souled things into this house. Milagros will have your head." She shot a disapproving look at Mako.

"Not haunted, yet," Mako said.

"You're not the one who has to hear about it. She'll be sage cleansing. It'll smell like a wood burn in here for days."

"Poor Gran. Maybe I shouldn't have brought you these."

Gela squealed like a young girl, so strange for a woman with crow's feet as deep as the earth, and picked up the hardback. She carefully spread the book open in front of her on the coat, lingering on the pages and caressing the faded print. The spine creaked as she inspected the cracked cover and worn edges.

"I didn't know if you have them already," Mako said.

"I have two copies, but it's always better to have more than none these days. I've almost completed copying the book of essays," she said proudly.

"Keeping the written word alive," Mako said.

"The old books don't hold up. I preserve what I can. It's important to save all these stories—you never know who they might belong to. The plastic peddlers don't have paper anymore so I make my own, but it's rough compared to this." She ran her hand back over the pages.

"Go wild," Mako said with a sideways grin that slowly faded. "Gran, I *am* sorry."

"You should go upstairs," Gela said, closing the books carefully and stacking them near her elbow. "Milagros is in the garden. Replenish what we used on you."

Mako nodded, stood, and placed the vial in front of Gela. She covered it with her hands, her body trembling, her eyes squeezed tight. Mako inclined his head for Thresher to follow. Thresher didn't understand their exchange—was this forgiveness? Mako didn't sound sorry in the way Gela wanted him to be, and it didn't sound as if Gela had forgotten what Mako had said. He tossed the squat bottle of corpse wax in his good hand. Thresher stood and followed, his legs complaining as they climbed two more flights of stairs. The stairway ended, and Mako opened the top door to a breeze that ruffled the longer hairs on top of his head. Thresher stared, stunned once more, and wondered if the amazement would never end.

Looping vines, vegetables, and herbs crowded the tall, crisscrossing wooden stands holding up the awning. Rust colored ceramic posts hung from the top. Flowers bloomed from square garden plots. The air smelled so good. An empty stack of deep bowls, tubing, and ivory mesh sat near a pump. Thresher grinned at the ingeniousness of it. Big bowls collected rain, which then filtered down the tubes into the mesh, where it could then be pumped from the small reservoir bladder. The whole roof felt like a dream, stitched from his books and imagination. He spun slowly to take it all in, while Mako beelined for a puttering woman in black with a pail slung over her forearm.

"Mama Milagros," he said. Her head perked up, and her arms opened wide in welcome. Mako filled the embrace of this small-statured woman. Thresher noted the sloped curve to her shoulders, the dark tan of her skin, the way Mako held her like fulgurite. Mako treated her more like a respected elderly companion than a mother figure.

Her black eyes stripped Thresher down to his essentials, and he shuddered under her gaze. She motioned him closer with a long, gnarled finger. Thresher approached uneasily. Mama Milagros traced his facial features, her fingers fluttering over the bridge of his nose. He studied her just as closely. Small pink mouth. Sun-exposed skin wrinkled and darkened like sturdy leather. Deep crease-lines across her forehead, the sloping bridge of her nose, thick lashes, and hair grayed from the scalp but still raven-black at the ends. Wreaths of small blue beads crossed her neck. Big bone gauges stretched her earlobes. Black gossamer draped over her shoulders, covering all but her hands. Thick bronze rings—a raven skull, human skull, and turquoise stone—sat on each finger.

"A new prophet come to replace me?" She tapped Thresher's chin. "You've seen the bony girl, haven't you?"

A sweeping calm filled Thresher, like a blanket tossed over his shoulders in the coldest cell, and he swayed, holding her hand to his cheek and pressing hard. He didn't have to say a word, but he felt her inhale the extent of his damage, take it inside and nurse it. He reached for her, tasted her own past on his tongue: the desert skies and raven's caw, the pungent, sickly sweet smoke of a lit joint, and the dull chime of a bell rung thrice.

The hallucination he'd seen on the beach before Mako came into his life flashed through his mind: desperately crawling to a skeleton woman who wished to accept him.

Mama Milagros brought out a silver flask and sprinkled water onto her fingers. She stroked wetness over his cheekbones and forehead, murmuring under her breath in a language he didn't understand. It felt like hydrotherapy at the Facility when an orderly zipped a heavy canvas mat over him up to his neck and then he soaked in hot water.

He closed his eyes and leaned into the touch, felt her reach around and rub a hard finger down the length of his spine to rest at the lower lumbar curve. Tingling warmth spread throughout the tight muscles, which transformed into an ache bordering on agony.

Mama Milagros released him to pluck the grave wax container from Mako's hands. Unscrewing the lid, she sniffed the hardened white grease. "Good vintage," she said. She scooped out a dollop and smeared it over both her and Thresher's hands. The wax felt smooth, but suffocating, like putting on gloves too tight for his skin to breathe. She rubbed the tattoos on his wrists in gentle circles, and then flung more flask water over his hands. The droplets beaded on the wax, curling around the inked T until it resembled a fish.

"A shark," she whispered.

A glow smoldered inside Thresher, one that transformed the stress tightening his back into loose flexibility. He wanted to rub the glow in the scars Nika left in Mako. He wanted to gift handfuls of it to soothe the dry desolation in Mama Milagros.

Yet, Mama Milagros's face had gone grim. "*Two* sharks," she said.

The connection ended so abruptly that Thresher jerked. He looked down to see Mako's hand gripping Mama Milagros's wrist. Lazily, Thresher traced from Mako's wrist to his shoulder to his spooked face, noting the sliver of teeth behind his lips.

"Trinity's sake," Mako whispered and Thresher, indulgent, leaned down and put his forehead against Mako's. He shared the peace, the serenity, the soft wonder of life.

"*Trinity's sake,*" Mako asked again, voice pitched higher than usual. "I need to get back into Gela's good graces before I handle any mojo from you two."

Thresher drew back, remembering Mako's rules of interaction consisted of limited touch and dagger sharp remarks. Mako walked farther into the garden, picking specific leaves and flowers from different pots, a healer's bouquet growing in his hand.

"She came to you?" Mama Milagros sounded shaky. "Did she speak?"

"She…wasn't put together correctly," Thresher stumbled over his words, bewildered at how she could know of something he had never spoken of. "Her bones didn't align properly. She wanted me to follow, but I wasn't fast enough."

Mama Milagros wiped Thresher's hands, removing much of the wax. "I don't understand what the Bony Lady is trying to tell me. We'll talk later. Downstairs, with you."

Mako returned, his face tight. "Starting to hurt all over."

"Only now?" Thresher grinned.

"Apparently," Mako snorted and nudged Thresher's shoulder with his good one, piloting him toward the door. Thresher left the outdoors with a sigh of regret, wishing he could have hung his head over the side of the rooftop and see if it felt like flying.

Back downstairs, Gela kneeled in the center of the room with the panels of Thresher's coat dismantled and spread out on the floor as if on display for public punishment. A startled gasp of distress slipped past Thresher's throat, and, horrified, he watched her line material along the curve of what used to be the shoulder and snip around it with scissors. A ball of tangled red string rolled near her hand. Mama Milagros scooted around them, her nose scrunching up in distaste. She knelt by Gela and touched her chin until Gela looked at her. Thresher's heart skipped a beat. Of course Mama Milagros would notice the traces of tears and grief from Gela's rocky homecoming with Mako. She leaned in and laid a soft kiss on Gela's mouth.

Thresher blushed at the intimacy, looked back down at his coat, and became completely mortified all over again. He turned a pleading eye to Mako, who pursed his lips in sympathy and put a steadying hand on his shoulder as if to say, *Be strong, man.*

"Don't worry, sweetheart." Gela laughed as if she didn't know what she had done. Mama Milagros cupped Gela's face, thumbing at her cheeks. "Looks alarming now, but it'll all be better in the morning, I promise."

"Mako," Thresher whined, thinking, *Make it better. Make it whole.*

"It's gonna be okay," Mako said. "If she fucks up, I'll give you mine."

Tension eased out of Thresher. He'd keep his fretting internal. If Mako bet on Gela's skills to resurrect his coat, Thresher would have faith too.

"Language," Gela said, determined to keep a civil household. "We have company."

Mako stiffened. Thresher followed his line of sight to the young woman sitting in the faded pink chair near the disemboweled coat on the floor. A green shawl lay across her shoulders, lighting up her copper red hair. She uncrossed her buckskin-clad legs.

"Hiya there," she said, her gaze fixated on Mako.

"Anna-Skye," Mako rumbled, drawing a shield of cockiness over him like the fastest gunslinger at the show. "Nice to see you again."

Thresher catalogued her physical flaws and perfections. He absorbed Gela's secretive smile, Mama Milagros's silence, and Mako's strut—a walk Thresher knew well, which had been fading little by little over their journey—as he greeted the woman. No sense of ease here or comfortable familiarity. The air was thick with faint attraction and heat like a cat brawl.

He had never personally witnessed a feline fight, but he figured they smelled like the restrained sexual tension running rampant at the Facility when springtime rolled around. A very confusing time for Thresher, especially when he'd been restrained in his bed after knocking another experiment down for looking at him wrong. His orderly brought in a guard from another ward and the two of them made sucking, popping sounds together out of Thresher's sight, but hardly out of his mind. Immobile, Thresher fixated on the warped ceiling, enthralled with the quiet moans and muffled grunts from the hormone-enraged teenagers—a sentiment expressed by his psychiatrist one session. He tried hard to stop yearning. He rode out the sensation and mentally shackled his body from undulating. If they so much as suspected he wasn't drugged out of his mind, they would leave and never come back.

But he knew the lingering scent of it, crowding the back of his throat, both beloved and insidious. When Mako dragged his hand away from Thresher to embrace Anna-Skye, Thresher wondered if he could endure it again—only sensing, never seeing or participating. He grimaced. Loyalty restrained him in choking cuffs. Jealousy gnawed at him like rats. Emotions—running him into the ground, making him consider things he never should.

27

Nika woke to gulls cawing, the ocean roaring, the wind whipping up a torrent, and the Enders brewing what smelled suspiciously like tea over a low-burning, cautious fire. Beau handed her a bent metal cup. The steam broke up the congestion in her nose and chest as she drank deep and felt her roughened tongue sting from where she'd burned it the night before.

Walker slept hard. She touched his shoulder on and off until he roused, then handed him the leftover tea. His eyes widened, fascinated, as he tasted it.

"This is all new to you, isn't it?" she asked quietly.

He swallowed. "Have you been to this part of the world before?"

She shook her head. The apology stuck in her throat and came out as, "You're a dunce, you know that?"

"Sticks and stones, baby." He smiled, taking the last gulp.

"You know that's all my backwash."

"I don't mind."

The rest of the Enders' olive branch was crispy fish burned at the edges, flakey squares of what she assumed was dried algae, and two badly crunched biscuits. She scarfed her portion while scrutinizing Walker, who took time to actually taste the lint on the bread.

Nail marks scabbed his cheeks. She'd hurt him more than she realized. "I'm sorry," she choked out.

"Guess I wasn't something you needed," he said and held his hands over the fire, bending his fingers like they hurt.

Nika's fingertips were cold as ice. She couldn't imagine what the night would have been like without clothing. Death by hypothermia, probably. She remembered Milo's worried statement, *if she is Manahatta*, and hoped for something good.

"I'm not very good at taking care of what I need," Nika said and swallowed hard. "I see the bad. Everywhere. I used to think I was a positive person, but I'm the worst of the bunch. I don't see the good, even the good in you."

He hesitated. "I understand."

Suddenly, Nika could breathe again.

Jake nudged Milo. Milo bent down to look Nika in the eye. A curve of carefully wrapped fishing line stuck out of his pocket. "There's a storm heading our way," he said, and motioned to the sky. She looked up, but couldn't tell the difference from the blue sky of yesterday to the one of today. "We're going to a trade post and you're coming with us."

"We're going *home*," Nika said.

"You're coming with us," Milo reiterated, his eyes narrowing with an imperceptible nod, like she'd follow his lead if he looked convincing enough.

"Think again, sweetheart." She bared her teeth at him.

"I could hog-tie you. Drag you myself. Are we clear?"

Nika glared at him. Food and sleep strengthened her fire, but Milo grabbed her and swiftly tied her hands. She kicked his shins, pleased when he grunted in pain.

"Where's our home?" Walker asked, as Milo did the same to him.

Nika realized with a start that she'd included the experiment by saying *we*. "West of here."

The Enders were quiet on the trek from the beach into the pine barrens. It didn't escape her notice how the group forced her and Walker in the middle. It also didn't escape her notice how Maggie Mae was in that middle group too.

Maybe she wasn't *just* a Manahatta screwball after all. Maybe, she scared them straight.

28

N ika hadn't been paying attention, completely lost in her own thoughts, to notice anything beyond the endless trees. She took stock of her breathing, her footsteps, and the background shuffle of Walker beside her, but her chest ached, like she couldn't catch her breath. It made her dizzy. Her rib cage inflamed with a sudden nameless pain. A gentle clinging bump to her fingers had her clumsily holding Walker's hand.

Two cleared parallel paths cut through rounded humps of overgrown grass. Track marks. The trees on either side of the road weren't tall, but they twisted over and around each other, creating a canopy penetrated by shafts of light. "Where are we?" she asked. As the pain in her chest grew, she gripped Walker's hand.

"We're going to see the mother of monsters," Tobey growled, prodding Nika's shoulder. "Hurry up. I don't want to be outside when night falls."

Maggie uttered a sharp word but turned a reassuring smile on Nika. Small jagged lines of dim light folded in the curves of her curly, glossy hair. *What a lovely girl,* Nika thought, *there might even be a backbone hiding in her somewhere.* She even surprised herself by gifting Maggie a small smile back.

"Place giving you the spooks?" Maggie asked her.

Tobey rolled his eyes. "Really?"

"Something like that," Nika said, watching Maggie lower her head, mouth pursed.

In all truth, the place reminded her of an abandoned spot that was still being picked over by things that didn't mind doing what needed to be done to survive. Like the collapsed subway tunnels running underneath the city where big slabs of concrete had crushed a thousand people. She had ventured underground once, and it had been as quiet as this end-of-the-line lane. Rats as long as her forearm, fat with black hides, crawled in and out of the dusted bones of those forgotten folks.

"My grandmother used to tell a similar tale about a battle between man and monster," Nika said softly. "It was an old tale passed down from when the earth was new."

"Maybe," Maggie said, "before the volcano blew, our ancestors were friends and they traded stories. Tova is a kind of...*witch*, after all."

"Witch?" Walker inquired. "What's a witch?"

"Didn't have any books on mythology, huh?" Nika said and nudged Walker, somewhat delighted in his concern and the way he didn't pull her closer, only held her hand like he could put all his comfort into that small contact.

"Tova fought in the war against monsters and ate the grandfather of monster's brains," Maggie said. "Digesting all that knowledge and craft drove her crazy. Now, she believes she can speak with their spirits and harness their dead energy."

"Yet she runs a trade post." Nika bit back a smile. These Enders might be suspicious, prophecy-believing fools, but Nika grew up with Mama Milagros and knew about living with so-called magic users. *Bruja*, her young self had teased Mama Milagros, who sharply corrected her with *curandera*. She remembered how Jake looked at the end of her tale: horrified at the truth that the Facility captured outsiders and turned them into guinea pigs.

The shade created cold spots that chilled her. Long skinny reeds shimmied between the twisted boughs, rustling like muted maracas. The road widened, revealing a wide square beach house at the end of the lane. Campfires littered the worn grounds around the house. Small groups and loners pitched tents or built lean-tos. Low voices conveyed an ambiance of anxiety, and they all looked to the sky with grim faces. Nika couldn't blame them. She wasn't a weather bird, but she understood the ominous threat on the horizon, swirling gray clouds and a patch so dark it could be black. Storm on the way. Milo had been right.

She studied the people for a familiar face, but everyone was a stranger. It figured, this being a trading post for the Eastern Islands. The Manahattas had their own post with a plastic peddler, and maybe he had made sure he didn't tell her tribe where he got his goods.

"Back so soon?" A woman with black skin and even darker hair broke from one of the smaller groups and stepped in front of Jake. She must have been five inches shorter than Nika, but she looked polished and lean compared to Jake's long silver-streaked hair and the deep lines creasing his face. "Didn't think you'd fulfill a bounty so quickly, Jake. I'm impressed."

"It's one way to provide, that's all, Taysha."

"Which bounty was it?"

"Runaways."

Nika kept her head down, warm hope blooming in her chest. The woman looked like a warrior with hard leather covering her chest and arms.

Taysha rubbed her full lips. "Don't remember that one. What are they paying? I'll double it if you give them to me. Won't tell a soul. Just give me the lead and you can even have everything I came with."

"Why so eager?" Jake asked, and patted his pockets, looking for a smoke.

Nika felt Taysha's gaze on her. Sizing her up. It wasn't the same as the Facility. It felt worse. "Woodland wars are getting bad," she said in a harsh whisper. "There aren't enough people to fight. I need to bring back new blood who can hold a knife."

"Not for sale," Jake said, gesturing for her to back off.

Her lip curled. "I've got cloth, food, paper. You can have it all. I have to go back with something."

"Woodland war isn't my fight," Jake said with a huff. "We had our tribal wars—they're ended. Hell, my people have been fighting wars on this land long before the volcano blew."

"Jake, this is a good deal."

"I never gave anything to those wars. What makes you think I'll start now?"

"You've stuck your nose in before," Taysha snarled. "I've heard the stories."

"There's always been a reason, but when I did, I almost lost my whole tribe," Jake said, stepping into Taysha's space. "Back down, *girl.*"

Taysha slumped and put a hand to her hair, braided tight to her scalp, the curly ends gathered into a large bun on the top of her head. "You change your mind, you know where to find me."

"Get out of the rain, pup," Jake said, pointing to the sky. "You think this hurricane's bad? I don't want to imagine what's coming your way."

Taysha made a gesture Nika didn't understand, some kind of goodbye or curse, but Beau tugged on Nika's rope and brought them up to the house. Peeling grayed paint crumbled in Nika's hands as she was ushered inside. She grimaced. It wasn't any warmer. A layer of grime had worked into the floorboards. People crowded into the kitchen, sitting on cracked countertops beside piles of dishes and clutter, waiting in line. Soft conversation permeated the room. She leaned into Walker's side, stiff like a board.

"I remember you," Tova said. "Reckowackies brought you in. Had a nice bruise on your forehead. Didn't look too good, but a bounty's a bounty, and we exchanged goods. It's interesting to know how much you can go for. You were worth a lot."

"You knew who I was," Nika said. "You knew I was an outsider."

"I earned a lot of quality goods for you. Probably what I would've made on you, Milo."

"Far as I can tell, you're not worth the dirt on my boots," Milo growled. "You're nothing but a liar and a charlatan. Jake, we don't need this. Let's *leave.*"

"I have such a soft spot for an End man," Tova crooned. "It's a good thing we've got such a lovely history, Jake, and I love making you happy. Otherwise, I'd have thrown Milo to the Woodlanders. They'd love a leader like him, someone who knows how to kill."

"Milo is an Ender," Jake said.

"You truly are the mother of monsters," Nika whispered.

"It's not an easy world to live in," Tova said. "New liars emerge every day. A month ago, the Shinnecoes betrayed our treaty and traded directly with the Promised Land, but it looks like they got theirs. Something wiped them out. See, I'm the only one that trades with the Promised Land. With what they've given me, they can have anyone they want. I sold you, just like I sold the girl before you. Just like I'll sell the next one they'll need."

"Did you lie about the prophecy?" Milo asked. "The sharks on the cards?"

Tova sighed and reached for the deck—a set of thick, ragged-edged paper with nothing but smeared fingerprints decorating the back—and laid out a spread. Nika didn't understand this ritual, but as Tova flipped the cards, she figured it was something akin to Mama Milagros lighting different colored candles at her altar. A tea-stained smudge shaped like a fish hovered in the corner of each card. "They read the same," Tova said, looking at Jake with sadness in her eyes.

Milo shoved the cards off the table. Tova didn't move, the sadness sinking into her mouth, leaving it half-open as she sighed. "Hocus spells," Milo roared. "It doesn't mean anything but to scare us, make us think we're in danger, keep us coming back here, using your *sight* to avoid the so-called monsters—"

"Milo." Jake crossed his arms and leaned back. Nika realized that Milo had crossed a line disrespecting someone much more powerful than he. Beau looked scared. Maggie pulled her lip in between her teeth and gnawed it red.

Tova fingered one of the scattered cards before giving it to Milo. He crushed it as his hand curled into a fist. "You'll meet with the Wallabout contact, who has informed me their ship is en route to capture the original bounty. Barter what you will with them and then bring that male to me. Leave these two and I'll trade them back to the Facility. The bounty for them will be released soon, I'm sure of it. We'll forget this whole thing happened."

Outside, the thunder roared and rain pounded the windows. The room seemed smaller as the candles flickered. The house shuddered and the glass shards swayed, one dangling just above Nika's head. Her reflection came in and out of view. She put a hand on Walker's knee and squeezed. *Be ready.*

"Don't think so," Nika said and leapt to her feet, pushing the table over. Cups and the pitcher shattered in time to Tova's screech. Launching over the couch arm, Nika snapped one of the shards from the ceiling. The glass sliced her hand. Her elbow jammed into the stomach of one of the young Ender pups. She tripped another one and sliced wildly with her new weapon. Her shoulder slammed into the swinging glass doors, and she felt Walker's weight behind her make the door crack and collapse. She leapt out and into the rain.

The storm soaked her instantly. Covered fires of the mother of monsters' tradesmen—worshippers, for all she knew—scattered around the browned lawn. Someone grabbed her arm and she punched out, her fist thudding into something hard. She heard a cry, but the rain obscured her vision. She bolted, the pursuit loud behind her. It terrified her that Walker didn't follow, but at least she hadn't left him to the wolves this time. The pine barrens loomed around her. The taste of iron flavored her fear in the back of her throat. Branches slapped her face. She stumbled again and almost rammed into someone—the Woodland woman, Taysha.

Lighting flashed, outlining Taysha's grin. She dove for Nika's wrist and dragged Nika deeper into the woods. Nika yanked back, sending them both tumbling into the mud. The wind howled, bending the trees low. Taysha shouted, and Nika knew Taysha wanted to capture her to sell her down to the Woodlands and make a warrior out of her. She lashed out, kicking Taysha in the knee. Taysha screamed, and they rolled in the muck until Nika's head was wrenched to the side, pain radiating from her scalp. Nika thrashed and realized she was screaming.

"It'll be over soon," Taysha said. "Stop fighting, you stupid bitch. Use it for the war."

Mud filled her mouth. The hurricane felt as if it lifted her, and she wished Taysha would float away with the force of the gale. She couldn't see, but the painful pressure was suddenly gone, and through the wall of rain she watched Milo punch Taysha, sending her to the ground. He grabbed Nika by the shoulder and hauled her to her feet. Fear made her comply. She'd rather be with the Enders, with Walker, than sent down the coast with a gun or sword at her side.

Milo slipped as he dragged her forward, and she surprised herself by steadying him instead of using it to run. Ahead of her, the collectors hovering under shelters by their fires had broken into a riot. The house swarmed with people. Tribesmen ran from the house, goods tucked under their arms or shoved into packs. Licks of fire had caught an edge of the house. Maybe Tova would burn in it, and then the monster mother would never sell another soul. Never put a price tag on anyone else.

Although she was still an End captive, still a failure at escaping, when Milo shoved her forward in front of the other Enders, her heart unclenched. Walker, kneeling and bound, looked up at her with relief. She would lose more freedom, but doubt shone in Jake's eyes as he backhanded her and that felt like the greater victory. She had hooks in them. Her hope brightened. She would tug on their heartstrings until she ripped their hearts out, if she had to.

29

Finally alone in his childhood room, Mako perched his elbows on his knees and studied his boot-clad, cockeyed feet. Exhaustion warred with the desire to undress. It felt so hard to lean over and pick at the mud-caked laces. He couldn't imagine the last time his feet had felt clean air. His toes wiggled in anticipation, but his gut churned with dread from the evening's events. "Damn the trinity," he said.

He always knew Gela was sneaky, but he never pinned her as diabolical. It was the main reason he had been such a bastard, but he knew she would distract him with something like this. Tribal protocol and rules. Family respect. She moved faster than anticipated, reminding him of Manahatta culture—anyone who leaves the island should be mourned as dead—because *nobody* came back, even though he brought her Nika's vial necklace as evidence. Gela make damn sure to remind him why he should stay. Barely home a day and she had already arranged a blind date with Anna-Skye, no less. Anna-fucking-Skye.

Not that she wasn't a lovely piece of work. She always had been. Cute button-nosed ginger had matured into the gangly girl-woman he fucked against the wall *one* night after he burned his throat sneaking her father's homemade booze. After, she made him swear in a panicked squeak that he wouldn't rat her out, and the promise had been easy as pie to make. He didn't want the word getting out about their little love fest, either. Only the trinity knew what Nika would say, but Mako had a pretty good idea none of it would be nice, even if she *was* bosom friends with Anna-Skye.

To make matters worse, Anna-Skye's beau, Elliott, was Mako's friend, and the thought of his friendship with his boys—Tarek, Elliott, and Mako, *how they ruled the world*—destroyed by a half-hour fuck made his stomach twist. He'd been twenty, stupid, had hair a girl would die to touch, and he felt too old to wait any longer to lose his virginity. The memory burned like hasty shots taken from cracked glasses. Liable to cut your lips, make you bleed.

It all came down to responsibility. Kids were revered for their hope in the future almost as much as elders were for their wisdom of the past. Ever since he hit seventeen, the subject of children had crept into plain conversation.

Anna-Skye had been a subject then, too, but in a way that she was a lost opportunity. She had promised herself to Elliott, whatever that meant. It wasn't like marriage was a big deal when there was barely anyone out there *to* marry. It wasn't like they arranged unions between tribes, but Gela still wheedled ideas of: *Oh Mako, the plastic peddler told me a rumor about the MacPhearson daughters in northern Manahatta. What do you think about taking some milk and butter and see if they feel like trading?*

He hadn't cared one bit about the MacWhatever girls. He cared about completing his chores and romping around the island doing the shit kids do to stay entertained. Nika flirted with Tarek in a way that had Mako grinding his teeth, but she had similar sentimentality about the subject of love and sex: who the fuck cared?

That was before his world collapsed, of course. After Tarek and Nika disappeared, Gela, hung up on one true love, fretted that they had run away together. Mako knew better. Nika loved Tarek, sure, but she wouldn't *abandon* Mako. Sure, Gela and Milagros weren't the same after, but losing Nika meant Mako couldn't function.

He felt her all the time. Her rage, confusion, and fear pooled in the center of his chest with no outlet. He climbed to the top of the highest building and screamed himself hoarse to take away the hurt. It didn't help. No one believed him. They gave him sympathetic looks as time slipped by, clearly hoping he would get over it, but he was still stuck up there, screaming away her pain.

But then he found clues and crafted a plan that lead him to Soul-Dago and into a haint's future where he butchered people for words and strings of sentences.

He toed his boots off, leaned back in just the right way to make the familiar bed springs creak, and bounced gently up and down. Part of the room had been transformed into Gela's paper-making studio. A scraggly screen full of clumped pulp stretched over a pan of stagnant oatmeal colored water. He could only imagine the mess when she made her own ink.

He nudged his socks off. What an odor. His shoulder ached as he pulled his sweater carefully over his head and exchanged it for a worn long-sleeve, briefly patting his marked stomach. His coat hung on a nail beside the door, a small patch sewed over where the arrow had pierced the leather. His muscles clenched weakly, permeated with deep soreness.

Anna-Skye might not be so eager to get him alone if she knew how bad he stunk. He chuckled half-heartedly. She smelled like tulips, pine needles, and something harsher that he couldn't put his finger on. They had acted their parts perfectly: the returned son and the waiting, secret lover. Mako had even dutifully completed small talk. He even asked after her father, for the trinity's sake.

She answered succinctly, eating Gela's prepared dinner all lady-like while Mako devoured the servings of eggs, tomatoes, cucumbers, and thickly buttered bread like he'd never tasted anything so good. He even sacrificed his third serving to Thresher. Why? Because he was a fucking saint, that's why, and Thresher had faded into his introspective observation mode where Mako's every movement had a thousand different meanings, and Thresher compiled every possibility for further analysis.

Drove Mako crazy, made him act different just to screw up Thresher's internal filing system. He didn't understand his own need to annoy the shit out of Thresher, but he'd learned that ignoring the impulse usually lead to him pissing Thresher off on a grandiose scale further down the road. Like flinging the grave wax at him.

Mako frowned. Grave wax. He didn't like that stunt Mama Milagros pulled on the roof, either. He never doubted her. She was a second mother to him, but she kept giving Thresher suspicious, sidelong glances that Mako didn't get. She had always been the type for prophecies—*Mako, read the foretellings in the melted candles*—but this felt different. By the trinity, he didn't understand it and he wasn't going to abide by it, until he did.

As the dread continued to build, Mako laid down. Everything seemed smaller since he had left. The quilt didn't cover him, his elbows stuck out the sides like fitting a fledged hawk back into its nest. He closed his eyes, intent on ignoring his behemoth feelings, and commanded sleep to overcome him.

His legs twitched and begged to be stretched. Overtired, his mind blabbed, intent on reliving the night. He groaned.

Anna-Skye had pulled him to the window after dinner, while Gela nudged Thresher into helping her clear the dishes. Mama Milagros rolled a cigarette in front of her altar. The paper-thin curtains had been drawn, but Mako could still see half of his reflection cast black and glowing in the sparse candlelight. Anna-Skye never showed her teeth when she smiled, and Mako compared this introverted young woman to the wild thing he had known in his youth. She'd hardened, he knew, was exhausted, he assumed, and the weight on her mind created age lines around her mouth. Maturity looked good on her. He wondered if she was just as displeased with Gela's hasty matchmaking as he was.

"It truly is good to see you," she said softly. "I wondered if I ever would again."

Mako rested his palm on the glass, letting the cold outside soak up his heat offering and leave his handprint for a ghost's moment.

"I miss Nika, too, you know," she said.

Mako's throat clogged up. She could never know the true loneliness of missing someone who had been with you since day one. "I miss Elliott, too. Any idea where he is?" Mako asked and felt a flush of shame. It wasn't her fault their friendship had fallen apart. They should have banded together, but it was as if the glue holding them together had cracked like the spines of Gela's books. Without it, they didn't know how to be friends anymore.

"You weren't the only one grieving," Anna-Skye murmured.

"Is that so?" Mako turned to her. "I lost my *sister.*"

He didn't mean to sound so harsh, but see, something wasn't right.

Mako lived by his gut and his feet. Right now, his feet angled toward Thresher and his gut rolled uneasily. He couldn't put his finger on why, but Anna-Skye had him on his guard. He had the ridiculous idea that he should usher Thresher under his arm—if one could fit a huge monster like Thresher under one's arm—and tuck him into bed. Then, he'd have it out with these women who made it their mission to turn the world topsy-turvy on him.

Plus, Thresher wasn't *that* tall. If Mako stood up straighter, they'd be level.

Anna-Skye glared at him. "She was my best friend, too, Mako."

"I know," Mako said, knowing his selfishness had caught up with him. "I'm sorry. I've been a real ass lately."

"What's with your friend, then?" she asked, his apology silently accepted.

"What about him?"

"He seems," and here a soft pause as if she didn't know if she should continue, "different."

"He is."

Now don't be coy, said her raised eyebrow.

"He's had a rough life," Mako admitted, watching Thresher methodically wipe a plate dry.

"We've all had rough lives," Anna-Skye snorted. "Not an excuse."

"I don't mean like that, I mean…" and here Mako trailed off because he heard warning bells again, gut wrenching sirens telling him to keep his mouth shut. It wasn't his story to tell. He shouldn't be prancing it around like the latest gossip, but Mako was an idiot—that had been proven true many times before—so he carried on. "He was experimented on in some kind of institution. They did things to him. A lot of bad things."

"Like what?" Anna-Skye asked, curiosity killing her cat.

"I don't know." Mako told the truth. "But it comes out sometimes. Like, he's here one minute and gone the next, and I know he's reliving some sort of traumatic shit. He gets all pale and sweaty, eyes gone off like he's not seeing me in front of him."

Anna-Skye frowned. "You've been traveling together for a while, yeah?"

Mako shook his head. "Barely. I found him trying to eat a fucking piss-clam. Raw."

Anna-Skye exaggerated a retch.

"Exactly," Mako said, with a pointed finger. "Exactly."

"For the trinity's sake."

"I know," Mako said. "I don't get it either, but that's what I mean. He knows so much, but it's like he's never applied it to the real world. Sometimes I can't tell the difference, but then something will cross him and it's like a whole new facet of the universe opened up."

"Maybe he's just brave. Maybe he'd been dared."

"No. He genuinely had no idea." Mako paused and caught the string of her amused reminiscence. "Just because you decided to eat one and get dog sick does not mean I'm at fault for daring you."

"Oh, fuck off."

Now that was an oldie but one damned goodie, and Mako smiled wolfishly at her, bared teeth and all.

"Tell me one thing that's changed his world in a good way," she said.

Touch, Mako wanted to say. "Clothes."

"Clothes?" Anna-Skye laughed.

"I'm serious. Boy was buck-naked on the beach when I found him."

"You know, you would be the only person to find," and here she ticked off each descriptor with a finger, "a buck-naked man, dumb enough to eat piss-clams, crazed from experimental treatments, and decide to fix him up suitable enough for your grandmothers."

"When life gives you lemons," Mako said and ended the quote with an opened armed shrug.

"Think he's dangerous?" Anna-Skye asked. "Maybe he escaped the Wallabout and he's deceiving you."

"That's what I thought at first, but he doesn't have the look of a hardened ocean warrior."

"Or murderer."

"Or rapist."

"Or pedophile."

"Or extortionist."

"What would he extort?" Anna-Skye demanded, an old glint shining up her gray eyes.

Mako squinted. "Larceny."

"You lose."

"I do not, I thought of another crime."

Anna-Skye harrumphed. "Not quick enough. Thought you had a set of brains on you. Guess you lost them in the wild."

"Oh, fuck you."

Oldie but a goodie. He saw it in the way she smiled. "Missed you, too."

"Yeah, yeah," Mako said. "Only reason you're here is for Gela to pretend she has a chance at great-grandchildren."

"Oh, lay off the old lady. She's been lonely."

"She's got Mama Milagros."

"I know that," Anna-Skye said, "but I think you'd want everyone you dearly love close to you when you're nearing the end."

"Trinity, why would you even say that?" Mako's stomach flip-flopped again, only this time it felt like a steel band dug into him from the inside. His feet tapped like he needed to walk a hundred miles.

"Just an observation," Anna-Skye said quietly.

"Who made you so morbid?"

"No one." Her voice was thick.

Mako's eyes zeroed in on Thresher stacking plates neatly in the cupboard. Thresher cast a quick look in his direction, and Mako felt an itch in his fingers, like Thresher had him all figured out despite Mako's valiant attempts at subterfuge.

"You'd tell me if anything was actually wrong, yeah?" Mako asked.

"'Course," Anna-Skye mumbled. "It's only sometimes, I really hate living like this."

"Like what?"

"From the scruff of our teeth."

30

A nna-Skye's last sentiment rang in his head until he sat up in bed, his head pounding. Footsteps pattered back and forth in front of Mako's room. Thresher.

He stood, opened the door a sliver, and made sure he had a perfect squinty-eyed annoyed face on. Thresher jumped at the sound, crossed his arms, and scowled.

Mako couldn't help his unrestrained smile. "What's got you walking walls?"

"It's quiet," Thresher whispered back. The small, straight scars around his mouth had pinkened from the sun. "Kind of..." he moved his hands as if to emphasize everything was too small and too big all at once.

"It's supposed to be. Middle of the night, remember?"

Thresher swallowed and gave a half-perceptible nod.

Something in Nika's old bedroom must've triggered this. Thresher's face was tight and sharp in a way that said he saw old ghosts like he had in the cemetery.

"I'm climbing walls, too," Mako lied and snagged his coat from the hook. He closed the door behind him. "Kind of feel boxed in, yeah?"

Thresher's blue eyes flickered around the small hallway. It played in the downturned tilt of his mouth how trapped he felt.

"Feel like getting out of here?"

"We shouldn't leave." Thresher seemed baffled at the suggestion.

"I don't mean *leave* leave," Mako said. "Just...come with me."

Thresher hemmed and gave Mako one of those looks that said Mako was planning on doing something ridiculous, and Thresher wasn't completely sure he was on board. And yes, Mako was, but he didn't like being so transparent.

"Trust me," Mako assured him. "Grab a blanket."

It was incredible how he was transported to his youth, attuned to the sounds of the penthouse, hoping not to hear Gela's yawns or Mama Milagros's slippers sliding over the floor. Thresher, a living, breathing force, kept close to him. In the kitchen, under the cupboards, steady as clockwork and just as old, was Gela's hidden stash of gin bought off of Anna-Skye's father. He shook the bottle at Thresher, sloshing the liquid inside. "Hey, hey, hey. What do we have here?"

Thresher leaned in to get a better look at the nondescript brown bottle. "What is it?"

"Courage, my friend. Liquid courage."

"Oh, so that's where yours all went."

"There you go again, being smart," Mako said and was rewarded by a flash of white in the dark.

They snuck out of the penthouse into the stairway, and out to the rooftop garden. The temperature change stunned him. He slipped his coat on and zipped it up tight, the sheepskin a trusted layer against the elements.

Mako began to walk toward the garden, but turned, suddenly bereft of Thresher's gargantuan clinging presence. Thresher had his head tilted way back, his mouth slightly open. Mako looked up, thinking how strange it was that even though this was the same night sky he saw from the ground, it felt bigger up here, *closer*, like he could see more. Long river-wide strips of twinkling stars shone between the parted, gray clouds. "Your eyes are going to fall out of their sockets," he told Thresher. Thresher walked over in a stilted gait, still preoccupied with the heavens.

Mako took the blanket folded in Thresher's arms and spread it over Thresher's shoulders, wrapping it like a shawl. "Cold," he said, hating that he even said it. What an overprotective mother hen he'd turned into, but when he looked up, he had Thresher's attention again. "C'mon." He guided Thresher to the spot between the wooden racks full of vines and the skyscraper's ledge. He pushed pots out of the way and scooted up against the wide ledge's flowery whorls and decorative cornices that kept him from falling back. Thresher settled stiffly across from him and relaxed against the tall racks in jerking fractions. His legs crossed and their knees touched.

The bottle nestled in the triangle of Mako's bent legs. He pulled on the cork until it popped. The scent of juniper and pine wafted towards him. He breathed it in, held it, and then swallowed a bitter mouthful. "Here." He shook the bottle at Thresher until he took it. Thresher jerked back with a sound of disgust at the smell.

"Don't breathe it, trinity. Swallow quick," Mako said. "Just a mouthful."

Thresher fit his mouth around the bottle and tipped it back. His eyes tightened and Mako imagined the booze sliding down his belly as scalding fire. "Hold your breath," Mako said. "Open up your throat. Don't taste it. Swallow it."

Thresher complied and passed the bottle back to Mako with an unhappy grimace like he'd been tricked. Mako touched the slick shine of Thresher's saliva on the bottle's rim.

"What is that?" Thresher demanded.

"Gin. Good for the soul."

"It's terrible."

Mako took another hearty swig and couldn't disagree. Anna-Skye's family was full of drunks that wouldn't give up spirits no matter what nature threw at them. That didn't mean they were good at making the stuff. He passed the bottle back to Thresher and Thresher gingerly accepted it. "Puts hair on your chest," he said, instead.

"Sears them off more like."

"Stop pussy footing around and drink."

Thresher's gag was like music to Mako's ears.

"Do you want to play a dumb game?" Mako asked, feeling warmth coat his insides. Everything had a ludicrous edge to it.

Thresher wiped his mouth. "What kind of game?"

"Truth or Dare," Mako grinned sloppily. "I'll go first. Truth or dare?"

"Dare?" Thresher asked, attention straying to the bright sprawl of constellations above him.

"Okay, I dare you to hang your feet over the edge," Mako said, tapping the wave shaped cornice near him.

Thresher's eyebrows narrowed. "Why?"

"That's the game. If you don't do it, I win, and you're chicken shit."

"And these are all bad things," Thresher stated.

"Not from where I'm sitting."

Thresher huffed and scooted forward so his leg stretched out past where the cornice ended. He wiggled his feet in the open air and Mako felt the stakes rise as Thresher shot him one of those come-at-me challenges.

"Your turn," Mako told him. "Ask me truth or dare."

"Truth or dare?"

"Truth."

"At the Facility, there were shelves and shelves of books, but they all came from..." and here Thresher paused as if he didn't know how to describe what he wanted to say, "before this era. They're like the ones you found for Gela. I read all of them, so I know much from back then—about the rise and fall of many empires—but I don't understand what happened to that world or what happened after it to make it like it is now. Tell me what happened."

"That's not how the game works," Mako said crossly, imagining Gela's glee if she got her hands on those stuffed bookshelves. She had only one bookcase built from driftwood. "You're supposed to ask me something personal."

Thresher blinked at him. "But that's the truth I want to know."

"I would've told you that even if we weren't playing a game."

Thresher, his feet still dancing in open air, slouched as if ready to hear a good story. "I asked the question. You have to answer it true."

"It came down to an environmental holocaust. When the Yellowstone volcano finally erupted, it created a domino effect that caused all of the other dormant volcanos along the fault lines to blow. The explosion took out most of the west, sending us into a volcanic winter," Mako said. The truth felt like a campfire tale. "The canyons in the Midwest splintered as tectonic plates shifted, and since we had mined so much from the earth, they buckled easily. Nuclear reactors blew, contamination from plants and drills spilled everywhere, polluting the water table with so many chemicals that irrigation killed hundreds of miles of farmland, and anyone who drank the water died within months. It caused a famine.

"The volcanos caused a tsunami that hit the islands on the other side of the world. Took many of them out," Mako continued. "I'm not as versed on this, mind you, but I do know that when we used to be a country, we called out for help, but there wasn't any to give. The water level rose. People fled their homes. No one wanted to take them in. Too scared of limiting already rationed resources." Mako took another drink from the bottle, remembering when Gela spoke of some great-grandparent who missed his chance to board a ship sailing toward a friendly ally, only to find out later that the passengers were turned away to starve on the journey back.

"This whole island used to be bigger," he said. "There used to be a green lady who stood at the end of it. She's gone now. As for after, families formed communities who formed tribes and reclaimed land. For our family, we'd been here even before all that, so we decided to stay here. It wasn't long before we fought for water rights and defended our homes. That's how the tribal wars started, which ended in an uneasy truce. Never really stopped warring with Bruykleen, though."

A pause, pregnant with the decades of destruction, hung between them. Mako wished Thresher hadn't brought it up. All the silly drunk bubbles beginning to carbonate his blood had turned morose. "That question doesn't count though. You have to genuinely ask me something personal, otherwise it's no fun. I want a dare this time."

"Come sit by me and put your legs over the ledge," Thresher said without looking at him.

"You are the worst at this game," Mako said, but complied. He wasn't going to be the chicken shit, no siree, and he jostled Thresher's shoulder as he sidled up next to him. He tried not to notice how much further Thresher's legs stuck out than his. "What the hell did the Promised Land feed you to make you grow so much?"

"Is that your actual question?" Thresher asked, knocking Mako's leg with his own.

"No," Mako said quickly. "Truth or dare?"

"Dare," Thresher said, and Mako rolled his eyes, desperately wanting a truth, because he had plans, loose-tongued plans.

"Drink the rest of this," he said, taking one long pull from the bottle before handing it off.

Thresher's eyes saddened and the edges of his mouth tightened. "It's a drug, isn't it?"

"Technicality." Mako brushed it off.

Thresher rubbed the curlicue around the bottle's lip. "It's making me feel funny." His voice was soft.

"It's supposed to."

"My fingers are numb, but my stomach is on fire. Makes my head spin."

"You wanna tell me every hypochondriac thing that's wrong with you?"

"You don't have to drug me to make me do things for you," said Thresher.

It blindsided him. Mako gaped, knowing he must have been dropped as a child to be this stupid, this uncaring. He didn't think, didn't even put two-and-two together that Thresher must have been drugged all his life, held against his will, and here Mako was doing the same thing, forcing him to ingest something that would alter his state of mind in the pursuit of having a good time.

"It's not like that," he said weakly, wondering when he became such a bad, bad man that had no right to drink or deserve a person like Thresher in his life. "It won't hurt you. I mean it will if you drink too much, but I'm drinking it too, so it's not like I would let it get that far. I mean, it's..." Mako fumbled—such a clumsy idiot—to the finish line. "I wouldn't give you something like that. I wouldn't hurt you like that."

Thresher didn't say anything, and instead, took three gulps before Mako could stop him. "Not a chicken shit," he said. The empty bottle swayed sideways in his lap. "Truth or dare."

Mako's chest hurt, a thick pain that expanded with each breath. "Truth."

"Are you in love with Anna-Skye?"

Mako snorted and ended up coughing on his own spit. "Trinity, no. I mean, I love her like a sister, sure, but I'm not *in* love with her. I've never been in love before."

Thresher was silent. Mako wondered when his plan had gotten so twisted that he was the one spilling his guts. Verbal diarrhea, his drunkenly vice, and even though he knew it, it didn't stop him. "Gela's got all kinds of books, right? Lots of literary nonsense, all back when stories were written more so than told, but one time, I must've been eleven, I found this novel nestled out of the way. I thought it was a transcribing project, right? It was pure filth. All sorts of nasty sexual fantasies. I devoured the whole thing in one sitting. Gela's handwriting didn't even turn me off. My point," Mako said, realizing he should have a point in this ridiculous diatribe, "is that Anna-Skye and I fucked once and that was it, and yeah it was great, but it wasn't love. It just felt good."

Thresher shifted and let out a deep sigh, like blowing smoke from the deep recesses of his lungs. "She's very beautiful."

"She's a babe, don't get me wrong." Mako held up his hands in peace. "I just don't want to spend all my time with her."

Thresher went quiet, internally filing away everything Mako said, but at least his eyes had glazed over.

Now they were getting somewhere. "Your turn," Mako breathed, "and I want a truth."

"Fine then, truth."

"What are you reliving when you zone out? I mean, what did the Promised Land do to you?"

Thresher fell into a fit of laughter, sounding so young. "You want to hear all about my trauma, Mako? About all the horrible things they did to me so you can pretend they're doing them to Nika?"

"No, trinity, no." Mako retreated, addled. He didn't understand how Thresher could make these connections, these twisted webs, when Mako truly wanted to know about Thresher's scars, inside and out.

"Be specific, then. I thought you knew how to play this game." His blue eyes pinned Mako down.

"Your mouth, then. How'd you get the scars on your mouth."

Puzzled, Thresher touched his lips. "What scars?"

"You have scars," Mako said, baffled. "Here." He touched a small faded line near the corner of Thresher's mouth. Thresher jerked back like he'd been electrocuted. Breathing heavily, Thresher fingered his mouth carefully. "I didn't know," he said. "Probably from the gags. Or biting my lips. It was the only thing I could do when I was restrained. Do they look bad?"

"No," Mako said, his chest pain almost throbbing now, "but you have a lot of them."

"Oh," Thresher said, sounding so lost.

"They're here," Mako said, using his forefinger to draw the scars on his own mouth. Two parallel lines on either side of his lower lip like double fangs. The shorter ones along his upper lip, more numerous in the corners.

Thresher mimed Mako, some scar-counting version of Simon Says, and Mako imagined someone shoving something between Thresher's teeth to keep his tongue down, stretching his mouth out wide enough to split the delicate skin.

"I never felt threatened, you know," Thresher said. "I can see it on your face sometimes. You think I was some kind of victim. It wasn't like that. It was like..." He petered off, and Mako watched those baby blues flicker back and forth across his face. "...like I was in a pack and I didn't want to be an omega. None of us were alphas of course, but you could sense the weak and frail. I hurt some of them bad enough to prove I wasn't like them. I knew when they punished me, I deserved it."

"That's not an excuse," Mako sputtered. "That's not a reason."

"Before I figured out what it meant to explore the feelings building inside me, I wasn't punished," Thresher said. His face was close to Mako's. His cheeks flushed, and he seemed to grasp for words. Alcohol was in his veins, stripping him of sense, leaving him bare. "I was coddled. Never drugged, restrained, or isolated. It wasn't until I struck out and hurt someone who tried to intimidate me that they took away my touch, my words, even my senses."

The scent of pine lingered on the air. Thresher slumped into Mako, his head resting on Mako's shoulder. Both of their legs dangled in the open air, pushed this way and that by high winds. Thresher tapped his calf against Mako's ankle.

"It's different," Thresher said again. "In there, I was an experiment in the whole sense of the word. Out here, the emotional freedom, the words—even the flashbacks—make me more. I wouldn't want you to know the experiment I was in the Facility. I wouldn't want you to know Subject T at all."

Mako finally decided he had a good enough answer. "You can't say stuff like that and expect me to be okay with it."

"Once you've accepted it, let me know." Thresher yawned.

"I met Subject T. He was washed up, eating piss-clams. By all accounts a fucking idiot. Kind of like you."

Thresher laughed, and Mako thought it was nice, sitting on the roof, warmed by body heat. Something he wouldn't mind doing again. Thresher's dark brown hair smelled like oil, real and tangible.

"This feels like a good drug," Thresher murmured.

"Yeah," Mako agreed, the stars spinning concentric circles above him. "It does."

31

Thresher woke with a kink in his neck. His spine felt compressed, the discs out of place. A stiff ache radiated up his left side, but he accepted the pain, because Mako's head rested on top of his. He blinked at the dawn. Stars still twinkled through the fading night. His legs swayed in the open air, while his left foot flopped uselessly. Moving sent a tingle down his thigh to his toes. His mouth felt cracked and dry, and his head throbbed like a giant hand squeezed the back of his skull. Shivering, he touched his forehead. Sweaty and cold. He still wasn't sure how he felt about the drug gin. Extracting his head from under Mako's, he swallowed a groan of pain. Mako grunted and tilted away. One arm crossed over his stomach and the other lay flat, cradling the empty air where Thresher used to be. Thresher watched him with a kind of intensity that startled even him, noting the way Mako's eyebrows twitched as he came out of a dream, and Thresher hoped that, for once, it had been a restful sleep.

"Mornin'," Mako drawled, stretched, and moaned as his spine popped. Thresher ached for that kind of flexibility. His lower back felt like it had been branded with hot pokers. "Thirsty," Thresher said.

"Me too." Mako rubbed sleep from the corners of his eyes. "All dried out." He ruffled his hair, making the strands stick up straight.

Thresher raised a hand and Mako obeyed, helping him stand. Thresher leaned against the rack as a whimper escaped; he willed his back to relax and chastised his stomach muscles for slacking on the job. Mako's hand hovered over his shoulder.

"I'm okay," Thresher breathed, scrounging up the remains of a smile. "Need to loosen up."

"Stiffness is for old men," Mako said.

"You're calling me old now?"

"But a man." Mako grinned, helping Thresher across the garden. "Be grateful."

In the lightening sky, each flower petal and vegetable bud looked vibrant, like pill colors.

Mako stopped next to the water pump and cleared the grit out of his voice with a cough. He pumped the handle and a burp of clear water surged up the pipes, filtering down into a mesh filter stretched over a bucket. The ingenuity of the rain harvester amazed Thresher. It was an invention he would never have come up with on his own.

Mako fit Thresher's hands around the pail and helped him drink. Thresher could have mocked all he wanted—after all he didn't exactly need help—but he felt warm inside in a way that made him shake. Perhaps this was coddling or fussing, but whatever it was, he let Mako go the extra mile. The metallic tinged water sloshed in his belly.

Mako drank, spilling water down his jaw. "Why're you grinning like that, huh?"

Thresher realized it wasn't fussing or coddling at all, but simple fondness coloring the way Mako set the bucket down, tucked the blanket closer to Thresher's trembling body, and kept close as they walked back inside. Thresher wondered if Mako knew what he was doing, caring like this, *gentling* like this.

Back downstairs and into the Saddlerock home once again, Thresher's ears rang in the dim quiet. The need to sleep overwhelmed him, but the thought of going back into the bedroom made him pull away from Mako.

Annoyance crinkled the faint crow's feet beginning to trace Mako's eyes. "C'mon, I'm exhausted. Rooftop doesn't exactly give you the best night's sleep."

"I'm gonna sleep out here," Thresher said. "In the chair."

"Nika's room is perfectly fine."

Thresher sucked the corner of his mouth under his canine. He wouldn't go back into the small closet room full of burlap dolls with hand stitched black grins staring down at him from mismatched button eyes. Hospitality was a beautiful thing, but the walls had claws, and Nika's personality was imprinted on the sheets like a ghost.

The final straw has been his nightmare, a Facility horror where he sat in a plastic chair with a doll in front of him, scissors in one hand and tweezers in the other, and he took that doll apart, ripped the mouth open and pulled out the stuffing through the split opening, turned the sack inside out and handed it to his psychologist like destruction was something he should be proud of. "Still gonna sleep in the chair," he said.

"Fine," Mako snapped. He stomped into the hallway while Thresher stifled the need to cower. It was impossible to pretend that this was a test to see what Mako would do. Once, if Mako had pushed hard enough, Thresher would have gone into the bedroom, but now he felt that boundary of want and dislike, the flexing of expectation and self-care, and realized he might now have a *backbone*.

"You're a pain in the ass," Mako said, reappearing with blankets and pillows. He tossed them on the couch and the chair, his wounded shoulder hunched. "Like I'm gonna let you stay out here alone. Can you imagine the trouble?"

Thresher pinched the corners of his lips in to stopper his smile and watched as Mako huffed and puffed his way into a comfortable sprawl on the couch. His coat now off, he pulled the blanket up to his chin and punched the pillow like it had done something offensive. Thresher settled into his chair, feeling the old give of well-loved cushioning, and spread the blanket over his knees. The pillow propped his head to the side. Thresher could smell Mako embedded in the cotton next to the old scent of washed but unused linens. Musty.

"More flashbacks?" Mako yawned, his eyes already closed.

"Yeah." Thresher felt raw and exposed just talking about it.

"What set it off this time?"

"Dolls."

Mako laughed, but dropped off quickly when Thresher didn't respond. Thresher's eyelids drooped, and he woke off and on at Mako's soft snores, half-convinced Mako slew dozens of tree-sized clapping dolls with the pots and pans in Gela's kitchen.

A soft touch at his shoulder. Mama Milagros's sun-darkened hand crinkled his borrowed shirt. "Shhh," she hissed, padding forward and leaning over Mako's slumber. His feet stuck out, and he gripped the blanket close to his mouth. She made a pleased hum and smoothed a slash of hair off his forehead. Thresher marveled at the softness, how in one familiar move she had made Mako a young boy. Her beads rattled softly as she backed away, her black shawls brushing the floor like the bristles of a broom, and her small, otherworldly smile brought Thresher into abrupt wakefulness.

She knelt before her altar and with a raised hand motioned for Thresher to join her. He carefully slipped out of his chair and stood behind her, feeling the weight of whatever she wanted to say in his chest. She lit the candles around the robed skeleton. Smoke curled from the tiny dancing flames, and Thresher sank to his knees beside her.

"It's a shame," she said, so quietly Thresher wasn't sure her voice was real. "A shame about the Saddlerocks."

"What do you mean?" Thresher asked, whisper-soft. Hearing Mako's family name felt like a jolt in his heart—Mako was connected to a generation of people who loved and reproduced and the culmination of their gene pool slept on the couch behind him.

Mama Milagros unscrewed the jar of corpse wax and smeared some over her face, making her skin glisten in the candlelight. Thresher scrunched his nose up at the smell, but when she offered the jar to him, he mimicked her. The wax felt thick and suffocating on his skin. Mama Milagros waved a finger over one of the candles, making the flame dip and dive. Thresher couldn't help but be mesmerized by the flame like the first time he'd seen fire. Primal, delicate, consuming, and he touched his chest, still feeling the weight. The smoke spiraled and disappeared.

"When I found the twins, not two minutes an orphan on a bloody road, Nika was dead set on the whole world knowing she'd lost her mother. Her grief had a voice and a name. Mako, on the other hand, buried his sadness and panicked in silence until the pain had to come out. Same thing happened when Nika disappeared, only this time when he ran away, we didn't *have* Nika to find him."

She tugged on her stretched earlobes. "Before them, I'd only had the divine love of the Bony Lady, and that love wasn't something I could lose. I grew up in a cult of women who'd survived the world's devastation by the grace of the Bony Lady." Mama Milagros nodded to the daffodil-eyed skeleton. "Every generation, a girl would be blessed by the Bony Lady to hold all the sadness and loneliness of our denomination; a girl devoted to her so that she would continue to keep evil away. She swore an oath to never love any but the Bony Lady, and once she could survive on her own, she would be chased from the land. This was my fate. Alone, with the world endless before me, I knew I'd never lose my faith or become blind to the truth of the Bony Lady's existence. Yet, I couldn't imagine feeling loss like either of the twins did, even when spurned from my mothers. Can you?"

Thresher felt like everything inside him ballooned out of his veins. He respected the Facility, similar to the way she loved the lady of the altar, but he'd never loved something that could destroy him by its death. "Don't own much to feel like that," he choked out.

"Exactly." Mama Milagros twisted a plait of herbs into the flame. The scent of rot and moss intensified. "There's a holiness in being forgotten. We are completely dedicated to the higher beings controlling our lives. The Bony Lady didn't like that I soiled the sanctity of that loneliness by taking in two children. Some part of me wanted to bond with them, but they weren't *mine*."

"Mako says you're like a second mother to him." His wax mask felt sticky, alive, and clinging, as if the Bony Lady used it as her skin to touch him.

"When Gela found us, I'd never seen anything so ferocious. Nothing compares to a mother who's just lost her own baby and then her daughter's children. You can't imagine the fire in her eyes. Suddenly, I wasn't the Bony Lady's anymore. Just like you're no longer part of whatever god you used to serve."

"The Facility wasn't a deity," Thresher said. He couldn't breathe.

"But it defined you, made you who you are, scared you of anything outside of it. I didn't understand how naïve I was until Gela pinned me down, hand at my throat, knife at my stomach. It was like I didn't exist. I'd never felt so insignificant. She held my life in her hands, and the only thing she cared about was the welfare of her grandchildren. I was instantly addicted to her fire. Somehow, she had claimed me, more than the Bony Lady ever had. You understand that, don't you?"

"Yes. I think about it all the time," Thresher said in a rush. She understood the devotion he felt, a loyalty forged through terror of being alone. Mako had a way of living with conviction, a strength that Thresher wanted. He hadn't just been surviving. He'd been learning *how* to live. How to truly shed Subject T.

"We were nothing before the Saddlerocks claimed us," she said, and her eyes averted away from the lady of the altar as if ashamed.

Thresher could feel his teeth imprinting on the inside of his lower lip. "Yes, we were. We are. *I am.*"

Her dark eyes widened when she turned to him, like she saw something else than him. To Thresher, she was a vision of black and tans, her skin a translucent sheath over her bones.

"The twins clambered into Gela's arms," she continued. "I slunk back, waiting for the abandonment I wasn't ready for. Gela was outlined in the doorway. When she looked over her shoulder, Mako and Nika were two moon-eyed circles peering over each one. 'You comin' or what?' she asked. That sealed my fate. The Saddlerocks have a habit of taking in wild things like us."

A rolling threat of bile crawled around Thresher's stomach like the big black spiders that used to hide in the Facility. He could see their long spindly arms in the smoke. "We aren't pets," he stammered. "We can leave them. They can leave us."

"I tried to, once. The Bony Lady showed me Mako, only he had the teeth of his namesake. He tore my legs to shreds. The Bony Lady stabbed him through the heart from behind, and when he fell, it looked like he'd been chewed up. She leaned over me, close enough to kiss, and I knew that danger was coming, and a Saddlerock was destined to die. How could I tell Gela? How could I live with that in my dreams? I left, only to crawl back with a lie on my lips to explain my absence. Couldn't stand the look in Gela's eyes. She'd had people leave her before. She knew what it looked like."

She closed her eyes. "I thought the Bony Lady had taken Nika as her next priestess. Nika heard her mother in the bones, and when she disappeared, I thought the Saddlerock sacrifice had been fulfilled. Now I know Nika's alive. Her mother's bones fill this home once more, making me see sharks everywhere. In the smoke, in the wax. They came back when we first met, when you had the Bony Lady's touch on you. She showed you to me as a catalyst, a lost thing cooped up and confused in a cage made of love and affection. Mako's affection. What sacrifices would you make for him?"

"We're not...not in...it isn't like that," Thresher stumbled, barely understanding how she could compact his and Mako's relationship into a simple four-letter word.

Because Mako was a four-lettered word, like fuck and shit and hold and help and love. Four was as holy as a trinity, a quadrality that couldn't be broken.

Thresher was an eight-lettered word. Too long to make anything real worth feeling, too mutated compared to the simplistic clean lines of four. Eight was too much, double the fuck, double the shit, double the love.

"Lost things aren't supposed to love like that, but we do. Saddlerocks take in strays, but they never think anything bad will come of it. Will you be the shark that kills Mako? Or will Mako's love become another cage that you have to escape?"

Thresher shivered and an absolute *no* vibrated in his chest. He didn't want to be spoon fed, re-tattooed, and drugged in oxytocin. He wanted to be a whole person, someone with backbone and strength. He couldn't believe in these prophecies, these symbols and dreams—he didn't understand the science behind them—but he did believe in the emotional chains spun around him, stronger than anything he had ever felt before.

He couldn't see the sharks swarming the smoke, but he could see the tears in Mama Milagros's eyes. She had accepted her cage. He now knew what the feeling in his chest amounted to, but he couldn't understand how all his tests and experiments had added up to this.

He rushed to the kitchen and wiped his face with a cloth. The wax left a brown smear. His breathing sounded abnormal in his ears. Mama Milagros's words jumbled in his head, feeling like she had spoken another language to him. But one thing was clear: she thought he had traded one type of confinement for another, and while the Facility had physically locked him up, Mako would shackle him through *dependence.*

He clutched the rag and turned back to see Gela, her hair mussed like a cloud and a ratty pink bathrobe with sleeves that barely covered her elbows wrapped tightly around her waist. She looked like a belligerent old flamingo with bald spots where feathers had fallen out. He bit back a laugh at the unintentional parody of the extinct creature, stunned at how he could race from anxiety to flabbergasted hilarity within moments.

"A little early for prayer, isn't it?" Gela asked, waving the smoke away and bending down to wipe the tears and wax from Mama Milagros's face.

"More bad dreams," Mama Milagros said, leaning forward to blow out the candles.

"They're coming back." Gela pushed Mama Milagros's wild black hair out of her face and gently kissed her, whispering something in her ear. Mama Milagros clutched Gela's hand, briefly nodding, and released a shuddering breath.

Thresher's heart leapt into his throat. This was what...*love* was supposed to look like. He had paged through the fairy tales, old, preserved stories of knights slaying evil and maidens locked in dark towers. They were supposed to teach *empathy*, and he read enough to know that love was instinctual and instantaneous, not...whatever Mama Milagros had implied. There wasn't anything in those tales about being confused and scared, of feeling lost—not just physically, but deep down, in his soul.

"Didn't mean to wake you," Mama Milagros whispered.

"It's nothing, sweetheart," Gela said. "Sun's up, so am I. Unlike this piece of work." She thumped the couch. Mako stirred, blinked owlishly, and sat up. His hair plastered to one side of his head.

"Not a child anymore," Mako said, pawing at his eyes.

"Respect, boy. Don't forget you're meeting the plastic peddler with Anna-Skye this morning."

Mako pulled the blanket up over his head with a groan. "You *made* me make plans with her. Trinity, I'm still a little hungover."

"Hungover? How did you manage that in the first place?"

Silence from under the blanket. "You're right. I should be disappointed in myself."

Gela stomped into the kitchen. Shelves rattled and banged open. Mama Milagros lifted Mako's feet and settled on the couch, laying his legs in her lap. She caught Thresher's gaze with her head cocked, and he absolutely hated her for her secrets and spells and especially for *what she'd put in his head.*

Gela held up the empty booze bottle and glared. Mako cringed. Mama Milagros soothed. Gela made breakfast. Thresher's belly plummeted when Mako caught his eye within that moment of Saddlerock household normalcy, because yes, he finally did see that all this bundled irritation, exasperation, adoration, and worship meant Thresher wanted to spend all his time with Mako. He wasn't sure he could stomach it, the way he'd traded one institution for another. He didn't feel safe. An abyss opened in front of him, an unknown blackness made of the future and unsaid words. He wished they could all be packaged back into the pages from whence they came, where self-sacrifice broke enchantments and safety could be found in the arms of another. Where Thresher wasn't the impetus for Mako's fate, wasn't an easy guide to Nika, and wasn't a Promised Land pawn.

"How are you feeling?" Mako shot him a sloppy grin.

"Fine," Thresher said, short and slanted, delightfully unhappy at the way Mako's face shut down.

Thresher choked down his biscuits and tough fish grilled with egg yolk, letting his taste buds enjoy the flavor while his stomach reeled.

Mako kept glancing at him, small lines appearing between his eyebrows and across his forehead. He held a long, chipped platter questioningly toward Thresher and asked for the hundredth time, "Do you want more?"

Of course he did. What an idiotic question. Thresher wanted the whole world, but he bit his tongue and wondered if he would have scars that matched the ones on his mouth from holding inside everything he suddenly wanted to say. He accepted the second helping.

Anna-Skye arrived after the plates had been licked clean and the smells of hot frying pans and cooled butter lingered in Thresher's nostrils. She looked put together, he thought, watching her from his seat near the window. Copper hair combed into a neat ponytail, loose coat buttoned up her middle, and an indulgent smile when Gela pulled her into a conversation. She handed a brown bottle to Gela, who counted small misshapen white and purple shells into Anna-Skye's cupped hand.

Mako hovered between Thresher's chair and the kitchen table, sweeping invisible crumbs from the tabletop. He approached Anna-Skye comfortably, and Thresher threw a snarl at Mako's back. He wanted to hurt Anna-Skye badly at that moment, not only for being Mako's savior from the awkward situation Thresher had created, but because she sucked Mako toward her like a vacuum.

Thresher retreated into the hallway, emptied and hollowed from these people who meant so much, made him think so much, uncovered things he didn't clearly understand about himself, and thrust it under his nose for immediate analysis. He careened into the small bathroom, shut the door, and stared at the familiar flush toilet, only the water had been replaced with wood shavings and the excrement slops had to be cleaned out. He turned and pressed his forehead against the yellowed wall tiles. The cold cradled the front of his skull.

He wondered again what it would be like to creep back to the Facility and confess, let them wrestle all the emotions out of him.

The doorknob rattled, then the door pushed open and Mako slipped inside. He leaned against the closed door, barricading them both inside the bathroom. "Good thing you're not taking a crap," he said breathlessly. "Otherwise that might have been awkward."

"Isn't this supposed to be a private room?" Thresher demanded, outraged at the intrusion. Couldn't he have a moment alone? Space where everything wasn't branded with Mako?

"Wanted to see what was up. Did Milagros say something to you? Gela said she's been acting *morose* all morning."

"Nothing of importance," Thresher said. He turned back to face the wall.

"Hungover, then?"

"I don't know," Thresher muttered, rubbing his forehead back and forth against the tile.

"Look, I just wanted to make sure you were okay."

"I don't need you to check in on me all the time." He didn't want Mako anywhere near him. He wanted room to be able to breathe, *think,* to try and find that person Thresher had been: the Thresher who had a modicum of control, who had experimental rage to survive, who didn't need a fucking hero to check in on him.

"Don't give me that bullshit," Mako hissed, standing over Thresher's hunched shoulders. "You're acting…strange."

"I'm not."

"Pissy, even. Is it Anna-Skye? She throw you off somehow?"

"I don't even know what that means, Mako."

"Trinity, don't say it like that."

"Say what?" Thresher asked, turning his head.

"My name."

"What do you want from me?" Thresher yelled. Mako's eyes widened in a way that told him to keep it down, this was weird, *I followed you into the bathroom and now I regret it.*

"Nothing," Mako snarled, sliding hipshot against the wall.

Such a liar. Thresher cocked a grimacing smile, something ugly to match his insides. Mako's eyes narrowed in frustration. Bent down close to him like this, he could almost believe Mako was taller. The aroma of breakfast lingered on Mako's breath, and Mako's blistering body heat made Thresher feel like he had a fever.

And well, he was devastated at how close Mako was, a grounding point that stilled Thresher like he'd been hunted and cornered, where freezing seemed like the best solution to an outcome that would end bloody. "It's a little overwhelming," he said, straining to hear sounds beyond the bathroom through the intensity building between them.

Mako shivered and his eyes rose from Thresher's scarred lips. "What is?"

"You," Thresher finished.

"Me?"

"Yeah," Thresher said, dry-mouthed. "You're stupid and you're obsessed with finding your sister, and because of that, you've put me in this cage when it would've been better if you'd abandoned me, at least then I might've become independent—"

"I wouldn't abandon you, trinity, who do you think I am—"

"—and you're arrogant and obnoxious, and you drive me absolutely up the wall, and I get it now, how you're training me and punishing me and conditioning me—"

"What the hell? *Conditioning?*"

"—trying to make me this perfect sacrifice to exchange for Nika, and I don't want to be back in prison, *any* prison, and I don't want to hurt you, but I don't want to love you, I want to be, no, to *understand* myself, and I don't want to be another one of your strays—"

"What? Strays?"

"—because I'm a wild thing that the Bony Lady wants to use. Don't you see that?"

"Shut up," Mako growled. "I'm not fucking conditioning you for anything. I'm not planning some diabolical scheme to trade you in for Nika or any other conspiratorial plot you might've imagined. You're acting fucking crazy—"

"I am *not*—"

"Can't you shut your mouth for one minute and let me talk?"

"No," Thresher said. "Not anymore—" But he swallowed his words when Mako slipped his mouth onto his, close-lipped and world ending. Mako's fingers tucked in the short hairs at Thresher's neck. Mako adjusted, slanted his mouth for a second, better angle over Thresher's, while Thresher's buildings collapsed and a rolling fog grounded all of his brain activity.

Mako broke the kiss. Dazed, Thresher counted the freckles marching up the bridge of Mako's nose.

"I'm not going to sell you out, okay? Not gonna do anything except keep you here, so shut up already," Mako said, almost too fast, linguistically tripping.

"Keep me. Yeah, *this* time," Thresher croaked. Stunned. Talking nonsense. "You're still not right about everything. I am not crazy."

Mako's crooked grin looked just as devastated and aghast at what had happened as Thresher, but in for a minute in for a mile, and Thresher felt like he'd been hit with a sledgehammer. "I gotta go," Mako whispered, sounding as if he'd been brought to his knees by the consequences. "Anna-Skye."

"Yeah," Thresher said, because he could do nothing but agree these days.

"We good?" Mako whispered, his hand on the doorknob.

"Yeah," Thresher said to the empty room, imprinted with the seconds of before.

32

Mako never meant to do that.

He'd done...*it* to shut Thresher up, but in no way had he planned it. The transformation from terrified beach creature to whatever fiery thing that had *yelled* at him in the bathroom had compelled him to take it that far. His body had taken control and the...the...whatever *it* was seemed like the logical action to stop getting yelled at. It hadn't really been a true...*nothing* with tongue, trinity, he couldn't think of it like that. Simply put, it had been an honest display of affection to shut Thresher the fuck up. He didn't regret it, but he damn sure didn't know where it left them.

If honesty was the key here—and Mako went ahead and assumed it was—Thresher had been way off base saying *any* of that to him. No way was he going to trade Thresher like stock for Nika. That scenario hadn't even crossed his mind. Whoever put those thoughts into Thresher's head needed to be taken behind a shed and shot.

Stupid. Ridiculous. Promised Land crazy.

Walking behind Anna-Skye, Mako realized he had fallen into a familiar rhythm where his feet led the way as his mind puzzled over the sensations still tingling on his lips. He wished he knew how to stop the drop in his stomach when he mentally replayed it—and he replayed it all right. His mind was like Thresher's motor mouth. It wouldn't *stop.*

He hadn't been this unaware of his surroundings since the Woodlands. He looked up and squinted at the flattened land, ashamed at his inattention. Anna-Skye's lengthy strides ate up the jagged concrete. The place looked familiar, but this whole island had been his playground for so many years, everything was familiar. His memory felt hazy, which irritated him more. It wasn't fair that he could recall the Woodlands in stark detail and not home. Maybe this was a different, better route, than the one he'd trekked as a youth to the plastic peddler's wheelbarrow. He tried very hard to remember, but he'd been cursed with inattention as a kid and had never looked up until he caught sight of the peddler's patchwork jacket and the displays of plastic utensils, faded toys, and hundreds of different shaped bottles. He should ask Anna-Skye about the route, but for some reason, he felt uncomfortable talking to the girl he'd grown up with.

Good advice. *Grow up.* He cleared his throat and hurried to catch up to her. Her lips upturned in a ghost of a smile. "Lost in that head of yours?" she asked.

"Can't seem to remember this way," he said. His feet urged him to flee in another direction. The pit balling in his stomach warned of *wrongness.* He didn't understand why he was fighting his instincts so hard.

He thought perhaps it had been the kiss—see, he *could* take responsibility for his actions—but the wrongness clenched as he gazed at Anna-Skye. Another familiar sight, but this time he saw her as she used to be, lit by firelight, the way her face hadn't grown into itself yet, when she sat next to him at the bonfire celebration nights around the big pit.

All the nearby families participated by bringing food, goods, and crafted booze to trade. When business concluded, the adults wrangled the children around the blazing fire that summoned dancing shadows on the tall skyscraper walls. The rising hoots and hollers reverberated off the broken windows and crumbling façades. Drums and guitars enchanted the crowd. Then, the stories would begin. Old stories, new stories, stories that had only been written down, stories that had only ever been told.

Gela, the favored minstrel, spoke in cadence with the acoustics as she wove Mako's favorite tale about the battle of monsters. Adrenaline surged within him as he imagined man and animal forging a pact to destroy the grandfather of monsters. He could almost taste the silvery tang of the monster's blood in his mouth when man and animal decapitated the grandfather and tore his body asunder. The blood ruined them, transforming the tribe until they were unable to speak with the animals. Thus, they unintentionally severed their connection with the earth. The story traded to the next teller like a game of hot potato until the fire burned out.

Mako had cornered Anna-Skye in the shadows afterwards and sucked on her fingers like the boy in the next tale who licked the other children's fingers and left them black and stiff. That had been the beginning of the terrible incident with Anna-Skye, the first bit of foreplay before their sexual encounter years later.

"I'm not taking you to the plastic peddler," Anna-Skye said, slowing down and angling her feet toward the surf. "I thought we should talk, instead."

Bells rang in his head. He felt like a painted target. "What about?"

"Your experiment," she said. "I think we need to have a chat about him, and about you, and about me."

"Go ahead," Mako hedged, feeling as in the dark as when the old Woodland haint mistress had put a carved doll in his hand and told him to cut. "What do you have to say?"

"Don't you want to know why I split from Elliott, first?" Anna-Skye climbed up one of the algae covered concrete boulders sticking out of the waves. "Remember how dramatic I'd been?"

Mako stared up at this untouchable queen of the hill. "Sure."

"I fell in love with someone else. *Something* else."

"Oh yeah, like who?" Mako fought the lump in this throat and desperately hoped it wasn't him. He hunched his shoulders against the cold, hoping the next gust wouldn't steal all his heat. The ocean swelled against the horizon, and the old saying resonated in his ears: *big waves come in groups of seven.*

"I fell in love with a different way of life." Anna-Skye's eyes locked on the horizon. "I hate how we live, day to day, the same grazing and hunting and gathering. When do we ever make something? Create something meaningful that can be looked on generations from now and be thought of as something great?"

He squinted, following her line of sight. Terror clawed up his throat as he caught the decipherable sway of a ship mast rounding into the bay. "Holy shit."

"Gela has all these books from decades back and some of them are still beautiful and most are rotten, but you know what? They last. That's immortality. That's the kind of life I want. I want to make something, Mako. Something that sticks, that can be found a hundred years from now and will survive a hundred more. I can't do that in this world."

"Anna, get down, we need to get away from here," Mako said, panic lacing his order. He hadn't felt this scared since a Woodland warrior nearly butchered him in two. They needed to run and hide. They needed to get back to Gela, Milagros, and Thresher. "That's the fucking Wallabout." He reached up to grab her ankle, but she edged out of his reach, stepping onto another concrete boulder jutting further into the water.

"I know it is," she said. "It's coming for me."

"What the fuck are you talking about? Get down. *Now.*"

"The thing about the Wallabout," she paused, "and your Facility for that matter, is that they aren't any different from us."

"You better explain yourself right now," Mako shouted. He wanted to leap on her and drag her down, but she'd said *Facility* and the only ones who called it that were the Bruykleen slave-dog and Thresher.

"They're a tribe, like the rest of us. Stuck in the same situation. When the caldera blew up in the West and the food shortages starved this land and those across the oceans, when the nuclear power plants melted and it was one disaster on top of another, the acting government put all the delinquents of their society on a prison ship for safekeeping. When that government collapsed, the Wallabout had to fend for themselves. That was the best decision they ever could have made, you know? The Wallabout's great-grandparents might've once been killers and thieves, but now they've created their own tribe and society, like we did. They evolved."

"Wallabout is a horror ship," Mako said. "The government hoped they could starve them to death where it wouldn't be seen. They're crazed, violent, like the shit you hear about from the Woodlands. You know the stories. They're to scare children into behaving so the Wallabouts won't come and get them."

Anna-Skye shook her head. "It's so much more than that. So is the Facility. It's not a torture chamber or a death sentence. It's not something to run away from. They were scientists trapped together who evolved a culture based on science. They knew how to make antibiotics and grow food, knew to raid the hospitals for supplies and machines instead of the clothing outlets. Thresher isn't a poor man doled out a dodger's luck. He's worthy of something great."

"You're telling me that experimenting on people isn't a crime? Isn't sick? What do you know about the Promised Land, anyway?"

"He's not a real person, Mako. Let me be clear. The Facility's goal was to preserve their livelihood. Science became their religion. One of their psalms was to repopulate the earth and restore humanity. Growing people and making them compatible with the outside population isn't a twisted plot, it's part of their damn bible, written by their founders and supported by their prophets. They don't want land, food, or war. They want to create something good from our species. Thresher is one part of an overall mechanism to complete that prophecy. Don't you understand that? They want to make people immune to the diseases and conditions of this world, send those man-made experiments out to the tribes and repopulate with us so we can *be* something again. So we can have that immunity. Thresher is a piece of the puzzle that you stole, gave a name to, and imprinted with a personality."

"Anna-Skye." Mako breathed her name in disbelief.

"I know you're thinking about morals. About Nika. We don't have to dance around this. Wadi blacklisted me, after what you did. Just like that." She snapped her fingers. "Said I sicced a shark on them."

"You're working for them?"

"I'm not working for them. I'm working *with* them."

"What have you done to Nika? Where is she?" His fury exploded into his veins and he could taste the future where he slaughtered her. Messy. Ugly. *Horrific.*

"She's being used for good. They have her, Mako, and now, they'll have Thresher too."

"What are you going to do to Thresher?"

The Wallabout sped past them, the wind billowing its sails, the hull slicing through the water faster than Mako had seen before. Figures dove from the bow, sliding through the water, and Mako almost welcomed the Wallabout warriors' arrival.

"Where do you think the Wallabout's going, Mako? I called in the bounty on Thresher's head. They're merely making a pit stop to pick him up."

"You lying, manipulative *cunt.*"

"I gave Nika to the Facility to prove my loyalty. They needed a specific breed only I could provide, but when I came to them a year later, so lost and confused about my own identity crisis of just what was the fucking point, I caught sight of her there. She wasn't happy, but when are martyrs and saints ever happy, Mako? When did someone do something extraordinary beyond the concepts of their body and soul and be happy about it?"

"You left her there! You sold her there!" Mako leapt up onto the rock, ready to take her down. His unsheathed machete felt hot in his hands. "I'll fucking destroy you. You want to know why Wadi blacklisted you? It's because I'm a mean sonuvabitch, Manahatta made, but Woodland forged. Prisoners of war screamed when they saw my face. They would do anything to make me stop, but once I showed them the dolls I had carved of them—showed them exactly what I planned to do to them on those pieces of wood—*nothing stopped me.*"

"You're so narrow-minded, Mako. You don't see the whole picture because the people you love blind you. You'd let us all burn for them, even if it meant wiping out what chance we have at civilization." She cupped her stomach. Protective. "I won't have my child growing up in a version of your world."

Mako didn't register her words, could only see the years he had *without,* and swung his blade at her. She put her hand out to stop him and he felt a slight give. She screamed, holding her bloody hand to her chest. *Fingers.* He wanted her whole arm.

The sound of splashing made him glance away from her. Men rose from the waves like ghosts and ran toward them. Anna-Skye scrambled across another concrete jut, slipped, and landed hard on her knees. Mako swayed, his balance precarious from his wide swing, but he leapt to the same rock. Betrayal curdled his stomach, the same wild, bloodthirsty trance he felt when he fought the Bruykleeners crawled up his spine into his consciousness. The only thing he wanted was to look into her eyes and see her terror before he ended her life.

A Wallabout man reached up for her first, yanking her down into the surf. Mako jumped off the rock, his machete clashing with the Wallabout's spear. The shaft splintered and cracked in half, his blade lodged in the wood. Anna-Skye slogged through the waves further out, water up to her thighs, fighting against the tide pushing her back towards Mako as he fought with the Wallabout warrior.

The Wallabout grappled with Mako, trying to pull him closer, the wet dagger shining in his other hand. Mako yanked his blade free from the broken spear and dove into the dagger's embrace, sliding in the sand before the warrior lunged to chop into the Wallabouts' kneecap. The man shrieked, raising his knife to plunge into Mako. The tide roared forward, sending them both to the ground. Mako gasped, spat out sand and water, the taste of rotted fish and chemical tang flooding his mouth. His shoulder seized in pain, but he stumbled to his feet and staggered to the writhing Wallabout struggling to rise. Pushing the man over and holding him down, he wrenched his machete out of the Wallabout's leg and slid the blade into his throat. The waves frothed red. His shoulder had become numb.

Three more Wallabouts rose from the ocean. One grabbed Anna-Skye, sweeping her behind him. Mako wished he had a gun, any instrument that would send death across the wide distance between them and make her fall limp into the ocean. Mako decapitated their friend out of spite, the only way to relieve the *want* embedded deep in his mind—conditioned through war, hungry from loss. He would fight until the sharks rose to feast on the Wallabout carcasses.

You'll destroy anything in your way, and I won't give you this instrument to do it.

The ship turned, catching wind that took it far from their band of warriors, heading straight to the heart of Manahatta.

Thresher.

Retreating felt like panic, but he ran back along the coast in the direction of the ship that would take Thresher away from him, the prison ship that would send Thresher off on a terrible journey back home.

33

Feel like taking a walk with me?"

Looking out the window at the crisscrossing streets below, Thresher imagined Mako striding along the tiny avenues with Anna-Skye. His heart tasted as stale and smudged as the window.

Gela rubbed his shoulder to get his attention. She asked the question again, softly.

Thresher flashed a sick smile of agreement at her, thinking: *Your grandson just kissed me.*

When she smiled back, he saw the faded freckle line bridging her nose. He thought how sacred and wise she must be to have survived for so long. "Wonderful," she said, talking sweet and quiet to the flight risk caught up in the tingling sensation coating his mouth.

Mama Milagros prayed over her altar. Thresher wondered if they prayed for the same thing. Wild things, after all, have wild gods. Gela interrupted her with a kiss. Mama Milagros's cheeks flushed as she whispered, "Always taunting the Bony Lady, aren't you?"

"Keeping it interesting," Gela said.

Downstairs, light filtered through the windows. Gela wound a tether around her wrist and coaxed the cow from her indoor stable. Thresher double-checked that the safety of his gun was on and stroked the cow's neck, feeling giddy. She hadn't rejected him.

Outside, wind pushed volcanic thick clouds across the sky, bathing the crisp day in shafts of bright and shadow. "I never liked Mako's father," Gela said as they walked down the street. Thresher glanced over the cow's swaying head at her. "He brought me around after a few good years—very much the smooth talker—but I knew there had to be something wrong with a man who hunts water beasts for a living. My baby girl was gone on him though, thought he hung the moon, no matter how many other suitable matches I suggested. Sharks got him when the twins were barely four years old. That's what he gets for killing one too many of *their* tribe."

"Did Mako look like him?" Thresher asked.

"Nika's got the look of him," Gela admitted with a restrained shrug. "Mako's all his mama."

Once again, Thresher felt haunted. He wondered when he looked at Mako, when he kissed Mako, how much of Mako's mother stared back at him.

"I like *you*, though," Gela added. "Little quiet. Little strange. But I like you."

"Little wild," Thresher said.

"Nika was wild. *Is*." Gela sighed. "In my heart, I buried that girl. I know that's brutal to say, but you lose a lot of what makes you whole after a while. I lost my daughter, my man, my parents. It's life's big joke to give you everything in the beginning when you can't appreciate it, and then rip it away piece by piece."

"You didn't give up on them when they were young. Why give up on Nika now that you know she's alive?"

Gela controlled a sob by exhaling slowly. Thresher counted the hitches. A sharp, searing agony of guilt clawed his side. "When I was young, my grandparents terrified me. You couldn't look up from the floor without permission or they'd slap you for disrespect. I swore I wouldn't be feared. I'd be beloved and the respect would ride on those coattails. I'm glad I brought my children up the way I did, but right now I'd kill to have that respect to make Mako obey. What he wants to do will start a war between Manahatta and all the tribes he crosses." She opened her clenched fist to reveal the silver vial in her palm. "Last month, I delivered triplets to a friend's daughter. *Triplets*. I can't make them motherless by raising a Manahatta war tribe. I'm not strong enough to fight. But to leave Nika *there*? To do *nothing*? My heart and mind are at war. Tribe or family?"

"Gela," Thresher choked, spiraling, because the truth rested with him. A simple tell or don't tell, a truth or dare, and all of a sudden, Mako's life lay golden and throbbing in his hands. The most brilliant and vibrant soul he had ever held. "I don't know how to get back to the Facility."

Gela threw her head back and laughed, something sharp and ugly. "Does Mako know?"

"I haven't exactly confirmed or denied my navigation abilities."

"He's working under assumptions." Gela ran her hands over her face. "I don't blame you, honey, but what does this mean? Is this some twisted form of universal guidance?"

The clouds whispered over the sun, outlined in blinding yellow and white. The cow nibbled on a vine curling up from underneath the concrete. Gela wiped her nose across her forearm. "Luck's been on his side for so long, it's bound to turn. He hasn't been the same since Nika disappeared, but I would rather have him damaged and here rather than dead and whole."

"It's hard to lose what you've found, isn't it?" Thresher asked, his tongue nearly numb in his mouth. It scared him, how close his teeth clapped around it, almost like he could lose the power of speech between the spaces of a sentence.

"I can't fathom it. I won't survive it, but I don't think I'll survive *doing nothing either.*"

Suddenly, Thresher knew he wasn't a wild thing. He was the most docile and kept creature, bound to a cage of his own making. He shuddered at the thought of the truth in Mama Milagros's prophecies, at the genesis of Mako's nightmares, and at needing to know if he had been released as an accident or an experiment. "We have to go. I don't know how, but we have to try. This isn't divine intervention speaking, but experience. The Facility isn't a place where Nika should be. She should be here with her family."

Gela swept around the cow and engulfed him in a tight embrace. "You'll take care of him," she said into his chest. "You'll *all* come back home."

Awed, Thresher sheltered her in his arms. She felt small but wicked, sharp but accepting. She gripped his shirt. Tears stained the cloth like an inkblot test.

Out loud, he sounded insecure. "I'll try."

Gela gave him a self-deprecating smile. He couldn't imagine a more beautiful woman. It seemed the world listened to her alone. She smiled, wide and gorgeous, and took his hand. Fingers entwined, they lead the cow in silence. Sunlight glinted off the lapping waves of the bay as blinding starbursts. The smell of dirtied ocean coated his throat. The desolate city rose on every other side, and he couldn't help but think of it as their island alone.

Gela broke their walk with a long pause, a question in her tilted head. She inhaled deeply, and he wondered what she had sensed that stole her tranquility. Thresher had the sense that the sun was setting far too soon.

She shoved him hard to the side with a scream. Unbalanced, he skidded to the ground with her on top of him, the pavement burning the first layer off his palms. Shock rattled the bones in his wrist. "Get up, get up, *run,*" Gela screamed in his ear as arrows pelted around them. Finally, his brain accepted her war cry: *Run, motherfucker, run.*

He fled blindly, trying to get her under his bulk when an arrow speared his calf so suddenly it brought him to his knees. His anguished cry melted into a victory yelp far away. Gela pushed him, as if she could cover *him*. The scent of cloying copper infiltrated the stale air. Blood.

Gela mouthed curses and commands. Their hands grasped each other, sweaty and hot together compared to the dry cool touch of before. He had no survival skills, no sense for danger. He would have walked into that trap with an unsuspecting smile on his face. Gela had a long blade clutched in her hands, useless in anything but close combat. In panicked flashes, he saw shadows rise from the water and glide toward dry land.

"Who are they?" he panted.

"Don't know," Gela growled, looking over her shoulder. "Fucking ambushed on *my* land? Motherfucking *bastards* of a whore."

Adrenaline pounded through him like a migraine. He felt rabid, his hackles rising as more mermen rose. He could barely walk now. The cow mooed in agony, her head tossing as she fled in another direction. Arrows peppered her rump. A second arrow pierced his thigh. Blood drained from the wound as Gela wrenched him down an alleyway. The back of his mind calculated his injuries: two arrowheads, shin splints, possible wrist sprain, *be careful not to twist an ankle.*

Gela sprinted down the alley and into an open crossroads, yelling, *"Son of a bitch!"* before diving into a second alleyway, sticking close to the shaded sides. Iron in his nostrils, the back of his throat clogged, Thresher heard the mermen's calls everywhere, wondering if these creatures were herding them. He flicked the safety off of his gun.

Gela abruptly stopped, and unable to veer away, he barreled into her. He grabbed her, ready to pull her any which way to safety. She clutched her chest where a spear stuck out, her glassy eyes fixated past the buildings to a dilapidated harbor where a vast ship rocked side to side. Blood bubbled on her lips. The vial dropped from her hands and shattered on the pavement.

Thresher howled as she collapsed in his arms, but she was too heavy to lift. Another arrow thudded into his shoulder. Arm numb, he fell down and over her, wondering how such a woman so beautiful minutes ago could become lifeless.

Footsteps surrounded him. He fixated on Gela's slack face, the way her neck tilted sideways as if she had to turn away. His grief evolved into rage, the mutated end result of everything.

Staggering to his feet, he finally had a good aim and shot one of the warriors advancing on him. The blast deafened him, but the man clutched his stomach and fell. The trigger felt hot in his hands as he frantically tried to shoot once more into the throng of men surrounding him, but the gun clicked empty. Ropes twirled in their hands. A wide, looped circle landed over his head and shoulders with a thump, the slipknot tightening. His gun clattered to the ground. Wrangled. The smell of wet algae made him nauseous, yet he still emitted a hoarse scream and charged. Another noose slipped over his head and tightened around his neck. Tethered.

He rolled on the ground like an animal, thrashing until he couldn't breathe. Black splotches bloomed in his vision before the handler loosened the noose incrementally, and he sucked in a burning breath.

Expert tugs kept him balanced on the edge of unconsciousness paired with flashes of razor sharp focus when he had the chance. Hands trussed his limbs. He lunged away, barreling headfirst into the cement, yanking on his leash hard. More rope connected his neck to his ankles and he squirmed to keep his legs up. Putting them down tightened the noose, making him responsible for his own fate. Someone carried him with a grunt to a set of rowboats surrounded by tribesmen holding spears. Far beyond, a massive ship cradled by the waves, the sun crystal clear, and it suddenly seemed very important that he watch it set. It might be the last one. It probably was the last one. He fought against the burn in his legs until his ankles slipped down, pulling the slipknot tight against his throat until he fell over the precipice.

34

Mako's heart thudded frantic beats, so loud he could hear the whoosh of blood being sucked and expelled inside that damnable organ clenched tight in his chest. His imagination dealt in hindsight these days, and he replayed what he should have done, even against the odds: mutilate the Wallabout warriors, capture Anna-Skye, and get all the information out of her. She was vulnerable. She was pregnant.

He tried to drown his regret with justifications, but the fuckers had fins now. Shame and panic made him picture Wallabouts holding his grandmothers and Thresher hostage. Thresher would gladly let those monsters rip him open if it ensured Gela and Milagros's safety. The knot tightened inside his stomach. A fresh flush warmed his cheeks as he ran faster.

He met Mama Milagros on the staircase to the fourth floor. Her dark eyes flickered over the sweat dripping down his neck and matting his hair, the way his chest heaved, eyes wild and spooked. "They've been gone too long," she said, her lips pinched into a hard line.

All his terror solidified with that one sentence. Mako's heart stopped. The knotted hurt in his belly slithered into his lungs to make him gasp even harder.

"They took the cow out," she said, and flashed him her tri-cornered blade hidden underneath her black cloaks.

"Anna-Skye," he panted, "sold us out to Wallabout. They want Thresher."

"Why?" she asked, automatic and soft, but they both knew why.

"What do you do with an escaped, dangerous prisoner? You hire the reckless pirates of the ocean to bring the runaway back." Mako turned and bolted back downstairs, hearing the familiar brush of Milagros's dress sweeping the floor. The one thing he needed to do right now was find his loved ones quick and maim whoever thought they could put him through this kind of emotional torture.

What had Anna-Skye said? *You'd let us all burn for them.*

"Don't be foolish," Mama Milagros whispered behind him as he slammed the front door open.

"We need to find them," Mako said, zig-zagging between fallen debris. He knew the path Gela liked to walk. He had lighter fluid in his blood, hot with revenge and ready to burn.

He piled the growing *what-ifs* behind a dam of denial. He couldn't dwell on the double loss. Thresher, so new to Mako's future, was supposed to be in his life for the long haul. Mako felt that in his bones, now. He couldn't go on existing with this tall experiment-shaped hole, always feeling off-kilter as if something crucial was missing.

And Gela. The familiar beloved, singular to Mako's identity. He couldn't imagine a time in his life without her. She made up all the facets of safety, love, home, and he swore to any deity—the trinity, the Bony Lady, *whoever*—that he would settle down, get married, have a few kids. He would do anything, just please let her be safe. Let her be alive.

The cow's flayed, open carcass chilled him. Her body had been gutted, huge quarters of meat carved out from the flanks in a shit butcher job. Black flies buzzed close by, sucking up the scent and ready to start the decay. Mako felt cold spots encompass his whole body. This attack meant he was going to war.

The cold shredded the edges of his *self* and severed all emotions until he was nothing but a ball of uncaring, bloodthirsty want. *Hainted.* When Nika disappeared, Mako thought he might do something suicidal. That's how little he cared about himself. It scared him badly enough that he broke the rules, made deals, and walked the earth despite Gela's protestations. To quest for his sibling and find the man he used to be. Instead, he had found the depths he could go, the pain he could inflict, the drive that narrowed the world to a single purpose.

Once, he would've been ashamed. Now, he praised the cruel man he had become.

He sidestepped the dead animal, scanning the loose arrows puncturing sun-bleached wood or shattered on old brick. He scooted around the debris, breathed the fight still fresh in the air, and caught sight of a path of trailing blood droplets. He whistled. Mama Milagros rose from her prayer over the cow with a raised eyebrow. He tilted his head. They followed the sprinkles leading them across an alley with a bloodhound's focus, through a crossroads, and to the crumpled body he'd know anywhere as his grandmother.

"Gela? Gela!" Mama Milagros pushed Mako aside and fell to her knees beside the body. One of Gela's hands gripped the spear carving her chest in two. The other laid out flat, as if reaching for someone.

Head turned to the side with a soft look of horror. Half of her face was red and blue from hitting the ground, as if she had been tossed away unceremoniously.

Mako wanted to hide his face, but he made sure he remembered every last detail. Even as he felt like he was being drawn and quartered, his organs burned to dust, because this was his grandmother, his Gela, and he realized he was saying *no, no, no,* to the fact that *yes, yes, yes,* she was dead and gone.

Mama Milagros's death keens ricocheted between the tall buildings. She took Gela's hand from the spear and cradled it to her cheek.

Mako couldn't look. He broke away, his eyes landing on a white starburst on the ground, the tiny shards of glass, the crumbled silver casing. Trembling, he dipped his fingers in the bone dust, and the ancient grief of his mother's death crashed into him again. It felt like she had died all over.

Messy blood splatters continued further down the street. Gela's knife was too far away from her body. Large smeared pools on the ground ended the trail. He bent, touched the thin layer of blood like it was paint. He rubbed it on his finger, hoping it would stain his skin. Thresher. The Wallabouts had taken him, just as they had taken his grandmother and Nika. This was it. For this, he would burn the whole world.

35

Thresher greeted his awakening like an old enemy, a routine he handled automatically, as easy as clockwork.

He had gone down choking, blackened panic puncturing his memory like bullet holes. His throat burned as he took in a deep experimental breath until his lungs couldn't hold any more. It felt like hitting a wall inside his chest.

"—gonna have to verify it's him. You have any idea what he was tested for?"

His bruised windpipe held in a rusty whimper. He used to have similar damage around his neck, thicker and wider from leather collars or slender and deep from restraints. He would press into them when he was free, just to feel it.

"—didn't have to stab him, good god, monkeys all of you—"

Three throbbing points of pain: calf, thigh, shoulder. This, too, felt familiar, the exchange of conversation above his head like he didn't exist.

"He put up a fight, Carey," a second, younger voice defended. "Good legs on him, ran like the wind. That old lady, too, fierce as a whip, had this look that made me cold—"

Gela. He cracked his eyes open and gazed at a ceiling crisscrossed with wide wooden beams. Lumpy burlap sacks were stuffed up in the corners and linked chains dangled down. Tentatively, he tried to pull his legs and arms down, but they were manacled at each end, securing him to a wooden plank.

"What happened to the woman?" a female asked.

"What do think happened to her?" the young male snapped. "She got in the way."

"Idiot. You weren't supposed to kill anyone," the female hissed. "You've likely started a tribal war with Manahatta."

"They shot first." A clatter of metal, as if something had been dropped on a table. The gun.

"That thing is worthless. See if we can do anything with the spare parts," the female said.

"He's waking up," he heard the older male, Carey, say.

Grief cut Thresher, slicing a new hole to fester in. He took a second deep breath and swallowed, feeling his throat scrape against the familiar collar barrier. Back in bondage. The whimper finally escaped. Light shone in his eyes. He blinked as the imprint burned his retinas.

"Can you hear me?"

"Yes," Thresher wheezed.

"Do you know where you're at?"

He didn't—how could he?—but his stomach rolled to the ebb and rock of the boat and the swinging chains. He mewled in embarrassment and tried to turn over on his side, stoically refusing to be sick.

"You're on the *Wallabout*."

Prison ship. This was where Mako first thought he had come from.

"We're taking you back home. Do you understand that? We're taking you back to the Promised Land."

The Facility. He remembered emerging newly minted into the outside to the car's old engine rumble and the flat cushioned seat he had sprawled on while drugged out of his mind.

"Do you remember who you are?" Carey asked, his wrinkled bronzed skin filling Thresher's clearing vision.

"Yes." Thresher almost sobbed.

"You're Promised Land's property," Carey stated, his cracked lips carefully enunciating. "You've been stolen and released prematurely. We've been commissioned to bring you back home. There's a bounty on your head. Do you understand?"

He wanted to speak—who knew how many more words were at his disposal—but his voice wouldn't cooperate.

"You're part of what's going to bring civilization back," he heard the woman say, sweet as if reciting a long loved tale. Her hand rubbed at his temples. She fixed her nails into the soft spots along his forehead that brought brief reprieve from the overwhelming nausea.

Anna-Skye.

Thresher gagged, bile fouled his mouth and burned his teeth as a small liquid stream puddled past his lips. A hard grip on his bound arm wrenched him flat. Carey, thin and strong, fiddled with the crook of Thresher's arm. He screwed a glass vial against a long needle.

"Where did you get that?" the young male asked.

Carey shot him an annoyed glare, despising the disrespect. "They give us equipment in exchange for our services."

"Doesn't look like my life is worth one flimsy sewing needle."

"It's a hypodermic needle, you uncultured reject," Carey snapped. "It serves more of a purpose than your arrow-slinging arm ever will."

Resentful silence followed as Carey tapped a vein in Thresher's arm and inserted the needle's angled tip with a quick pinch. Thresher wrenched his head around to watch crimson seep into the glass vial.

"Paul's been worried," Carey said quietly. "He thinks you're putting too much stress on yourself."

"What do you think?" Anna-Skye said, hand curling over her stomach. Bloodstained bandages wrapped around her fingers. *Some were missing.* "You're supposed to be the doctor, aren't you?"

"You knew the woman who was killed, yes?"

Anna-Skye swallowed hard. The other male crossed his arms.

"I recommend taking a break," Carey told her, kind and firm. "Take time to mourn."

The needle pulled out, and Carey swabbed at the leftover bead of blood with a gloved finger, then tilted Thresher's wrist to the light.

"I don't need to be coddled," Anna-Skye snapped.

"Paul does. You've been gone for most of the pregnancy. And when you do come back, I have to waste precious resources on making sure you don't get infected and croak." His eyes directed to her hand. "Paul's been going out of his mind with worry, and I don't blame him."

Anna-Skye bit her lip, took the glass vial, and held a strip of paper against it. "Name?" she asked.

Carey traced one finger methodically over Thresher's tattoo. "Experiment T."

Tears crept over Thresher's tightly squeezed eyes. A hatchet to the chest broke the fundamental blocks he'd built on the outside until he was a zoned and flattened city.

"Have you had extended contact with the experiment?" Carey asked Anna-Skye.

Her gray gaze glossed over with hurt but was edged in determination. "Some," she breathed. "He's adapted well to our society."

"Recommendations?"

"I think he's forgotten he's an experiment."

The other male spit on the floor. "Filthy mutation."

Carey nodded and stuck another needle in a small clear vial and filled up a syringe. Thresher thrashed because he knew the oncoming obsolete darkness of the shot like the back of his hand. "Please don't," he croaked. "Anna-Skye, please don't, I'm begging you, please don't do this."

Carey frowned and tilted Thresher's head to the side with a moist palm on his forehead. Thresher emitted a strangled moan as the tip pressed into his neck. The skin gave way, and the cooling sensation injected into his bloodstream. Eyelids drooped. Quick.

Maybe it was all a dream, this adventure of his, where Subject T played the hero. Such an imagination he had, such a mind for stories, creative to lose himself in fake memories, because it was easier to pretend and lie than live and weep—

36

Mako's arms throbbed as he carried Gela, nestled limp like a child, her head turned into his chest as if asleep back home. Before Mako cradled the stiffening body, Mama Milagros had pressed her eyelids closed and laid a lasting passionate kiss on her still lips. Now she walked beside him, gripping the spear in her hands. Knowing her, the bloodied wood would be whittled into a charm reminding her of a love passed.

He clenched his jaw so hard he heard it click. All the missed minutes and hours he spent *without* added up to a painstaking totaled number of lost moments. Crossing his home's threshold, he lowered Gela down to the swept floorboards. The chickens clucked and bobbed around their pen, the smell of sharp urea and dusty feathers coating the air. He wished it smelled like flowers. He wished he could have carried her up the stairs without resting. The sharp tugs from the stitches in his shoulder relaxed. His teardrops splashed like liquid jewels on Gela's face and he smeared away the bereavement, but it continued to build until he covered his mouth to hide the single sob that grew into a gasp.

Mama Milagros dropped to her knees and gently pulled Gela into her arms, her misery somehow greater than his, and whispered into her hair. With heavy legs, Mako blindly walked the endless flights to their penthouse to gather the wrappings, the ocher, holy water, anointing oil, and the shroud. The home, dark and silent, felt as if it waited for their return, prepared for new and now impossible evenings filled with laughter and arguments. Thresher's coat rested on the back of a chair, rebuilt with thick black panels. Mako balled the coat up and buried his face in the scentless wool. It didn't smell like either of them, but they had both put their hands on it at some point, Thresher's warmth and Gela's precision binding it all together.

He pulled away, his knees too weak. It was one of the greater efforts of his life, the will to momentarily let them go so he could function and complete his task. Gela's past lingered: her hanging pans, the ridiculous pink robe, the bookcase stuffed with recorded stories. He wasn't sure if he could do this, bury the woman that had made his home thrive. He laid the coat over the chair and smoothed the wrinkles. A rough tremble shook his hands. He didn't think it would stop anytime soon.

Back downstairs, he heard Mama Milagros sobbing. He'd never seen her stripped bare like that, emptied from the inside out. Kneeling, he used her tears and water to wipe away the blood from Gela's face. Mama Milagros battered his hands away, clutching Gela closer. "No," she said, her hair covering one eye.

"I don't want to, either," Mako said, "but we have to."

"It's not fair," Mama Milagros whispered. "It's not right that she's been taken from me. I've been good. I deserve more time."

"You've always been good." Mako barely got the words out.

"I wasn't supposed to love anyone like this," she said. "I'd been brought up as a revered child high on a pedestal, always knowing I was bound for sacrifice. My priestess left me in the desert, and I hid under the shade of a cactus for days, desperate for water, when the Bony Lady chose me. She sat beside me, and I promised her I'd be hers alone if she let me survive. It rained the next day—a flood that swept me out of the desert and into a valley. I kept my promise. I traveled, I lived within holy loneliness, only speaking with the Bony Lady, only loving *her*, until I found you two, until Gela found me." Mama Milagros covered her mouth. "The Bony Lady was jealous, but I broke my oath anyway, always knowing I'd pay the price, but I thought the price would be my life, not hers. I can't live without her."

Mako knew it would take hours to overcome what had to be done and shake him from the disbelief that today was the day he would send his grandmother to the afterlife. He stroked Gela's hair, the small exposed skin on her neck, while the hole of loss inside him whispered that there was no afterlife, that all of her personality was powered by electricity and sparkplugs, that souls were earth-bound and firecracker bright like stars. She had told him once that those twinkling lights in the night could very well be dead and what he saw wasn't actually alive, just a remaining resonance. That's what Gela had become. A resonance lighting up his past and projecting into his future with triggers like the rounded sponges of her homemade bath soaps, *rosehips*, the way her smile got when she drank too much gin, *pine needles*, and the slick beaded sweat coating her exposed shoulders when she worked in the garden too long, *rich transported dirt*.

"I know you can't," Mako finally choked out, "but you have to."

"It isn't fair. I prayed constantly. I should've known when Thresher arrived that he was the new prophet for the Bony Lady, and that she would take from me, remind me that I owed her a life because I didn't give her mine until death."

"Thresher?"

"He said he saw her," she whispered, leaning down to lay kisses across Gela's cheeks, down her neck and arms to the palms of her hands. "She came to him in his most desperate hour. Full of loneliness. Longing for love. He must've made a pact with her and she sent him you, Mako."

Mako dipped his fingers in the small vial of crushed red ocher and drew lines from Gela's eyes out to her hairline. He pushed until her head pointed to the east. It would take hours, but Mako refused to truly break down or digest Milagros's tale until Gela was ready. He eased off her well-worn boots to hold her heel in his lap.

Mama Milagros looked at Mako, her eyes red and shiny, irises dark pools that Mako could drown in. "Go outside, boy," she said roughly. "Go outside and wait."

"I can help," Mako said, flat and dead.

"It's my duty to dress her. She's my woman."

Mako nodded, despondent, trying not to shut down, but he couldn't quite control what he did and didn't do anymore. He petted Gela's feet and calves until Mama Milagros reached over and slapped his away, like Gela wasn't his loved one as well.

Shock. Maybe this was emotional shock. He frowned at Mama Milagros until she stood, pushed him outside, and sat him on the stoop. He watched the sun take away hours well into the night. He felt loose, flying, rattling, like internally he was nothing but broken glass that couldn't fit right together again, cursed with seven years of this. Seven years sitting on the porch sunk in loss like tar, thinking how to survive the next tragedy, devising an exit strategy to stop feeling this ever again.

37

Godspeed.

The cold air seared Thresher's nostrils, burning down his throat to coat his lungs with razors, making him wheeze. He dragged his despondent body over patches of rough and smooth sand and concrete, his fingers scraped raw. He didn't know where, only forward. Saliva trailed from his lower lip to the ground. His head rolled, too heavy for his neck, and he paused, feeling queasy.

Good wishes, his mind gasped. To a person starting a journey. *Godspeed.*

All the chained, memorized words zipped through his brain. He opened his mouth to release them, but his tongue had been trained in silence. He could only lay his open mouth to the ground in a penitent scream. The doctor had driven off in a cough of exhaust. He could still feel her handprint burning into his shoulder as she whispered, *Godspeed.*

Patches of blankness permeated his vivid motion sickness. His knees fishtailed back and forth, gravel shredding his skin. Each new sensation gripped him violently. The filtered, re-circulated air had vanished. His land of high concrete walls and stale cotton sheets disappeared into a wide, endless, uneven landscape. The arm curled under his chest ached and he looked up, trying to comprehend the wavering, distant shape standing like a tower far in front of him. He gagged on the vile stench of old vomit and dirty teeth. The mirage flickered, as if the body of bones was built of horizontal planks and those near the stomach kept getting shoved off-kilter to the side. She beckoned to him, and he crawled faster, sick on hope that she might be real, that she would wrap him in the cloak draped over her head and tell him he was safe. He craved safety like he never had before.

A careful touch made him open his eyes, the darkness cold and devastating around him. He squinted into the dim candlelight wavering above him. The ends of Anna-Skye's copper locks tickled his face. Her eyes flickered over him in pity, and he noted her yellowed skin, the dark circles, her teeth-scratched mouth downturned in a frown. Crouching, she filled the opened door of his cell, cradling her hurt hand. The bandages had been replaced and still looked clean. He watched her sway in time with the rocking of the ship.

"Do you have to go to the bathroom?" she asked.

Still gagged, he nodded. Mentioning his bladder, no less his colon, made him feel full enough to explode, even as his stomach gurgled with emptiness. She reached in and grabbed the knot between his bound hands and hauled him up. His knees ached, and an uncomfortable tingle flooded his numbed hands. She took the end of the loose noose slung around his neck and tugged. He moaned as his legs nearly buckled, his shoulder smacking the metal spokes of the cage. A cow being led to slaughter.

She stayed three steps ahead of him, rope curving into a slack U between them. The chain hobbling his ankles clanked on the mismatched wood and metal planks. He sucked in deep breaths smelling of mildew, tangy body sweat, and the permeating presence of ocean salt. She guided him up a narrow set of rickety stairs out into the blinding sunlight. Red splotches burned the inside of his eyelids. He couldn't handle the brightness after his time below decks, and he squinted at the oversaturated world.

Large sinewy men—wearing tattered, mismatched rags, knives strapped to belts, tattooed shoulders—glared at him in passing.

Blink.

Tall masts creaked above him, swaying with the breeze. Open and full, patched sails bulged like a belly.

Blink.

He put so much trust in his captor, to lead him safely.

Blink.

The nose of the ship dove frighteningly into the oncoming, white-capped waves. One broke over the top and wiped the deck with a film of seawater. Thresher lifted his toes up and away from the cold.

Blink.

To his right, a young man, his leathered skin roughened elderly, knelt over a bucket. Black rags moved from the bucket to the deck, sweeping refuse down into the open slats overlooking the ocean.

Blink.

The man wore a red coat. Thresher stared at the tarnished buttons, the way the coat tails slopped against the back of the man's thighs, darkened and sopping with feces and urine.

Anna-Skye prodded Thresher forward, and he hobbled out as far as his chain would allow. She angled her face away. Thresher understood, just as he would if food were placed in front of a blindfolded starving man. He fumbled with the linen pants barely staying on his hips, slid them down to his knees, knotted hands pawing at each leg. The stench of rot and sun-warmed shit made him wince, just as the toss and roll of the dipping bow made his stomach flip-flop. He tottered on uneasy legs, hoping that his squat wouldn't push him into the ocean.

"You're a curious experiment, aren't you?" Anna-Skye asked, voice pitched higher for simple conversation. "Were you trained to infiltrate the tribes and assimilate into our culture? Make us at ease with what you are?"

Thresher didn't respond, his bowels aching with relief so close at hand. He wondered if he should take the risk and leap over the side. Would he be able to paddle to shore? Or sink and drown?

"I don't see how they thought we would accept outsiders when we enslave our enemies." She jutted her chin out to the cowering redcoat, who bowed his head so far down his hair trailed in the waste. Thresher blanched, even as he felt a powerful release inside him. The ocean churned below, and he watched the blue splatter with brown and black.

Anna-Skye gently tugged on his chain reminding him he wasn't better than that slave. No, he was below that.

"This boy's great-something-grandfather used to be a guard on this ship, one of many fooled into thinking he would return to the mainland after they set the convicts out to sea. It was an equal oppor-tunity world, you know, men and women alike responsible for the prisoners."

Thresher stood and fumbled with his cock, desperately trying to aim where he wouldn't dribble down his leg.

"After the revolt, the guards became the zoo animals. The new Wallabout tribe bred them to be good, taught them to be loyal, showed them they were society's dregs, too, ironically handpicked to deal with criminals."

Thresher winced, feeling a days' long burn shoot out, too yellow. He shuddered, completely empty now, and felt grateful when a wave splashed over the bow, the cold cleansing him. He pawed his pants up, and tried to slurp back the trails of saliva dripping from the gag that dug into the corner of his mouth.

"It terrified me," she whispered, "that a thing like you, with the disease you have, got out before you were modified. I hate that you made it to my home, defiled my people, and made me have to tell Mako about Nika." She yanked the chain, making Thresher touch one knee to the floorboards to catch himself. "You're part of the reason Gela's dead."

"Anna, what are you doing?" A broad man removed the lead from Anna-Skye's grip, fixing her with a glare. "You should be resting."

"No time for that," Anna-Skye snapped, hand to her belly. "I'm not an invalid."

"We can't take the chance," the man hovered over her, not touching, but seeking reassurance until she twined her good hand with his.

"We're alright," she said, smile fluttering between sweetness and beloved annoyance. "Nothing's going to happen, Paul. Carey did good work on me. I might be a few fingers shorter than when we met, but chances are you'll still love me."

"You can't take chances," Paul repeated, tattoos on the tops of his shoulders. "What if something happened, what if that creature attacked you..."

She smiled fully and kissed him.

Thresher looked down, words like *inbred* and *incest* flipping to the forefront of his brain. Paul's worry made sense. A ship was a nasty place to care for newborns, rife with infections after the woman's birthing trials, especially with minimal nutritious food and barrels of poorly cared for water. Generations of living in one clan all in one space could cause genetic mixing, unintended or not. He wondered if maybe the enslaved guards were bred as pack mules for labor, but that still wouldn't stop the crew's lineage from going extinct.

This was why the Facility outlawed touch, made sex a hush-hush topic the experiments were too confused to sift through. They wanted to select the genes. They wanted evolution to hand over the reins.

If the Facility truly had their hands on him, he would be steam-cleaned, shaved, scrubbed, and stuck in a decontamination chamber for days as he sweated out the toxins, eradicating every speck clinging to him, scorched-earth style.

Once they finished with him, he would find Nika, track her down, and get her out. Hopefully, she would have a sense of direction once she was on the outside again. He'd find the doctor who released him and demand to know what she gained from giving him freedom. All wasn't lost. Stepping over the bow in an act of quasi-suicide would be stupid. He could almost see the alarm on Mako's face and tried not to smile.

Thresher's time was up. Paul handed the lead back to Anna-Skye. Thresher waddled back, barely sparing a glance at the man cleaning the deck. Anna-Skye pulled her lower lip between her teeth. Thresher tried to memorize anything beyond the cell she was sentencing him back to. Sunlight warmed his cheeks. He counted four clouds whipped a creamy white. Eyes raked over him from all corners, but he ignored the intrusiveness.

Anna-Skye pulled him back into the darkness, stuffy with stale fear and straw. The door to his cell creaked as she opened it. Black moss covered the bars. Her hatred seemed to have softened.

"I almost feel sorry for you," she said. "I don't think it's right for an animal not to know his fate when he can understand and sense death. You have ALS, Experiment T. Carey told me today. You've got ALS."

The verdict hit Thresher in the gut like a punch. He remained suspended between exhausted collapse and a high recovery, thinking there was no way he could've known. He had never known an experiment with amyotrophic lateral sclerosis, only knew those affected with those kinds of disorders—the kind that stripped away control, left the senses intact but transformed the body into a prison—were taken away to be cared for gently when the disease got bad. It made sense. The numbed mouth. The shaking weakness he felt on and off.

When Subject V forgot his name and smiled dumbly before slapping Thresher hard enough to draw blood, the attendees took him away carefully, muttering that his Alzheimer's had progressed too far, never to be seen again. Thresher knew those experiments had their last contributions added to their chart before an orderly pulled a mask over their nose and mouth to welcome a drug-induced coma in the forgetting room.

That was his fate.

He didn't fight as Anna-Skye put him back in his cage and shut the door, or when she undid his gag and placed bread on his twitching tongue. He understood now, what it meant to be doomed, and wished he had no knowledge of it at all.

38

When Mako turned fourteen, Gela showed him the family gun.

Nika sat next to him on Gela's bed, her leg bouncing in anticipation. Gela opened the ancient safe embedded in the bedroom's wall. *An heirloom,* Gela explained, as she popped the gun's case open and removed the weapon from its cushion. *The last of its kind.* The magazine fell out with an oiled click. She emptied it, made them inspect the bullets, taught them how to load, how to shoot outside.

Pulling the trigger caused vibrations all the way into his ribs. He tried to keep his wrists steady and absorb the recoil. When Nika shot, he noticed the differences between them, something that reflected himself but made her a separate person. She hated the gun. Said the gunshot sounded like a pop in the universe, but he knew the real reason lay with the falling thumps and blasted holes in the debris they shot. He thought it too—same sound as when their mother collapsed, same jarring shock of her skull cracking open.

The gun never scared him. In his hands, he had the power to protect.

Gela collected the shells and showed them how to clean the gun before nestling it back beside the stacks of glossy ammunition boxes. Practice kept the knowledge fresh, but it had been two years since he'd felt the smoothed handle.

Now, the gun eased into his hands. Battle ready. He tucked it into its hip holster and packed away his grief, readying his bags like he wouldn't see home for a very long time. He closed the door, noting that with the shades drawn, the place felt so lonely.

A void encompassed him, into which he placed everything that didn't center on retrieving Thresher and Nika. To lose one was unacceptable. To lose two was fate pulling his chain. He intended to respond with war.

Downstairs and outside, he met the warm embraces and tears of families he hadn't seen in so long. Mama Milagros knelt before Gela, now committed to the sky. The tribe milled around him to say their respects and recall tales of Gela the storyteller, Gela the wordsmith,

Gela the mother, but they also whispered, *Mako, what happened? Mako, where have you been?*

He put a hand over his mouth. Hot breath made his palm sweat. "It was the Wallabouts." He repeated it, his voice stronger. "The Wallabouts attacked our land, our people." He stepped up onto a pile of bricks and looked out over the familiar faces he'd grown up with. "They killed my blood, one of our tribe's wise women who sought to make us a better people, make Manahatta a better place. They captured a dear friend of mine. We must fight back, prove we are not to be preyed on."

As a child, Mako had heard a similar speech when the tribal wars neared a bloody end, but instead of fierce, dedicated cries, he only saw resignation.

Anna-Skye's father, Ian, stepped forward to clap Mako on the shoulder. "We can't," he said. "The Wallabouts are transient. How would we attack them? Track them? Defeat an enemy with the water smarts they have?"

"Your daughter allied with them," Mako hissed. "She's a traitor to the Manahatta way of life, to its people."

Ian's face tightened as if Mako had punched him. "Don't speak lies, son. You disrespect your grandmother."

"What truth do you need? She told me. I watched her betrayal with my own eyes. She helped attack and capture my friend. She brought this war on our heads!"

"No one will pick up weapons, risk our children, abandon our gardens to battle. You're a child of war, Mako. It's all you know. You lost so much to it. Now, we have children of peace. We won't stand with you and lose what's ours." Ian stepped back.

The elders turned their backs first, a sign of rejection, until everyone faced away from him. Mako wanted to scream. Where had their warriors gone? He'd said it to Thresher, once. *We're a fucking island, a fucking rock, nothing can touch us.*

Except for fear.

He should've seen it in their rules, how they gave up on those who strayed from the island. He felt like he'd been thrown off a cliff, and wished Thresher was here to tell him, *I'm on your side.*

Mako would never get used to that, but he had a kiss to reconcile and his family to save and avenge. He knew what he had to do. Where he had to go. The water beckoned him to cross it, and step foot where his enemies were in power and his life lay on the line once more.

Mako paused as he pulled the canoe free from its ties, motioning Mama Milagros to stay back. The dead Shinnecoe woman still lay under the twisted tree, tacky blood staining the ground around her, her arms crossing her stomach. He should have felt a pang of guilt, but the sentiment was so far back on his list of priorities it only registered as uneasiness. Mama Milagros peered over his shoulder. "A warning?" she asked.

Mako shook his head, but he didn't want to tell the truth about the slain woman. "I've angered the Bruykleeners enough that they'd rather slit my throat than leave warnings."

Mama Milagros bit her lip. "What are we walking into, Mako?"

Mako helped her into the canoe. "I made deals that I broke. I killed many Bruykleen tribesmen. If we aren't shot as soon as we land, I'll be surprised."

"But they helped you before, when you searched for Nika."

"Soul-Dago helped me," Mako clarified. "The Bruykleeners probably would've punished him if they knew. He brought me clues, made the introductions to the slave traders, but I never knew where he got his initial information. This time, I don't have years to waste navigating to the Promised Land. He's the only one I can think of who knows where to start."

Milagros made a sound in the back of her throat. The dog-human slave's wild rambling filled Mako's mind. The rest of the journey continued in silence until the canoe sluiced through the final wave and scraped onshore before dusk. Bay water splashed his boot leather dark. His body strung tight as a wire, he waited for a war cry, the twang of a released arrow, and expected to see a spear penetrating his chest like Gela's. He had sailed slowly enough that any scouts would have had time to report, but nothing met them except silence.

Mama Milagros tottered out, as edgy in the water as Thresher had been, and stretched her legs. Mako dragged the hollowed log safely into the brush. He swallowed hard, and carefully picked his way up the hill, keeping Milagros behind him. Each step had the hairs on his nape standing up. His hands itched to hold his knife, but he kept them loose and at his sides. Shadows crept over the beach. A ringing took up in his ears.

They scaled the hill and followed the pathway leading them further into the tribe's dilapidated city center. Mako remembered the odd concrete circle that might've been a park or a monument at one time.

Once, Soul-Dago had brought him through it when they snuck out to meet with the Reckowackies. Now, it felt like he knowingly followed a path leading to his own execution.

Buildings rose on all sides of them. He squinted, looking up, seeing the broken windows fill with faces. A chill ran up his spine. Out of the alleys, Bruykleeners emerged. His stomach dropped in fear and he pulled Milagros closer. They wouldn't have a second chance. If the tribe fought them, there would be no escape.

Inside, his gut urged him to fight. His feet squarely faced his enemy as his old rage used his fear as kindling, fanning into flames. Even if he was a child of war, it still wasn't fair. He had lost almost everyone, his tribe had turned from him, and now he was forced to crawl and beg *again* for help from those who slaughtered his mother. If the Bruykleeners wanted to attack him, he would go down fighting, but he didn't want to waste precious time *playing games.*

"Soul-Dago!" he yelled. "I call on you, Soul-Dago!"

His voice reverberated off the buildings. The peering faces glared at him in silence.

"You helped me before," he screamed. "You told me you did it because you tasted the blood of my mother when she died and you always felt her grief. Grief destroys me now. I come without the blessing of my tribe to ask for your help."

He felt as if he could hear the whole tribe exhale as one. Silence persisted. Mama Milagros clutched his wounded shoulder, sending a throbbing ache down his arm. For an instant, he was paralyzed with the belief that his enemies had turned their backs on him too. "You owe me this. Maybe, when you lose what you've earned, we can stand on the same field and call it even ground."

The crowd parted. Soul-Dago strode out, his black hair pulled tight and braided, black and red paint splitting the symmetry of his face. Mako smirked, remembering when Soul-Dago donned the paint, so long ago, the red a tribute to his homeland, the black to those who had been lost. "I owe you *nothing*," Soul-Dago roared.

Mako's chest heaved. He felt out of breath. "Where did you get your information? Who put you into contact with the slave traders?"

"I saw you coming, Mako Saddlerock," Soul-Dago said, pointing his finger, his eyes flaring in anger. "I asked my seers why the Manahatta shark won't leave me alone. It's because you aren't tied to the land. You're rudderless, a wanderer without a purpose."

"I have a purpose," Mako snarled and slapped the pointed finger out of his face. "I need to go to the Promised Land and save my sister and my friend."

"Your friend," Soul-Dago scoffed. "The one who killed our people? Why should I help you find more Bruykleen slayers?"

"Do you know how to get there?" Mako asked, hating the rough edge of desperation making his voice hoarse. He grabbed Soul-Dago's shoulders, nearly shaking him.

Soul-Dago smiled at him.

"What do you want?" Mako asked. "I'll give you anything. Do you understand? *Anything.*"

"Join my tribe," Soul-Dago said, breaking Mako's grip. "You're a strong warrior, a good leader. Renounce your Manahatta ties and come under my command."

Revulsion instantly filled him. "Never."

"You're a handful of contradictions, Mako."

"I'll give you my water rights to Manahatta's freshwater." He swallowed hard. His tribe would never take him back. Anna-Skye was right—he would always be reckless and burn the world for the select few he loved.

Soul-Dago rubbed the back of his neck, as if trying to conceal his pleasure. The Bruykleeners hooted in approval. "And the rest of the night with your bruja."

"*Fuck you.*"

"I want to know her prophecies," Soul-Dago said. "My seers say a tribe will perish in the Promised Land. Does your bruja foresee that the sharks will make a wasteland of us? That's what I've been told, and I believe it, like I believe in the ground beneath my feet. Like I believe that the world has died, but it is surviving like us, trying to live like us."

Mako heard Mama Milagros gasp. Her hand tightened on Mako's shoulder. "Yes," she whispered, too soft at first. "Yes, I agree to this."

Mako shut his eyes, hated that he still trusted in Soul-Dago's *integrity*, but Mama Milagros pushed him out of the way and stood before Soul-Dago. "We accept your deal."

39

O nce upon a time," Soul-Dago said, "this island was a sanctuary, but even before the environmental holocaust, it became infected with the souls of disease-ridden ghosts."

Mako rolled his eyes and matched Soul-Dago's rhythm as they paddled toward the small island between Manahatta and Bruykleen. He was head-sick of all the tarot-reading bullshit, heartsick for Gela and Thresher, and plain sick from a night spent sleeping on the concrete, going crazy thinking about what Mama Milagros was doing in Soul-Dago's home.

"What happened last night?" Mako asked in a low voice to Mama Milagros, who sat next to him.

"He wanted me to read his future," she whispered.

"You don't do stuff like that."

"I speak with spirits," she said. "I see the dead. I was raised to be a prophet, Mako. I saw the same things his seers see."

"Have you read my future," Mako said, "and not told me?"

"Of course." Mama Milagros smiled sadly. "You want to know what I saw? I saw Thresher."

"Fucking sharks." Mako's jaw clenched in frustration and he wondered how he was supposed to ask the real question burning in his gut. "Did he...are you...?" He paused. "Are you okay?"

"Yes." She put her hand on his arm "Yes. I love you, Mako."

He opened his mouth to say it back, but the canoe scraped onshore. A wall of freezing air hit him as he stepped on the muddy bank, and he helped Soul-Dago pull the boat into the vivacious overgrowth. Stretched spider webs brushed the back of his neck, sending his skin crawling.

Mako scanned the leafy trees and white-flowered bushes, his body strung tight and shoulders hunched up high. He could feel the wrongness of the place under the façade of peace. Suddenly the cream petals were bright, curious eyes, and he swore something substantial with teeth stalked him from behind.

"You wanted to know where I got my information. It comes from there." Soul-Dago pointed to a huge, ivy-strangled building near the bank. Brown bricks, too small for their crumbling mortar and rounded like river stones, snuggled against grayed-white ones.

"Who lives there?" Mako asked, a tingling sensation encompassing his mind. The haunted presence reminded him of the swamp woman who had taught him the ways of a haint.

"You'll see," Soul-Dago said, with a snide smile. "Something wrong, Mako? I thought you'd give anything to know what I do."

Mako smiled, knew it to be ugly, and recalled the snap of breaking bones. "Still holds true."

Soul-Dago's look turned to one of concern, but he bade them follow him into the huge house. Inside, a collapsed roof made a ragged O peering up into the sky. The floor, rotten and soft as corkboard, creaked alarmingly under Mako's feet. He nudged rocks, dirt, and the slivers of picked over mice bones. "This is Kashana's lair," Soul-Dago said softly. "I befriended her a long time ago, when I needed guidance. She will know what you seek."

"Mako's mother still haunts you," Mama Milagros said softly.

"Her death was brutal." Soul-Dago flexed his hand into a fist.

The staircase's banister lay splintered on the ground. Mako swayed from one skeleton of a step to the next, suspended above the earth that wouldn't hold him if he fell. Mama Milagros's black cloak snagged on splinters sharp as stakes until she gathered the material and held it in one hand. She bent down with a small sound of surprise and picked up a cracked porcelain face of a doll.

Moldy wallpaper hung in strips off the walls. Dried leaves, some bright orange and yellow, others gray as ash, piled in the corners. Old books, with wasted paper and covers broken down to cardboard, lingered half-open. He caught sight of fragile, spindly chairs, shards of broken glass kicked in from the windows, and the curled remains of a songbird.

He thought there would be more silence, but he filled the space by breathing, the rustle of his sleeve brushing the crumbling corners, his slow step as he tested his weight on the water-damaged floorboards. His heart galloped in his chest like wild horses.

Soul-Dago paused in front of an open room and motioned for them to stay back. The door jams had rusted off. "Kashana," he called. "Soul-Dago has come with friends, seeking your wisdom. May we enter?"

"Yes," a soft voice said. A strange whirring emanated from the room, followed by a yellow glow flickered out into the hallway.

A tic started in Mako's jaw. Soul-Dago met his eyes, as if to confirm his commitment, and Mako nodded. Soul-Dago motioned them to follow him into the room, which looked like a new world compared to the derelict house. Bright lights strung across the ceiling, kept alive and together by wires connected to a big box with spinning gears. A tall woman—Kashana—bent over a long bench full of book stacks and odd equipment. Bulbous tumors covered her face and pushed against the thick, metallic collar swinging around her neck. Behind her, a map crafted from torn out paper was tacked up on the wall, looking like a malformed claw reaching into the ocean.

Kashana carefully placed a small vial into a machine made of cobbled together parts and closed the lid. The machine whirred and Mako shuddered, wondering if this was something from the past or future.

"Kashana," Soul-Dago said, "we come for your knowledge of your homeland."

"You came once before asking for knowledge of the west and south," she said, her voice lovely and strong. "Now you wish to know more of the east? Soul-Dago, it seems to me you have a wandering soul." She stepped away from the bench.

"It's for my...friend." He gestured to Mako.

Mako pushed down the lump in his throat when he saw the misshapen string of numbers and letters tattooed on her pustuled skin. *Do you want to know all about my trauma, Mako?* "Did the Promised Land do this to you?" he whispered.

She looked taken aback for a moment and then burst into laughter. "Unfortunately, it was your outside land that did this. I drank water directly from the back canals. Dying of dehydration will make you do stupid things."

Mako blanched. Nothing would induce him to sip from those black-tainted waterways. In his mind, Gela's voice recited the old story of the monster beneath the bridge.

"I still remember how it tasted," Kashana continued. "Disgusting. Someday, these things will grow so big that they'll push against the tracker and I'll suffocate or the pressure will break my neck." She tapped the collar. "It stopped sending data back to the Facility years ago."

"Are you..." Mako swallowed hard, "a slave like the other experiments?"

"You know a lot for an outsider. I was one of the first batches released from the Facility. They wanted to test how far we could go, map our location, see if any of the tribes would integrate us. From what I've seen of the subsequent releases, the experiments have gotten dumber and crazier, or maybe they're simply untrained. At least I knew how to find food and water. Not the right kind, mind you." Her blue eyes twinkled in humor. "I found this spot, made it my own, and lived in relative peace until the Bruykleeners started leaving offerings for me. Soul-Dago's the first one to brave speaking with me."

"My tribe is superstitious," Soul-Dago said.

"*You* are superstitious," Kashana said fondly, "but I value your company."

"Mako wishes to reach the Promised Land," Soul-Dago said. "His friend has been captured and he needs to free him."

Kashana's eyes narrowed and she pushed her brown hair out of her face. "I understand now. I assume your friend was a Facility experiment, then?"

Mako nodded. Mama Milagros grabbed his hand.

"Interesting. You don't resemble the other tribes I've known, so he must've gotten farther than most. Are you sure he didn't go back to report? Perhaps he'd fulfilled his purpose?"

"No," Mako said sharply. "He didn't want to go back."

Kashana shrugged and lumbered back to her bench. The strange mechanics made a loud click and the top popped open. "They won't trade you anything for him."

"I don't intend to trade," Mako snapped. "I'm going to take him back, by force if necessary."

Kashana shook her head in amusement. "What will you trade me for my information?"

Mako clenched his fist and locked eyes with Soul-Dago. He hadn't brought anything of value, he didn't know what Kashana valued in the first place.

"Mako volunteers for experimentation," Soul-Dago said.

"Excellent," Kashana said.

What the fuck does that mean? Mako mouthed to Soul-Dago.

"I've been working on a new vaccine," Kashana continued. "Two women from the east came my way riddled with a new disease, and I tested it on them, but I won't ever know the outcome. You have to promise he'll come back so I can gather the data."

"Of course," Soul-Dago said. "He'll need the medicines that work, of course, if you want him to come back alive."

Kashana pursed her lips. "I didn't think of that. The Facility *is* full of biohazards. I'll be low on supplies, afterwards. Maybe you can bring me back some things? I'll make a list."

"Sure," Mako said. "If I'm going to be pricked and riddled with Facility shit, I might as well make a day of it." He shoved Soul-Dago's shoulder. Immovable as a rock.

Soul-Dago glared at him. "You said *anything.*"

Kashana opened an ice box, pulled out racks of tubes, and began warming them with her hands. She motioned Mako to sit on a rickety chair. Mako took his backpack and satchel off, rolled his sleeves up. He shivered in the cool air, but shot Mama Milagros a winning smile.

"What are you doing?" he asked, as Soul-Dago knelt between his knees.

"Trust me, you'll want me here." Soul-Dago wound a thick piece of rope around Mako's biceps, making his veins bulge, and then bound his wrists to the chair.

"I don't trust you."

Soul-Dago bared his teeth as Kashana walked around Mako and began pulling liquid from her tiny vials, humming as she tapped his veins, and slid needles under his skin.

"What's she putting into me?"

"All *kinds* of things," Kashana said. "I've never had this opportunity before. I'm going to use it to the fullest potential."

"Mako." Soul-Dago snapped his fingers, distracting Mako from the needles sliding in and out of his arm. "I wanted to ask you about your time in the Woodlands."

"You always know how to say the right thing to piss me off."

"You nearly crushed my skull when we last met," Soul-Dago said. "I've never seen such fury from you. You've changed since you left the islands. It's the last thing I'll ask for."

Kashana's voice spoke above him and mingled with Mama Milagros's tone. "Is she getting the directions?" Mako asked.

"Yes," Soul-Dago said. "How do you feel?"

Mako laughed, wanting nothing else than to shock Soul-Dago and downright terrify him. A familiar sensation began to creep over him. The same kind that filled him when he put on the mask of the haint, letting it control him so he could pretend it wasn't Mako slicing tied-up men, wasn't Mako torturing souls in a swamp where no one could hear them scream. He lunged forward, lurching the chair, and knew he possessed the storytelling chops to horrify the Bruykleener warrior.

"I was forced to fight in the Woodland wars, and when I was captured, I wasn't slaughtered or turned around and forced to fight the army I had just come from. I was taken to a swampland, where I met a woman, alone like this, cruel like this. She tied a mask to my face. My breath bounced off the inside of it and covered my face in hot dampness. In that time, I felt *Mako* become a passenger. I thought I could do anything when *he* was hidden."

He fought to touch his face, but Soul-Dago held him down. He suddenly wanted to bang against the walls, break down this old mansion even more, part the silence and howl into it. Kashana had awakened the haint in Mako's body with her needles and potions and tests. How could he describe what it felt like to be hainted? He would show Soul-Dago, like he'd shown those poor bastards in the swamps who brought their long deaths upon themselves—they should've told him outright what he wanted to know, not make him carve it out of them—that this Woodlands-bloodied Mako Saddlerock was not to be played with.

"She told me to *open up*. Feel the in-between. She said to me: *I would've told you the consequences, but you wouldn't have listened anyway. The spirit is coming. You've opened up for it, so easy, so good for it, and it's coming in quick. You'll be ridden hard, but you must remember your name.*"

He would have laughed if he didn't feel so unsettled. Something had gotten in the marrow of his bones to kick out blood cells malformed with this strangeness growing inside. He swallowed hard and felt every bend in his body itch for a stretch, from his knuckles to the backs of his knees.

"Mako," Soul-Dago commanded, grabbing Mako's head and holding him steady. Mako twisted, arched away uselessly.

"*This isn't going to be easy, but it will* feel *easy, do you understand?*" Mako continued quoting, mimicking the female voice. He felt dizzy and full, like something else had settled inside him and tested the small confines of his body. "I got good at it, at the torture she showed me. I'd have a human tied up before me. I'd bring out a small wooden doll and show them exactly what I was going to do to them and then I stretched it out for days. They always knew what was coming but didn't know when. Do you have monsters in your old tribal tales? I became those monsters. People were deer that I stalked with panting breaths. I wanted them in my mouth. Wanted to taste the way their flesh surrendered under my teeth.

"It took days to break the slavers who traded Tarek to the war. Hours to learn Nika wasn't among them. Soon enough, simply seeing my face made the Woodland slavers scared enough to set up a meeting with the Reckowackies."

The binds around his wrists loosened. The world wavered. Mama Milagros stood in front of him, her mouth moving, but he had a hard time listening. He didn't know what to do with all the sensations around him. She gripped his shoulders hard enough to knead the tight muscles into a bruise. He wanted to look at the moon in ways he never thought possible. A sweet smell wafted up his nostrils. The world sharpened so that his head spun before narrowing down to Kashana drawing a trail with her finger along the map on the wall, tapping a spot near the sharpest point of the claw. He had the unmistakable urge to run east.

He felt lanky, powerful, on edge. He could smell fear in the air, marinated with expectation. A low growl rumbled in his throat. Mama Milagros clutched papers, instructions, and directions. The white showed around Soul-Dago's dark eyes, but he grabbed Mako and dragged him out the door, away from the science witch.

What was the old saying? The game, oh yes, the *game* was afoot. Mako grinned a rictus skull smile.

40

A sharp grip on Walker's arm made him think it was Nika roaring awake from a second nightmare, but she was still soft in the cradle of his arms, her eyes blue moons from sleepless bruises, soft hair piled like a pillow under her cheek. Sheltered under a lean-to the Enders had built after they fled the mother of monsters' home, Walker glanced up and saw Tova leaning over him, fever heat radiating from her hand and into his shoulder, spreading like an injection.

She put a finger to her lips. "Need to talk to you," she whispered. "Without her."

Walker hesitated. He didn't have instincts; this he knew. He would have drunk to all the Enders' health had Nika not put a hand over it and bade him wait. He didn't have survival instincts like she did, leaving him raw and innocent to the brutality of the *outside*. He didn't believe Tova would hurt him but wasn't sure. She had cut his bonds, at least. He now thought in terms of "what would Nika do?" in such situations. He had also learned that what Nika lacked, he more than made up for in wonder.

"Okay," he told Tova, extracting himself from Nika. The rest of the End slumbered in a pile away from them. Walker thought someone had been on watch.

Nika pretended not to care, made sure Walker knew she didn't need him, but when it came to times like these, bedtime comforts, she made sure he stayed close. It gave him the shakes, that absolute certainty that he was *needed*, and he complied in any way he could. He watched her like a hawk, offering her strength in the exact moment she craved it, and loved the way the crease digging a deep crevice in her forehead eased smooth when he succeeded.

Although he had engaged in simple comforts like that with his doctor, with Nika, comfort felt more basic, more innocent, like something that would have been shared with someone who had come to expect it from a young age, maybe for forever.

She was deep asleep though, and he took the extra moments to soothe her subconscious, mentally telling her he would be right back while piling his cloak around her shoulders. He stepped outside, eyes immediately going up.

It astounded him, the openness of the sky. In between slashes of thick gray clouds, he could see sublime glimpses of stars. Sometimes he wanted to go to his knees with the amount of love he had for them.

Tova touched his shoulder, guiding him deeper into the darkness.

"You're one of them, aren't you?" she asked. Her hair had been singed and wet ash covered her face like a mask.

"One of what?" Walker asked, playing coy, tilting his head down so his hair fell over his forehead. Made him look young. Made him look pretty.

"One of the Facility's experiments gone wrong."

"Not wrong at all," Walker corrected. "You have to know the exact environmental conditions to predict if you're going to come out right."

He never felt wrong. He wasn't right on the outside—not quite male and not quite female—but inside, where it counted, he never felt like an abomination.

"But they grew you with something else, didn't they? *Compassion. Wonder.* Like a sun spot on your soul." She held up her cards and tapped the dark splotch in the corner. It looked bigger this time, the fish-shape bloated until it resembled an infinity sign.

Walker's eyebrows came together. He didn't understand these prophecies and legends that permeated the air. They filled the tribes with fear and put them on edge for no good reason.

"I think you're going to toss their little scientific methods to the wind," she continued, eyes bright with inner light. "The monsters told me so. I saw you—the future you—in the broken mirrors when you entered the room. The Facility thinks they need a solution built on breeding and bone, but they've crafted a leader, instead."

Maybe it wasn't the smartest idea to come out here. Walker hedged back toward the shelter. Back toward Nika.

"They've probably made the most important human of our generation," she continued, voice pitched low, "and they don't know it yet because you're not *perfect*."

"What am I supposed to do with this information?" he asked. He didn't understand what to do with the data she just handed him. It was an outlier.

"I don't know," Tova said. "When I learned that the water beasts were coming for Jake, I told him. Now I'm telling you. You're meant for great things."

He nodded and walked back to the lean-to quickly, filled with an unnatural uneasiness he couldn't quite place. He glanced back one last time. Tova settled on the ground, her head up to the sky. Waiting.

Inside, Nika sat up, eyes haunted and wide.

He slid under the cloak and felt her heat like a furnace. She folded into his arms like she had been waiting a very long time. He knew this softness wouldn't last, but the night sometimes gave him miracles.

"Dreamed I was chasing something," she whispered against his collarbone.

"What?"

"Dreamed I took it between my teeth and tore it to bits. Felt frenzied. Felt unhinged."

He stroked her hair and tried to ease the fine shivers running up and down her body.

"Probably Tova's throat," he finally said. "You don't particularly like her."

Her soft laugh eased his apprehensions. Miracles and terror, that was all the night was good for.

Nika's scream of rage launched Walker out of his slumber and he bolted upright. He saw from the shelter of the lean-to Nika on her knees, her hands bound once more and a rope around her neck. The tribe fanned out around her, bracketing them on all sides. Nika's lip curled in distain. Jake furiously smoked through two bible pages before Milo took the tobacco pouch away. Jake coughed, the last dregs of gray smoke huffing out his nose. The noise sounded wet and rough, alarming.

The taste of smoke and ashes lingered in the back of Walker's throat, a roughness that made him try twice to find his voice. He stood and walked into the drizzle of rain. "What's happening?" he asked, but by the pleased look on Tova's face, he already knew it could be nothing good.

Tova smiled when she saw him and beckoned him over.

"If you do this, you're no better than the Facility," Nika growled, and it sent chills up Walker's spine to hear that edge in her voice. He had heard it in the Facility, a kind of rough, creeping insanity that flavored her tone when she nearly killed his doctor.

"Think about it," Tova said to Jake. "I know you have a sweet heart, Jakey, but let these two go free and the next thing you know, they're singing like larks and selling information, leveraging your lies to earn preferential treatment with the Promised Land. They'll take everything from you. Best thing to do would be to integrate them."

"Gotta protect ourselves," Beau said from behind her.

"You've a smooth tongue, Tova." Milo's fists clenched, but it seemed he learned his lesson from his previous outburst.

"It worked out well for you before," Tova said, gesturing to Milo. "Your killer child has turned into such a man."

Milo grimaced. "My tribe was dead."

"Yet you took to the End life, as will they. After all, the rest of you are related in one way or another. What will that do to the integrity of the tribe?"

Nika screeched and fought against her bonds. "I'll never be your slave. I'm *Manahatta.*"

"Milo turned into a natural leader," Tova said, putting a hand around Walker's shoulders, "and this one has incredible potential."

Walker couldn't help but smile at the praise, but it died when Nika's eyes shot daggers at him. Her teeth bared in a snarl, and the memory of her surrounded by this outsider tribe, exchanging her Facility clothes for theirs, her naked skin lit with gooseflesh while a coal-tipped stick threatened his vision hit Walker like a bolt of lightning. Ferocity, thy name is Nika.

"Who wants to integrate?" Jake asked quietly and everyone but Milo and Tobey raised their hands.

"If you decide you don't want the girl," Tova said, "we can trade her to the Wallabouts. My people regularly exchange goods and bounties with them. We're supposed to meet in a few days' time. But," Tova looked around sadly, "my people have abandoned me. If only I knew an escort who could guide me through these woods."

"Why should I take you anywhere?" Jake asked, but Walker knew the weakness shading his eyes. Affection colored Jake's frown, and whatever hold the red-haired monster mother held on him was deep and old. Walker wielded power like that once with his doctor and shuddered with aghast pleasure to think that Nika held it over him.

"I have a reputation to maintain, trade post or not. I'll need to rebuild my empire," Tova said. "Can't do that without something to barter. Maybe I'll be able to negotiate for some of those medicines you've been needing. I'm sure they have something for that leg pain of Maggie's."

"So, you're going to sell us back to them? Think you'll get a nice dress for me? One fucking cigarette?" Nika said.

Jake nudged Milo as Milo's mouth crooked up into a small smile. "Just one, eh? I bet we could get *two*."

Tova grinned at her. "Not much has changed." She turned back to Jake, spoke to him in hushed tones about directions while Milo glared at her and drew up to his full height, seeming to shelter Jake.

Walker pushed his glasses up and knelt beside Nika, careful not to spook her, and reached for her. Her fire crazed him. It was one of the reasons he was obsessed with the outside, a place where nothing was clean, everything was live or die, and the earth seemed endless. Here he was finally living, instead of tasting. He'd be happy to stay with this tribe, learn their ways and customs, but Nika had a family waiting for her, a brother who existed on the other side of this world.

She jerked away from him. Fury colored her cheeks. He thought of leaving her, forging his own path, but his gut clenched, reminding him that she knew how to sate the wanderlust igniting his veins.

Beau stood in front of him. "Do I need to tie you too?" He sounded tired.

Walker held out his arms. "I guess you better."

41

Mako couldn't quite remember anything, but he knew everything in the exact moment it happened. The unforgiving concrete shifted gradually to malleable earth. He smelled fish rotting in brine, listened to the uncharacteristic silence lingering—like a low laying mist—on land that was unable to support life, and watched Mama Milagros and Soul-Dago lead him east.

Foreign exhaustion overwhelmed him. He finally crashed, his legs twitching and soft as jelly as he rolled his back against the trash and decaying detritus. He thrashed, half-convulsing with ecstasy and the urge to run. Mama Milagros stroked his neck while Soul-Dago thrust a leather piece in his mouth that he clamped on instantly. He growled, the moon a sliver in the sky, overwhelmed with a sudden punch of loneliness as sharp as the moon's tip. He wanted his people with him so acutely it transformed into an ache. His ribs heaved with uneven pants as he tried to remember who he was amid the hot fever coursing through him.

Saddles.

He dug rocks out of the ground and clutched them tight.

Mako.

The moon and sun rose and fell all too quickly. He couldn't keep up, but he had to get up. His tongue lolled between his teeth and his body moaned in dehydration. Soul-Dago tried to make him lay down, but there wasn't time. At some point, he couldn't make sense of Mama Milagros's panicked face and her frantic chants to the Bony Lady to *spare him*.

He couldn't hear or taste, his eyes had swollen to slits, but he remembered old, lingering scents. Bruises and blood, brimstone and embers. Thresher's gin-soaked breath and a deep, choking perfume of Promised Land wrongness that had faded to a man who had his teeth in Mako deep. He remembered the second scent, one without a name because it was just like his own. He had grown with that scent in the narrow canals of the womb. He laid his head back and keened—it had been so long since he recalled Nika so vividly.

Soul-Dago laid a hand across his forehead. His eyes widened, a show of concern Mako never thought the Bruykleener would have for him. "You have to rest," Soul-Dago said.

He growled rough like gravel in the back of his throat. The urge to keep going turned into a compulsion, but instead of a direction he had a destination. Landmarks laid out in front of him after Mama Milagros spread the rudimentary map she had copied and pointed out their path. He brought his machete up and put his face close to Soul-Dago, realizing that his enemy-friend had a scent, too, musky, woody, the old scent of cave-rocks radiating from the paint peeling off his face. "You remember the old Mako," he said. Soul-Dago swam in his vision, and Mako blinked, unable to make sense of the rolling world around him. "The Mako who didn't tear guts out of warrior's stomachs or slice off fingers until that one, valuable sentence of information eked out through the screams." He laughed. "I'm a haint, Soul-Dago. I kill people now."

"You're hallucinating," Soul-Dago said. "Don't die on me before I get your claim of freshwater. Your tribe would kill me if I went to Manahatta without you to vouch for your deal."

"My tribe," Mako smirked. "My tribe turned its back on me. They're *weak*."

A cool hand slid across his forehead and he leaned into the touch. Mama Milagros peered into his face. "You have to slow down," she whispered.

"Can't," he said. "Nika needs me. Thresher...I kissed him, Mama, and then I left, and he doesn't know why."

"You can't let that make you kill yourself."

"I think I understand it now, your sharks of the wastelands. It's a feeling right here." He thumped his chest. "I'm starting to see them, like you taught me to see shapes in the wax. They're scavenging the dead moments passing us by, the things we didn't say or do, and everything after the present belongs to them. We can't remember fully, can't experience anything a second time. They have to eat to survive, but they're so lonely, Mama, being locked in the past."

"Mako, you'll fry your brain, and then there will be nothing of you left to give to Thresher."

"I can't stop." He pulled away from her. So many miles of his journey still lay before him. "Don't make me leave you."

42

T hresher had never been one for denial, not when the facts erased any shadow of doubt. He was accustomed to diagnosis. After all, doctors were rarely wrong, rarely took back their reasons for their experiments' existence. Each had a purpose.

A death sentence was still a death sentence. It shook him to the core.

He looked at his hands, numb from the bonds and slightly blue at the tips, thinking how life was so temporary. He had been loaned this body and would be getting a new one shortly. That was denial.

He stared at his black-stitched wounds. *This was it.* His minutes ticked by in solitude. He created nothing, *did nothing* but eat once a day and starve for the other twenty hours.

He counted time by Anna-Skye's stomach. She bulged, her pants lower around her hips to cup the baby. She stroked the growing life within her.

He had strange urges to touch her belly and bless the child within its watery cradle, because he was dying now and the child's life had not even begun.

Paul watched Anna-Skye with certain franticness.

Calmness descended on her. A secret smile curved her lips when she pressed one side of her stomach and her hand bumped back in resistance. When Paul slipped his hands over her belly, she repositioned him so he could feel the kicking feet. Three fingers on one of her hands were puckered stumps now, red with new, healthy skin.

Thresher heard it all. "If it's a girl, I want to call her Gela," Anna-Skye said.

"Where did that name come from?" Paul asked, fondness softening his mouth.

Anna-Skye hid her face. "I just like it."

It fascinated Thresher, in a far-off way, how Anna-Skye could continue to incarcerate him with such disdain and dote on the child trapped inside her.

He wasn't a person, though. He was something abhorred. A contagion they'd been exposed to.

He forgot how to speak. He drooled and picked at his itching hurts. Gela felt like a hallucination, something outrageous crafted by a mind too high on medicine.

The day the ship scraped on land, Thresher felt it deep in his sleep like a shock of ice. He bolted upright, slamming into the bars of his cage, desperate for news. Footsteps thumped above him, followed by unnatural silence. He banged the bars with the side of his bound hands, feeling them bruise, but needing to celebrate the coming of change.

The redcoats came for him next, hurriedly unlocking the door and motioning him without words to stand and follow.

Where's Anna-Skye? He moaned through his gag. *Where's the baby?*

Their hands fluttered over his body like they needed to be reassured of his health. Thresher fumbled to his feet, tripped up the stairs, and once again, felt like a lowly behemoth. Tentative guiding touches kept him upright.

He expected more. He was prodded into the sunlight and onto a rickety boat where he cowered next to the booted feet of his captors. The dinghy tilted alarmingly to the side as it lowered. A splash crossed Thresher's face, and he tasted harsh sea salt. Someone tightened the rope around his throat and handed it to Anna-Skye. His handler. Shame warmed his cheeks.

With a few strong strokes of the oars, the dinghy cut through the waves and slid on pale sand. Thresher crawled out, his knees soaked, rough grit on his palms to the conclave of men onshore. A jerk on the rope told him to keep his eyes down, but defiance felt too good.

The Wallabouts stood apart from this new tribe, and Thresher stared, shell-shocked, at the woman bound like him and kneeling in the sand. He was glad he was on his knees, otherwise he would've fallen.

He would have recognized her anywhere. She had darker hair and a wider face, but she had the look of *him*. It was the way she held herself, cocky with a shielded glare. He desperately wanted to unwrap the bandages around her hands, finger the veins tracing up her arms and know that the same blood ran through her as her twin.

Mako, she's alive.

43

S omewhere between Nika's threats and sullen silences, the drizzle had lightened, and the sun broke through the clouds, turning into a moment of beauty as they traveled farther up the shore. The ocean rolled against the sand. Broken branches and debris from the storm stretched over the dunes like a veil, a unique sight for Nika. A white owl soared through the dune valleys, disappearing into the brush.

She scowled at it. A frantic knot tugged in her chest, making her consider dangerous, ridiculous things. Leaping on Tova's back and yanking out her red hair with Nika's bound hands remained high on the list. She had pulled the escape stunt one too many times and could feel the eyes of Tobey and Beau boring into her back.

Walker walked beside her silently. The afternoon light glinted off his glasses, highlighting the smudges and smears. How could he see at all? Her teeth gnawed her lip and the betrayal she felt when he stood beside Tova still felt fresh. Even though Walker had chosen her, she couldn't stop thinking about it, the way he had smiled at Tova when she said he had *potential*. She always held onto things for too long.

She bumped his shoulder, a little harder than intended. He smiled, as if he had been waiting for her.

"Knock it off," she whispered, but even she could hear the lightness in her voice.

"You finally came around," he said. She caught the tease, a strange mix that sounded like her, but now had a specific Walker quality.

"Can't help your chivalrous nature, can you?" She paused. "You could've joined their tribe, you know."

"I like the one I'm in."

Her eyes narrowed, but before she could retaliate, Tova held up a hand. Tobey kicked Nika to her knees. A huge ship loomed in the distance, casting a long shadow across the blue water. A smaller boat crossed the space between, the oars breaking the glitter off the waves, and finally slid on shore. Nika shaded her eyes to see the figures stepping out. The Wallabout leader approached with the stance of a queen.

"Anna-Skye," Tova said, holding her hands out in welcome. "It's a pleasure to trade with you again."

The superiority in Anna-Skye's eyes made Nika tremble. Anna-Skye's captive crawled on hands and knees. The experiment had his head down low, connected to her on a leash. Nika wondered where the loose girl she had grown up with had gone, replaced with this merciless, adept slave-trading *lady*.

She realized a small bubble of hope still existed within her, and it had popped with a blink of finality. *"You fucking bitch,"* she hissed, but the words didn't sound as angry as Nika wanted them to.

Seeing Anna-Skye stunned her, almost to the point of making Nika want to stumble to her and take those familiar hands in hers. In one moment, that she-devil was the closest thing to home Nika had seen in a long time. Finally, she understood how the poachers knew where to capture her and Tarek, how chance had been a sweet belief that hid the truth: an old friend had stabbed her in the back.

"Did you do this to me?" Nika said, her voice breathy on the verge of screaming. "Did you sell me to the Facility?"

Anna-Skye faltered, her pretty mouth frowning in despair like she had been caught and they were fourteen again, giggling at the top of a skyscraper, passing booze between them, only Nika wasn't an empty bottle Anna-Skye got beaten over. She was a human being who came with all the contradictions. As much as she wanted to wring Anna-Skye's neck, she wished to feel that Manahatta sisterhood again.

Anna-Skye took a deep, shaky breath and looked away from Nika. Her mutilated hand clenched into a fist. "Tova, I've fulfilled the bounty for the Promised Land." She nudged the experiment. He was curled at her feet like a dog that had been kicked one too many times. His shoulders heaved with breath, like he could barely get enough. "Does our deal still hold?"

Nika shuddered and slowly got to her feet, knowing she was a second lowly companion to this *experiment* to Anna-Skye. She tried to pretend like Nika wasn't there, but Anna-Skye didn't understand injustice, couldn't comprehend the black rage that consumed Nika now.

"Midwife services for me when my time comes," Anna-Skye said, looking pale, her throat moving frantically.

"Of course," Tova said, smiling. "Some place friendlier than your ship."

"Tarek's most likely dead," Nika shouted, for once delighting in the cracked edge of oncoming madness coating her tone. "When they brought me to the Facility, they tried to make me as pregnant as you. They stripped me down. Tied me up. Tried to make me accept it."

Anna-Skye closed her eyes, lines deepening around her mouth, the kind that said she was set in stone.

"You've taken part of my life." Nika realized she was on the verge of a long, deep breakdown. "Do you see Mako every day and pretend like I'm dead? Do you spend afternoons at Gela's and talk about what I used to be like, and the whole time, you knew where I was?"

Anna-Skye looked at Nika then, tears filling her gray eyes. "Gela's dead, Nika."

Nika's breath hitched alarmingly. A wretched sob tore from her throat in an ugly release. "Did you do it?" she gasped, her hand seeking her chest, feeling like she might collapse.

"Not directly, but the Wallabouts—my tribe—killed her. I loved her like a mother. She'd want you to know."

Nika couldn't speak, but her body knew what to do with all that black-rage fuel. She ran at Anna-Skye with her head tucked down and barreled into her stomach, viciously glad to feel a crunch as they collided. Give her the opportunity and she would destroy Anna-Skye after what she had done—even if that meant sacrificing her baby.

Anna-Skye collapsed with a scream. She thought she could whittle Nika down, but Nika was driftwood, contorted and beaten by the relentless ocean surge. Arms surrounded her, pulled her off, threw her to the ground. Ferocious Wallabouts surrounded Anna-Skye, protecting their traitorous leader.

Nika's lip was split. Blood coated her mouth. "I hope something's broken in there," she snarled before the Enders yanked her back by her shoulder and held her down. She could only imagine what she looked like, but it didn't matter. She felt empty, like a hole the abyss wanted to possess too fast with crushing loss.

"I'm not sorry," Anna-Skye said, as she was helped to her feet. "I told Mako the same thing. I understand the truth behind sacrifice. I don't know how you escaped, but Tova will take you back. Remember, your pain is worth it, even if you don't understand why." She tossed the leash lead of her slave toward Tova, who picked it up. "Remember, witch. I'll be at yours in five months' time."

Tova nodded and smiled, pulled the experiment closer. Wallabout warriors eased Anna-Skye into the boat. Dusk raced across the rippling waves to coat them in an orange setting light. Nika watched them go until they were mere pinpricks lost against the ship's shadow, her smile twisted as she caught sight of a stain growing on Anna-Skye's pants.

44

Who was that?" Walker asked as he brushed away the tears on Nika's cheeks.

"A traitor," Nika whispered, captivated with the ship until it disappeared from view. "She's responsible for my grandmother's death."

"I'm so sorry."

She knew he couldn't understand the concept of Gela or the dreams Nika had of being enveloped in Gela's tight embrace. Swallowing a lump in her throat, she laughed when Buck undid her bonds in pity and turned to see Jake kneel in front of his new cargo, placing a gentle hand on the experiment's back. His shoulder blades seemed to cut through his shirt to lay shadows like the stubs of broken wings.

"Sit up now," Jake said gently, cupping the experiment's arms and helping him roll over. "There you go."

The experiment spasmed in pain as if his legs wouldn't work. Blue eyes eerily landed on Nika. It gave her the chills, but it didn't stop the inexpressible urge to go to him.

Jake fingered the leash. Nika knelt before the experiment and reached her hands out, suddenly needing to do something useful and humane. The experiment flinched, eyes closing momentarily. She tried again, this time slowly so he could see her stretch around his head to undo the buckles on the gag. His lower jaw hung open until he crooked it side to side before closing it. White scars surrounded his mouth.

"Better?" Nika stretched the gag out on her lap. Damp.

The experiment nodded. His dark brown hair stuck out in unruly spikes. Feeling motherly, Nika smoothed the wild locks down. He shrank from her, but endured the touch, eyes a bit too wide. A kindred spirit, lost in the world.

"What a mess," Milo said, squatting down next to them. "What are we going to do now that your tribeswoman expects us to take you back to the Promised Land? We can't integrate them, now."

"Not much else we can do," Jake breathed.

"You have to take *him* back, at least," Tova said, inclining her head toward the new experiment. "We can't ruin our relationship with the

Promised Land over a measly experiment. He's the chance for me to rebuild, start over. Whatever you want me to bargain for, Jakey, I'll do it."

The experiment raised his bound hands, as if pleading to be released.

"I do this," Jake said, holding a knife just too close to the experiment's eye, "and if there's any funny business, I'll cut your balls off. Do you understand me?"

The experiment nodded.

"And the leash stays on."

Jake sawed the rope in two. The experiment shook his blue hands until they took on an angry reddish hue. He turned his head to look toward the ocean, allowing her to glimpse the black letter touching the nape of his neck.

"Can we make camp?" Beau whined behind them. Nika threw a handful of sand at him.

"Set it up, kiddo," Jake ordered. "And a stake in the ground. We'll bind this one to it."

"Here," Milo said, thrusting the boots in Nika's hands. "Put these on him."

Nika realized for the first time that the experiment was barefoot.

"Let me." She drew the experiment's foot into her lap.

His face scrunched with pain and he leaned back, like he couldn't hold himself up. She carefully rubbed his foot warm in her palms, then unwound the gauntlets covering her hands and ripped the gag apart.

"It'll keep from rubbing your feet raw," she explained, and nearly caught on a sob. The experiment's lips opened slightly in wonder. His foot gave a small jerk as she massaged the instep. She wrapped the cloth around his foot like a mummy, padding the heel, before tying it off at his ankle. She smiled and slipped the boot over his foot and tied the laces. Ironic, she thought. All this time the Facility tried to knock her up and only *now* did she exhibit classic maternal signs. Irony at its finest.

It didn't feel like irony when she took the experiment's other foot in her lap though. It felt like kindness.

They retreated behind the dune line for shelter, using low brush to create a deep-set fire that illuminated everyone's faces in an orange glow. The young pups had gone hunting and returned victorious with long strips of seaweed and two striped bass. The fillets cackled near the fire, spitting oil into the flames. Nika's stomach uttered a treacherous growl.

The experiment sat too close to the fire. Cheeks flushed with heat, the light illuminating his blue eyes. He jumped when she sat cross-legged beside him. The leash lay down his back and stretched out to a stake hammered into the sand behind him. Walker pushed his glasses back up his nose and sat on the other side of the experiment, draping part of his cloak over the experiment's shoulders.

Perhaps it had been kindness, too, that made the Enders keep her unbound for now. She tried to contemplate escape—seduce one of the eager boys and take advantage of his youth before banging him unconscious and scampering to freedom—but the thought made her skin crawl. Grief numbed her more than any Promised Land drug. Sharp sudden pain raced through her split lower lip and she realized her teeth had re-drawn blood. She couldn't imagine trekking into the dark night alone. Images of her mother's death filled her head, only now, Gela joined the bloodshed. She imagined both women, lifeless, cold, and broken on Bruykleen concrete, and had to stuff her fist in her mouth to stop from screaming.

"I have to piss," she choked out.

Milo shot Jake a look and nodded, helped her stand. "I'll escort you," he said, his voice hushed. "Take your time."

It made her start to cry, this touch of compassion. Milo understood what she needed. Darkness within which to weep.

Walker wondered if he had looked as half-eaten and raw when he had escaped. He breathed out slowly as he studied the experiment's curving jawline and blue eyes all too common in the Facility's experiments. Must be a rampant gene, something recessive that couldn't be washed away.

Too thin. Too numb. Walker remembered that state. Living moment to moment from the cold intake of fresh air, to the tingling warmth of body heat, to the demanding growl of his empty stomach. He plucked a roasting fish fillet from the coals and, tossing it hand-to-hand, held the boneless offering to what he could only think of now as his brother.

The experiment—and wasn't that a laugh, calling him that when they were almost the same—zeroed in on the food. He took the fillet from Walker's burnt fingers and stuffed it into his mouth. His cheek bulged. Walker smiled kindly, flickering his gaze over the scars. Could it be like looking into a mirror? He knew phenotypically they should be different, but how varied could the Facility's generated gene pool be? They very well might have had the same biological mother.

He had a sudden urge to touch the experiment. This was his first true encounter with a creature from his home out in the wild. A brotherhood must be established.

"Environmental?" Walker whispered out of the side of his mouth.

"Blind study," the experiment said hoarsely. Walker watched him run a thumb along the letter on his wrist. "Genetic disease."

No wonder they had never met. Completely different realms of study.

"I have ALS," the experiment blurted out. He glanced sidelong at Walker. The corners of his eyes showed signs of crow's feet.

"Positive expression?" Walker knew the diagnosis shouldn't be met with sadness. After all, they were simply protocols in a much greater research scheme. All the same, his chest clutched.

"I think so," the experiment said.

Walker heard it again. Numbness. It felt like an eternity, but he remembered when his doctor had come to him, defeated after a failed round of tests. His subjects had all died within the first three months of conception.

His doctor hadn't wanted to look at him, only take him from behind and let loose his failure on Walker's body. Walker opened up to it, let it happen, and found some kind of ecstasy in the bruises left on his body. Like he had taken his doctor's pain and physically transformed it into deep yellow and purple marks that would, in weeks, disappear and be forgiven.

He didn't understand it, but it felt good to be a vessel in which others could give their pain that he could absolve with his body. He suddenly wanted to do this very badly for the experiment.

He reached out and placed his whole hand over the experiment's, sliding the experiment's stroking finger off the tattooed letter.

The experiment sat as still as stone. His hand curled into a tight fist and he breathed out hard.

Walker dimly remembered this, too, how first kind touches felt. His was his doctor, of course, who had cupped his jaw and brought their faces together, cheek-to-cheek.

"How'd you find out?" Walker asked, pushing his glasses up his nose.

"Tested me. On the *Wallabout*. The ship."

"How'd you...get out?" He didn't mean the ship.

The experiment licked his lips. Walker removed his hand. "Had help." His face screwed up in an expression of pain. "Thank you. I'd almost forgotten what..."

"I know." Walker cleared his throat. "Nika calls me Walker."

"I used to be called Thresher."

"Then Thresher it is."

"Nice to meet you," Thresher said shakily, as if it was his first time testing out the saying. His mouth stayed flat as a line, solemn.

Walker had read that book on mind and manners too. "Nice to meet you too."

By the time Milo brought Nika back, Walker had begun to pace. Her swollen face, reddened cheeks, and Milo's downcast eyes proved that she had slunk off like a cat to mourn alone.

The other Enders had slipped into sleep. Jake smoked as they waited, and Thresher pondered the fire. Nika slumped next to Walker and gave him a tiny, exhausted shadow of a smile.

Milo and Jake fell into a hushed, intense discussion. Walker knew they spoke about what to do with their prisoners. With them.

Thresher reached across Walker and laid a tentative hand on Nika's shoulders. He licked his lips, paused as if debating and then whispered, "Mako is coming for you. He knows what's happened to you and he's fighting everyone to bring you home again."

Prickling jealousy graced Walker's conscious as Nika's face softened in wonder. Nika clutched his hand frantically, her eyes flickering to the End leaders. *"How do you know?"*

"Mako saved me. I was traveling with him before the Wallabouts came. I was with Gela when she died."

Nika's cheeks flushed, tension radiating from her as she leaned even closer. "We can escape." Her voice was charged, determined. "You know where he's going. The Enders want to integrate us, but sell you to the Facility. We have to think of a way to get out of here and find him."

Thresher shook his head. "I have to go back to the Facility."

"Trinity, why?"

"I was released on purpose by a doctor," Thresher breathed out. "I need to understand why she did it, and the only way I can is if I return. I have limited time to accomplish what needs to be done."

Nika went abnormally quiet, still like Walker had never seen before. When she looked up, her eyes looked clearer than they had in days. That old fire that he had been drawn to when he first saw her, made a tightness he didn't know exist ease in his chest. Thresher had found kindling to ignite in her guttered soul, and Walker could have kissed Thresher on the mouth for this gift of hope.

"Mako will go to the Promised Land. It's the only location he has to find me, right?" Nika said. "We'll meet him there. As long as you swear he's coming for me, I can go back to that place of damnation."

45

We'll stop here," Milo announced, standing in front of a tall, crooked house. Light remained for their journey to the Promised Land to continue, but by the way Jake lagged and Maggie limped, Nika understood Milo's decision to rest.

She listed against Walker. In her exhaustion, she felt like she had regressed.

"Pups in one room," Milo shot over his shoulder. "Maggie, find Jake a mattress. I'll take first watch."

"Not broken," Jake said under his breath.

"You want to sleep on the floor?" Milo snapped. "'Cause when the cold gets into your bones—and trust me, it will—I won't be getting up to help you."

Jake rolled his eyes. "You get more opinionated every day. Remember when you were small and barely spoke at all? I'm starting to miss that."

"Shouldn't have been so nice to me, then. Should've left me in Tova's care to be sold to the Woodlands." Milo cracked the broken door open and disappeared inside.

Buck shifted side to side as they waited. "This is ridiculous."

"Boy has to check the perimeter. It's how it's done." Jake crossed his arms.

"But we've been here a million times," Buck said.

"And every millionth time we've ensured it's safe for us."

"Milo's paranoid," Buck said. "I get it's from all that kid-soldiering he did with his old tribe, but *still*."

"Milo's an End through and through."

"I know, Jake. Didn't mean he wasn't." Buck sounded contrite.

The experiment—no *Thresher*, as Walker had instructed Nika to call him—stared unblinking. She grimaced, concluding that Milo had once been like her: part of a tribe, then kidnapped, sold upriver instead of down, and embraced by the Enders, then brainwashed to become one of them.

Milo emerged through the front and motioned them inside. Maggie directed Walker and Nika into a small room with a broken window covered with rusting, spiraled bars. A hide had been tacked over part of it, letting a beam of light illuminate the scratched floor. Nika shuddered at the mouse pellets scattered about and imagined she could hear squeaking in the walls.

"There's a pillow in the closet," Maggie said. She hesitated and then tried to hold Nika's gaze, but failed. "Don't think about escaping, okay? It's a hassle for all of us."

"Wouldn't dream of it," Nika sighed, intending it to be harsh, but somehow, the comment made Maggie give a small huff of laughter. Nika smiled, after all, she had made the decision to see the Facility walls again, even though the thought paralyzed her with fear. She caught sight of Thresher being led away before Maggie locked the door shut.

The air smelled dense with dust. Walker sneezed as he rummaged in the closet. Yelping in surprise, he took a quick step back.

"Mice have the pillow, don't they," Nika said in a dead voice.

She didn't even have to see him nod. Filthy rats.

"I hate vermin," she said, sitting hard on the floor. Her knees creaked in protest, and wouldn't it be funny if, after all this, she died before her time because she had gotten too old for this life.

Walker spread the cloak and wrapped them both in it. Nika grimaced as her hips protested against the hard floor. She grunted and rocked back and forth to ease the ache.

"What are we going to do?" Walker's question vibrated under her fingers on his chest.

"What do you mean?" Nika said, although she knew damn well what he meant. She grimaced. She didn't like playing dumb.

"I love the space and exhilaration of the outside. I don't want to go back to the Facility."

"You think I do?"

Walker's chest rumbled in frustration.

"You think I have all the answers?" She hissed. "The only reason I'm going back willingly is to find my twin. If he's there and I'm not—" She turned over so she wouldn't have to face him. Those thoughts left her shaking. "I couldn't live with myself if he was captured."

Walker touched her hunched shoulder.

"Don't touch me."

A small disapproving grunt fluttered against the nape of her neck. "Why not?"

"Because I don't like it."

She could feel the high voltage crackle charge the room when an argument was brewing. Add a spice of resentment here and a dash of cruel words there, and what a fine making for a truly disastrous fight.

Walker rolled away from her and onto his back. His warmth disappeared. She felt adrift. While he was merely a hand span away, it felt like a sea between them.

"Do I repulse you?" he asked softly.

She cringed, unable to reconcile her wants and her insecurity. She curled even more into a ball. "Why would you say something like that?"

She heard his shoulders scrape on the cloak as he shrugged. "I never thought of it before, but perhaps I'm unappealing to you."

Nika floundered.

"I don't mean physically," he broke in. "I mean mentally, psychologically, spiritually. My doctor once told me that was why he and I were so perfect together. Because we matched all those things."

Nika found she could rally. "Did you feel that way?"

Again, the soft shifting sound as he readjusted. "No. But that could be because I didn't quite understand what it meant." He paused. "I feel that way about you."

Nika couldn't breathe. She suddenly needed very much to be free from the cloak and bathed in fresh air. She flung the cloak off and scrambled to sit cross-legged, far enough away so she could see Walker prop himself up on his elbow. The shadows hid half his face, but she could tell by his pinched lips he might be grieving.

"You don't want to be any of those things with me." She had to get the words out before they choked her. "My head's all messed up, and my heart's in a thousand pieces, and I can barely stand living in my own skin."

He toed the cloak off his body and crept on all fours toward her. Panic blazed in her head, but she was rooted to the spot. A small part of her mind babbled that he was seducing her, or at least trying to, that he was one of those men who knew how to smile crooked in just the right way, how to put all that want and need into his eyes, knew how to be close enough to make her imagine what it could be like if he came any closer. Even if he didn't have the equipment to prove it.

She smirked. Honestly, that played in his favor.

He folded his limbs in front of her but didn't touch her. She eyed his long legs. He cocked his head to the side and peered into her face. "What if I told you right now I wanted to kiss you?"

She snorted. "You can try. Might have a black eye in the morning."

"What if I told you that I wanted *you* to kiss *me?*"

Now that was a different story. She bit her lip and imagined rising to her knees to stand over him, grabbing a handful of his hair, yanking his head back so his neck was a long line, and covering his mouth with hers.

The bright electricity of panic zipping along her nerves quieted. Maybe, if he fought back or tried to change the tables on her, she could tug on his hair until he submitted. She swallowed hard, wondering in a panic if she should be taking what he had to give in this way, twisting it for her purposes like his old doctor-lover.

Walker looked like he could wait decades for her answer. Maybe, he was the one using her.

"You…you have to let me control it," she whispered. "You can't try and…take what I don't want to give."

"Okay," he breathed.

"Can you do that? Can you let me do absolutely whatever I wanted?"

"Of course."

"I don't want you to touch me." She sounded ragged. "I don't want anything close to being inside me."

He dropped his head a little, as if proud. "I don't have anything to *do* anything like that."

Relief. She sighed because, strangely enough, he was safe.

Walker's blue eyes were a glossy summer sky as she got to her knees and did exactly what she had imagined. He remained motionless as she put her lips against his. His mouth parted and her tongue moved languidly against his, angling him the right way to make a spike of painful heat strike her abdomen.

"I want you to get undressed, okay?" she asked breathlessly.

He nodded, hands obeying, and soon enough she had yards of Walker-legs bent in front of her. He had managed not to touch her.

"Hold your hands above your head and lay back."

So good, he did it. His knees bent and slightly spread. She could see the scrambled mess between his legs trying to rise to the occasion. He barely extended longer than her thumb. Nika ran her fingers up his calf to the crook of his knee, watching him shiver slightly. His hands clenched. She circled up his thigh and stroked the smooth skin just before running her hands underneath him.

She felt settled in a way she'd never been before. Walker twitched, and she tightened her hold until he let out a little wanting moan, but he didn't try to roll on top of her. So far, he'd kept his word.

Another sharp spike of arousal careened inside her. She thought about putting her mouth on his neck, kissing his chest, but she truly didn't want to do that. After all this time, she wanted it fast and over before he did something to ruin it, before he touched her in ways that would make her regret.

She tried and failed to be detached. He fascinated her. She rolled her fingers back and forth across him, tugging on his small cock slightly, engulfing him with her hand. She touched the mayhem below it, fingered the loose flesh and spread it until she could see the soft hidden indentation. Pressing her finger into it made him buck, but he strained to stay still. She wasn't sure if it was a malformed vagina or a sensitive spot, but it ended beyond her first knuckle. She spun her finger, pulled in and out. His breathing came out fast and quick. Good signs, but if she was going to do this, she wanted to do it right.

"Being good for me, aren't you?" she asked him.

"I am?"

"Yeah," she said. "Is this good? Is this what you want?"

"You tell me," he said.

She pushed harder into the hole and his head tipped back. "I want you to stay hard." She pulled her fingers away.

He made a low sound of denial, but she had to stop the heat inside her. Her fingers knew where to go. When she touched herself, for once it didn't feel wrong. Walker's hips undulated in small sharp thrusts to the rhythm of her hand down her pants, but he never faltered. His hands remained far away from her.

It almost felt better before she came. A slow tingling built up in the bottom of her spine and rushed in her bloodstream. A gentle release made her legs sag. But that was it.

"Please," Walker asked, and she realized with a jolt, that she'd left him wanting.

Power danced on her fingertips, giving her a greater rush than satisfying basic biological needs. Darker arousal. To touch or not to touch. "Spread your legs farther." She wanted to see him stretch. His breath hitched, *like she knew what she was doing,* and she tugged and stroked, cupped and thumbed.

"Want to touch me, don't you?" she asked, harsher than intended.

"No," he gasped, "this is perfect. Watching you get off…ah… perfect."

She bent over him, so if he moved an inch, their bodies could touch. "Come for me."

He obeyed immediately all over her fingers, his face transforming from urge to bliss. He relaxed on the floor, his knees knocked together to the side, mouth slightly parted.

Nika wasn't sure what to think or do. She had spunk on her hand.

While she stared blankly, her mind rebelling against action, Walker suddenly crouched in front of her. He had a piece of browned cloth that likely came from the rat-infested pillowcase in the closet. He wiped her hands clean in two quick movements and tossed the foul cloth away.

She smiled, grateful in ways she couldn't express, and had an overwhelming urge to reward him, to show him she knew he could be trusted. "You...you can kiss me."

He didn't ask questions, only leaned forward. She felt his breath on her cheek and panic flared again. She hadn't specified what kind of kiss.

Close-lipped. Soft and dry. He kissed her gently, holding onto the contact more than she ever thought someone could without shoving a tongue down her throat. In that moment, she realized she had a lot to learn about intimacy. He broke the kiss with a sigh and the spell of the night shattered, passing them back into the realm of normalcy.

He put his arm around her to tug her down onto the cloak. She came willingly, because when it mattered he had obeyed, and she let him wrap his nude body around her clothed one. He blazed with heat, but felt pliable in a way only sex could give. She tentatively laid her head next to his, allowing him to put his leg between hers and interlace their fingers. His sleep felt contagious, but she knew she would be up all night thinking about what the trinity had happened.

"I can hear your thoughts," Walker murmured.

"Oh, yeah?" Challenging.

"You're thinking I *really* am an action verb."

Laughing hadn't felt so good in a long time.

46

I s this what defeat looks like?" Tova asked, her voice low but mocking. She reached out to touch Nika's hair.

Nika jerked away with a scowl. She didn't want to give this trade post witch anything, but it pleased her to know that her faded resistance translated to her being broken. "Get away from me."

"I had no idea Anna-Skye was your tribeswoman," Tova continued, attempting a bright smile that only increased her appearance of sunken exhaustion. The long relentless days trekking across sand and pine barrens took a toll on everyone. "Back then, she sold you to me without any remorse, but she'd also been incredibly eager to prove her worth."

A crazed, inner whisper urged Nika to slap Tova across the face. "You two share a trait. Boot licking never came naturally to me, I suppose."

Tova leaned in and pointed into the sparse tree line. "Do you see that? The contraption in the trees?"

Nika squinted, but finally caught sight of a dilapidated structure barely balanced between a set of branches. It looked like it had been pushed over by the wind.

"That trap use to be tied to a tripwire, and when someone unwanted crossed it, they fell into a pit. Then, it would catapult a net on top of them. Sad. The Promised Land doesn't replace things like they used to."

One of the reasons she had been able to escape. Lessened vigilance. Snatches of adrenaline-fueled terror and tunnel-vision focus suddenly overwhelmed her.

"How did you get on such good terms with the Facility?" Nika asked. "They pay for women. Why they didn't snatch up a rare specimen like you baffles me."

Tova flashed a smile. "Charming. I proved I could be more valuable elsewhere. For a tribe as isolated as the Promised Land, sometimes a familiar trader is worth more than gold or medicine."

"Would you sell Jake to them?" Nika asked, wanting to know where Tova's morality lay. "What could you get for Maggie?"

"I would do no such thing. Jake and I are old sacred lovers. Maggie's the runt of his sister's litter. They mean something to me."

"And Milo? Poor bastard. Separated from his tribe, believing the Enders *care* for him."

Tova's eyes flashed. Nika knew she'd struck a chord. "Milo was an accident, a feral child raised to be battle-fodder. His people—I hate to call them a tribe, those rough barbarians—either died or abandoned their so-called children to the wolves. Milo was just another *thing* with a target on his head. Jakey's soft heart made Milo human, made him the man he is now. I like to make sure Milo remembers where he came from in case he goes back to his old bloodthirsty ways. I wouldn't trade him, but only for Jake's sake."

"What trinity-blessed saints you all are."

"You, on the other hand, have given me nothing but trouble. I wouldn't mind being rid of you. I'll keep your man, though. He's got something in him. Real potential. A specific kind of light you don't see every day."

Nika couldn't stop the growl from leaving her lips.

"Don't worry," Tova said. "Jake's too uncomfortable to sell you back to the Facility now that he knows you're an actual outsider. Guess Anna-Skye did you some good after all."

"What about Walker?"

"Oh honey, I'd buy him off Jake before I let the Promised Land take him."

"More integration, huh? Diversification? Same line as the Promised Land. Jake's cut from the same cloth." She had said it to her psychologist, hadn't she, that the tribes were getting too small and children were too hard to have. Even so, she would never become an Ender.

"Better in than out," Tova said and broke stride to catch up with Jake. Nika desperately scoured the woods for any sign of Mako, wishing he would emerge from the shadows and fulfill the newfound hope inside her. Walker, keeping close to Thresher's side, must've sensed her distress and came to stand next to her. She breathed out a sigh, refused to believe it was one of relief. His hand slid through hers and squeezed even as she caught sight of a roof skimming the top of the trees, giving her the impression of a widespread sprawl, something industrial that had let the forest overrun its boundaries. The foliage cleared and the looming, gothic building came into view.

"Ready for this?" Walker asked.

"Always," she whispered. In reality, she wasn't ready for anything. Dread sat inside her belly. *They can't control me.*

The Facility's ambassadors, three men and one woman in frayed lab coats, waited in front of a rusting chain link fence thrown open in greeting. A big wooden box sat next to them. The woman put a hand on top of it protectively. Buck, who had gone on ahead to announce their presence, stood slightly in front of the four. A stormy expression marred his face and his black hair looked oily under the smoky light.

A group milled just inside the fence, a mixture of orderlies and, by the sparse clothing, experiments. Nika quickly averted her eyes. She had never seen experiments willingly *left* outside the Facility. They swayed and gathered in clumps as if terrified.

Tova and Jake approached the Facility's tribe—how the thought curdled in Nika's brain—with Thresher in tow. Thresher descended to hands and knees, the leash straining between Milo's hand and his neck. Small gasping sounds whistled through his mouth as the rope cut off his windpipe. Nika couldn't imagine willingly counting the steps to your death.

Maggie peeked out from behind Beau and Tobey, who stood in front of Nika and Walker as flaky gray dust floated in the air like snow. Clothing, her armor, hid her identity. She had scratched the tattoos on her wrists so many times they'd become painfully red and raised. Even as she realized all she could do was wait and endure, a roaring took up in her ears next to the beating of her heart. She could barely focus. Was the man on the left looking at her? Did he recognize her?

Swallowing hard, she focused on the Facility's shattered windows. Debris clogged the browned, sagging eaves. A piece of dust landed on her shoulder and she frowned at it. Ash. The smell of chemical fire created a prickling sensation between her shoulder blades. Against Tova's braying laugh, something felt *wrong*.

Walker focused intently on something in the distance. Following his line of sight, Nika saw a scaffold behind the negotiators near where the mish-mash group waited. Squinting, she made out a human figure hanging from a hook screwed into the wooden overhang, hands bound in thick rope over his head. He should have been swaying with the breeze, but a pile of bricks dangling from the rope binding his feet weighed him down. It wasn't right, how long his arms looked.

Jake's voice rose, and he shifted his weight, as if ready to flee. Tova handed Thresher to the Facility woman, who looked wan. A set of sores traced down her cheeks.

Nika readied to speak, remembered why she couldn't, and nearly screamed as Walker bypassed the young dogs, heading straight for the scaffolding as if possessed. His hand rose to cover his open mouth, aghast. Heat washed over her in a dizzying wave as he crossed the no-man's land between them and the Facility. Nika's feet rooted to the ground, but no matter how hard she tried to break the fear, she had already had this revelation—she couldn't walk to the gallows out of free will.

"Stop him," she whispered, and yanked on Milo's arm, tried her voice again. *"Stop him."*

She wondered if Milo felt the same sense of danger because he didn't question or frown, only leapt after Walker, trying to cut him off as he got closer to Tova and Jake, who watched him approach as if he were a ghost. The negotiations had been tense to begin with, but now they shivered with suspicion.

Walker's cry of denial confirmed what Nika didn't want to know. Walker's doctor, his lover, hung in front of the Facility as a traitor for all to see. She had expected lethal injection for his actions, something clean and swift to match the cool clinical ways of the Promised Land, not this barbarity.

"What have you done?" Walker screamed. "What have you done to him?" His hands rose above his head as he passed through the gate and to the foot of the scaffold. The Facility's leaders regrouped into a neat square around their box. The Enders watched Walker with the dread of a hurricane that couldn't be escaped.

Fear for Walker overpowered her, but still her terror immobilized her. The broken windows might not be shattered by accident, there could be guns peering out of that glass or bows with notched arrows aimed at each of their foreheads. She wanted to delve into the approaching disaster, but her body obeyed her frantic instincts that remembered being trapped, chained, dehumanized, manipulated, instead of the logic telling her Walker would die if she didn't do something.

One of the leaders intercepted Milo as an orderly from the crowd gripped Walker's shoulder. Walker's sobs tore at her heart. The orderly swept aside Walker's hair to check the back of his neck. "He's one of ours." He sounded breathless, as if the revelation jarred him like Anna-Skye's betrayal had her. "He's one of ours!"

Walker thrashed, but the orderly punched something into his neck—an injection, perhaps—so violent and quick that Nika felt stunned. The female doctor's face screwed up in rage. "You think you can use us like this?" she shrieked. "Stealing our people and selling them back to us? Is that how you introduced your outside *sickness* to us?"

"Nothing like that," Jake said, putting precious space between them. No wrath like a woman's, and this Facility doctor had the fury of all of them combined as she wrenched Thresher's leash tight, effectively strangling him.

"You fucking outsiders," she screamed. "Worthless leeches of society. You've been working with traitors like him to smuggle our experiments out, haven't you?" She pointed at Walker's dead doctor.

"Let us explain," Tova said.

"You can explain how you have one of ours!"

"Take them. We'll give both experiments in good faith," Tova stammered, and for once, sounded unbalanced.

The Facility woman put a protective hand on the wooden box. "I thought you were trustworthy, Tova."

"How can I make this right?"

"Your girl," the woman said. Nika's knees turned to water when she pointed at Maggie. "Give us your female and we'll forget this. You get off our property and we won't destroy your whole tribe."

"No fucking way," Tobey shouted. Maggie's widened stance began to tremble and she ducked behind Beau.

"You want a war?" the woman said. "We'll take her, just like you took ours." A shaky smile parted her lips, like she had suddenly had an epiphany and for once, all the pieces fell into place. Like she might come out on top.

Walker crumpled into a heap on the ground. Nausea twisted Nika's stomach as loss wrenched her uselessly. She couldn't do anything but think: *not again.*

Beau's grip on Maggie's elbow tightened as he tried to shield her and steer them away. The group of anxious orderlies and experiments broke from the chain link fence and advanced quickly, as if possessed with war-rage. The experiments hedged, but with furious cuffs from their fellow orderlies, stumbled forward, confused. The experience of freedom seemed to steal any sanity they had.

"Rise!"

Nika dove to the ground at the piercing cry and crawled to the tree line. Darts thudded around her, streamlined and small enough to be thrown or shot through a device with force. A cold shudder engulfed her. Probably tipped with a sedative or non-lethal poison, something to make the enemy submit as the orderlies, who had been trained to restrain and restore order, could collect them. Make them brand new experiments.

The sound of breaking glass and small contained explosions made her glance behind her. The box had been opened and experiments laughed wildly, throwing beakers full of chemicals at the fleeing Enders and at each other. When the beakers broke, circles of green-burning fire erupted in the grass.

Nika now understood Jake's reluctance to let her leave, his fear of her flapping her mouth. The End, for all their bravado and treaties, maneuvered peace between the violent Bruykleeners, the terrifying Wallabouts, and the manipulative Facility with a reputation based on trust and reliability. She and Walker could've put the End tribe too close to the spark for a war they had no hope of winning, being surrounded on all sides by war-like tribes.

They weren't winning now. This fire looked like magic, shooting high into the sky and burning out quickly, an unearthly color stranger than any shade of grass. It reminded her of polluted water. Nika scrambled to her feet, saw Maggie struggling with two others who punched her hard and hefted her over a shoulder. A larger man lorded over Buck, bloody-faced, before Milo crashed into him, sending the three of them to the ground.

Chaos made a battle where they were outnumbered. Nika remembered this, too, being overrun, cornered, and helpless as others surrounded her and charged her with deafening war cries. She remembered watching another tribe take from her until she had nothing left to give.

A young Promised Land orderly rushed towards her, raised his hand to throw the beaker, and slammed into her side. They tumbled to the ground. She heard the crunch of glass, and the chemical splashed everywhere. She rolled, terrified that the mixture would melt her skin, a phantom feeling crawling along her spine.

The orderly screamed as the chemical fire erupted on his hands, spreading up his arms and eating through his clothes. He began to sob, the pustules on his face popping with the heat. She couldn't let him come after her again. She grabbed one of the thick shards from the broken container and jabbed it into his stomach, feeling slight pressure and then a pop as she punctured something. He screamed, crying out for his mother. Fire licked at her clothes, trying to leap between them, but she pulled away quickly, battering at green sparks until they died out on her arms.

Nika ran, an inner voice firmly instructing her that she couldn't look back. She would end up like her mother, stranded bones in a vial somewhere on a beach desert, or back in chains where she didn't own her body anymore. If it came to that—being selfless and worthy and honorable—she would take the easy road out every time. She couldn't do it. She just couldn't.

Heavy breathing behind her, blood in the back of her throat, and her thighs ached. Her skin itched and burned from where the chemical fire had touched her. She wondered at the causality count, but it didn't really matter because they had Walker.

Walker and his stupid ideas of adventure, beauty, and truth. Walker, who loved a bastard enough to expose himself to the enemy, who couldn't keep his shit under control and who was gone, like Tarek, like Mako...

She sobbed, heart beating loudly in her ears. Her breath, too shallow and fast, made her dizzy. She counted the limping End shadows retreating with her.

The Facility wouldn't keep pursuing. They had their female. Nika knew, to the trinity and back, what they would do to her.

47

Thresher jerked awake, mouth fishing for air, and dragged a deep rattled gasp down his bruised throat. In flashes, he saw fellow experiments collapsed against the wall, tended to by the exhausted slump of doctors and orderlies. Everything *looked* disorderly, barely under control, a frenzied atmosphere that felt more like the soul of the outside than what he had grown up in.

Unconsciousness sucked him under again until he woke up coughing, phlegm crawling up into his mouth. A metal pan appeared in front of his face and jiggled impatiently.

Muscle memory. Thresher spat out the gummy mess and flicked his tongue to get rid of the iron taste. Crust congealed in the corners of his lips. He was strapped to a metal bed, and he shuddered when the reddened blaze covering his vision lifted.

He smelled a sickly odor when he should've smelled earth, remembered with a rising sense of dread that he had been choked unconscious before he saw what happened to Mako's twin.

Bodies were piled up in the corner. Sallow faces, pustules weeping on their skin, the unmistakable pallor of illness making his mind frantically think *plague*. A furnace blazed, and the woman tending to it threw one of the bodies inside and slammed the door shut. The metallic ring made Thresher wince.

She turned and Thresher's heart climbed up this throat. His fingers clawed on the metal bench. One of her eyes had been scooped out. The engorged eyelid barely covered it. Sores littered her mouth. He had seen such a thing before on the Shinnecoes, but this was worse, bulging and inflamed, as if the ordinary sickness of the outside had transformed into a behemoth pestilence.

"Do you remember me?" he gasped.

She paused in her shuffle to the bed, leaned over him, scraped at his skin, and emptied the flesh sample into a vial.

"You released me. You drove me in a car out into the middle of nowhere and left me."

A nasty smile curled her lip. He heard a snip along his scalp. Hair sample.

"Did you release me as a test? Was I your experiment? What was I supposed to bring back?"

She paused, her gaze roving over his face. "No experiment," she said, her voice scratchy and raw. "One of human compassion, I suppose. I remember you now. You had a level of emotional intelligence I didn't often see."

"Is that why you chose me? So I might...connect with the outsiders better?"

"There used to be a man who lived here," she said, her hands shaking as she continued to take his heart rate and scrape underneath his nails, "old when I was young, who said the world had ended to purge itself. We, as the Facility, are trying to re-create something that was gone. Living in the past. Do you see this?"

She held up a metal contraption, her two fingers through the wide circular holes and her thumb resting on a plunger. A needle screwed in the top. "This was stolen from a museum as a precaution for when our state-of-the-art tech failed. It's more than three hundred years old. We're still using it to do what humans do best. Dissect each other." She stuck the needle in his arm, attached a vial for blood. "I released you for your own sake, to see what would become of you. Life's the experiment. It shouldn't be contained and played God with. But what did you do? You came back. You'll always end up coming home. You asked for this death. Look around you. Disease has infiltrated our sterile ecosystem and wages war on our weak immune systems. Nature, purging us again."

"What kind of disease?" Thresher couldn't keep the horror out of his voice.

That ugly smile danced across her lips again. She stuck him with a second needle. "You'll be fine. You've been outside and come into contact with who knows what. At least I gave you that, but because of my experiments—because of you—I'm forced to work here until I collapse of fatigue or sickness, forever taking samples and recordings of what finally killed the Promised Land while I shovel bodies into the furnace. Sometimes, I wish they'd hung me like that poor bastard and let the weight at my feet crush my lungs."

She stepped back. A door opened behind her and the shadow of two people stood in the doorway. "Goodbye, Subject T, and godspeed. I hope you lived while you could."

A hand patted Thresher's shoulder, and then latex gloved hands turned him onto his back. He blinked into the bright industrial light and tried to bring his hand up to shield his eyes. Hands attempted to soothe him as he fought to rise, pushing him into a bed padded soft. His head lolled, and he squinted past the angled lab coat clad doctors at the beds lined up in a row, heads against the wall.

No.

There had to be dozens of hospital beds perched on rickety metal stands with wheels for easy maneuverability, all full of experiments who had become too sick to live, too mentally unstable to control, who needed to be quieted before their organs could be harvested for analysis. Blue cups, misty with condensation, covered mouth and nose. IV stands with carefully repackaged coma juice sent each and every one of them into a blissful sleep they would never wake from. A whimper of denial crept out of Thresher's mouth. Terrified, he felt the hands holding him tighten as he convulsed.

It was too quiet in the room, no audible breathing, nothing but the violent straining of his hospital bed, no his *coffin*, as he kicked and twisted side to side. The walls were faded white tile. Goosebumps broke out over his arms. The room was cold enough for preservation.

He let out a guttural scream as his arm was yanked straight and taut, the familiar prick of a needle injected medicine that would render him limp and docile before he fell into the nevermore. He barely registered fingers stroking his hair, like they were sorry for what they were doing. It was their job. The Facility would run until all the parts rusted. Thresher was no longer usable—he was an experiment who had failed to cure his disease or prove immune to it. It was time to put him down and figure out *why*.

He felt sluggish. His legs calmed to a twitch. The petting became softer and longer. He was crying. Deep inside, he was a man blackened with unrealized potential that would never be nurtured to grow. He was one blip of data clustered on a graph, used to draw a line, helpful when calculating slope.

The mask stretched out above him like a spider covering his face. His head tilted forward and the elastic bands fit uncomfortably tight around his skull. As soon as the respirator settled over nose and mouth, he heard his breath as if from far underwater, gasping, panicked, and petrified.

He felt heavy, slightly numb, and tingly. He wasn't ready for this. A spike of grief drove through his chest. He had forgotten—a lifetime ago, so far away in a dream, and always too late—where he had laid a bent picture of a beautiful man and woman white and wrinkled from age on top of a dresser that belonged to a lost girl. Before he had lain in Nika's bed, he studied the picture, swearing that he would survive until his body collapsed. His golden thread wouldn't be cut. The spool would simply end.

A sharp pain slipped into the top of his hand, followed by the unmistakable tidal wave of coldness flooding his veins. He wanted to shudder, but he couldn't move. His head settled back on the fluffed pillow. Tears dried gritty on his eyes. A black heaviness tugged. His eyelids fluttered. His breathing dragged roughly.

He couldn't, he mustn't, he hoped…

48

T hey've got Maggie." Beau's hands perched on his hips and he stood, looking ready to take the Facility down brick by brick. Milo paused, a curved bone needle with black thread mid-stitch in Buck's forehead.

Jake rubbed a hand down his face, dragging at his mouth and wincing as he brushed the black bruise blossoming on his chin. His long hair had been singed, and scorch marks covered gnarled hands that patted the dented satchel at his hip. He pulled out his shredded bible. Even Milo couldn't begrudge him a cigarette. Jake tore an uneven strip and spread tobacco over the psalms. "I know," he said. "We got careless. A tribe's not bound by promises and words, and now our girl's been taken." Ash from his cigarette fell, curling the turf.

"I can't believe they did that," Tova said, her voice shaking. "I've always been able to come to some agreement." She plucked Jake's smoke from his mouth and inhaled deeply. Jake pulled her into a rough hug and held her for a long time.

Although the secondhand smoke tickled Nika's lungs, it calmed her. Nestled in the long grass shaded by a scraggly overgrowth, a place they had rested before their meeting with the Facility went sour, Nika felt slightly safe. The Facility remained out of sight, but its presence lay beyond the leafy brush and vines. A tangled mess of shame choked her. She could've done better, *been* better. For Walker. For her own self-respect.

Jake released his trade post witch and peered through the smoke at Milo. "You got the stash?"

Milo sucked in his lower lip. "Might not be good anymore."

"Ow, careful." Buck winced.

"Stash?" Nika asked, imagining rolls of parchment with stamped and notarized treaties that Jake could throw at the Facility's doorstep.

"What do you care, you Manahatta shit?" Buck snarled at her. "If it wasn't for your stupid *boyfriend* we wouldn't have lost Maggie in the first place."

"Maybe if you had the balls to defend your *girlfriend* properly she wouldn't have been hauled off," Nika said.

Buck jerked to stand, face red and murderous, but Milo pushed him down, tied off Buck's stitches, and wiped his knife, tacky with blood, on the ground.

"Tova," Jake said. "You know the land better than anyone. What's the best way to get inside without anyone noticing? I'd like to keep the rest of my hide, thank you."

Tova rubbed her arms, grabbed a stick, and cleared a spot in the dirt. She talked as she etched a blocky blueprint of the Facility on the ground. "The basement would be the hardest way to enter, even though it's mainly storage. The north end's abandoned, while the tribe resides in the eastern corners. Experiments are held in the center, surrounded by the living spaces of the rest of the tribe. Better to keep what you can control surrounded on all sides. Maggie has got to be somewhere secluded, but I don't know where."

"No," Nika said, her certainty like a black hole. "She's gonna be up near the top. They won't let her interact with the other experiments."

"Why's that?" Jake asked.

"Contamination," Nika said with a sick smile. "The whole point of having an outside female was to successfully breed her with the experiments. See if our compatibility would jumpstart the human race. They won't risk putting her with experiments that might ruin that possibility."

"Stealing tribesmen." Jake nodded.

Nika spread her hands. *Told you so.* "They won't hurt her, at least, not in the way you might think."

"You know your way around?" Milo asked.

"Get me in there and I'll recognize things." She pressed her palms together, feeling the slick slide of cool sweat from fighting off her fright, and suppressed a shudder. She pressed her hands into her eyes, imagining that the Facility had no pity for runaways.

"Do you know how to use a gun?" Milo said, flipping his knife closed.

"I've pulled a trigger once or twice." She imagined the family heirloom, the loud blast, the shattered thump of destroyed debris clattering to the concrete. Those weapons made her ill.

"Better than these youngsters." Milo sighed and itched his sandy beard. He dragged a red metal box into the light and snapped open the dirty metal clasps. The box, crusted over with packed mud and grime, creaked as it opened. It smelled like deep earth, rotten dampness, and sewage. Nika peered inside at the carefully laid guns, machetes, and violence.

"What is this?" she asked, awed.

"This is my past that I unburied at the safe house," Milo said. "Instincts told me to bring it along. Good thing I listened."

"I said I could shoot a gun. Not direct an army."

"Good thing for you, I can do both." Milo checked the smooth load of one of the guns. The click of the safety coupled with the sliding barrel made Nika uneasy. Too easy to kill with it, but she would do it anyway.

"Jakey, I can't go through that again. I've never shot anything, I can't fight—" Tova buried her face in her hands to muffle her sob.

"No one said you had to, Tova," Milo said, uncaring. He turned to Nika. "You thought our stash was nothing but a box of rocks to hurl at the enemy?"

"Yeah," Nika said, stunned. "I've never seen so many guns before in my life."

He grinned. "Don't I know it. Gun safety in ten minutes. We attack after that."

49

Walker pretended to be asleep. He concentrated on staying dead weight, letting his knees be hinges for his swinging legs. His lovely outsider clothes had been replaced with thick paperweight pants and shirt when he'd *actually* been unconscious. The orderly dragging him across the grainy tile floor couldn't stop cursing about *the piece of outsider shit.*

Unceremoniously shoved against a wall and left in a puddle of limbs on his side, Walker cracked an eyelid open. Within the shabby examination room, two orderlies from the End negotiation paced. A lightbulb flickered sporadically. An oval piece of equipment hung from the ceiling. A thick tan computer box perched on a wheeled cart. A chair stood behind the examination table. Ethanol permeated the air. Walker tried not to wrinkle his nose.

"This is insane," said the orderly with a smeared blood splotch on his stomach.

"Calm down," the other one said.

"It's not something to calm down from, Tom! Everything is falling apart!"

"We've got a viable female to continue testing—" Tom said.

"Testing should be abandoned! We should've transitioned to purge protocols after the first wave of plague set in. We haven't just lost half our experiments, we've lost half our staff."

"We only need one viable implantation, Jeff," Tom continued.

"You know last week I had to look Tina in the eye and tell her both her boys were dead? Do you know how that feels? After all we've done, we get wiped out by the damn flu?"

"So, what is it?" Tom finally snapped. "Is it the plague or is it the flu."

"Either way it's killed us."

"Evolution for you, baby."

"Fuck evolution."

"Evolution fucked us," Tom corrected. "Even viruses and bacteria mutate. We aren't dealing with the same shit that affected our grandfathers. This was a possibility. It was why we kept everything here locked up tight from everything out there."

"We should abandon integration protocols and cleanse. Who knows what else those outsiders brought in with them? Most of us aren't going to survive this epidemic."

"It's not only the outside," Tom said, tapping his mouth. "You know what Adam did. Then there was Bible-thumping Rachel before him. At least she got what she deserved. I'm surprised she hasn't croaked while incinerating all the plague patients."

Jeff's lip curled in disgust. "At least Adam confessed that he'd been fucking around with an experiment. A mutated one at that. I can't imagine it."

"To each his own, I suppose."

"That's like screwing around with your children. You think these experiments can think? They're nothing more than brain-damaged kids."

"You've been in the mental ward too long."

"That was the *only* blessing of the sickness." Jeff looked forlorn. "Took those poor ones out of their misery."

"Shhh." Tom looked over his shoulder. "Here she comes."

The woman who had conducted the negotiations shoved the door open, hitting Walker hard in the shin. He bit down on his tongue to keep from crying out in pain. Only bruises. Bruises fade. Bruises heal.

She dragged Maggie, dressed in a loose, open-backed robe, inside and threw her on the examination table. Stuffing poked out of the cracked plastic covering. Maggie whimpered.

"Lie down," the woman ordered. "Don't move." Maggie shook like a leaf, but obeyed. The three doctors put silver saggy bags over her stomach, throat, and private parts. The woman wiggled the overhanging equipment over Maggie's body and rolled another half-broken machine closer. She shooed the two men out of the room and followed them out, dimming the lights. Walker closed his eyes and tried to be as small as possible. Three clicks followed by a deep rumble like a door breaking under a battering ram emitted from the cart.

The doctors reentered and lifted the bags, helping Maggie sit upright on the table. The woman waited by the computer box, her fingernails tapping on the dull plastic.

"Feeling lucky, Jen?" Jeff asked, shifting from foot to foot.

"We'll see," Jen said. "Lucky we got a viable specimen. Unlucky that we've pissed off the Enders."

"We need only one, right?" Tom asked.

"If she's good, we'll inseminate her. It's our last shot since most of our tests were duds." Jen turned to give Maggie a soft smile that ended up looking manic. "We'll let you go home soon enough."

Tears slipped out of Maggie's reddened eyes. Her arms wrapped around herself and Jen smirked, looked back to the computer. Walker imagined Maggie's insides translating into codes of data. He knew computers were beautiful machines that rarely worked anymore.

"Shit!" Jen banged her hand down hard on the cart. Tom gaped at the screen.

"What is it?" Jeff asked. "Not my specialty, looking at bones."

"Her leg," Tom said, pointing to the screen. "See that? Big mass there? Could be cancer."

"Does your leg hurt?" Jen demanded, looking like she might attack Maggie. "Answer me!"

"Sometimes when I walk it feels swollen," Maggie stammered.

"Could operate," Tom suggested. "She doesn't need her leg to be pregnant."

"It could've moved to her bones by now. She could be dead within weeks." Jen sighed, her head slumping forward. Her fingers dug into her scalp.

Maggie paled, her mouth pinched tight. Her small legs dangled above the ground, swaying back and forth like she was her own ticking pendulum.

"Do we terminate then?" Tom asked.

"She's our last chance," Jen said. Blood covered her fingers. "The other girl escaped when Adam fucked up by screwing around with his experiment."

"We're going to have to purge," Tom said. "I know we never said we would, but we need to eliminate everyone who's infected."

"Thank you," Jeff said, slamming his fist in the air like he had won an award. "Finally, someone has the decency to say it."

Jen looked ill. "After all this time, it's going to end like this? We've worked so hard for so long. We had decades of hopeful science, and now we end up in the darkness with the rest of them? I wonder if the Greeks knew it, when their civilization was about to collapse. If the Egyptians knew they were going under. I wonder if it felt like this for them."

"Recovery would be too long if we amputate," Tom whispered. "We should do it, anyway."

"Might die of infection on the table. Best to leave it on," Jen said, turning back to look at the screen. Her mouth had deep lines around them, as if she frowned too much.

Maggie's high-pitched cry startled Walker to his very bones. She leapt off the table and dove for the skeleton chair, picked it up, and smashed it over Jeff's head. The man crumbled.

Walker jumped to his feet and in two strides, cocked his elbow back and punched Tom so hard in the face he wondered briefly if his knuckles had collapsed. He bellowed in agony, but he had one job to do. Take them out so Maggie could escape. His fist collided with the doctor's face again and the two slid to the floor. Walker held the doctor with his knees as bone crunched and the nose collapsed in a heap of flattened cartilage. Blood spackled his face. Small ragged gasps wheezed through Tom's broken teeth, but when Walker pulled back, he wasn't sure if Tom was dead or simply unconscious.

His hand throbbed and began to swell. He glanced around wildly, finding that Maggie had mangled Jen's head with the computer box. Sparks shot from the cracked screen. Blood soaked Maggie's robe and left her bare arms and hands glossy red.

"Don't say anything about my leg, okay?" she said, her voice breathy and panicked as she wiped as much blood off as she could with the hospital gown, before stripping Jen, and yanking the stolen shirt over her head. "I don't want the boys to know."

Walker's gut twisted in immediate admiration and fear. "I won't say a word."

Maggie swallowed hard, as if trying to find her voice, and nodded. "Good. You know the way out, yeah?"

"Yeah," Walker said. "I have to get Thresher first."

"Where's he at?"

Walker could see Maggie barely hanging on, that this small, prematurely white-haired beauty was no longer the quiet thing he had first met on the beach. She had taken Jake's advice to fight her own battles. "Probably the intensive care unit."

"What's that?"

"It's where experiments are taken to die," Walker said, the throbbing flare in his hand matching the pain in his heart. "He's got ALS, see? He's dying, just like you."

Maggie pursed her lips and didn't respond. She pattered to the door and looked through the window. "Let's go, then."

50

Walker remembered the hallways quiet with respect for the experiments, but never eerily abandoned or full of chilling ghosts. He checked each room, convinced he would startle a nurse taking an experiment's blood pressure. Instead, the clean sterility had been marred by disorder. Locked rooms held nothing inside but bursting orange biohazard buckets. Precious medical supplies had been spilled across the floor, once-reverent equipment overturned on the floor, and the uncanny quiet of barricaded rooms stuffed with the slack-mouthed dead. They snuck past a couple of doctors dressed for travel, frantically stuffing supplies and folders into bags.

"Something's wrong," Walker said, strangely unsettled at the disruption of the place.

"You think?" Maggie hissed behind him.

She didn't understand. She didn't know it *before*, when things worked as well-oiled machines and doctors of care and treatment floated from room to room. He couldn't imagine a virus demolishing a place that had fought so long and hard to rid itself of modern-day ailments and long-standing diseases, but it was like Tom had said. Evolution.

He rounded a corner, trying to calculate the fastest way to the basement. He had never been inside that specific ward, but he knew it was like an oubliette where once the door shut, it never opened again. It terrified him but in an addictive way. Adrenaline poured in his bloodstream. Every sound that wasn't him or Maggie brought him on a razor edge where everything sharpened intimately. Maggie's breathing heated the back of his neck as she fought not to cry. He could smell and taste a thousand times better. Right now, the air was chock full of spilled lemon sanitizer and an underlying scent of rot.

Walker held the door to the stairwell open for her. His feet made slippery sounds against the stone stairs as they descended. Maggie cleared her nose with a loud snotty sniffle. They hit the last step with nowhere to go but out into the final hallway. Trepidation egged Walker on. His purpose to save Thresher made him anxious, but Thresher was a brother, someone who couldn't be left behind.

Grief suddenly shook him. He leaned into the door's handle, unable to turn it, imagining his doctor strung high on the scaffolding with a pitiless ashen light behind him. His knees nearly buckled. His doctor who loved chocolate and the aftermath of sex, who liked to kiss him soft on the mouth, now hung among the elements with one eye pecked out by the crows.

Walker gritted his teeth. He understood now what it meant to be responsible for others, how he had used love to get him out. Nika was right when she said they should've killed him. It's what a good man would've done for his cherished ones.

He pushed the door open and felt along the wall for the light switch. Clicking it, a familiar generator whir turned the electricity on. The lightbulbs flickered, bathing them in an off-white sickly light. Maggie gripped a handful of his shirt between his shoulder blades.

Barrels of preserved stock food were stacked against the wall alongside mouse-chewed boxes full of empty syringe packaging and thumb sized glass vials whose contents had evaporated. Mold darkened the plaster between the wall tiles. Black rubber skid marks, dust, and mothballs floated across the floor like a desert's tumbleweeds. Walker hoped the light would still hold until they reached the end.

The junk dwindled away, revealing at least thirty hospital beds stacked next to old, incompatible equipment. Maggie's hand tightened in his shirt. Walker approached the young man in the first bed, somewhat in shock over the worse-for-wear conditions of the room. A wrinkled plastic bag flooded clear liquid into the man's veins. Walker touched his hair, felt the brown strands cling to the spaces between his fingers, and accidentally pulled out a handful of thin locks. The contact between the pillow and skull had already rubbed part of him bald.

"What *is* this?" Maggie said, glancing into the faces of the next two hospital bed occupants.

"I'm sorry," Walker said gently. Bedsores covered the sallow shrivel of muscle. He showed no signs of aging, but Walker knew his avenging disease required containment. Alzheimer's? Huntington's?

"They've fucking…"

"Atrophied," Walker finished for her. The pain in his chest couldn't expand any farther and set up house in his gut. He went to the next two beds, checking for Thresher's dark hair and scars.

The fourth was dead, judging by the ripe smell, the way the saline and food bag had been drained dry. Souls packaged into comas.

"This one's dreaming," Maggie said quietly, three more down. "Her eyes are moving."

Walker wanted to unhook them all from whatever dark dreams they wandered in, but time was short. He didn't know how to handle waking up an experiment that could no longer walk due to their inactivity. They might be brain dead, too, and stare at him through glazed eyes with vague understanding. Again, he felt the low blow of responsibility. He wanted to be better than the doctors who left these experiments to be forgotten among the rest of the outdated, broken equipment, but he walked among them with his choice to wake one and leave the rest.

"He's here," Maggie called, five more down. "What do I do?"

Walker jogged to Maggie. Thresher looked almost peaceful, his dark lashes a smudge against the purple rings under his eyes. His long legs stuck over the end of the bed. His mouth parted slightly underneath the respirator.

Walker brushed Thresher's dark hair off his forehead and circled the T on his wrist, strummed the fine ligaments there like a guitar. He wondered if it was a kindness to bring Thresher back to the pain, horror, and simple strength required for survival. Wouldn't it be better to rest than be filled with life's fury?

He recalled the first whispers of rain. Cold, refreshing, and humid. He remembered Nika holding him in the ocean, floating like he was flying with the pushing tide. He memorized her mouth, the fear of her displeasure amplifying his pleasure. He wouldn't give that up. The fury was worthwhile.

"Help me," he said, bringing Thresher's head forward and loosening the elastic bands. Maggie worked the buckles loose. Walker carefully eased the IV out. The liquid squirted on the floor. A small pinprick of blood welled out of the wound.

"Thresher," Maggie called, shaking his shoulder. "Wake up."

"It's going to take a moment."

"We don't have a moment."

"The drugs have to work through his system. Give it a few minutes. He'll wake up."

"And if he doesn't?" Maggie asked. "If we're stuck down here when they find us?"

Walker took Thresher's hand and squeezed tight enough to feel Thresher's bones creak. "He'll wake up."

Thresher was in the black until he was in the light—red, bright, and painful against his eyelids. He craved water with a ferocity that scared him. The black had drained him of liquid, sustenance, and hollowed him out to fill him up as part of the darkness.

He might have wanted to stay in the black if he wasn't so thirsty.

Someone called to him, using that old name bestowed upon him by a beloved—fifty-three freckles at last count—begging him to open his eyes.

He felt cold and his first escape rushed back, how he had been stranded where the Bony Lady's mirage beckoned him to the sand and the ocean—oh, water, how he *needed* water.

Stickiness like tape along his eyelids. His lips smacked like a newborn. With delight, he realized he could move his arms and legs.

"Wake up, Thresher, wake up."

There was no disobeying the Bony Lady. She brought him so much joy when he followed her instructions. He could discern her slender ribs caging her heart, the long white line of her femur, her painted skull under a cowl. She reached inside him, lifted him up with the light, and spread a brand of silence in his marrow.

"It's been too long, he needs to wake up *now*."

"Thresher, *Thresher*..."

He blinked, opened to the sun, and saw Walker nose-to-nose with him. "Hey, there," Walker said. "Sleep well?"

"Water," Thresher begged.

"I'd like some too," the female, *Maggie*, said, tapping her foot. "If you get on your feet, I promise I'll get you some."

Walker helped slide him to the edge of the bed and put Thresher's arm over his shoulders, hefting his weight. "Are you hurt?" Thresher asked. He couldn't feel his mouth. His tongue tingled, but he seemed obliged to address the mottled red splotch coating Walker's chest.

"Not mine," Walker said. "Borrowed clothes."

Thresher's awareness narrowed dizzily down to those two words. He talked like Mako.

"Who's Mako?" Maggie asked.

Thresher didn't realize he had said it out loud and tried to stop his feet from waddling. He paused, staring at the bodies lined against the wall.

"I was one of them, wasn't I?" he asked, failing to stop his voice from trembling.

Walker hesitated. "Yes. But we got you out. *We got you out.*"

Thresher began to cry. "I want to go home."

"Is that who Mako is?" Maggie asked. "Your home?"

"Yes," Thresher cried. "I want to go *home*."

51

Nika cradled the gun strapped across her body like a newborn as she maneuvered through the barbed fences to the boarded-up door hidden behind vines and castoff junk on the Facility's northern side. A sheen of sweat glistened on the butt of the gun from her hands. A grenade waited in her pocket. Milo's crash course in gun safety flipped through her mind, and unlike the gnarled trees used as target practice, it didn't seem likely that an attacker would wait for her to line up the tiny notch at the end of the barrel with their heart.

Jake guided them through another defective trap attempting to block and ensnare them. She couldn't imagine anything more important than defense, but when one lived in a golden castle, one tended to forget about what dangers might be evolving on the outside.

Crushed glass sprinkled over the debris-covered floor and cast rainbows on the peeling walls. Beside demolished equipment and thick, frayed wires, small bird corpses no bigger than her wrist curled under drifted brown leaves, fragile feet crinkled into tight Os.

Milo stopped in front of two tall double doors. Sweat wetted his hair a dirty yellow. "Release anything and anyone that'll create chaos." It sounded like he had given these orders before. "It'll be easier if the Promised Land loses control internally *and* externally."

Nika knew going inside would be the biggest mistake of her life, but her wrongs had to be cleansed. She had abandoned Walker one too many times for fourth and fifth chances. They only masqueraded as promises, anyway.

A gleam lit Tobey's eyes like he might just enjoy this *mission*.

"Don't shoot unless necessary. Use your cover," Milo continued, refusing to look at any of them directly. "You're *nothing* to them. Don't think you know more than you do, but remember what they took from us."

"Yes, Milo," the End pups echoed.

"Gonna be okay," Jake whispered, putting his hand on Milo's shoulder.

"I don't want to do this," Milo said suddenly, angrily. "I don't want to be that child again, fighting because I need to eat, killing because I'm told to."

Jake's hand tightened. "You've made me prouder than I care to admit."

Milo's jaw clenched with a click and he let out a deep breath through his nose. His hand covered Jake's as if finding comfort in the touch. "Let's get our girl back."

Planks, nails, and rusted metal piled up as the End pups dismantled the door. Inside, the darkness had the sterilized smell that tried to hide the stench of disuse. The Facility had always given Nika the impression of hugeness: chock full of bustling doctors, experiments shuttled from the recreation room to the exercise room, and the ever-present threat of watchfulness. She assumed she had seen only one part of a sprawling enterprise. In reality, she had taken the full tour without realizing it.

She had to applaud them. Not only had she been manipulated physically, she had gone through the whole mind fuck too.

It didn't take her long to get her bearings once the hallway emerged into the cafeteria's back kitchen, a place where the scent of oats and wilted vegetables wafted, where she had peered around countertops and pots, straining to see what pills would be in her cup for the day.

Jars of preserves and pickled food were strewn across the floor, a nauseating mixture of vinegar and jam. Linoleum tables were bent in half and thrown to the side. Ash overflowed from the black-scorched fireplaces. The place looked picked-over. Looted. Further out into the main eating area, clumps of motionless bodies slumped against the chairs and tables. In all her nightmares, she had never imagined such eerie silence. She peered into the face of an experiment, eyes half-open with sores marching down his temples and along his mouth. Her eyebrows drew together. The open wounds looked familiar. A child's disease, something she had had multiple times growing up, and now here in a new, terrible form.

"Is that spotted flu?" she asked in a hushed voice.

Milo gave her a strange look. "Don't know the term."

"It's a childhood sickness, like chicken pox," she said. "I had it when I was really young. Gave me sores everywhere, but no one worried about it since it was simply one of those things that kids got. I was better in no time."

"We call it spotted fever," Beau said quietly. "This...this *has* to be something else."

Nika shook her head in denial. Milo bumped her gently, and she motioned silent directions by the crook of her finger until they entered her old ward. It was like stepping back in time. The divot in the wall was still there. The raised floor tile near her room still waited to trip orderlies new on the job.

Experiments and doctors alike were collapsed against the walls or curled in the beds, the spotted pustules leaking from the mouths and noses of the fallen. Others were curled together, as if having sought comfort before the end. Doors had been locked with people inside, as if trying to keep the infection contained before they realized the endeavor was helpless. Nika covered her mouth with her sleeve. Silence hung in the ward, ultimate and absolute, and the tribe backed away from it. Nothing remained there.

Nika wracked her brain, wondering where Maggie could be if not here. This sickness had ruthlessly swept through the Facility, and she knew of only one place where they'd take someone as precious as a fertile outsider. The doctors' mecca, a place of study and camaraderie that she'd heard of but never been inside.

She squeezed Milo's arm in reassurance. His pinched face relaxed a bit. Back downstairs on the ground floor, Nika guided them past quarters that always remained closed off and secret, but she knew the library by its tall, exquisite doors, unique to the rest of the unadorned Promised Land. She pulled on the door handles and felt a slight give, as if barricaded from the inside. "Notes on tests, past documents, successes, failures are all kept here," she said. "If Maggie's anywhere, it's here."

Jake placed his hand on the door, his gun like a pointed accusation. "Maggie Mae, be still," he called. "We're coming for you."

Nika swallowed hard and took the grenade out of her pocket. The rest of the tribe backed away, finding shelter around the hallway's offshoot. Pulling the ring, she dropped the small bomb in front of the doors, and scrambled to where Jake and Beau took cover. Jake's lungs rattled as he struggled for breath, noticeable only because she was next to him.

A pop sounded in her ears. The explosion blew heat, splintered wood, and shrapnel down the hall. Smoke billowed around the ceiling like the reaching hands of a monstrous shadow. Jake screamed something Nika didn't understand, but she knew the tone, even with her muted, damaged hearing. How tempers led to triggers. A battle cry.

The Enders surged into the library and coalesced into a square with weapons raised and aimed. Nika felt safe in the back of the formation, wishing she had *her* tribe at her back.

Bookshelves and metal cabinets lined the back of the room, higher than she could imagine. Big windows reflected the oncoming twilight. The electric light had a soft quality compared to the flicking industrial lightbulbs outside. Faded colored portraits graced the walls. The sacredness of the place where doctors came to shake hands and talk, act out their ceremonies on scratched chalkboard surfaces, hit her like a hammer.

In front of them, toppled bookcases, desks, and chairs had been pushed together to create a barrier. Debris and thick splinters impaled the walls and mismatched furniture from the grenade. Mechanical clicks filled the room, and it took her a moment to understand the sound of guns being cocked and loaded before the world shattered around her. Bullets from behind the barrier rained around them. Holes riddled the wallpaper. A desk, shredded to pieces, smashed against a window, leaving a spider web crack in the glass. Papers floated to the floor. A haze like dissipating fog enhanced the groans of the undecided victor. The fight had become gritty and dirty too fast.

Nika ducked behind Beau, her mind going black even as her body took control. She crashed against the wall, sliding behind an overturned examination table while furniture turned to firewood around her. Clapping her hands over her ears, she screamed as Tobey smashed into the space with her and she fought hard to take deep cleansing breaths. His fear amplified her own. Remembering she could fight back, Nika fumbled with her gun, heard the unmistakable scream of the dying, even as the assault relentlessly continued. Her head leaned back against the tacky blue plastic and she stuck her eye to the open space made between the table's hinge and cushion.

Out of the wreckage, she saw a familiar face rise up from behind the wall of the Facility's last resort. Her psychiatrist fired the final rounds of whatever weapon he held and threw it aside, ducked back behind the wall to grab another. Terror rolled through her like a punch in the gut. She whipped away from the viewing hole, her back pressed hard to the table as sweat dribbled down her spine. She covered her mouth to seal in the whimper, hard enough to bruise. She couldn't make a sound or else her psychiatrist would see, *he would know where she was...*

Another ream of bullets cascaded around her, louder and petrifying, until she realized whichever Enders had their heads on straight were fighting back. Tobey slid the barrel of his gun over the table. His gun rattled off, the slight kick thudding into his shoulder.

Her own gasps toned with those dying pants until she couldn't tell where hers began and theirs ended, until hers were the only ones left. "Mako," she prayed to the ceiling. "I'll kneel in front of the Bony Girl and say right to her withered face that she's right and I'm wrong if you come find me right now."

A tight pain spiked through her. She wondered how long Tobey had been digging his fingers into the meat of her shoulder before another round of bullets shattered the remaining cover and split his skull in two. Blood coated her face, thick brain matter sliding down his ruined face, as he collapsed.

A sound of victory drew her attention to the wall where her psychiatrist reloaded an ancient weapon. Fury filled his eyes when he caught her gaze, and she knew with her cover gone, he would have his sights set on her before she could make it to safety. She rolled, nearly vomited from the adrenaline coursing through her, and cradled her gun close.

She had entered a new game of survival.

Her psychiatrist came for her, trading blasts with other shooters, his dark skin beaded with blood. Nika scrambled into the hallway, not just running from him, but from the pit where he had bound her, asking if giving up control was worth being treated like an animal.

Sliding behind a hallway jut, she tried to calm down, thought of it as a quiet game. Simple really. Except this had a little bit of hide-and-go-seek mixed in with it.

No problem. She was a pro at hide-and-go-seek. She remembered Mako trying to find her, thinking he could outsmart her, that she was stupid enough to hide somewhere so easy. Then, she'd shoved her hand over her mouth to stifle her giggles.

She wasn't giggling now. Those were real screams bottling the back of her throat, but if she let them out she would lose. She hated losing.

The black butt of her gun ground into her pelvis. Her finger thumbed convulsively over the safety, even as she kept her trigger finger alongside the trigger itself because *if your finger gets twitchy you're going to shoot your own leg off, so get your finger off the damn trigger.* Right, Milo. You're so right. Good pointers.

She brought one shaking leg up slowly and twisted to until she perched on her knees. She wished the Facility would give up. She couldn't handle the ringing silence between gunshots and wanted to put her hands over her ears, lay her forehead on the ground, but that meant she would have to let go of the gun, ha, like that would ever happen.

As she put the gun against her shoulder, she heard the whisper of her psychiatrist's feet against the floor. He never called out to her. He wouldn't waste his breath explaining anything to her anymore.

She bared her teeth, felt the sweat on her upper lip wet the tip of her nose. *He* was the animal, a monster who had put a fear in her belly that she couldn't shake.

Lifting the gun up, she set the monster's forehead dead center in the notch and fit her finger snug around the trigger. The recoil was hard enough to send a numb tingle sliding down her arm. The bullet puffed into the ceiling tile with a rain of plaster.

"Shit!" She pressed the gun against her cheek so hard she thought she might break skin. Her location revealed, he ran for her, his own gun lifting to take her life. She fired two more shots at him, wildly missing each time. She was doing it right, *she was aiming through the fucking notch*, but Milo's voice in the back of her head roared that she was jackrabbiting the trigger, jerking her arms up in preparation for the recoil, get a hold of yourself and *do it smooth*.

She lined up the shot—his gun nearly towered over her—breathed out and pulled the trigger so slowly she could almost count the seconds until it fired. Her first true shot clipped his eyebrow ridge, sending a triangle of bone and brain matter ricocheting against the floor. Her cry of victory was drowned out by the slew of fire as she unloaded until the gun clicked empty. Her ears had been blown by gunfire.

Her psychiatrist spasmed, and something inside of her cut free, a tense terror feeling with the death of a man who had caused her so much heartache and misery. For a span of moments that stretched a lifetime, elation rushed through her, a kind of peace that told her she could learn to *live* again. She twisted to her feet, her gun emptied and forgotten. The pitter-patter of gunfire ricocheted behind her. With her back turned to the carnage, she apologized to the Enders. She couldn't become one of their tribe. She had her people to find. Death hadn't marked her, yet.

52

Mako slid his machete against the red-haired woman's throat and pulled her back against him. A husky cry escaped her mouth, but she went limp and didn't struggle. She had been sitting in a small glen looking out towards the building that belonged more in the city streets than this wilderness.

Mako envisioned Anna-Skye's neck under his blade in place of this red-haired woman's and knew that if he turned this woman around to face him, he would stare into the dim gray coins of her eyes and wouldn't be responsible for his actions. "Are you one of the Promised Land?" he crooned. She quivered as he pressed the blade harder against her bobbing throat, making her utter a squeak of fear. Soul-Dago emerged in front of them, and Mako gave him a vicious smile, playing a bit. "Answer his question," Soul-Dago said.

Could *exhaustion* be shading Soul-Dago's eyes? His black hair was wild and matted, an unhealthy leanness starting to show in his body. Perhaps Mako had finally worn him down as they covered extensive ground to the eastern lands.

"No," the woman stuttered. "I'm not one of them. I show fealty to no tribe but myself."

"Liar." Mako nicked her neck. "I haven't seen *anyone* new since Manahatta. If you're not part of the Promised Land, why are you here?"

Her choking cry made Mako cringe. Fever still raged inside him, but it had become manageable, despite the shivers and aches. He was glad Mama Milagros had taken the time to gather herbs for his illness, glad she wasn't here to see him.

She might've been right about his brain being fried. He saw sharks everywhere. Swimming through the trees like the earth was their ocean, flashing in and out of sight as bright bursting blinks of pain blinded him. These predators of the past haunted him, curious yet wary, frenzied and alone in a sea of timelines.

"Who are you then?" Soul-Dago asked, snapping Mako out of his reverie.

"I'm a trader." Her soft sobs interrupted her sentence. "Please, let me go."

Mako eased back, letting her breathe, and made his hand, shaking in disgust, still.

"What do you trade?" Soul-Dago asked.

"Anything. Whatever the Promised Land wants, but they don't own me."

"Do you know how to get inside?" Mako asked.

"Weak spots," Soul-Dago added. "Places we won't be noticed."

"Have your man let me go and I'll tell you," she said.

Soul-Dago quirked an eyebrow, a question instead of a command, and Mako nearly laughed, remembering how angry he had been when Soul-Dago asked for his fealty. Now, it was simply *assumed*. He released her, stepped into her view, and pointed his knife at her.

She pressed on the cut. Her eyes shone with a cunning that made Mako's bones itch with the same crazed urge to run. She frowned at him. "I know someone in the Promised Land who has the look of you."

The small, guttural keen in Mako's throat shamed him, but he couldn't help his hope. "Nika?" He sounded breathless, but the sharks couldn't take her from him. She was part of him—not only his past, but his future—and she still lived.

"Manahattas everywhere," the woman uttered.

"You have no idea," Soul-Dago said dryly.

"Where is she?" Mako asked. Soul-Dago rested a warning hand on his arm, but Soul-Dago didn't understand. If Mako sat still for too long, the sharks began to circle him, eager to devour him in his fatigue. "How do you know her?"

"She was…involved in my trade."

"How do we find her?" Mako wondered if Soul-Dago had a touch of the hainted in him, too, a bloodlust that could pinpoint a drop of havoc from miles away. "Or are you loyal to the Promised Land?"

"No," she snorted. "Take the south side. It enters the morgue." She paused. "I hope you find her. Her tribeswoman betrayed her. I…know how that feels."

Soul-Dago nodded, forced her hands behind her back, and tied them swiftly together. Mako placed a makeshift blindfold over her eyes while she struggled on the grass. She wasn't worth the risk if she'd lied.

Soul-Dago pressed a hand on Mako's chest. "Wait for me, Mako."

"I can't," he said, thumbing his machete.

The pressure increased. "You can. Let me collect Mama Milagros."

Mako felt his heart bleed, knowing he had to staunch the wound with revenge, but he clung to his identity instead, the man who loved and lived in the moment, who could wait if asked.

Edging out of the forest, Mako felt exposed as they snuck across the clearing to the large industrial doors. The leaves Mama Milagros had forced down his throat left a bitter aftertaste, but his head felt clearer. They slid against the wall as the doors opened and a woman emerged, the same sickness of the Shinnecoes lining her face. Mako slit her throat before she could cry out. Mama Milagros's face paled as the girl convulsed, but she still followed them inside.

Bodies, more than Mako could count, waited in rows on the floor. Calmness overtook his insides, and he would soon be lost within numbing violence.

The haint had followed him inside the Promised Land, its streamlined gray-blue body giving up fins for legs, a bone mask keeping its true face obscured. It looked around the corner and fixated on him with one clouded eye. Underneath the unmoving milk, something round and black shifted focus, as if it weren't just *one* starting at him, but two. Strips of meat and white cartilage hung from the corner of the its jaw. Mako trembled, touched his forehead to feel the hot spike of fever, but calm acceptance still filled him. Once, he would have denied this hoo-doo vision, but that haint was a piece of his excavated soul, born in the Woodlands and brought to life through hallucination. It was the thing he became in the Woodlands: the masked killer, the heartless torturer, the man driven insane from loss.

The walls of the Promised Land whizzed by him as they crept further inside. A doctor slumped against the floor, a needle eased into a deceased experiment's tattooed arm and left hanging from the vein. "Purge protocol," the doctor whispered. An empty vial, marked with skull and crossbones, rolled out of his hand. The haint opened its razor-lined mouth around the doctor's head and Mako acquiesced. Purge protocols worked both ways, apparently.

The doctor was one of many that Mako passed by among the coughing, the shaking, the weak. *Purge protocol* they must have declared before ending the lives of those around them, but when they saw Mako now they wept and pleaded, *"Oh god, oh god, I don't want to die."*

His soft questions were never answered. Flesh parted underneath his machete. The piles of dead grew. In the distance, the sound of a bomb thundered through the hallway.

"Where do you keep the outsiders? The newly returned?" he thundered.

Blood coated Soul-Dago's chest. Mako smiled at him, and Soul-Dago grinned back, making Mako wonder what the future held in store for them as they encountered more doctors fleeing in one direction.

Some stopped and brandished surgical saws at them. One frantically loaded an old shotgun. Shells tumbled to the ground with small pings as Mako and Soul-Dago advanced. Mako's hungry machete clashed with the pristine steel of the saw.

"Where do you keep the outsiders?" he yelled into his opponent's face. The doctor wasn't strong enough to keep his blade matched with Mako's. The haint loomed above him, and Mako laughed, something wild, unpredictable. The doctor weakened. Mako struck.

The sound of the shotgun suddenly deafened him from behind, a momentary silence like a single gasp before the ringing whine made him shake his head and turn from the newly impaled doctor sliding down his blade.

Backed against the wall, the doctor with the double barrel wrestled with Mama Milagros, the gun like a tug-of-war between them, trying to point the long barrel into her chest for the second shot. Plastic shells rolled across the tile. Her mouth bared in a snarl, but before Mako could reach her, the end dipped down, close to her hip, and another blast echoed throughout the hallway.

A splatter streaked the wall as she collapsed, the smell of gunpowder and blood thick in the air. Mama Milagros's agonized scream was a sound he had never heard from her before.

The doctor shoved Mama Milagros off, scrambling for another shell, but crumpled when Soul-Dago slit his throat. Soul-Dago's long finger pointed at Mako. "Get the rest of them," he commanded and Mako spun back to see the remaining doctors skidding away. The haint raced away from Mama Milagros, anxious to devour the carnage of the anticipated battle, impossible for Mako to resist.

The doctor's companion uttered a high-pitched yelp as he caught sight of Mako, and cried out, "He's coming."

"Shuddup, *he'll hear you.*" A woman muffled him with her arm and pulled them down a short hallway as if to hide. Mako breathed hard as he caught and held her eyes, the way her mouth tightened knowing he was right on their heels.

The haint stood over them as they launched into a room with wide grated glass panels. The woman managed to slam the door in Mako's face as he charged them. Waiting to be fed, the psychopomp's hot exhale warmed Mako's cheek as if ready to consume the leftovers of Mako's violence.

"I don't want to die, oh god, leave us alone!" the man cried.

"Where do you keep the outsiders? The newly returned?" Mako bellowed.

"The library," the woman shouted. Only one pane separated her from Mako.

"Tell me where."

She rattled off directions as her companion clutched her shirt. His eyes rolled, white as any stallions. "Please let us go, we'll do anything *please—*"

The haint's howl nearly deafened him, so desolate and lonesome. The glass shattered. Warmth radiated from the gun barrel in his hand, and Mako realized he had shot just to get to them, even though they told him what he wanted to know.

"Don't, please don't!"

They tried to run, screaming like fighting cats cut off by a drowning crunch. Warm iron blood mixed with the gutter smell of loosened bowels, the stick-snap of bones splitting, the sloppy mush of intestines being rooted through, coupled with the reedy gasp of someone watching themselves be disemboweled.

"Mako," a soft hushed whisper said. He snarled at the voice, but through the inhumanity of blood and fury, it was impossible to deny the woman in front of him, her familiar golden-brown legs, the brown mole on her forehead, and the scatter of freckles dotting her face. He had personally witnessed those limbs developing out of a cluster of cells, even if he didn't remember it. They shared everything: first breaths, first cries, first words. He would know his twin anywhere, from her dark hair to their matching eyes.

Trying to obscure her, the haint's skull cracked, shiny pink muscle and a lipless mouth shaping words he couldn't catch. The ghost reared back, skidding in a puddle of leftover organs, its skin peeling back like ripped cloth, exposing a dark veined sheen that was smaller, fragile. The back stretched like a cat, spiny knobs rising from the flesh and popping back into place like cracking knuckles. The last half of the skull—*a mask*—clattered to the floor as the haint faded and absorbed back into him.

"Nika." His voice broke. He felt *whole,* but self-loathing rolled through him as he looked at what his hands had done. How utterly he had followed the easy trail of destruction laid out by the haint. This vicious, bloodied man wasn't her twin. He hated that after all this time, the first thing she saw of him was the ugly lair of his soul.

His twin shuffled forward into the gore and enveloped him in a hug. "You smell like a toilet," she sobbed. "And your breath reeks, but I'm so happy to see you." Slickness coated her arms, making her reunion slippery business.

"You're here." Mako's voice sounded harsh and guttural as he clutched her to him, the grounding point within the lightning bolt of his insanity. After so long, her presence sucked the scattered pieces of his life back together. She held him so tight his chest struggled for air. *"You're here."*

"They thought you were a girl," she said, almost shouting. "All this time, the doctors thought *my* twin was a *girl.*" Her weeping dissolved into thick, breathless laughter.

He hung onto her every word because she was something beyond this world. He knew her inside and out, from the womb and beyond. He couldn't let her think he clung onto the soul-scraps of her brother by a thread. Her Mako would laugh in the face of danger. Her brother wouldn't have given in to the haint. "Must've been bad doctors to get such an inaccurate family medical history."

"And you know what you've done, don't you? Beyond slaughtering all those people, you *scared* me out of my mind."

He shuddered, but when he looked at her, he realized that everything bad had been worth it. "Feeling is...mutual."

"Don't do it again."

53

N ika's hand hooked around his, exactly how they had once held hands when their mother took them to a cove where the water filtered from toxic green to a nice teal, where the mud had reverted back to sand. Together, they rose from the tiled floor, slick with the haint's slaughter. Mako looked anywhere but there—not because he didn't understand the ramifications of his actions, oh no, they were seared into his mind—but because he didn't want those people-turned-meat to haunt him. Arms around each other, the twins stumbled into the hallway.

Soothing coos vibrated between Mama Milagros and Nika as they embraced, but Mako couldn't release his twin's hand. He swayed beside them as Soul-Dago helped ease Mama Milagros into a lost-and-found wheelchair.

While bone poked out of her femur underneath the tourniquet Nika had tied. Black blood trickled out of the wound. Her knee looked like it had been gouged out with a spoon and the rest of the leg flopped sickeningly loose. Her lips, slightly blue, sent Mako careening into panic. Her necklace had been ripped from her throat, and when he reached to pick out the beads tangled in her hair, she cringed.

His heart ached, wrung like a dirty rag. Mama Milagros had been the one to teach him about indestructible love. Yet now, she feared him.

Nika's halting words chased away his hurt as she traded her story for her grandmother's. When she finished, she squeezed his shoulder. "You okay?" Her eyebrows drew together in concern.

Now that he had his twin at his side, Mako started to fade, the eroded pillar of his willpower beginning to topple. "I don't know." He had an odd sense of absence, and that to be more *Mako*, he should've smiled broadly and lied.

"Rethinking if all this is worth our water rights, Soul-Dago?" Nika asked, giving the Bruykleener a nasty wink. Nika's age-old hatred had woken, and while she might resent the Bruykleener's presence, Mako felt strangely relieved. Soul-Dago didn't seem to hate him any more than usual, even with offal staining his fingers.

"I'll be bathing in that water soon enough," Soul-Dago growled.

"We can't leave, yet," Nika said. She had two soft lines forming in the corners of her mouth, so much like their mother. "I've met Thresher, Mako. He's here."

He grabbed Nika's hand tight—mustn't let go, mustn't lose her again—and suppressed a full body shiver. He felt like he might come out of his skin. "Where?"

"I don't know where they are, but any logical being would migrate to the big explosion I created earlier." She grinned and turned, guiding them deeper within the Promised Land.

"Chin up, Manahatta," Soul-Dago whispered as they followed Nika's lead, grabbing Mako's elbow, keeping him steady, as he pushed Mama Milagros down the hall. "You look like shit warmed-over."

The scent of honey iodine and the cool iron of a fresh scab intertwined with baser distress and yearning. Around him, the Facility crumbled: bald-headed experiments darted between rooms in terror, doctors collapsed and gasped like beached trout, equipment was overturned and goods scattered across the floor in disarray. Mako covered his nose with his sleeve against the overpowering odor of illness. It moved quickly, this bacterium, or virus, or trinity-forbid some mutated super-powered combination of the two. The Promised Land. Killed by the invisible.

Soul-Dago suddenly yanked him against the wall. A rumble vibrated from Mako's throat as he heard unknown voices arguing a few doors down from them. Bad mistake, rookie error. His inattention could've put them all in danger. He closed his eyes to gather his wits, remembered he only had one task left before he could leave this cursed place forever, listened hard and heard a familiar lilt.

He pushed Soul-Dago away and barreled into the room where the ceiling had half-collapsed. He barely spared a glance at the startled, long-haired man and the frightened young woman, who both tried to bolt at the sight of him and drag Thresher along with them. He crashed into Thresher, hating that his knees decided to give out, and brought them both to the floor.

"Shouldn't try and run," Mako roared in Thresher's ear. "Should've known I'm only gonna chase you."

Thresher's baby blues narrowed, his elbows dug into Mako's side, and the giant had the audacity to fight Mako's embrace after all Mako had done. Mako pressed every inch of his hot weight into Thresher's chest until the world stopped spinning. Vaguely, he heard voices shouting directives above him and easy-to-ignore hands scrambling at his back.

"Stop fighting me," Mako snarled, feeling that small piece of himself that used to be the haint twitch awake.

"It makes me feel better," Thresher uttered even as he placed his one free arm that wasn't chicken-armed by Mako's stomach on Mako's shoulder. "Don't need to be saved all the time."

"Do too," Mako nearly thundered, remembering their last time together, how Mako had kissed and run. It was no wonder Thresher despised him.

Thresher hissed, and he tilted his head back a fraction, lengthening the blue traceable vein leading down to his clavicle. Mako wanted to grab a fistful of that short dark hair and make Thresher dizzy and pliant for Mako to do what he needed to. Thresher stared at him through a smudge of dark eyelashes, shiny with held back tears. Mako realized his experiment was close to breaking, that he had erected this façade because that's what the Mako Thresher knew would do, so *this* Mako leaned forward and placed a gentle kiss on Thresher's exposed neck.

An exhale shuddered under his lips. The grip on his shoulder tightened before a sob wrenched from Thresher.

"Get off of him, you're hurting him—"

"Mako, don't hurt him, okay, listen to me—"

"He's got ALS! You think it's a game to push neurodegenerative affected experiments to the ground like that?"

"ALS?" Mako asked. "What's ALS?"

Thresher's mouth twisted in a grimace. He looked as if Mako was blowing his world up one question at a time.

"It's a disease," Thresher shouted, eyes widening to stop the tears. "Attacks nerve cells in my brain and spine. Soon enough, and I mean one-year soon, I'll be completely paralyzed. I won't be able to eat or chew or swallow or breathe. *That's* what ALS is." He hid his face in Mako's chest, wrapped his arms around Mako's waist.

Ice slipped into Mako's veins. "We'll find a doctor." He kissed the top of Thresher's head. "This Facility was built to eradicate diseases, right? They must have a cure. Trinity, they've probably got some all-encompassing elixir held hostage, and all we have to do is find it, okay? That's all we have to do."

It scared him, the strength of his own convictions.

Thresher looked up, oddly distant, as if searching for a different answer. Mako would find a treatment even if he had to burn the whole Facility to the ground. He planned to nail Thresher's very soul to the earth.

"Okay," Thresher said in a quiet far-off way. Mako felt like he had failed somehow, that he finally held the colossal swirling colors of Thresher's spirit for a split second, and now that he *decidedly decided* Thresher would not die, the experiment pulled on his armor to lock Mako out.

It made him want to punch a wall hard enough to dislocate his fingers. It was a good thing he was sitting because his knees would have given out again. All Mako had was the word *can't* and he was convinced it could move mountains.

"We need to stick together and be *careful*," Nika said, her hand on her hip. "We don't know who survived the standoff. The Enders might've retreated completely."

"They wouldn't leave without me." Maggie took a step into Nika's space. "We don't leave each other behind."

Nika's eyes narrowed. "You don't understand. It was slaughter on both sides. There's good reason to think no one survived."

Walker's hand rose to rest on Nika's shoulder, wishing her to be kind, but at Mako's curled lip, the hand dropped. Somehow, within minutes of bursting into Walker's life, Nika's twin made split second judgments Walker was desperate to negate. Nika had a way of being tender with Mako, and Walker wanted to tap into the why of it, study it, and above all things, mimic it.

Success remained out of reach. Mako kept what he loved—in this case Thresher and Nika—close. He had a way of lifting his chin defiantly when he spoke about finding a doctor until even Walker believed Thresher could be cured.

"You're a piece of work, thinking I'd ever leave my tribe behind," Maggie sneered. "We *have* loyalty, unlike you Manahattas who sell their own to places like this."

The argument escalated quickly. Mako added his two cents, saying he didn't care *where* they went unless it was to the damn medical records. Chin tilt. Shoulder jostling Nika because by default, she would be going with him.

Thresher stayed silent. Walker wondered if he felt the running heat of the outsiders as acutely, the way the Manahattas and Enders argued about the tactics of approaching the library as if it were the most important, singular decision in history.

A small sound startled him, shrill as a bird, just underneath Nika's scathing shout. He cocked his head to listen, letting the clogging smell of disarray and fading disinfectant wash over him. An unnatural silence waited in the spaces between the yelling. His mouth softened in a half-open question, and he turned to ask if Thresher had heard anything.

The question died on his lips. Guilt, sharp and small, made him decide not to break Thresher's stunned expression. Walker couldn't imagine being taken to the forgetting room and then resurrected. He wondered if Thresher had made it all the way back.

The sound again, but this time it was more like a stifled sob. The Bruykleener, Soul-Dago, glanced up briefly as Walker left Nika's side. Walker's foot nudged aside medical sundries as he picked his way to the room adjacent from them. He peeked inside.

The room might've been a study once. A fire scarred desk filled the room. Loose papers littered the floor like snowfall. A small rectangular window in the top corner shed murky light into the already darkened room. Within the shadows, Walker could see a set of darker shades huddled together, heard their rough breathing, and a sudden quiet that hoped he might not see them.

Two bald-headed experiments, he presumed female, tracked him with terror. They sat close enough for safety, but didn't touch each other. Touch was foreign, unfamiliar. He remembered that from a long time ago, when a young doctor laced his fingers with Walker's and shakily asked him if that was okay.

Walker knelt before them. They scrambled to get out of the way, as if there was anywhere else to go being squished into the corner like that. A sharp scent of urine filled his nostrils. He pulled up his sleeve, baring his wrist to the strongest beam of darkening light. "It's going to be okay," he said. "Look. I'm just like you. I know you're scared. It seems like the end of the world, but I promise, there's much more waiting for you. You don't have to be scared of the outside. It won't hurt you." He smiled. "I've been there. I can lead you through it."

A thought began to take shape in his mind, hardly concrete, but full of so much potential he almost couldn't keep the quiver out of his voice. He thought of all the experiments, lost and hiding in the fading Facility because of the propaganda about the outside, all the beautiful minds that would never *know* because they couldn't fight off preconceived notions.

He could. He could show them. Was this what Tova meant? Could he remake the Facility into a new tribe, one that bonded with the others? Maybe he could do what the Facility had sought to do all this time—make the human species stronger. Create peace.

"I'm giving you a directive." That was how the Facility spoke when obedience was imperative from an experiment. "Gather all the remaining, able experiments within this Facility, even the doctors if they'll listen to you, and meet me outside near the front courtyard. I know it's terrifying, but I promise I'll find you and show you how to live in this new world."

The girl on the left had glazed eyes, too glossy with fear to understand him. The other gave a slight nod, as if agreeing would make him leave quicker. "Please," he said. "It's important."

He stood and stepped back before turning around. Nika watched him from the doorway. Her eyes coldly flickered to the experiments and back to him. "We decided to stick together," she said, victory a lovely color on her.

Walker put his hands on his hips and tilted his chin. "Never really had a choice in the matter though, did they?" His lips spread into an overwide, crooked smile.

A beat before Nika stepped in front of him. His smile slipped. Her fingers bracketed his jaw. "Don't," she whispered. "Just be you, okay?"

Walker turned his head into her hand and kissed her palm, wondering if it was against the rules since she hadn't ordained it. A hopeful hurt stretched his stomach. Her small smile made everything in him tighten with words too big to say. It was there, all for him. Tenderness.

54

Nika stood over the body of her psychiatrist and felt like she had returned to the scene of a crime. With half of his face blown off, she barely recognized him, except for his hands that clenched the bent remains of a musket. It seemed wrong that a man determined to shape the future died defending himself with the archaic.

"It doesn't make sense that a facility dedicated to the pursuit of science has an armed militia," Soul-Dago said, standing beside her and crossing his arms. A deep wound across the top of his shoulder bled down his arm. "In a way, they were like us."

Nika snorted, knowing the Bruykleener was trying to make friends with her but for whatever reason she couldn't fathom. Soul-Dago tracked Mako closely, wary yet intrigued by her twin. Nika understood. Mako had transformed since they'd been apart. His bones remained the same, but the man on the outside had been renovated, balanced on the brink of extremes. "The only reason you're here is to get what you're owed," she said. "No need to pretend otherwise. We don't have to be friends."

Soul-Dago grinned. "As prickly as your brother. Understood."

"Your tribe killed my mother. Not a good starting point for friendship."

Maggie came up beside them and touched Nika's arm. "Enough of this let's-wait-and-see bullshit. I'm going in."

Nika swallowed hard, imagined another force waiting to ambush them, and wondered why it felt important to keep track of this wayward girl.

Two men crumpled against an overturned table. Brain matter and black blood made the manila envelopes tacky. Nika nearly slipped on a stack as she followed Maggie farther inside. Nika turned to Mako, feeling her eyes widen impossibly and gathered strength from his hardened mouth. Thresher had fallen into step behind Mako like it was an unknowing, unbreakable habit.

She heard cries of the dying and stopped, frozen in place again when she saw Milo bent over Jake. Maggie pushed Nika out of the way. Jake's head, cradled by books, rolled back and forth. His hand, slipping every once and a while, pushed at a gushing wound in his side, like he could knead the dough of his skin back together. His eyebrows tightened in overwhelming pain.

"Don't you dare," Milo chanted. "Don't you fucking *dare.*"

He dabbed the tip of a cracked bottle of superglue to the spaces between the uneven stitches he'd made with the bone needle and catgut thread. Trying to sew Jake back together again.

"Fucking sharks," Jake coughed, choked on spit-up blood. "That's what Tova said, didn't she? Two sharks would rip me apart. Use those nasty teeth to swallow me whole and take my whole tribe with it. But that's what a prophecy is, Milo. The future coming down the pipe."

"Stop moving," Milo said, wiping his forehead with the back of his hand and leaving a long streak of blood. "Prophecies are bullshit."

"Oh," Jake said, turning to look at them, his dark eyes fever bright. "There's my girl."

Maggie sobbed and took Jake's outreached hand with her own.

"Told you we'd find her," Jake said, laying a kiss on the back of her hand.

"Stop moving." Slick blood and thicker fluid from Jake's stomach painted Milo up to his elbows. A quiet sob wrenched from his mouth, as if hope and terror strangled him. A mask of dirtied sweat and bloodied fingerprints coated his chin, like he couldn't help touching his face, couldn't stop Jake from helplessly touching, either.

Nika tallied up the body count with one quick glance around, making her sick to her stomach. Please, don't let Maggie look anywhere else but Jake. The boys, oh god, the End boys...

But Maggie had a mind of her own, stronger because of her grief, and Nika watched as she saw Beau's collapsed body, his arm blown to a stump. Tobey with half his face missing. Buck with his chest clear open. She closed her eyes and gasped, hand clutching Jake's.

"I'm so sorry," Nika whispered.

"Fuck you," Milo screamed, finally looking up. "If it weren't for you we wouldn't *be* here. If it weren't for you *we wouldn't all be dead.*"

Nika took a step back, feeling his rage like a physical punch. She couldn't breathe from the guilt and relief that she still had some of hers.

"Milo." Jake tried to grab Milo's shoulders and stop his frenzied doctoring. "Not going to make it better, pup."

"Don't you say that," Milo said, putting both hands over the wound as if he could physically be a bandage. "We don't say things like that."

"It's the end of an era," Jake smiled. "Was even warned and still walked right into it."

"Shut up. We'll get out of here. This is not going to happen here. It just *can't*."

"Thought it was going to be tobacco that killed me. Joke's on you." Jake laughed, his mouth a weak line.

Milo tied off the final stitch. "You're not leaving me."

"When I found you, you were so bloodied," Jake continued, eyes beginning to glaze and fade into the distance. "Couldn't feel a thing, didn't know what kindness was, nearly slit my throat a few times. Now look at you. You're strong. You'll lead our tribe fine."

Milo's hands shook on the tattered rags of Jake's clothes. His tears retraced old tracks down his cheeks.

"You're my son, you know, and I'm so proud of you," Jake said.

"We're getting out of here," Milo said, soft now, gathering Jake into his arms and laying the old man's head in the crook of his elbow. "Gotta see the sky, yeah?"

"I'd love that. I really would."

"We can't *leave* the rest of them!" Maggie hissed as Jake's hand slid from hers.

"You want me to take care of the dead now?" Milo snarled, pressing his shirt to Jake's stomach until it molded to the stitches. Jake coughed wetly and his dark hair swept over his shoulder like a cover. "Not here, Jake," Milo gritted out. "Not in this shithole."

"Is this what you did with your other pack?" Maggie's eyes flashed. "Leave them out in the open for the crows?"

Milo's face whitened, but he cradled Jake closer. "I promise I'll come back for them. I'll bury them right, but Jake's dying. Maggie. *Maggie.*"

She hovered over Beau, his thick beautiful hair matted across his forehead. Her hands shook over his face as if she couldn't quite touch him. Two fingers hovered over his open eyes.

"Maggie," Milo said again, jolting her from the grief she had drifted to.

"When I die, I don't want to be left someplace like this," she said, looking at Jake's silent form and wondering when Milo would understand that it was just the two of them now.

Mama Milagros cried out, her hand clutching her destroyed leg, as her face screwed up in a paroxysm of agony. Mako wheeled away from the dying Enders, stumbling to where Thresher knelt by her.

Nika gripped his arm as Thresher stroked Mama Milagros's face and curled his body as close to hers as he could to keep her warm. She gave Thresher a dull smile. "The Bony Lady's new prophet. Come to take me away? I couldn't stop Mako's slaughter." Her voice cracked with sorrow.

Thresher shook his head. "His soul is still bright as the sun."

Mako nearly vomited at her relieved smile. His hand curled into a fist so tight he had blue half-moon bruises in his palm.

"Gonna have to take the leg," Mama Milagros said. "I can't feel it anymore."

"I don't even know..." Nika trailed off before glancing at Mako.

At least their thoughts were in the same place. They were both hunters. They knew how to quarter a deer: cut around the hip joint and saw through the tough tendons, cartilage, and soft muscle, wrench the joint out of the socket and cut the remaining loose fibers before cauterizing it. Hopefully, she had the constitution to pass out from the pain.

Thresher laid a hand on Mama Milagros's forehead. "Shock," he said.

"The leg will hold for now," Nika said. "We've got time. Not a lot, but some."

Time ticked and evaporated like scalding steam. He couldn't hold it or ensnare it and yet it burned him all the same. His mouth opened and he didn't sound anything like himself. "I'll find a doctor."

55

Mako fisted the collar of the flagging doctor in one hand, a lounge chair in the other. He had found the man passed out from a head wound against a tilted bookcase and revived him by playing suffocation: hands over the doctor's nose and mouth until his survival instincts kicked him out of whatever coma he had been climbing into. Bullets had shredded the chair's stuffing, which hung out the punctures like cattail cotton wisps.

He tied the doctor's wrists to the chair arms with yellowing cracked zip ties and patted the doctor on the knee. He wasn't sure if the man was a bonafide physician, but odds were good after he had taken a look at Mama Milagros's leg and stuttered out, "Surgery."

Mako dragged a simpler metal chair in front of the man and perched on the edge of it, clasping his fingers loosely together. All-encompassing warmth flooded his veins, snaking to his brain to cloud all semblance of control, something wholly unlike the haint's calmness. He flashed back to the destroyed End tribe, the way holding Gela's weight felt like a punishment he would endure forever, and what it would be like to wake beside Thresher and find stillness instead of the thriving drums of life.

His throat closed. Life kept dealing him shoddy cards, but he kept waiting for a lucky streak. The pot may be battered and used gold, but he didn't give a shit about secondhand wins when love was on the line.

He calmly explained the facts. His mind continued to test him, throwing up twisted *what if* scenarios, and Mako knew he would do every wicked, irredeemable one.

A thicket of beard surrounded the doctor's shuddering mouth. "I can't," he said, his face whitening in fear of what this off-his-rocker toxic-addled outsider would do.

It wasn't one of Mako's *cant's*. His heirloom gun felt warm in his palm. Still loaded. "You fix this," he said, standing. "You must know how."

The doctor's eyes darted around the room. His fingers purpled from cut-off circulation. Mako didn't care. He had barreled past humanity, sped beyond the moralities of war, and picked up desperation at a trade point. There wasn't time for niceties, no consoling arguments of *think about your family, they won't want to see you dead*. Mako was at the point where he was going to start taking off fingers and shooting kneecaps.

"Is there a cure?" Thresher asked from behind him. Mako almost turned on him, wanting to shout *how can you be so calm when you're dying?* The thought made him put the barrel of the gun against the doctor's forehead.

"There isn't one," the doctor sobbed. Thick tears mixed with the bloody snot running down his nose.

Mako smirked when he smelled piss. "You give your people diseases to learn how to cure them, right? You're telling me you don't have a solution for one little sickness?"

"It isn't *little*," the doctor gasped.

"What *have* you accomplished, then?"

"It's a neurodegenerative disease." The doctor's cheeks flushed. "It's not like the measles where you can isolate the cause and vaccinate for it!"

"You're not so good at that either," Mako taunted. "This whole place is diseased." He leaned closer until he smelled metal on the man's breath. "What fucking good is your science if you can't save your own family?"

The doctor strained against his bonds, bellowing in rage. "You *filth*. It was those Shinnecoe outsiders giving us infected trades—"

Mako held up his hands. "I'm only trying to save *my* family. Now, tell me how to cure the disease."

"There isn't one! It attacks your brain and spinal cord. It kills the motor neurons. You can't cure the composition of your entire body, it's fucking genetics!"

"I know how it paralyzes you inside your own body," Mako shouted. "I know how it takes years, but you still lose all your muscle strength until you can't swallow or breathe. I don't need *you* to fucking tell *me* what *it is*. I need you to tell me *what I can do about it*."

Thresher had gotten very quiet behind him.

"Every patient is different." The doctor's chest heaved. "It could happen anytime—four years or even eleven. I can't tell how his particular disease will act. He's dying every day, anyway. He could walk outside and fall of a cliff. You never know how much time you have left. None of us do."

Mako was close enough to see the doctor's blown pupil and brown iris. "Walking off a cliff is not the same as ALS," he said, pressing the gun to the doctor's knee and pulling the trigger.

Blood splattered up his chest and neck. The doctor screamed, the shattered bone and ruin of his leg coating the floor. From far away, he felt Thresher touch his shoulder. Mako didn't shrug it off, but he didn't stop either. "Tell me how to cure it or I'll take off the other one. Do you hear me? You'll have to crawl out of here."

"The drugs," the doctor gasped as he convulsed, almost upending the chair. His nails embedded in the armrest. "Riluzole. Baclofen. Diazepam."

Mako glanced over his shoulder at Walker and Nika. Nika's hand covered her mouth, but Walker had a dead look in his eyes that said he understood Mako's unspoken command. It was all part of the outside, where you break bones for the people you love and bring them back to life by stuffing them full of expired chemicals because when you lose them, you only lose them once.

"There are other clinical trials," the doctor said, staring rapt at his mangled knee, "and paperwork. His charts."

Walker gave a quick nod and grabbed Nika's hand, steering her among the fallen cabinets of a secretary's apocalypse, paper sweeping up with their steps like fallen leaves.

"This is all your fault," Mako said, realizing he had started to cry. *"Trinity damn you."*

"I wasn't his doctor," the doctor said, as if stunned at the accusation. *"He wasn't my experiment."*

"Is there another hidden disease left inside him I should know about?"

"No." The doctor's mouth screwed up in an ugly snarl. "All aggressive forms of ALS patients have died with too many variables to add anything else."

"What else do I need to know?" There had to be more than a handful of pills that didn't make anything better, but only kept what he had stable for as long as possible.

"Nothing," the doctor screamed. "On a molecular level, his cells don't have any defenses. They're increasingly programmed for cell death. *Nothing* will help."

"Fuck you," Mako roared.

"I swear, there's nothing else. Let me go, *please*, I need medical attention."

"Mako," Thresher whispered.

Mako turned to him, staring at that beloved face: blue eyes dripping calm sorrow, his mouth a straight line, dark brown hair sticking up all over the place.

"I don't believe in god," Mako told him, his voice hitching. "I believe that *this* is it. We get one chance. There's nothing after but blackness and a grave and decomposition. Souls don't get transported anywhere, *they just die.*"

"I know," Thresher said, not trying to touch him anymore.

"There won't be an afterlife for us." Mako choked. He knew Thresher lied. Thresher thought souls were bright as suns, the fool. "There won't be any reunion. No rebirth. We get, what, a year at most to be together? It's not enough. It's not enough for me."

"I know," Thresher said, and he almost smiled. "You think it is for me?"

The world disintegrated under Mako's feet. Half of life contained wishes for something he hoped would come and the other half had dreams that had passed and wouldn't come back. He couldn't stop looking at Thresher, but the rage demanded satisfaction toward a world that took things just when he had made peace with the fact that he couldn't live without them.

He emptied the gun into the doctor's body: head shot, heart shot, throat shot, an interesting shot that exploded the ribs. There was no god to feel responsible towards and, even if there were, well then, Mako had a few things he'd like to discuss. It would probably end like this, too, him putting a whole other round into a god's body.

56

Walker could barely stand the sight of the Facility. The hushed quietness got under his skin like a rash that couldn't be soothed. He didn't want to go outside, either. Even that held a stark reminder of a lover's ruined life, a hung shadow tattooing the sky. But the outside had fresh air, a chance to clear his lungs from the stuffy heartache crowding him. He could get claustrophobic from it, given time.

He wasn't strong enough for this kind of living. He could feel the weight of the textbooks in his arms, the covers lovingly cared for, even as the pages were littered with faded yellow highlight and notes scribbled in a hundred different fonts in ballpoint, fountain pen, or pencil. Nika left file cabinets open when she had finished with them, the stack of manila envelopes growing higher in her arms. When the gunshot fired, she didn't even look up. Didn't even flinch.

"What was that?" Walker asked, thinking of escape routes as the flickering lights lit up the darkness like sunbursts.

Nika stared down the empty line of books. "Grief," she said flatly. "Check that cabinet."

Walker waited for more, but continued researching when she didn't elaborate.

"Do you want to learn how to dress a deer?" she asked, instead. "It'll be ugly."

A tingle worked up his spine. "Why?" he felt on edge and too nervous.

He discovered the answer later, when Nika placed the books and papers down and personally handed Thresher his file. Thresher held a useless Mako in his lap, trying to coax the human back into his eyes. Mako looked far away, cloudy-eyed, and on this side of too wild with the blood painting his front.

Nika stood, too pensive for Walker's liking. He touched her arm, tried not to look at the collapsed corpse on the chair, and gave his answer. "Yes."

Sharp knives and saws removed the wiry sinews holding Mama Milagros's leg together. Walker still felt the impossible resistance as they wrenched the leg, the wet pop as the joint twisted, yanking one ball and socket from one woman's hip. Mama Milagros had swallowed a handful of white pills earlier and that, plus the small amount of morphine siphoned from the forgetting room, kept her under and still.

Walker had never felt so shaken, desperately trying not to pray to a higher power. They might turn an eye on him, decide he hadn't suffered enough, and it was about time he learned what it meant to call on a god only when he needed it.

The room grayed out when exhaustion took its toll, washing his brain numb and receptive only to Nika's low-key commands. Finally, he held the dead weight of Mama Milagros's free leg in his arm, clammy like a marionette joint and bending as if it had no sense or control. He placed it far enough away to forget it, letting it become a ghost of the Facility. He wiped his bloodied hands on his pants. Nika set the fire-stoked iron against Mama Milagros's skin, filling the air with the fumes of burnt flesh, angry glowing metal, and the sound of sizzling meat. Smoke drifted from the stump.

He needed air. Which was how he ended up here, sun rising to start another twelve hours, bathing his aching eyes with a light too bright to look at.

He let himself cry, then. The dawn felt cold and new on his skin. He sobbed for the lost Enders, for the experiments too scared to *know*, the doctors pressed to the point where eradication had been the best policy. He felt beaten and blindsided by a tremendous pain, but he knew on the opposite side of this brutal luminous day still lay a star-filled darkened night.

A soft touch on his shoulder made him cringe. Opening his eyes, he saw a man who gifted him a fatigued smile. Behind him, gathered in a huddle, stood five experiments. "Hello," the man said. A strange clarity reflected off his green eyes. Black ash colored his neck and streaked his cheeks. "I hear you're the one who's going to save us."

Walker ogled them, his mind full of disbelieved miracles. The two experiments from the office stared at him. One had a slight smile. The other's mouth hung open. The rest looked at him like he had kept an ancient promise. Walker mouthed a dry response. He never imagined something like this would happen. Something so true and good. A fresh start.

The man—no, the doctor—gave him an encouraging smile as if to relate: *I know, I never thought I'd be here either.*

"Yeah." Walker settled on as his first words as a messiah. "Yeah, that's me."

57

The doctor—and Nika grimaced, because the man *did* have a name, Matthias—laid out a dog-eared centuries-old map and traced an orange line called 495 down the center. Nika stared in awe at the geographical representation, now zoomed out to a bird's eye view. The sunlight, dimmed from the smoke puffing from the Facility, lit the other tiny black lines breaking off from the main line like rivers. Other roads, she supposed, were numbered like the Facility numbered its experiments. Somehow, the land, her home, seemed so small.

"We should go this way," Matthias said. "It would be the best course of action."

"Best course for who, exactly, doc?" Nika snarled. "Have you ever been outside these four walls? Oh wait—" Her laugh had bite, a nasty high-pitched sound sharp as a spear. "Did you think we'd take you with us?"

Matthias's jaw clenched and he glanced at Walker for help, confirmation—Nika didn't care. She wasn't having her home sullied by doctors and experiments—they could take Walker and Thresher, sure, those two had proven themselves, but that was *it*.

"Nika," Walker said softly, laying his hand across the map that was spread over a battle-broken chair as if he wanted her to meet him halfway. "They have nowhere else to go."

Nika crossed her arms, glaring at Walker and his outstretched hand, the experiment who had begged her to escape the Promise Land now standing all too close to Matthias. She didn't want to draw a line in the sand, but trinity-damned Promised Land doctors just ruined everything.

"That route would leave us out in the open," Mako said. "Vulnerable to attack. Who even knows if it still exists?" He flicked the edge of the map, his finger making a dull thwap against the thick printed paper. "We have no idea what tribal lands we'd be crossing. If the Enders didn't take that route when they came here to begin with, there must be something wrong with it."

Matthias took a deep breath and met eyes with Mako, making Nika want to hide her brother, keep him far from anything resembling the

Facility. "This institution has fallen apart," Matthias said. "Any experiments who have fled will take the easiest routes away from here, the only ones they *might* know of are old interstate roads from salvaged maps and texts. The doctors will ultimately take that road because..." He glanced uncomfortably at Nika. "Before we transitioned to on-site tests, we used to release field experiments into the wild. That road was where we'd first let them go, the only one that we thought would lead them into the tribal heartland."

A moan cut Matthias off and he turned, like a flower toward the sun, to walk to an experiment huddled against the open doors of the Promised Land. He leaned over the experiment, who reached toward him with a wasted hand. Matthias caught the hand, touched the experiment's forehead, and rummaged in the medicine box sitting near the experiment. Pulling out a couple of pills, he urged the experiment to choke them down, having him sip some water from a cracked cup.

Medical paraphernalia sat in a neat line on the grass around them, pills and a hot water basin and linens all laid out as per Matthias's direction. "All our field experiments failed," Matthias continued, leaving the experiment and dunking his hands into the basin, washing a hard lye soap all the way up to his elbows. "We know nothing of tribal boundaries, only the tribes themselves. If we take that way, we can find those who might've survived—"

"If they haven't been slaughtered or taken as slaves," Mako cut in. "All the other surviving tests you sent out into the wild belong to the Bruykleeners or have become isolated."

"There are survivors?" Matthias's voice went soft with awe as he rejoined the group.

"Not many," Mako said. "But a few."

Matthias bit his lip and glanced back to the experiment trembling in the doorway. "He won't survive," he said in a low tone.

"How come you're not sick?" Nika asked. "Hiding some miracle cure and keeping it all to yourself?"

Matthias gave her a small smile. "I have it now. I was one of the first doctors to trade with the Shinnecoes, the first to contract the illness. I almost died, and I must've infected many others, but I managed to pull through. I don't think the effects will go away soon, though." His fingers hovered above the pockmarks around his mouth. His tongue flickered out to whet his chapped lips.

"You look like shit," Nika said.

"*You* look like shit," Matthias said, indicating Mako. "You need fluids. Here." He dug in his pouch, pulled out two misshaped circular pills. "Take these vitamins with a meal."

Nika slapped the pills out of Matthias's outstretched hand, the white balls of health flung into the air and lost in the grass. "Don't you *dare* talk to him about what he needs. You try to touch my twin again, I'll skin you alive."

"I'm sorry," Matthias stammered.

"There's no fucking way you're coming with us," she said. "You can stay in your infected white tower and die."

"We can't stay here." Matthias sounded desperate. "You might have built-up immunity to the sickness, but the other experiments haven't. I don't have any survival skills. I can't skin a rabbit, or find fresh water, or make my own clothes."

Beside Nika, Mako shivered, as if he had heard the words before. She nudged him gently, and he looked behind them to where Thresher, Soul-Dago, and Mama Milagros helped the Enders bless their dead.

"But I can bring genetic diversity to your tribes," Matthias said. "I know of equipment here that can make Milagros's life easier, her pain manageable. You're sick with something, aren't you?"

Mako shrugged. "Who knows? But it was the price I paid to get out here. Come to find out, those isolated experiments make some mean concoctions of their own, and I let them stick it in me."

"Wait, just a damn minute," Nika said. "Mako, what—"

"I know how to monitor your sickness." Matthias overrode her. "Watch for any warning signs. I can help you understand the illness for Subject T, make both of your transitions easier when the time comes."

"Thresher," Mako snarled.

Matthias held his hands up. "Thresher," he echoed. "Please."

An oil slick of distrust and alarm curled like a snake within Nika's stomach. Matthias had seen the mess Mako had made of the doctors, and Mako had let strangers stick him with needles.

"We can help them," Walker said to her, nearly pleading. "They're lost. They have no idea what's out there."

"They can stay with the Bruykleeners then. Give them to the Enders. Why do they have to stay with us?"

Even as she said it, fear swung its head like a bull in a china shop. Could her twin be ill and fading from something unknown? Her eyes felt as wide and panicked as her heart, swelling with sudden terror, both for her family and what she might have to do to ensure their safety.

"We might need them," Mako said to Nika. "I promised water rights to Soul-Dago. The Manahattas might exile me when they find out. Or refuse to honor my pact and bring a tribal war on our heads. We bring them back with us as proof of my claims."

"And my existence isn't enough?" Nika said, bewildered. "Missing for two years and suddenly returned home isn't good enough to admit that you were in the right?"

"But with all this to trade?" Mako inclined his head to the lined-up tools of a healer. "It'd be like bringing home a treasure trove. Anything could be forgiven with all this."

"I promised I'd help them," Walker added. "I promised to stay with them."

"Over my dead body," Nika snapped and shoved away, holding her hand up to stop Walker from following her. "Don't even think about it."

She knew he wanted her to see what he saw, look down upon the poor orphaned doctors and experiments stripped of their needles and restraints and feel *compassion*. She felt the straightjacket strapping her arms down, the choking collar keeping her attached to the wall while those poor pathetic psychiatrists and doctors dug into her past. Compassion, huh? How about *humanity*?

She turned to Mako, gave the snake permission to strike, and punched him in the arm. It felt good to let a fraction of that anger out, and by Mako's hardened face, she knew he would take any and all of her rage, let her unload it on him and trinity, he'd fucking *embrace* it.

She stormed away. No one called out to her. The snake lashed around her spine and climbed up and out her mouth. *Hate.* How dare he—*how dare they?* She could never go home and see their Facility faces on the regular, remember everything they'd done to her day after day. Not with Gela dead. Not with Mako a scarred ruin from searching for her. They had stripped her of her future, her sexuality, even her inklings toward motherhood. And now they wanted to take her hearth, her *home*?

The smell of fire lingered in the air. Some doctors and experiments refused to leave the Facility; others had bailed and run into the woods, refusing to accept any help, even with Matthias's coaxing. She watched Soul-Dago and Thresher carry another dead End boy out into the sunlight, laying him on the grass with his brothers. Mama Milagros, her face wan as she sat in her wheelchair, prayed over the bodies. Maggie held her head in her hands, tears dripping through the cracks in her fingers.

Nika's lip curled. The snake, coiling in her belly, laid cruel terrible thoughts that yearned to become spoken words. She loathed how mean this hatred made her, even as she wanted to put her hands on Maggie's shoulders and be strong for her. In the distance, Milo's sandy hair caught her attention, his body knelt over what could only be Jake. He hated her, she was sure of it, and misery sure does love company. She changed course, heading toward him.

Milo had decorated Jake's long silvered-black hair with braided grass. Next to his body, a hole had been dug in the ground, showing the striations of a dark topsoil covering loose sandy bedrock. Milo looked up at her, his face washed in grief, and whispered, "The earth here won't hold his body. The soil's too loose."

Jake's eyes had been forced closed, his arms crossed over his chest, the blood cleaned from his face and neck. Even still, Nika could see the rips in his stomach that killed him, gut wounds that leaked blood and black fluid. No, the earth wouldn't hold his body—with any hurricane or heavy rainfall, the topsoil would wash away, Jake's body uncovered and rolled to who knows where.

"On my land, we have bad soil too." Her throat began to close. Tears pricked her eyes. "We build platforms for our deceased, let them rest in the air. Let the sky and elements have what they may and then bury the bones." She paused, Gela's smile so sudden and bright in her mind. "I could help you, if you'd like."

A soft gasp slipped past Milo's lips and he seemed to double over as if his sorrow would make him sick. "I should take him somewhere else. I should bury him with his sister on the family hill. That would be right, it would be *proper*."

"Is it far?" Nika asked, knowing it must be.

"Too far to carry," Milo whispered.

"What about that 495 road? Could it take us there?"

Milo slowly turned to look at her, shaking his head in disbelief. "That road leads back to your land, Nika. That crumbling, fragile piece of concrete won't be anywhere I'm heading. I think you know that."

"Take some of the experiments," she said, ignoring how his tone flared with fire. "They'll be able to help you carry Jake."

"I don't want any of your cast-offs."

"You could sell them."

"I don't have the stomach for it, but I wish I did. I wish I was years younger and didn't give a damn about death. I'd slit your brother's throat, and I'd sell the experiments to the Woodlands, and I'd do awful, terrible things to you. But I won't sully Jake's memory. I won't let you destroy what a good man Jake taught me to be."

Nika put her hand over her mouth to stop the snake oil dripping from her lips, the twisted things she said to ease her own suffering. "I'm sorry," she whispered. "I shouldn't have said that."

A hand touched her shoulder and she turned to see Maggie's dewy eyes. The apology choked out of Nika like a sob. "I'm so sorry. So sorry for your loss."

"You should be," Milo growled. He took Jake's hand and held it up to his cheek.

The snake had migrated to him, a slithering hatred binding them together, feeding on loss. *Compassion.* Nika clung to the word. *Humanity.*

"It's your fault we came out here," Milo said, his teeth bared in a grimace. "My tribe's blood is on your hands. Everything that made up my world is dead. I wish you'd died on that beach. I wish I'd never seen you, wish I'd never tried to help you."

Maggie's face crumpled as Milo named all his wishes, and Nika finally saw a flash of the cage-wild child he must've been. Turning to Maggie, hoping to spare her anymore ugliness, Nika wrapped her arms around the girl, tucked the Ender's wild curls down against her face, and let the girl silently sob into her shoulder.

"He'll be all alone," Maggie whispered hot against Nika's ear. "One day soon, there won't be anybody left."

"He has you," Nika said into her hair. "You're more than enough."

Maggie lifted her head, her mouth pursing into a thin, determined line. How had this timid girl become such a hardened creature? Nika wondered, her heart aching.

"It'll be alright," Nika said instead, because there was nothing else for her *to* say. She had damaged the day with her fears, and the only thing left to do was to make it right again.

58

Thresher wondered if he wasn't reliving history all over again when he looked back at the band of unlikely travelers following them. He fought hard not to look like the experiments, with their eyes pinpointed on the ground, experiencing the glorious *new* through the filter of their peripherals. Five of them, three men and two women, were laden with bags full of survival equipment. They plucked at clothes that the doctor had somewhat sterilized, washing off any lingering sickness carried from the Facility. Matthias kept a lookout for symptoms.

The concrete route opened in front of them, ending in a point at the horizon. Shortest distance anywhere was as close to a straight line as you could get, and Thresher hoped that mathematical proof proved true. He couldn't wait to leave this so-called best course.

The day had a hazy, deserted quality to it, like everything had fused with the land, from the rusted-out shells of equipment to the collapsed buildings lining the sides of the pathway. Vines grew lattice-like over bent and rusting guardrails. The path seemed to groan, and Thresher imagined the road was much like walking upon his own spine: a crumbling ladder made fragile by tiny black cracks, ready to buckle at any moment.

Near the front of the procession, Matthias raised a hand, bidding them to a halt. In front of Thresher, the squealing wheel of Mama Milagros's wheelchair skidded on the rocks as Mako stopped pushing it. Walking around the wheelchair, Mako knelt in front of Mama Milagros, opening a yellow bottle from his bag and slipping a pill between her lips, keeping her blissful on medication until she would wake, groggy, never remembering being unconscious.

Thresher squinted suspiciously at all the multi-colored bottles stuffed in Mako's satchel, jiggling like a tambourine as he walked. It was ridiculous the way Mako took responsibility for doling out medication for both him and Mama Milagros on such a specific schedule, to the point where Thresher dreaded it.

"We don't have time for this," Mako said, helping Mama Milagros take a drink from a water bladder. "We can't stop at every possibly habitable *shack.*"

"We have nothing but time," Matthias responded, his hunched shoulders defensive as he headed toward one of the houses.

"You've left messages all along this route for them, created a trail anyone could follow—a trail you said they would all take," Mako snarled at the doctor's retreating back. "Let them come to you for once."

In the beginning of the journey, Matthias insisted they stop at every crumbling structure, every underpass, yelling himself hoarse from calling out to any fleeing doctors or escaped experiments. They had found many deceased; only a few alive, curled in the rusted hulls of old machinery or hiding within the houses—some sick, others refusing to join them. Yet, as their travels to Manahatta continued, signs of Promised Land life had faded to a resounding silence.

Matthias's stops had become less frequent, but his hope remained strong. Thresher understood the doctor's desperation, especially the feeling that would probably never leave either of their marrow: being displaced and hoping against all odds that those who found you, claimed you as their own, actually wanted to keep you in the first place. Matthias would never stop looking for his tribe, just as Mako never gave up trying to find his sister.

"The doctor must make peace with his losses," Soul-Dago said, crossing his arms and coming to hover over Mama Milagros. "We should make camp."

"Don't tell me what to do," Mako said. Soul-Dago's full lips parted in a grin. Mako stood and pointed at the doctor. "And don't encourage him. He's becoming grief-mad like the Enders we left back at the Facility."

Thresher closed his eyes tight, but the memory rushed at him—the way he had been responsible for placing Beau's body in a straight line next to his other fallen brothers. Thresher had nearly lost the tight rein on his tears when he rubbed the blood from Beau's face using his spit, thumb, and sleeve. When he brushed the thick hair to the side and laid a gentle farewell kiss on his forehead, too cold and still for Thresher to feel anything but a tremor of horror in his stomach. Death might've touched down on black wings at the Facility days ago, but that moment had been branded in his memory.

Mama Milagros had slurred a prayer over each boy, making Thresher feel better that something was done for the empty vessels. He knew the action potentials building between their synaptic clefts, like a hellhound yanking at the bit, had ceased. That the magical cohesion of charges and chemicals had become toxic from glutamate overload. Like lightning, purple and intense enough to raise the hair on his arms, it never struck twice.

That right there was soul.

Thresher opened his eyes to see Nika and Mako standing shoulder to shoulder. Thresher wondered if words were worthless between them, that it was easier to communicate through the fluid flow of twin-ship. He never realized how much attention Mako had bestowed on him before, until it was missing.

Mako clenched and unclenched his free hand. He cracked his neck, pops ratcheting one on top of the other. Shoulders broadened and stiff as if expecting a blow. Thresher couldn't tell if he was angry or not. It was hard, studying out of the sides of his eyes.

The back of Thresher's throat tasted like iron. He couldn't quite breathe, but that was the cost of rifling for courage. His mind told him he deserved to take what was his. Life was short. Mako wouldn't break like glass, and Thresher didn't need saving all the time.

"We should help him," Thresher croaked out, catching Mako's gaze. "Too much ground for Matthias to cover on his own." Not waiting for a response, Thresher walked to Mako, gripped his wrist, and dragged him towards a lopsided house covered with browned vines. So easy—Mako followed, as if he had been waiting for Thresher's signal.

Nika's shout suddenly filled Thresher's ears, her sarcastic tone making him blush. "Oh, sure, I'll just make camp on my own, then! We'll all hold down the fort while you two make—"

Thresher shut the door of the dilapidated house before he could hear anything else.

59

Mako reeled around in the abandoned space that must have once passed for a sitting room. An unbroken window let in a dusky sunlight that illuminated the disturbed dust motes.

"I've never met anyone like you before," he said in a near-accusatory tone, furious at Thresher's cool silence, as if everything could be ignored instead of met head-on. He blinked back tears, feeling his face flush red. "I've never done anything like this before. Don't you get it?"

Mako realized he had crossed the angry pulsating space between them like it was nothing, suddenly holding Thresher's face like it might break, compulsively thumbing his fingers along Thresher's cheeks. "And if you..." He swallowed hard, couldn't speak because the truth was too hard to say out loud. "You can't. You just can't."

Mako's eyes flickered back and forth between Thresher's: one cast in shadow and the other lit blindingly blue. He was so brilliantly alive.

"I know I'm a selfish son of a bitch." Mako's hitched breath stuttered his words, but he had to get this out. "That I shouldn't be acting like this. I'm sorry for knocking you down, and I'm sorry for what happened in the bathroom, but I always told myself that if I was lucky enough to have something like this, it wouldn't matter really."

Thresher stepped closer so they were flush against each other.

"But by the trinity how are you doing it? How can you remain so calm? Aren't you upset?" Mako was crying now. "Aren't you *bothered?*"

"Let me in," Thresher said, scarred mouth opening from its pursed line. "Let me in, Mako."

Mako made a sound, some kind of interrupt in surprise or mid-sob as Thresher slotted between Mako's legs, and that was it. Mako was too far gone to look or think. Thresher laid gentle dry-mouthed kisses on his lips until Mako caught his breath and could slide their tongues together without falling apart. Thresher tucked his hands at the nape of Mako's neck, holding him hard and *there*, guiding him until his back hit the windowsill. There wasn't any darkness to hide in. Mako knew he would be able to see everything.

"Your jacket," Thresher muttered, nudging it off and making Mako raise his arms over his head to slide his shirt up and off. "It's ruined."

"I know," Mako growled. "All that blood and guts."

"I bet we can save it," Thresher said, as if continuing the conversation was as important as his teeth bruising Mako's neck and pressing their bare chests together. "I'd miss it."

"If we don't I'll be cold all the time," Mako said, shocked Thresher would state such stupid facts. He had a strange fascination with molding his hand along Thresher's hip and thumbing the bone. An odd catching tug had taken up in his chest, something wet and painful, as if his heart was the big fish that the old man had just caught.

"Mako." Thresher said his name like it was some kind of ultimate answer. "I need you on your back."

"Sure," Mako stammered, complying. "Of course, anything you need." He was simply grateful that Thresher finally *needed* something. He slid to the floor. The wood scratched his shoulder blades.

Thresher stretched Mako's bent knees to the side, kneeling between the V, and Mako tossed his head back, not sure what to say or where to look. This was the final fight before the old man reeled him in, gasping for air, into the boat.

"I don't think I can do this," Mako said on the verge of tears again. "I don't want it to be like this."

"Then, it won't. We won't," Thresher whispered. His hands stilled on Mako's skin, and Mako counted every way in which his mouth betrayed him. To a man like Thresher who had been bound and hurt, whose will had been forced from him, consent meant a great deal.

"Not like that," Mako wrenched out, his bravery like a cut fishing wire. Loose and dangling. His hands slid over Thresher's. "I mean I don't want to start something I can't finish. I don't want you to... leave." He couldn't say it. Couldn't say *I don't want you to die*.

"I understand," Thresher said, and Mako closed his eyes, hoped Thresher wouldn't see it as self-defense. Thresher's hands played along his ribs, touched the marks on his skin from a too-chubby youth who grew tall too fast, his mouth leaving marks on those lines. Mako couldn't think for multiple reasons besides life-defying diseases that turned beloved bodies into coffins for the soul.

"I've never. I haven't. I'm not inexperienced, but I guess in this particular scenario, I might not be—I might not have good advice," Mako said in a small voice. He wondered when Thresher would ask him to shut up.

Thresher rose to his knees, still between his legs. "Me either," he said, two fingers obnoxiously wet from his mouth. "But I know a lot about male anatomy. It won't feel right at first. You won't see stars, but I'll get better."

"I don't need stars," Mako choked, embarrassed he might start sobbing again.

Thresher smiled a heartbreaking smile, as if he anticipated Mako to have low expectations.

It wasn't bad, but it wasn't good, either. Mako grit his teeth and shut his eyes, opened in a way he had never been before as Thresher coaxed him to relax. "I need, I need," Thresher chanted.

"Anything," Mako insisted, just before it was perfect in every way that it wasn't. "Anything."

Mako knew he wouldn't be the same as Thresher created a place only for him inside of Mako. He breathed in time to Thresher's body pressing up into him, filling him, feeling just this side of too full. Mako fought to keep looking into Thresher's eyes, but ended up pulling Thresher down for a kiss, feeling Thresher's giant hand fingertip-bruise his hip, just as Thresher bit through his lip and went still with a shudder.

Mako tasted blood, unsure he could handle much more, and pressed the marks on Thresher's wrists until Thresher let out a small moan. Thresher shifted back and Mako could've died with shame that he wasn't hard anymore—but the strange feeling had hurt—and he wanted Thresher to know that it didn't matter, that he only wanted to let Thresher know that he—oh trinity, he couldn't say it.

"I—I'm sorry," he whispered, instead.

Thresher touched Mako with a deft hand, rekindling the desire, until Mako arched uselessly away, destroyed by the utter knowledge that this right here was the thing that would ruin him in the end. He wouldn't get away until it had been taken from him, and he wasn't sure what to do with that, not when Thresher handled Mako like no one ever had.

"This is for keeps," he gasped, banging his head against the floor because he couldn't let go of the plea to stay. He never was good with promises and keeping track of the things he couldn't live without.

Thresher covered him in heat and want. He kissed Mako hard. "Mako, shut up."

There it was. Mako had been waiting for it, needed it, and was glad for it because if Thresher hadn't said it he would've helplessly blurted out, *you're the love of my fucking life*, and Mako wasn't sure he could survive that, especially if it was there, out in the open.

So he let Thresher break him apart and rebuild him. Silently.

They traveled the mother road for a week before Soul-Dago detoured to Bruykleen lands, carrying a bag full of Promised Land treasures, with a vow he would be back to make good on Mako's word.

Thresher smelled familiarity, the curving dark sand coastline bracketing crumbling concrete. When he rubbed his chin on his shoulder he caught Mako's scent. He had a grin that wouldn't erode, fueling Mako's sharp-edged responses to *knock it off, do you want everyone else to think that we're some doe-eyed adolescents?*

There was sunlight in everything now, from the bare freckled curve of Mako's shoulder to the soft cries he made because Thresher made good on his promise to get better. Touch fulfilled him now. He could sink into it, let it linger and heat him up when he slept plastered to Mako. Mako had a habit of running—*too close too fast* as he would tell Nika frantically between moments of peace—but at night he kept his feet between Thresher's ankles, a low hand on his hip, sometimes just breathing against Thresher's skin even as he fought to angle the rest of his body away.

Dedicated to *taking*, Thresher didn't hold back anymore, especially after the first time Mako curled into him. Thresher put his shoulder up, like it might keep their happiness safe for a little while longer.

"It's not much of a chase," Nika commented to Thresher one night as they sat around a low burning fire. Walker had snuck Nika's hand into his to tug and stretch her fingers. Mako had begged off to go piss, quiet panic drowning his face. "He tries to put up a good fight," she added.

"You call this a fight?" Thresher asked.

Nika laughed, delighted, a full robust sound that startled him. Walker smiled in a desperate way. Thresher tried not to show his pity. Even though Thresher had asked Walker for advice, Walker was still a Thresher from long ago, craving to experience the wild outside life with the person he loved.

Mama Milagros had an infection and begged for a cup of water. The experiments gathered around her, offered her a battered cup, and waited for their reward of a story. Matthias took out a much-used notebook from his breast pocket, pen poised to write the tale down. When she began, Thresher wondered if it was one of Gela's old tales, passed down from when her lineage walked the islands before anyone else.

Thresher slipped away into the shadows. A piss really shouldn't take that long. He found Mako sitting on the grass, backed up against a smoothed pole with the remains of a bird's nest on top. Thresher eased down beside him and wrapped his arms around his knees.

"Isn't it weird," Mako said, "that the winter used to be in the summer?"

Thresher decided not to answer because season creep wasn't weird at all, not if you put into account all the carbon and ash shot up by the volcanic explosions, how the heat dried the soil and boiled the air.

"Gonna have to figure out what to do." Mako's hands clasped loosely in his lap.

Thresher shivered with an ill omen. He had been thinking that the rest of his life meant forever. *Figuring it out* had nothing to do with him. Maybe he had moved too quick, gotten too close, succumbed to the lovesick addiction without a whimper of protest, but he knew what he wanted. "What do you mean?" He looked everywhere but at Mako.

Mako shot Thresher a glare that possibly said *don't play coy with me.* Thresher wouldn't know. The stars looked particularly dull tonight.

"I mean I want to know what you want to do. We should stick around until Soul-Dago returns with his damned tribe and honestly, I couldn't leave Nika yet even if the Yellowstone exploded again, but if there's something, I don't know, that you want, we should do it."

"I want," Thresher said, more irritated with Mako than ever before, "for you to stop being such a terrified guppy and admit you love me already." Thresher's upper teeth fastened hard on his lower lip.

"A bit soon, don't you think?"

"Not for me."

The grass rustled as Mako scooted closer. "If I say it, it's all over for me. You'll actually be stuck with me and that's scary."

Thresher dug his hands into his thighs. There was shame and pride at feeling this intensely. "Stuck with you now, aren't I? You crossed all this land for me. Went on a crusade for me."

"Kinda did, didn't I?" Mako said, soft. Thresher finally glanced up at the familiar catch in Mako's voice to see him kneeling in front of him. Mako smiled matchstick white in the dark, something Thresher once read as Cheshire-wide. "Still don't know why I gotta fucking say it," Mako finished, "when I can just keep showing you."

He pressed fingers against Thresher's jaw, angling for a long cool kiss, until Thresher widened his knees for Mako to get between them. He didn't put up a fight, instead let desire roll through his blood like thunder.

"Remember," Mako whispered, "when I said I didn't want to spend all my time with Anna-Skye? What I should've said was I wanted to spend it with you."

That was something Thresher thought about often. Anna-Skye's baby.

Thresher bit his tongue and closed his eyes, notching his hips up and rocking against Mako, tight and violent.

"Good enough for you?" Mako asked. Thresher wanted to tell him to shut up, but he had an incredible fixation on how rough and graveled Mako's voice got in times like these. Sometimes he slipped, calling Thresher endearments that gave him chills.

"Good enough for now." Thresher's breath hitched, but he still managed to cock an eyebrow. "But you can do better."

"Trinity damn him and all Bruykleeners," Mako's voice cut through the air as the rumble of drums made the small pebbles dance around Walker's feet. "Soul-Dago beat us here."

Along the banks of a wide river separating the shoreline from Manahatta below him were Bruykleeners lined up in what he assumed to be full war regalia. They pounded their chests, smacked simple drums made of wood and taut cloth, even slapped the ground. Soul-Dago waited at the water's edge, flanked by huge warriors, fresh paint bisecting his face, his black hair piled up high on his head. The retreating light of dusk made the blade in his hand glimmer, out in the open for all to see. A shiver ran down Walker's spine—the Bruykleener appeared fearless, larger than life.

Water surrounded Nika's home, the final outpost for this fresh-faced melting pot Walker was now proud to call his tribe. A tribe which had at one time or another consisted of Manahatta, Bruykleen, End, and Facility; held by unity, carefully crafted and precariously maintained. Now, they stood together, preparing for what was to come.

Tova's words rushed through him. *You're meant for great things.* The task ahead of him yawned like a chasm. Walker would have to rely on these fragile amorphous concepts to achieve his last goal of delivering Nika back to her people, of ensuring the safety of *his* people: belief in the stories of others, trust between past enemies, the precariousness of human nature to slaughter instead of listen. Back when he only knew the Facility, he'd wanted to see the world. He never thought he would have to lead it.

"What's happening?" Matthias asked, tugging at Walker's elbow.

"He's cunning," Walker said out loud, inclining his head toward Soul-Dago. He bit his lip, the thoughts racing through his mind all variants of how an outsider would think. How quickly he had outgrown his Facility-shell, shedding it like a crab, ready for his new outsider armor to harden. "Soul-Dago has the advantage in every way."

Mako snorted beside him. "He always was one to make an entrance."

Nika gave Mako a hard nudge. "You promised him water rights. He's prepared to get them. Are you so surprised he got here first?"

An ache squeezed Walker's heart. With Mako so close-by, Nika had become distant, and it didn't help matters that Walker had thrown his weight behind Matthias and the other Facility-born. Loyalty was earned, he understood that, and even if she thought he didn't possess any, he would still be by her side until the end. She had earned it after everything she'd been through.

"If you back out of your promise, Soul-Dago will attack Manahatta instantly," Nika said, her lips pinching, making her face grim. "He'll even have the upper hand of being prepared to battle at night."

"Don't inflate his ego any more than it already is." Mako went quiet, his mocking tone erased. "Manahatta isn't prepared for war. Our people have become farmers, isolationists."

"We'll have to play by Soul-Dago's rules, then." Nika's smile looked wan.

"If Manahatta rejects your pact, Mako," Walker said, "we'll all be captured."

"What would happen to us then?" Matthias asked, his eyes wide. Silence met the question, but Walker could tell by Nika's narrowed eyes that the answer was nothing good.

"Look," said one of the female experiments from behind them, her finger pointed out toward the island where a large canoe launched from the shore, heading across the channel to meet the Bruykleeners. At the sight, Soul-Dago raised a white cloth high above his head, the wind catching it and sending it flapping back and forth.

"He's calling for peace," Walker said.

"He's calling for negotiations. Our elders will confront him," Nika said, squinting. "I see only one representative. And a wise woman."

"Trinity," Mako swore. "We need our curandera down there. They have no idea what's happening and Milagros is respected enough to make them listen. Is Mama Milagros awake?" He paused, his voice dropping low as if suddenly afraid. "Is she coherent?"

They turned as one to look at the woman sitting in the rickety chair not too far from them. She leaned forward, her hands clasped, the veils of her dress wrapped around her single leg. "Take me to him," she said, her voice stronger than it had been on the long journey back to Manahatta. "We must live with your promises, Mako. We found our lost ones, but we sacrificed our loyalty."

"I'll take you," Walker said, catching Mako's eye. "Matthias and I will explain what happened. We can prove our usefulness by demonstrating the gifts of the Facility."

Mako nodded slightly. Acquiescence without an argument from a Saddlerock? The unspoken praise warmed Walker's insides.

"The twins must follow. Mako, by the trinity if you can manage it, keep your sentences short and your temper cool," Mama Milagros said. Mako winced, and even Walker felt the whipcrack in her voice.

"I don't understand what's happening," Matthias whimpered.

Walker clasped his shoulder. "Be calm. It's your time to testify, doctor."

Walker took the handles of Mama Milagros's chair in his hands, navigating her down the slope to the water's edge. The Bruykleeners were silent as they passed, their eyes tracking them as they approached Soul-Dago, their leader. The white flag floated on the air. The Manahatta boat crept closer. Matthias's eyes widened, taking it all in. His hand fluttered to his pocket, the edge of his book peeking out.

"Not now," Walker commanded under his breath, feeling slight unease at the hard edge of his words.

Indecision flickered within Matthias's eyes—the experiment giving orders to the doctor?—but obeyed. Walker sighed with relief, clenching his hands into fists with a new kind of confidence. Integration was necessary. Matthias's disease was continuing to look upon the tribes as bugs or plants to be pinned or studied instead of becoming one of them. Matthias could no longer be above them.

They came to a stop in front of Soul-Dago. Soul-Dago knelt on one knee in front of Mama Milagros, laying his crossed arms flat over his leg, and lowered his head. "Prophet of the Manahatta tribe," he began in a booming voice, "relay the words and promises entrusted to me by Mako Saddlerock to his tribe. Take my seer as witness to your words. I trust you are true."

The formality of the ritual stunned Walker, adding a new complex layer upon the bloodied relations of the tribe he had known.

Mama Milagros touched Soul-Dago's wrists. "I will honor your request."

A woman emerged from those standing around Soul-Dago. A bone ring pierced her nostrils like a bull. The shawl covering her shoulders was brightly painted and well-cared for. She crossed her russet-brown arms and bowed before Mama Milagros. Like Soul-Dago, her black, braided hair was piled up on top of her head.

Behind them, the canoe landed. A grizzled man stepped out and helped an older woman from the boat.

"Lead us to our adopted kinsmen, Walker," Mama Milagros said. "Those with testimonies to relay will follow us."

Walker glanced behind him, saw Mako throw a silent snarl at Soul-Dago, who grinned like a wolf back at him. Walker wished Thresher was closer to ease Mako, but the former experiment had remained behind with the other Facility-born. The wheelchair stuck in the uneven ground, jolting Mama Milagros forward. She gasped in pain as Walker cursed his momentary distraction and eased the chair out of the rut. The Bruykleen seer remained silent beside them, keeping pace with them.

The Manahatta representatives stood close to each other, and Walker caught the puzzlement and wariness in their stature, but their eyes lit up with shock and acknowledgment as he brought Mama Milagros closer.

"Ian," Mama Milagros called out. "Even though I am a curandera and part of the Manahatta tribe through marriage, I insist that I represent this exchange with the Bruykleeners as the Manahatta wise woman."

The woman on Ian's arm lowered her head and stepped back in agreement. Walker saw a flash of light in her hands—a knife—just before she concealed it within her robes.

"What happened to you?" Ian asked in astonishment. "Your leg..."

"Listen to me, Ian. Look beyond my shoulders to the woman with Mako. Do you see her? Do you see that the dead have returned to their homeland?"

"Nika?" Awe softened Ian's voice. "Mako was right?"

The Bruykleener seer shifted but remained silent. Walker understood finally that she was only to hear what they said and report it back to Soul-Dago. But what a burden to bear!—she had to trust they wouldn't break tribal protocol and kill her.

"Yes," Mama Milagros said. "I beseech you, Ian. I know what this looks like—it's exactly how you ended the tribal wars with Bruykleen the first time, only you waved the white flag in victory. Do not think of that. Think of Nika, who was like a daughter to you. Wouldn't you cross an ocean for Anna-Skye? Wouldn't you go to the ends of the world for your daughter?"

Ian's breath hitched as if he might cry. "She left when Mako did. I didn't think she'd simply disappear. I thought she'd return to defend her name after what Mako said. I fear…if Mako is right about Nika, what other truths have I ignored?"

"Listen to me, Ian. I witnessed a deal Mako made with the Bruykleeners to find his sister. He promised his Manahatta freshwater rights to them."

Ian blanched. "Trinity, the boy has become crazed."

"We have two choices," Mama Milagros said, eyes flickering to the Bruykleener. "There's a war band in front of you. If we do not honor the pact, the Bruykleeners will kill us now and attack Manahatta. You know," her voice lowered into a whisper, "Manahatta is not prepared for war."

Ian clenched his hands, his eyes squeezed tightly closed. "Mako has no power to make such promises, no wisdom to demand Manahatta elders honor the consequences of his foolishness—"

"Or," Mama Milagros continued, "we honor Mako's decision and begin negotiations."

"We've brought you gifts on par with water rights," Walker interrupted. He heard Mama Milagros sigh in exasperation. He might not understand tribal protocols, but he had to be heard. "We are a lost tribe." He touched his hand to his chest and pointed behind him to the other Facility-born far behind him. "We hope to be integrated with your tribe as equals, but we did not come to you empty-handed."

Mama Milagros looked to the Bruykleener. "Hear this story," she said. "Prove that we are not deceitful. Tell your tale, doctor of the deceased Promised Land tribe."

Matthias swallowed hard and began to force out the saga of the Facility's downfall, how they had made trade agreements with representatives of the eastern tribes and violated them by making pacts with the Shinnecoes. Ian's eyebrows drew together when Matthias attempted to explain the Facility's purpose, finally breaking off to refocus on the plague, his voice wavering with sorrow.

"The burning bodies ashed the whole place. I can still feel it in my lungs," Matthias said. "Then the purge. Eradicate all who had been infected, all who were suspected of being infected. It was barbaric, but we didn't know what else to do. The illness began in the exposed first, then infected the young, then bounced to the young wards tending them, and finally sickened the rest of the experiments. Food-borne perhaps, but after a strict diet, it only worsened. Bad blankets? Everything had been washed in boiling water."

The tribes had required they shake hands at negotiations, and touch—as much as Walker knew Matthias and the other doctors despised it for all its germs and dirt, for all the caution they took to eradicate that particular form of transmission and attachment—touch had been their downfall. Matthias opened the bag strapped to his side and brought out tools—metal syringes, plastic bags, alcohol, medicine.

"He's a healer," Mama Milagros said. "I would've died from this leg if he hadn't helped me stave off the infection. The twins removed the limb, but I'm here, speaking to you, because of him."

"That is a gift," Ian said and paused, as if weighing his next words. "I cannot give the Bruykleeners full access to our water. The other elders would panic. Would the Bruykleeners accept an allotted amount per month out of good faith?"

"We must trust you will not poison it," the Bruykleen seer said, her full lips twisting.

"A risk worth taking," Ian said.

"Perhaps."

"Go then," Ian said. "See if Soul-Dago accepts our terms."

"He will." The seer smiled. "Although, I almost wish you had said no." She turned and left, walking quickly to Soul-Dago and whispering what had transpired in his ear.

Ian watched her and then shook his head at Mama Milagros. "What a mess your grandson has made."

"We've both raised reckless children," she responded, her eyes transfixed on the island in front of her. "I'm not sure I know mine anymore."

61

I think we're gonna go north," Mako said, leaning over the kitchen island in their Manahatta home, his arms crossed under his chest. "Think Thresher should see some of the world. It's been six months, after all."

"Hmmm," Nika said, matching his poise by leaning over the counter. Her finger pointed at the end of a sentence to keep her spot in the open book in front of her.

"I'm not asking," Mako said, fingering the edge of the book's cardboard cover and wiggling it. Nika's finger pressed down harder until her first knuckle bent. She frowned at him.

"I just wanted to let you know," Mako continued. "Walker's starting this new tribe thing with Matthias, you and Soul-Dago haven't killed each other yet, and I wanted to make sure I wasn't, you know…"

"Leaving me," she finished for him quietly.

Mako shifted. "I got two halves of my world. You and Thresher."

Nika smiled, small and close-lipped, but kind. "Nightmares are getting better. I know I spend a lot of time alone, but Mako, it's a *good* alone."

Mako peered at her. He didn't like it, the way she got lost in the city as if searching for something unrecoverable. He never got the sense that she found prayer or rapture, but she came back whole before time splintered her again.

"I need to heal," she admitted. By the tucked in corners of her mouth, he knew it was a hard admission. "On my own, you know? Without everyone asking me. A lot happened."

He knew, had dragged her after two nights home to the top of the wobbling skyscraper and made her tell him everything in halting tones. The wind howled and stole her tears, but after that, he felt like he had damaged her walls.

She took in a shuddering breath, and the afternoon light highlighted the green in her eyes. "I still can't let Walker touch me without…I still need control." She laughed. "He likes it. I think. Gets off on the fear."

"Or has a thing for demanding, troublesome women."

"Or that." She paused. "Don't worry. When you get back, I'll be better. I won't be who I was, but I'm still me."

To him, she would be Nika even if she lost all her limbs. Some things couldn't be taken away. "What about Mama Milagros?"

Phantom pains still woke Mama Milagros in screaming fits, clutching the empty air where her leg used to be and moaning for Gela. Mako had a terrible sense of premonition that the Facility's drugs were more addictive than he knew. He had started hiding the pills and weaning her off with the lasting remainders of Gela's herb stash—willow bark, peppermint, and arnica salves.

The Facility had taken more than he realized. A rift existed between him and Mama Milagros, like he had broken her love for him. Mako couldn't understand why the women in his family were of the silent nature. Without their words to anchor him, he remained adrift and lost, frantically trying to understand them.

Nika leaned across the counter to smack his arm. "She'll be fine. We'll all be fine. It's not like you're leaving forever, and Thresher should have this." The lines around her mouth softened. "I think you both need this."

Mako had gotten good at deflection, good at ignoring statements that could bring reality too close for comfort. He belonged in the dream business.

"Sometimes I think I need a wayfare myself, but I can't find the courage to leave. Been away from home too long already, yeah?" Nika said.

Mako nodded, heart crushing his throat. "I miss Gela. She'd know what to do."

"Think she would've liked Walker?

"No." Mako took her hand. "But I do. We're not easy, you and I. Not easy to please or live with or love."

"You did that so I'd lose my place, didn't you?"

"Guilty," Mako said, and shut her book, too.

62

Nika had a hard time smiling when her twin left, but she had a hard time frowning too. Thresher waved again, as if the first ten times hadn't been enough. If they returned, would Thresher be falling apart from his disease or already in the body bag?

She loved his child-like enthusiasm, his love of simple things like Nika's pancakes and the scissor's snip as she trimmed his hair. Two different breeds, she thought, glancing at Walker standing beside her. He had lost that quality along the way as he fought to create a life for those from the Facility among the Manahatta people. A sparse number of additional doctors and experiments had joined, those who had followed Matthias's trail and begged for shelter. They took them in. They always took them in.

She knew Walker wanted to ask her about introducing the experiments to the other families around the island, maybe get a celebration underway like the big bonfire nights she had told him about, but she couldn't fight the fear, the suspicion. She refused to have Matthias or the experiments stay in her home. While there wasn't room to begin with, now with Thresher and Mako on their honeymoon, there might be questions. Requests. She knew some of the experiments had great dreams of being asked to live in her grand house even as they made the buildings close to her skyscraper their homes. She could almost hear Walker trying to persuade her, saying she would have to get along with them sometime.

Nika didn't have to do anything anymore.

She overcame her fear alone, out in the open with the night sprawl above her. On nights when the clouds cut swatches across the moon to make it glow smoky, the remembrance of Jake's lingering tobacco musk almost overpowered her. Usually, she would let the cold burn of a fathomless abyss fill her up and remind her she was a universal pinprick. Her trials always became so trite, but Matthias always managed to reawaken her terrors.

Walker touched her arm, bringing her out of her memories of the past whirlwind months. He tried to hide a concerned grimace, a hidden frustration that had been gathering steam for the past few weeks. She couldn't give him what he needed until she was whole again, but that might never happen, and she couldn't make it without his love and kindness. She knew building a new structured tribe that integrated the experiments was hard, and being a liaison between the Manahattas and Bruykleeners was not something he had planned for when he helped her escape.

She touched his hand, ushering him upstairs, summoning strength to prove to him she wasn't going anywhere, that her distance didn't mean their relationship had frayed.

"Soul-Dago not here?" Walker nearly growled.

"Not today," she said. Soul-Dago's all-too common presence put her at ease, and she hated that they had struck up a strange friendship amid all the changes. Now that the Bruykleeners shared water rights, it was if they were all finally getting along.

"He's around here too often anyway."

There it was, her Walker red hot and piping angry like when she first met him and he had slammed into her, asking, *Where's your courage? Where'd it get off to?*

He let her push him back into the bedroom. The back of his knees hit the edge of the bed and he sat.

"If I asked you to leave with me right now, would you?" she asked.

Walker watched her skeptically as she slipped his shirt over his head and put his arms behind his back. "Why? Planning on going off with that Bruykleener and make babies together?"

She straddled his lap. This was good. He let out a breath too fast through his nose and glared at her. "How does he always know where to find you when I don't?"

Nika carded a hand through his hair, decided they needed this as easily as she decided what to eat for breakfast this morning. She put a hand on his chest, over his heart, and he shuddered. "I'll make you a deal," she said. "You can ask me anything you want and I'll answer truthfully. Anything you want."

"Will you kiss me?" he asked immediately, and oh, how she loved that, never can *I* kiss you, always letting her steer them. She obliged, something thorough until he broke away for air, his head tipping back so their chins touched.

"Where do you go when you disappear?" he gasped.

"All over," she said.

"You have to answer truthfully." He pouted, lifting his hips up. "None of this evasive shit."

Nika couldn't help but laugh. His mimicking had somehow transformed into his actual personality. "I get these images, flashbacks, and sometimes they're so intense nothing helps but walking until they go away. It's like being hunted. I get the shakes and feel so ill."

"Why don't you come to me?"

"What could you do? I feel better doing it alone."

"Soul-Dago follows you." Walker pointed out. "It's like he can sense when it's happening and he disappears after you. So no, you're not alone."

Nika took a moment to think. "Did Mako put him up to that?"

"Probably." Walker put his head on her stomach, rubbing back and forth, his voice muffled and agonized. "Are you gonna want kids one day?"

"Maybe," she said.

"What if I can't—"

"Not a reason to leave you." She threw her shirt off. "Unless you're a real asshole. Or fall in love with Matthias. You and doctors, Walker."

He laughed as she stripped him bare, touched him until he whimpered and groaned, hands above his head now, his hips bucking as she marked his neck. "I've never felt inadequate before," he whispered.

"You're not." She slicked her hands with oil.

"What do you think about when you're gone?" he asked, nearly biting the words off as her fingers explored and widened him. His head tossed when she rubbed that one particular spot inside him.

"A lot about you," she said. "Wondering when you'll get tired of me being unable to do things." She wasn't sure if she would ever be ready, but when she killed her psychiatrist, she felt some of her fear flee, knew it to be just a hurdle to overcome if only she faced the terror head on.

Walker moaned, said her name over and over until it lost meaning. She had the fly on her pants open, her free hand sliding down to touch herself. It never failed. Watching him come apart under her fingers made her release in an incredible way.

Afterwards, he sat up, his knees on either side of her, and took her hand, putting it to his face and inhaling deeply. She swallowed hard, wondering if he was going to ask the most important question.

"Do you love me?" he said.

She nodded, almost couldn't say it back, but she had to answer truthfully. Those were the rules. "Yes. I love you."

He smiled and kissed the center of her palm. "Is your favorite food really pancakes?"

She grinned as he flipped her. She didn't struggle or panic because it was *Walker*. "It's a close call if scrambled eggs are in the running," she said, cupping his face. Sometimes vulnerability was worth it. "It really is a close call."

— EPILOGUE —

Y ou're taking away my whole life here," Mako whispered into Thresher's ear. Mako's arm around his chest was scarred and much older than when they had first met, but still strong. Thresher leaned back, feeling the familiar thump of Mako's heartbeat. He looked at the setting sun like he had the first time, petrified and full of the sublime.

"I know," Thresher said. The use of his legs had been gone for so long, but he could relive the ache from walking too long, the exhausted shiver of spreading too wide. "I'm glad I'm not going be here to see it. You're going to be a complete mess."

He heard Mako laugh beside him. Warm breath and hair tickled his cheek. He had mapped out every freckle who knew how many times, knew every line and shape of Mako's body, traced his skin with his mouth and eyes. He said he didn't want to know when it was going to happen, didn't want to see it coming, wanted Mako to be ready for it, to take his life in his hands because Mako *always* held Thresher's fate. He wanted Mako to control this too.

"I love you," Mako breathed, and Thresher felt elated, like his whole life made sense, how maybe he had been created in a lab but he'd been meant for Mako. "Want it to be you and me always."

It will be okay, Thresher thought, He'll be okay. He'll be—

Mako cradled Thresher's limp body, the gunshot ringing like a bell, memorializing the enormity of what he had done. Thresher's blood and brain matter spattered across one side of his cheek. He thought about wiping it away, but it was Thresher.

This was the last time Thresher would mark him, own him, cover him with his body. He couldn't let him go so soon. The body slumped, listed to the side, still warm, cocooned, and safe.

It wasn't fair. It wasn't right that the best part of his life ended with a bang and not a whimper. He wished he could've done it the drugged way, the peaceful way, but there was nothing but bloodshed here, blood and love, and morphine was a luxury when bullets were cheap.

He had seven years to come to terms with this, but he procrastinated so much, shoved it off for another day until that day had come, the day when Thresher's breathing struggled and speaking sounded like he was suffocating.

Now, Mako couldn't hold the grief in, could only keen and know he was dying, real dying, the kind that ate you up, broke your heart, and stole your dreams with *not enough time* and remembered nicknames breathed in the dark.

Nika and Mama Milagros—wobbly with her cane and wooden leg—pried his fingers from Thresher's body. Mako wished the sun had burned his eyes out. A skull fragment, rounded and long enough to fit against his thumb sat on his coat. Picking it up, he wiped the blood away, picked at the skin clinging to it, but it would decay away soon, the gray brain bit spongy against his skin. He couldn't do this. But now he had a keepsake, a treasure, a memory to keep in his pocket and not feel so alone, a talisman to keep the hounds at bay.

"Running away isn't going to help," Nika said, her arms crossed. Mako stood in front of the suite's huge window, the sun barely rising and casting slants of brightness across his face. Blinding him so he wouldn't have to turn and suffer his twin's disapproval.

"I'm not," he said, tightening the gloves on his hands. He couldn't look at them, at what they had done, even though he knew it was a necessary evil. He wouldn't have balked from doing it anyway. It had been Thresher's request.

"Thresher and I talked, you know," she said, and he felt her presence behind him. "Since you both came back, I've talked to him about this moment. He knew you were going to do this. He knew you'd up and leave."

"I have to listen to my feet," Mako said.

"He wouldn't want you to do this."

"You don't even know where I'm going."

"Don't go back to the Facility. Don't go looking for Anna-Skye, trying to find some kind of vengeance. Don't try and find Milo or Maggie. It's worthless to keep repeating history."

"Thresher tell you to tell me all that?"

"No, that's directly from me."

"The End were eradicated," Mako said. "I wouldn't walk into the Wallabout's territory for nothing."

"Then where are you going?"

Mako smiled at his reflection in the window, half covered in shadow. He had Thresher's case files in his bag, all the details about Thresher as Subject T that he promised a long time ago he wouldn't read. Everyone had been grossly goody-two-shoes about promises. Even death had kept his little pinky-swear, but now Mako felt like there wasn't any point in respecting memory and honoring last wishes. He planned on finding a nice secluded place far enough away so that when he got through the boundless pages, he could scream himself hoarse afterwards.

"You're not going to kill yourself," Nika said flatly.

"No." Mako placed his hand against the cold glass, seeking some kind of comfort there. "But I need some time. I need…"

"We've all lost someone, Mako. You're not the only one."

"Christ, Nika, it's not that. It's just, it was *Thresher.*"

"What am I going to do without you, huh?"

Mako blinked away tears and leaned his forehead next to his hand. Her arms wrapped around his sides. She had made the last few months full of unity, blasting into his and Thresher's room, demanding they go and watch the stars, start a bonfire, get piss drunk together. He loved his twin with a ferocity that nearly made him double over.

Nika laid her forehead between his shoulder blades and sighed deeply. "We all loved him, you know. You aren't the only one in mourning. Don't make me mourn you too. It was fine when you left before, but now you'll be alone."

"I was so happy, and now I'm so unhappy." Mako's voice broke. "It's like I'm paying for those years."

"I know," she said, tightening her hold. He lost it, in every sense of the word, until he sagged, exhausted in her arms. He had burned up his strength.

"I have all this time left," he said. His breath fogged the window. "I don't know what to do with it. I don't want it."

"Don't leave."

His hot face pressed into his reflection. He hated what he saw. "We all know what happens when one of us disappears for long periods of time." He despised that he laughed, just a little.

"I will actually come and find you," Nika said. "I won't wait years searching in the wrong direction."

"You're a cruel woman, Nika Saddlerock."

Her arms fell from him, and he turned away from the window. Her hand cupped his face and she leaned up to place a kiss on his cheek. "Don't do anything stupid," she said.

"I won't," he whispered, promising it, not just to her, but also to Thresher and himself.

Looked like he hadn't lost his will to forge promises after all. He had heard of a wind called the west, another myth taught by this country splintered into tribes, lies that promised if he had feet and a destination, he could go anywhere and be free. He knew he would get lost in the calling, running from his grief until he could emerge from the other side, still with his sun exploded and all his stars burned out, but he would return. He would come back.

AUTHOR'S NOTE

When I lived in New York, I swore I wouldn't write a book about New York and then promptly did the opposite. From trash-strewn archeological beaches to gorgeous cemeteries to end point lighthouses, each place I wandered left me speechless and yet full of words. This, in turn, all rolled out as the post-apocalyptic setting for Mako and Thresher, Nika and Walker. Sometimes falling in love with a place means you fall in love with the stories it has to tell, and I was caught, hook, line, and sinker. Or at least, that's what it felt like.

While I laid the foundation, great thanks are in order to those who strengthened the walls, replaced the shingles, and cleaned the gutters. To Alana Joli Abbott, an exemplary editor, for her incredible insight and attention to detail and not murdering me when I accidentally spoiled the ending for her. To Elise McMullen-Ciotti for her phenomenal sensitivity read that left this tale richer than I ever could have imagined. To Jeremey Mohler for gorgeous artwork and bringing my garbled descriptions of *Urban! Nature! Wanderers!* into a piece of wonder. To Mike Brodu for lovely layout and patience with endless proofs. It takes a village to raise a book, and this team took my pile of words and created a piece of art.

To my husband, Shay, for unwavering belief in my writing. There's something to be said for someone who says, "You should probably write tonight." To Stephanie, for reading over four-hundred pages during her weekend to ensure not a comma was out of place and informing me she wouldn't be reading this book again because of all the weeping that was had. To Kellie, my guide from Queens, for letting me traipse her across New York on adventures when we were clearly very hungover, and only requesting a supply of goldfish to snack on. To my family, and always Janet, John, and Lucian for endless support and love.

A lot of this story is about place—a place to fall in love, a place to die, a place ravaged and destroyed but still beloved, a place that speaks to your bones and that sense of belonging, even if it is for a minute or a lifetime. I hope you found a place within these pages just for you, Reader. Thank you for reading.

ABOUT THE AUTHOR

Gwendolyn N. Nix has been an editor, casting producer, scientist, and social media manager, but always a writer. A born seeker of adventure, she saw her first beached humpback whale on a windy day in New York, met a ghost in a Paris train station, and had Odin answer her prayers on a mountain in Scotland. *The Falling Dawn*, her first fantasy novel, released in 2018 and her short fiction has appeared in StarShip Sofa, and anthologies such as *Where The Veil is Thin*, and *The Sisterhood of the Blade*. She lives in Missoula, MT. Find out more at www.gwendolynnix.com.